JOE GREY, P.I.

IT WAS NOT UNTIL THE NEXT MORNING that Joe, brushing past Clyde's bare feet, leaping to the kitchen table and pawing open the morning *Gazette*, learned more about the burglary at Medder's Antiques.

"What are you reading?" Clyde picked Joe up as if he were a bag of flour, so he could see the paper.

Joe dangled impatiently, twitching his tail, as Clyde read.

Clyde sat down at the table and dumped pepper on his eggs. "So this is why you've been scowling and snarling all morning, this burglary."

"I haven't been scowling and snarling. Why would I bother with a simple break-and-enter? The police can handle the simple stuff."

Clyde raised an eyebrow.

"So there's a new cat in the village. So are you satisfied? It's nothing to worry you, nothing to fret over."

Clyde was silent a moment, watching him. "I take it this is a tomcat. What did he do, come onto Dulcie?"

Joe glared at him. Stupid humans could be all too perceptive at the wrong times.

Praise for Shirley Rousseau Murphy's Cat Mysteries

"Not to be missed."
—*Armchair Detective*

"Magical whimsy and deft writing."
—*Cats* magazine

Books by
Shirley Rousseau Murphy

CAT IN THE DARK
CAT TO THE DOGS
CAT ON THE EDGE
CAT RAISE THE DEAD
CAT UNDER FIRE
CAT SPITTING MAD
CAT LAUGHING LAST

And in Hardcover

CAT SEEING DOUBLE

CAT
in the
DARK

Shirley Rousseau Murphy

AVON BOOKS
An Imprint of HarperCollinsPublishers

AVON BOOKS
An Imprint of HarperCollins*Publishers*
10 East 53rd Street
New York, New York 10022-5299

Copyright © 1999 by Shirley Rousseau Murphy
Cover illustration © 1999 by Mark Hess
ISBN: 0-06-105947-1
www.avonbooks.com

First Avon Books paperback printing: July 2001
First HarperPaperbacks printing: November 1999
First HarperCollins hardcover printing: January 1999

Avon Trademark Reg. U.S. Pat. Off. and in Other Countries, Marca Registrada, Hecho en U.S.A.
HarperCollins® is a trademark of HarperCollins Publishers Inc.

Printed in the U.S.A.

10 9 8 7 6 5

For those who wonder about their cats.
And for the cats who don't need to wonder,
for the cats who know.

And, of course, for Joe Cat.
And this time, too, for Luby and
skybound E.L.T.

And always for Pat for his laughter
in the right places
and his support and advice.

1

THE CAT crouched in darkness beneath the library desk, her tabby stripes mingled with the shadows, her green eyes flashing light, her tail switching impatiently as she watched the last patrons linger around the circulation counter. Did humans *have* to dawdle, wasting their time and hers? What *was* it about closing hour that made people so incredibly slow?

Above her the library windows were black, and out in the night the oaks' ancient branches twisted against the glass, the moon's rising light reflecting along their limbs and picking out the rooftops beyond. The time was nine-fifteen. Time to turn out the lights. Time to leave these hallowed rooms to her. Would people never leave? She was so irritated she almost shouted at them to get lost, that this was her turf now.

Beyond the table and chair legs, out past the open door, the library's front garden glowed waxen in the moonlight, the spider lilies as ghostly pale as the white reaching fingers of a dead man. Three women moved out into the garden along the stone path, beneath the oak trees' dark shelter, heading toward the street; behind them, Mavity Flowers hurried out toting her heavy book bag, her white maid's uniform as bright as moonstruck snow, her gray, wiry hair ruffled by the sea wind. Her white polyester skirt was deeply wrinkled in the rear from sitting for nearly an hour delving through the romance novels, choosing half a dozen unlikely dreams in which to lose herself. Dulcie imagined Mavity hastening home to her tiny cottage, making herself a cup of tea, getting comfy, maybe slipping into her bathrobe and putting her feet up for an evening's read—for a few hours' escape and pleasure after scrubbing and vacuuming all day in other people's houses.

Mavity was a dear friend of Dulcie's housemate; she and Wilma had known each other since elementary school, more than fifty years. Wilma was the tall one, strong and self-sufficient, while Mavity was such a small person, so wrinkled and frail-looking that people treated her as if she should be watched over—even if she did work as hard as a woman half her age. Mavity wasn't a cat lover, but she and Dulcie were friends. She always stroked Dulcie and talked to her when she stopped by Wilma's; Mavity told Dulcie she was beautiful, that her chocolate-dark stripes were as lovely as mink, that Dulcie was a very special cat.

But the little lady had no idea how special. The truth would have terrified her. The notion that Dulcie had read (and found tedious) most of the stories that she, herself, was toting home tonight, would have shaken Mavity Flowers right down to her scruffy white oxfords.

Through the open front door, Dulcie watched Mavity hurry to the corner and turn beneath the yellow glow of the streetlamp to disappear down the dark side street into a tunnel of blackness beneath a double row of densely massed eucalyptus trees. But within the library, seven patrons still lingered.

And from the media room at the back, four more dawdlers appeared, their feet scuffing along inches from Dulcie's nose—silk-clad ankles in stilted high heels, a boy's bony bare feet in leather sandals, a child's little white shoes and lace-ruffled white socks following Mama's worn loafers. And all of them as slow as cockroaches in molasses, stopping to examine the shelved books and flip through the racked magazines. Dulcie, hunching against the carpet, sighed and closed her eyes. Dawdling was a *cat's* prerogative, humans didn't have the talent. Only a cat could perform that slow, malingering dance, the *half-in-half-out-the-door* routine, with the required insolence and grace.

She was not often so rude in her assessment of human frailties. During the daytime hours, she was a model of feline amenity, endlessly obliging to the library patrons, purring for them and smiling when the old folks and children petted and fussed over her, and she truly loved them. Being official library cat was deeply rewarding. And at home with Wilma she considered herself beautifully laid-back; she and Wilma had a lovely life together. But when night fell, when the dark winds shook the oaks and pines and rattled the eucalyptus leaves, her patina of civilization gave way and the ancient wildness rose in her, primitive passions took her—and a powerful and insatiable curiosity drove her. Now, eager to get on with her own agenda, she was stifled not only by lingering humans but was put off far more by the too-watchful gaze of the head librarian.

Jingling her keys, Freda Brackett paced before the circulation desk as sour-faced as a bad-tempered possum and as impatient for people to leave as was Dulcie herself—though for far different reasons. Freda couldn't wait to be free of the books and their related routines for a few hours, while Dulcie couldn't wait to get at the thousands of volumes, as eager as a child waiting to be alone in the candy store.

Freda had held the position of head librarian for two months. During that time, she had wasted not an ounce of love on the library and its contents, on the patrons, or on anyone or anything connected with the job. But what could you expect of a political appointee?

The favorite niece of a city council member, Freda had been selected over several more desirable applicants among the library's own staff. Having come to Molena Point from a large and businesslike city library, she ran this small, cozy establishment in the same way. Her only objective was to streamline operations until the Molena Point Library functioned as coldly and impersonally as the institution she had abandoned. In just two months the woman's rigid rules had eaten away at the warm, small-village atmosphere like a rat demolishing last night's cake.

She discouraged the villagers from using the library as a meeting place, and she tried to deter any friendliness among the staff. Certainly she disapproved of librarians being friends with the patrons—an impossibility in a small town. Her rules prevented staff from performing special favors for any patron and she even disapproved of helping with book selection and research, the two main reasons for library service.

And as for Dulcie, an official library cat was an abomination. A cat on the premises was as inappropriate and unsanitary as a dog turd on Freda's supper plate.

But a political appointee didn't have to care about the job, they were in it only for the money or prestige. If they loved their work they would have excelled at it and thus been hired on their own merits. Political appointees were, in Dulcie's opinion, always bad news. Just last summer a police detective who was handed his job by the mayor created near disaster in the village when he botched a murder investigation.

Dulcie smiled, licking her whiskers.

Detective Marritt hadn't lasted long, thanks to some quick paw-work. She and Joe Grey, moving fast, had uncovered evidence so incriminating that the real killer had been indicted, and Detective Marritt had been fired—out on the street. A little feline intervention had made him look like mouse dirt.

She wished they could do the same number on Freda.

Behind the circulation desk, Dulcie's housemate, Wilma Getz, moved back and forth arranging books on the reserve shelf, her long, silver hair bound back with a turquoise clip, her white turtleneck sweater and black blazer setting off to advantage her slim, faded jeans. The two women were about the same age, but Wilma had remained lithe and fresh, while Freda looked dried-up and sharp-angled and sour—and her clothes always smelled of mothballs. Dulcie, watching the two women, did not expect what was coming.

"Get your cat, Wilma. You are to take it home with you tonight."

"She's all right inside—she'll go out later through her cat door."

"You will take it home with you. I don't want it here at night. There's too much possibility of damage. Animals have no place in a library. You are fortunate that, so far, I have allowed it to remain during the day."

Wilma laid aside the books she was arranging and fixed Freda with a level look. "Dulcie is not a destructive cat. Her manners, as you should have observed, are impeccable."

"No cat can be trusted. You have no way to know what it might do. You will take it home with you."

Dulcie, peering from the shadows, dug her claws hard into the carpet—she'd like to tear it to shreds. Or tear Freda to shreds, flay her like a cornered rat. She imagined Freda as a hunting trophy, the woman's head mounted over the circulation desk like the deer head over Morrie's Bar.

Wilma picked up her purse. "Dulcie has a right to be here. She *is* the library cat. She was appointed by the mayor and she is of great value to us. Have you forgotten that her presence has doubled the children's book circulation?"

"That is such a ridiculous notion. The library is a center for sophisticated research tools, Ms. Getz. It is not a petting zoo."

"This is a small village library, Freda. It is geared to patrons who want to spend a few pleasant hours."

"Even if that were its purpose, what does that have to do with a *cat*?"

"Our patrons like having a little cat to pet and to talk to." Wilma gave Freda a gentle smile. "You've seen the statistics. Dulcie has brought in patrons who never came to the library before, and who are now regulars."

"Ms. Getz, the city hired me to run a library, not an animal shelter. There is absolutely no precedent for . . ."

"You know quite well there is precedent. Do you think the libraries that keep a cat are run by idiots? There are library cats all across the country, and every one of them is credited with large increases in circulation. Do you think the librarians in El Centro and

Hayward and Hood River, in Niagara Falls, Fort Worth, and in a dozen other states would bother to keep a library cat if the cat did not perform a valuable service?"

"Very likely those libraries have a mouse problem and were forced to keep a cat. You are truly paranoid about this foolishness. I would hope your reference work is of a more scholarly . . ."

Wilma folded her hands loosely in front of her, a gesture Dulcie knew well when Wilma longed to punch someone. "Why don't *you* do *your* research, Freda? Library cats date at least as far back as the eighteen-hundreds, not only here but in England and Italy. There have been nonfiction books published on the library cat, a videotape is now being produced, and at least one thesis has been written on the subject—to say nothing of the Library Cat Society, which is a *national* organization of librarians and library cat supporters."

Beneath the reference desk, Dulcie smiled. Wilma hadn't spent thirty years putting down pushy federal parolees for nothing.

"Since Dulcie came," Wilma reminded Freda, "our children's reading program has grown so popular we've had to start three new groups—because of Dulcie. She draws out the shy children, and when new children come in to pet her, very often they discover a brand-new love for books. And they adore having her with them during story hour, snuggling among the cushions."

Dulcie wanted to cheer, to do a little cat-dance to thank Wilma—but as Freda turned away, the expression on the woman's face made Dulcie back deeper under the desk, an icy shiver passing over her.

If she had been an ordinary cat, Wilma would take her away for her own safety, because who knew what

Freda might do? How could an ordinary cat fathom the lengths Freda Brackett might go to, to get rid of her?

But Dulcie was not ordinary. She was quite aware of the woman's malice and, despite Wilma's worries, she knew how to keep out of Freda's way.

Freda, turning her back on Wilma, motioned her assistant to put out the lights. Bernine Sage hurried out from the book stacks, heading for the electrical switches behind the circulation desk, her smoothly coiled red hair gleaming in the overhead light, her slim black suit describing exactly Bernine's businesslike attitude. She was not a librarian but a computer expert and a book-keeper—a perfect choice as Freda's assistant, to bring the backward village institution into the twenty-first century. Bernine, during the exchange between Freda and Wilma, had stood in the shadows as alert as an armed guard ready to support her superior.

Bernine and Wilma had known each other for many years; Bernine was, as far as she could be, Wilma's friend. But friendship ended where her bread was buttered.

Dulcie's own relationship with Bernine was one of a fear far more complicated than her wariness of Freda Brackett. Bernine Sage had acquired her dislike of cats in an unusual way, and she knew too much about certain kinds of cats. If she got started on Celtic history and the ancient, speaking cats, and began spilling her theories to Freda and quoting mythology, she could set Ms. Brackett off in a frightening new direction. A real witch-hunt—cat hunt—focused on her; though she was neither witch nor witch's cat, Dulcie thought demurely.

But what she *was* could be no less terrifying to an unsympathetic and unimaginative human.

Now, as Bernine threw the switches for the overhead lights, the library rooms dimmed to a soft glow where a few desk lamps still burned, and the last patrons headed out. But Wilma glanced across the room to Dulcie, her message as clear as if she had spoken: She would not take Dulcie home—she would not give in to Freda. But her look implored Dulcie to go on out and let the woman cool down. Her gaze said clearly that she wouldn't sleep unless she knew Dulcie was safe.

Within the shadows, Dulcie blinked her eyes slowly, trying to look compliant, trying to ease her friend.

But she had no intention of leaving. Crouched on the carpet, her tail switching, she waited impatiently as Freda and Bernine, and then Wilma, moved toward the door. Bernine paused to throw the last switch, and the desk lamps went dark, casting the room into blackness. For an instant Dulcie was blind, but before the dead bolt slid home her night vision kicked in and the darkness turned transparent, the tables and chairs reemerged, and across the book-lined walls, the blowing shadows of the oaks swam and shivered.

Alone. At last she was alone.

Trotting out from beneath the desk, she leaped to its top and spun, chasing her tail, then flew to the floor again and hit the carpet running, racing through the reading rooms under tables and desks, tearing through moonlight and shadow. Around her, the darkened rooms seemed larger, as if the daytime walls had melted away into wind-tossed space. Leaping to a bookshelf, she pawed down a claw-marked volume. With a soft thud it hit the carpet.

Carrying it in her teeth, she sprang to a table where the moon's light shone brightest. Pawing the book open, she soon was wandering Africa, prowling the open grasslands, her nostrils filled with the sharp scent of wildebeest and antelope, and around her the African night reeled away to mountains so tall they vanished among the stars. Feasting on gazelle, she raced across grassy plains so vast that if Molena Point were set down there, it would seem only a child's toy village. Roaring and chuffing, she was a leopard padding among clay huts terrifying sleeping humans, leaving gigantic pawprints in the dust for unlucky hunters to follow. And when at last she was overwhelmed by Africa's immense spaces, she turned to the close, confining alleys of tenth-century England, to tales of narrow medieval streets.

But too soon those tales turned dark. Hecate wooed her. Evil beckoned to her. She blundered into stories of witches in cat-form and of cat familiars. Medieval humans stalked her, folk terrified by the sight of a cat and wanting only to kill it. Trapped by that era of cruelty, she was sucked down into darkness, unable to shake the bloody and horror-ridden images. These stories were nothing like the gentler, Celtic dramas that she liked to browse through when ancient peoples, taking cat-form, wandered down to a netherworld beneath the soft green hills, when the magical race that was kin to both man and cat could take the shape of either. When that ancient tribe of speaking cats to which she and Joe belonged—and of which they might be nearly the last survivors—had been understood and loved by the Celts. Unable to rid herself of the darker visions, she backed away from the open book, slashing at the offending volume, almost bereft of her reason.

Then she whirled away to crouch at the edge of the table, shocked at her own loss of control.

What am I doing? There is nothing here, only stories. Words on a page, nothing more. That evil time is gone, ages gone. Why am I crouching here trembling like a terrified hunk of cat fur? What set me off like that, to nearly lose myself? Shivering, she felt almost as if someone had fixed dark thoughts on her. Lashing her tail, disgusted by her pointless fear, by her sudden failure of spirit, she leaped to the floor and fled through Wilma's office and out her cat door into the night, into the soft and welcoming night, into Molena Point's safe and moonlit night.

2

IN THE BEDROOM of the white Cape Cod cottage, moonlight shone through the open windows and a fitful breeze fingered across the bed, teasing the ears of the tomcat who slept curled in the blankets, his muscular body gleaming as sleek as gray velvet. Beside him on the double bed, his human housemate snored softly, clutching the pillow for warmth, unaware that Joe Grey had clawed away the covers into a comfortable and exclusive nest. Clyde, naked and chilled, was too deep in sleep to wake and retrieve the blankets, but Joe Grey stirred as the breeze quickened, his white paws flexed and his nose lifted, catching an elusive scent.

He woke fully, staring toward the open window, drawing his lips back in a grimace at the stink he detected on the cool night air.

Tomcat.

The smell that came to him on the ocean breeze was the rank odor of an unknown tom—a stranger in the village.

Joe might not encounter a village tom for months,

but he knew each one, knew what routes he favored and which pals he hung out with, by the scent marks left on storefronts and tree trunks, aromas as individual as hand-lettered placards stating name and residence. He knew the smell of every cat in Molena Point, but this one was exotic and foreign.

Joe tolerated the regular village toms, because how could he not? Without some degree of civility, life would degenerate into a succession of endless and meaningless battles. One restrained oneself until the prize was greatest, until a queen in heat ruled the night—then it was war, bloody and decisive.

But no amount of civilized restraint among the village toms left room for strangers on their turf.

This could be a stray from the wharf who had decided to prowl among the shops, or maybe some tourist's cat; whatever the case, he didn't like the intruder's belligerent, testosterone-heavy message. The beast's odor reeked of insolence and of a bold and dark malaise—a hotly aggressive, sour aroma. The cat smelled like trouble.

In the moon's glow, the cottage bedroom was lent a charm not apparent in the daytime. A plain room, it was suited to a simple bachelor's spartan tastes, comfortable but shabby, the pine dresser and pine nightstand sturdily made and ugly, the ladder-back chair old and scarred. But now, in the moonlight, the unadorned white walls were enlivened by the shifting shadows of the oak trees that spread just outside the window, their knotted patterns softening the room's stark lines and offering a sense of mystery and depth. And beside the bed, a thick, ruby-toned Persian rug added a single touch of luxury, gleaming like jewels in the moonlight—a tender and extravagant gift from one of Clyde's former lovers.

Pawing free of the confining bedcovers, Joe Grey walked heavily across the bed and across Clyde's stomach and dropped down to the thick, soft rug. Clyde, grunting, raised up and glared at him.

"Why the hell do you do that? You're heavy as a damned moose!"

Joe smiled and dug his claws into the rug's silky pile.

Clyde's black hair was wild from sleep, his cheeks dark with a day's growth of stubble. A line of black grease streaked his forehead, residue from the innards of some ailing Rolls Royce or Mercedes.

"You have the whole damned bed to walk on. Can't you show a little consideration? I don't walk on your stomach."

Joe dug his claws deeper into the Persian weave, his yellow eyes sly with amusement. "You work out, you're always bragging about your great stomach muscles—you shouldn't even feel my featherweight. Anyway, you were snoring so loud, so deep under, that a Great Dane on your stomach shouldn't have waked you."

"Get the hell out of here. Go on out and hunt, let me get some sleep. Go roll in warm blood or whatever you do at night."

"For your information, I'm going straight to the library. What more sedate and respectable destination could one possibly . . ."

"Can it, Joe. Of course you're going to the library—but only to get Dulcie. Then off to murder some helpless animal, attack some innocent little mouse or cute, cuddly rabbit. Look at you—that killer expression plastered all over your furry face."

"Rabbits are not cuddly. A rabbit can be as vicious as a bullterrier—their claws are incredibly sharp. And what gives you the slightest clue to Dulcie's and my plans for the evening? You're suddenly an authority on the behavior of *felis domesticus*?"

Clyde doubled the pillow behind his head. "I don't have to be an authority to smell the blood on your breath when you come stomping in at dawn."

"I don't come in here at dawn. I go directly to the kitchen, minding my own business."

"And trailing muddy pawprints all over the kitchen table. Can't you wash like a normal cat? You get so much mud on the morning paper, who can read it?"

"I have no trouble reading it. Though why anyone would waste more than five minutes on that rag is hard to understand."

Clyde picked up the clock, which he kept face-down on the night table. The luminous dial said twelve thirty-three. "It's late, Joe. Get on out of here. Save your sarcasm for Dulcie. Some of us have to get up in the morning, go to work to support the indigent members of the household."

"I can support myself very nicely, thank you. I let you think otherwise simply to make you feel needed, to let you think you perform some useful function in the world."

Padding across the oak floor, Joe pawed open the bedroom door. "So go to sleep. Sleep your life away." Giving Clyde a last, narrow glare, he left the room. Behind him, he heard Clyde groan and pound his pillow and roll over.

Trotting down the hall and through the living room, brushing past his own tattered, hair-matted easy chair, he slipped out through his cat door. He supposed he should feel sorry for Clyde. How could a mere human, with inferior human senses, appreciate the glory of the moonlit night that surrounded him as he headed across the village?

To his right, above the village roofs, the Molena Point hills rose round and silvered like the pale, humped backs of grazing beasts. All around him, the shop windows gleamed with lunar light, and as he crossed Ocean Avenue with its eucalyptus-shaded median, the trees' narrow leaves, long and polished, reflected the moon's glow like silver fish hung from the branches—thousands, millions of bright fish. No human, with inferior human eyesight, could appreciate such a night. No human, with dull human hearing and minimal sense of smell, could enjoy any of the glories of the natural world as vividly as did a cat. Clyde, poor pitiful biped, didn't have a clue.

Trotting up the moon-whitened sidewalk, he caught again the scent of the vagrant tom and followed it on the shifting wind, watching for any stealthy movement in the tangled shadows. But then, hurrying past the softly lit shops and galleries, he lost that sour odor; now, passing a block of real estate offices and little cafes, sniffing at the doors and at the oversized flower pots that stood along the curb, he smelled only dog urine and the markings of the cats he knew. The tom had, somewhere behind him, taken a different route.

Approaching Dulcie's cat door, which had been cut at the back of the library into Wilma's office, he startled at a sound within—and the door flap exploded out and Dulcie shot through nearly on top of him, her green eyes wildly blazing.

She froze, staring at him. She said no word. She lashed her tail and spun away again, racing for the nearest tree and up it, swarming up to the roofs.

Puzzled and concerned, he followed her.

Was she simply moon-maddened, wild with the pull of the full moon? Or had something frightened her in the library's dark rooms?

With Dulcie, who knew? His lady's moods could explode as crazily as moths flung in a windstorm.

At least he hadn't scented the strange tom around her door, he thought with relief as he gained the moonlit peaks.

Already she had disappeared. But her scent was there, warm and sweet, leading away into dense blackness between a tangle of vent pipes that rose from a roof as silvered and flat as a frozen pond. Slipping between the slashing shadows, he galloped past a dozen east-facing windows that reflected a dozen pale moons. Rearing up to look across the roofs for her, peering beneath overhangs and around dormers, he softly called to her. He spoke her name half a dozen times before he grew uneasy, began to worry that the tom had found her first.

Most toms wouldn't harm a female, but there was always the nasty-tempered beast who liked to hurt a lady more than he liked to love her, the unusual, twisted male who fed on fear and pain—beasts little different from a similarly warped human. Except there were far fewer such cats than men.

Not that Dulcie couldn't take care of herself. There wasn't a dog in Molena Point who would tangle with his lady. But despite Dulcie's temper and her swift claws, Joe searched with growing concern, hurrying along the peaks and watching the shadows and calling. Beneath the moon's shifting light he could see nothing alive but the darting bats that skimmed the rooftops sucking up bugs and squeaking their shrill radar cries.

Suddenly the tom's scent hit him strong, clinging to the wall of a little, one-room penthouse.

Sniffing at the window, Joe could smell where the cat had rubbed his cheek along the glass, arrogantly marking this territory as if it were his own.

Peering in through the dusty pane, he studied the old desk stacked with papers and catalogs and the shelves behind, crammed with books and ledgers. What had the tom seen in there of interest?

Beyond the desk a spiral staircase led down to the bookstore below. Maybe this cat, like Dulcie and like Joe himself, found a bookstore inviting; certainly bookstores had a warm coziness, and they always smelled safe.

Maybe the cat had taken up residence there; maybe the two young women who kept the shop had adopted him, picked him up on the highway or at the animal pound. How would they know that Molena Point already had enough tomcats? And why would they care? Why would a human care about the delicate balance of territory necessary to the village males?

A nudge against his flank spun him around crouched to attack.

Dulcie bounced aside laughing, her green eyes flashing. Cuffing his face, she raced to the edge of the roof and dropped off, plummeting down into the concrete canyon—he heard her claws catch on an awning.

Crouching on the rain gutter, he looked down where she clung in the swaying canvas, her eyes blazing. Lashing her tail, she leaped up past him to the roof again and sped away. He burst after her and they fled along the rooftops laughing with human voices.

"You can't escape . . ."

"No scruffy tom can catch me . . ."

"No hoyden queen can outrun *this* tomcat, baby."

"Try me." She laughed, scorching away into the dark and twisted shadows. And who was to hear them? Below, the village slept. No one would hear them laughing and talking—no one, seeing them racing across the rooftops, would connect two cats with human voices. Wildly they fled across the peaks, leaping from shingled hip to dormer and up the winding stairs of the courthouse tower, swiftly up to its high, open lookout.

On the small circular terrace beneath the tower's conical roof they trotted along the top of the brick rail, looking down at the world spread all below them, at a vast mosaic stained to silver and black. Nothing moved there, only the cloud shadows slipping across and the little bats jittering and darting on the fitful wind.

But then as they padded along the rail, stepping around the outside of the tower's four pillars on a narrow row of bricks, something stirred below them.

In the sea of darkness an inky patch shifted suddenly and slunk out of the shadows.

He stood staring up at them, black and bold among the rooftops. A huge beast. Black as sin. The biggest tomcat Joe had ever seen—broad of shoulder, wide of head, solid as a panther. He moved with the grace of a panther, swaggering across the roof directly below them, belligerent and predaceous and staring up narrow-eyed, intently watching them, his slitted, amber eyes flashing fire—and his gaze was fully on Dulcie, keen with speculation.

3

ON THE ROOFS below Joe and Dulcie the tomcat sauntered along a sharp peak, swaying his broad shoulders with authority and staring coldly up at them where they crouched high on the rail of the tower. Though he dismissed Joe, hardly noticing him, his gaze lingered keenly on Dulcie, making her shiver. Then he smiled and, turning away again, began to stalk between the chimneys, his gaze fixed on a skylight's clear dome; crouched over the moonstruck bubble, he peered down intently through the curving glass.

From their high vantage, Dulcie watched him with interest. "Blue Moss Cafe," she said softly. "What's he looking at? What's so fascinating? They're closed for the night." There would not be so much as a bread crust remaining on the small round tables, not a crumb visible in the stainless steel kitchen; she and Joe had often looked in, sniffing the good smell of beef stew, watching the happy diners. The cat seemed to study every detail of the dim, closed restaurant, remaining so for some moments before he moved on again to peer into an attic and then into a darkened penthouse. There were apartments above some of the shops, and where a room was lighted, he kept his distance, circling around to avoid any wash of light spilling upon him. Approaching an angled, tilting skylight, he hunkered over the dark, dusty panes—and froze.

Whatever he saw below him down in the dusty-dim environs of Medder's Antiques had jerked him to full alert. Lashing his tail, he clawed at the glass, every line of his muscled body focused and intent, fixated on the little crowded antique store and its ancient, dusty furniture, perhaps studying some odd accouterment of human culture—maybe an antique rattrap or silk umbrella or silver snuffbox. A faint glow seeped up from a nightlight somewhere within, dully igniting the skylight's grimy panes and silhouetting the black cat's broad head and thick shoulders. Clawing at the metal frame, digging and pulling, he soon forced the skylight open.

Heaving his shoulder into the crack, he pushed the glass up, rolled underneath, and dropped out of sight as the glass thumped closed behind him; the leap would be ten or twelve feet down among dust-scented Victorian chairs and cluttered china cabinets.

"Come on!" Dulcie hissed. Leaping from the rail, she fled down the tower's dark, winding stairs. Joe raced close, pressing against her, gripped by a nameless fear for her; he didn't like to think what kind of cat this was, breaking and entering like a human thief.

Side by side they crouched over the skylight looking down where the cat had vanished among the jumbled furniture. Nothing moved. The reflections across a row of glass-faced china cabinets were as still as if time itself had stopped, the images of carved fretwork and tattered

silk shawls lifeless and eternal, a dead montage. A heap
of musical instruments, violins and trumpets and gui-
tars, lay tumbled into the arms of a Victorian settee. An
ancient bicycle wore a display of feathered hats sus-
pended from its seat and handlebars. The cats heard no
sound from the shop, only the hush of breeze around
them tickling across the rooftops punctuated by the
high-frequency calls of the little bats.

Clink. A metallic clunk jarred the night. Then a
familiar scraping sound as the front door opened, the
tinkle of its bell stifled quickly, as if someone had
grabbed the clapper.

Two men spoke, their voices muted. The cats
heard the scuff of shoes crossing the shop but could
see no one. Soon they heard wooden drawers sliding
out, then the ring of the shop's old-fashioned cash register as its drawer sprang open—sounds they knew well
from visiting widow Medder. Joe found himself listening for a police car down on the street, hoping that a
silent alarm might have gone off, alerting a patrol unit.

But would Mrs. Medder have an alarm, when she
didn't even have a computer or a fax machine?

Celia Medder had opened the shop a year ago, after
losing her husband and young child in a boating accident down near Santa Barbara; she had moved to
Molena Point wanting to escape her painful memories,
had started the little shop with her own antique furniture from the large home she no longer wanted, slowly
buying more, driving once a month up into the gold-
rush towns north of Sacramento looking for bargains. It
had not been easy to make a go of her new business.
The cats were fond of her; she always welcomed them,
never chased them off the sofas or Victorian chairs. She
would brush up the satin when they jumped down, but
she never spoke to them harshly.

The night was so still that they needn't look over to know the street was empty. No soft radio from a police unit, no whisper of tires, no footsteps.

"Why would a burglar break into a used furniture shop?" Dulcie whispered. "Why not a bank or jewelry store? And where did that cat come from?" She cut him a sideways look. "A trained cat? Trained to open skylights? I don't think so."

Below them the reflections jumped suddenly across the china cabinets. A dozen images flared and swam as a man slipped between the crowded furniture, edging between chairs and couches. A thin, small man—hunched shoulders, a slouch hat, a wrinkled leather flight jacket. The black cat joined him, circling around his ankles, rubbing and preening. Suddenly all the history of their ancient race tumbled through Dulcie's head—Celtic kings, underground worlds, sleek shape-shifting princesses—all the old tales that the rest of the world thought of as fairy tales and that she knew were not. And the idea that this black burglar might be like themselves both excited and frightened her.

Man and cat moved through the room, out of sight. Dulcie and Joe heard cupboard doors sliding, then the clink of metal on metal, then the buzz of an electric tool.

"Drill," Joe said. "Sounds like they've found the safe."

"They must have had it spotted. It wasn't that easy to find, hidden in the back of that old cupboard."

Joe clawed at the skylight, digging at its frame to force the glass open, but before he could slide in, Dulcie bit the scruff of his neck, jerking him away. The skylight dropped with a thud.

He spun around, hissing at her. "Thank you very much. Now they know we're here. Just leave me alone, Dulcie."

"I won't. You'd be trapped down there. They could kill you before you got out. You think *that* will help Mrs. Medder? You think getting dead will catch a thief? And they didn't hear a thing. How could they, with the noise that drill's making?"

But the drilling stopped. In the silence they heard a series of thuds and bumps. Dulcie crept closer, listening. "What did they do, drill the lock off?"

"I'm guessing they drilled a small hole—enough to stick a periscope inside."

She gave him a narrow, amused glance.

"Not kidding. Miniature periscope, with a light on it."

"Sure."

He sighed impatiently. "A safe's lock is made of flat plates. Okay? Each one turns when you spin the dial. When you get them lined up, the lock opens."

"So?"

"So, if you can see them from the inside, you can line them up. The burglar drills a hole, puts the little periscope in—Captain Harper has one. It's about as big as a pencil but with a flexible neck. You stick it into the safe and watch the plates while you turn the dial."

Her green eyes widened. "You're serious."

"Harper showed Clyde. He took it from the evidence room after it wasn't needed anymore."

"No wonder you hang around home when the law comes over to play poker. It's wonderful, the things you learn from Max Harper."

"You needn't be sarcastic."

"I'm not being . . ." She stopped to listen. They heard the front door open and close and footsteps going away. Leaping to the roof's edge, they crouched with their paws in the gutter, peering down.

Below them, the sidewalk was empty. No sign of man nor cat. But footsteps whispered away, around the corner. Joe crouched to drop down to the awning. "We need a phone—need to call Harper. Maybe a squad car can pick them up before they get away."

"Not this time," she said softly.

He turned to stare at her, his yellow eyes wide. "What's with you?"

"You want Harper to know that one of the burglars is a cat?"

"I don't intend to tell him about the cat."

"So you don't say a word about the cat. Harper picks up the burglar. You know how tough he can be. There's no sign of forced entry, and Harper keeps at the guy about how he got in, until he caves. Tells Harper that a cat let him in, that he uses a trained cat."

"Come on, Dulcie. The cat is his secret weapon. He'll protect that beast like Fort Knox."

She gave him a long look. "There'll be cat hairs all over the store, on the guy's clothes, and around the skylight. Even if the guy keeps his secret, Harper will be suspicious. You know how thorough he is—and how paranoid about cats. You know how nervous he gets when there's a cat anywhere near a case."

Over the past year, Joe and Dulcie's telephone tips to Max Harper, in the guise of interested citizens, had led to key arrests in three Molena Point murders, resulting in six convictions. But each time, the cats themselves had been seen in embarrassing situations. This, and the fact that some of their tips had involved evidence that couldn't possibly have been discovered by a human informant, tended to make Max Harper nervous. He had, in short, some well-founded suspicions involving the feline persuasion.

"We don't need to add to his unease," Dulcie said. She looked deeply at Joe. "Let's leave this one alone. I have a bad feeling about this."

"Dulcie, sometimes you . . ."

Below them a shadow moved in the blackness at the edge of the awning. The blackness exploded up at them and the black cat hit the roof inches from Joe, his fangs white in the moonlight, his claws gleaming sharp as knives, going straight for Joe's throat.

Dulcie charged between them.

The black tom froze, staring at her.

Joe and Dulcie faced the black cat, rigid with challenge.

Not a sound, not a twitch.

Then the tom relaxed, leering at Dulcie, his tail lashing provocatively, his neck bowed like the neck of a bull; when he smiled, his eyes burned keener than the fires of hell.

"I am Azrael."

Joe circled him, rumbling and snarling.

"Azrael," Dulcie said, moving between Joe and the black tom. "Azrael means Death Angel." She watched the cat intently.

The presence of another like themselves should be a cause for joy. Where had he come from? Why was he here in their village? As Joe moved again to attack, she cut him a look of warning. What good were teeth and claws, if they found out nothing about this cat?

"Azrael," she mewed softly, recalling the dark mythology. "Azrael of the million dark veils. Azrael who can spin the world on one claw.

"Azrael whose golden throne gleams in the sixth Heaven," she purred, glaring at Joe to be still. "Azrael of the four black wings and the four faces, and a thousand watchful eyes."

The tom smiled and preened at her but glanced narrowly at Joe.

"Azrael who stole from that store," Dulcie said,

trying to sound amused. "Azrael who helped that man steal."

The black tom laughed. "And what do you think we stole? That junk furniture? Did you see him carrying away old chairs and hat racks?"

"You took her money."

"If we did, little queen, that's none of your affair." His purr was a ragged rumble; he towered over her, slow and insinuating; his amber eyes caressed her, devoured her—but when he reached out his nose to sniff her tail, she whirled, screaming feline curses, and Joe exploded, biting and slashing him, sinking his claws into the tom's back and neck. The two toms spun in a clawing, yowling whirlwind across the roofs, raking fur and swearing until Dulcie again thrust herself between them, fighting them both.

They spun apart and backed off, circling and snarling, crouching to leap again for the tender parts.

Joe attacked first—blood spattered Dulcie's face. But the tom sent him flying against a chimney. Joe shook his head and bolted into Azrael, cursing a string of human insults until Dulcie again drove them apart, battling like a wildcat; neither tom would hurt a queen.

"You want to bring the cops?" she hissed at them. "There are apartments above these shops. You make enough noise, someone will call the station."

The black tom smiled and turned away. He began to wash, as casual and easy as if there had never been a battle. But soon he paused, and drew himself up tall and erect like an Egyptian statue carved from ebony. "You two little cats," he said, looking them over as if they amused him. "You two little cats—I see death around you."

He studied them haughtily. "Do you not sense death?" He licked his paw. "There will be death in this village. Human death. I sense death—three human corpses. Death before the moon is again full.

"I see you two little cats standing over the bodies. I see your foolish pain—because humans are dead." He laughed coldly. "Humans. How very silly. Why would you care that a human dies? The world is overrun with humans."

"What do . . ." Dulcie began.

But a whistle from the street jerked the tomcat up, a call as soft as the cry of a night bird. He turned, leaped down into the awning, and was gone. They heard a muffled *oof* of breath as he hit the street. Heard his human partner speak to him, then footsteps.

Looking over the roof's edge, they watched the two drift away, up the street into darkness. Joe crouched to follow, but Dulcie pressed against him, urging him away from the edge.

"Don't," she said. "Please don't—he frightens me." She was demure and quiet. If she had ranted and snarled at him, he would have been off at once, after the pair.

"He scares me," she repeated, sitting down on the shingles. Joe looked back at her crossly, knowing he'd be sorry he hadn't followed. But he was puzzled, too. Dulcie was seldom afraid. Not this shivering, shrinking, huge-eyed kind of fear.

"Please," she said, "leave him alone. He might be like us. There might be a wonderful mystery about him. But he terrifies me."

Later, in the small hours when Joe and Dulcie had parted, as she snuggled down in the quilt beside Wilma, she dreamed of Azrael, and in sleep she shivered. Caught by the tom's amber eyes, she followed him along medieval lanes, was both frightened of him and fascinated. Winding across ancient rooftops they slipped among gargoyles and mythic creatures twisted and grotesque, beasts that mirrored the black tom's dark nature. Azrael before her, drawing her on, charming her, leading her in dream until she began to lose all judgment.

She'd always had vivid dreams. Sometimes, prophetic dreams. But this drama woke her, clawing the blankets, hissing with fear and unwanted emotions. Her thrashing woke Wilma, who sat up in bed and gathered Dulcie close, her long gray hair falling around them, her flannel nightgown warm against Dulcie. "Nightmare? A bad nightmare?"

Dulcie said nothing. She lay shivering against Wilma, trying to purr, feeling very ashamed of the way the black tom had made her feel.

She was Joe Grey's lady; her preoccupation with the stranger, even in dream, deeply upset her.

Wilma didn't press her for answers. She stroked Dulcie until she slept again, and this time as Dulcie dropped into the deep well of sleep she held her thoughts on Joe Grey and on home and on Wilma, pressing into her mind everyone dear to her, shutting out dark Azrael.

It was not until the next morning that Joe, brushing past Clyde's bare feet, leaping to the kitchen table and pawing open the morning *Gazette*, learned more about the burglary at Medder's Antiques. He read the article as Clyde stood at the stove frying eggs. Two over-easy for Clyde, one sunny-side up for Joe. Around Clyde's feet the three household cats and the elderly black Labrador crouched on the kitchen floor eating kibble, each at his or her own bowl. Only Joe was served breakfast on the table, and he certainly wasn't having kibble.

Clyde said kibble was good for his teeth, but so were whole wheat kitty treats laced with fish oil and added vitamins from Molena Point's Pet Gourmet. Choosing between P.G.'s delightful confections and store-bought kibble was no contest. Two of P.G.'s fish-shaped delicacies, at this moment, lay on his breakfast plate, which Clyde had placed just beside the news-paper. Clyde had arranged four sardines as well, and a thin slice of Brie, a nicely planned repast awaiting only the fried egg.

It had taken a bit of doing to get Clyde trained, but the effort had been worth it.

Standing on the morning paper sniffing the deli-cate aroma of good, imported sardines, he read the *Gazette*'s account of the burglary. The police did not know how the burglar had gotten into the store. There had been no sign of forced entry. No item of merchandise seemed to be missing. Fifteen hundred dollars had been taken, three hundred from the cash register, the balance from the locked safe. The safe had been drilled, a very professional job. Joe didn't know he was growling until Clyde turned from the stove.

"What? What are you reading?" Clyde brought the skillet to the table, dished up the eggs, then picked Joe up as if he were a bag of flour so he could see the paper.

Joe dangled impatiently as Clyde read.

Clyde set Joe down again, making no comment, and turned away, his face closed and remote.

They had been through this too many times. Clyde didn't like him messing around with burglaries and murders and police business. And Joe was going to do as he pleased. There was no way Clyde could stop him short of locking him in a cage. And Clyde Damen,

even at his worst, would never consider such a deed—
never be fool enough to attempt it.

Clyde sat down at the table and dumped pepper on
his eggs. "So this is why you've been scowling and
snarling all morning, this burglary."

"I haven't been scowling and snarling." Joe
slurped up a sardine, dipping it in egg yolk. "Why
would I bother with a simple break-and-enter? Max
Harper can handle that stuff."

"Oh? Those small crimes are beneath you? So,
then, what's with the worried scowl?"

Joe looked at him blankly and nipped off a bite of
Brie.

Clyde reached across the table and nudged him.
"What's going on? What's with you?"

"Nothing," Joe said coldly. "Is there some law that
I have to tell you all my business?"

Clyde raised an eyebrow.

"So there's a new cat in the village. It's nothing to
worry you, nothing for you to fret over."

Clyde was silent a moment, watching him. "I take it
this is a tomcat. What did he do, come on to Dulcie?"

Joe glared.

Clyde grinned. "What else would make you so
surly?" He mopped up egg with his toast. "I imagine
you can handle the beast. I don't suppose this cat has
anything to do with last night's burglary?"

Joe widened his eyes and laughed. "In what way?
What would a cat have to do with a burglary? It's too
early in the morning for dumb questions."

Clyde looked at him deeply, then rose and fetched
the coffeepot, poured a fresh cup.

"You get the Sheetrock all torn out?"

"We did, and hauled it to the dump. No more
Sheetrock dust, you and Dulcie can hunt mice to your

little hearts' content without sneezing—until we start hanging new Sheetrock, of course."

The five-apartment unit that Clyde had bought was a venture Joe considered incredibly foolhardy. No way Clyde Damen was going to turn that neglected dump into a sound rental investment. The fact that Clyde was working on the project himself turned Joe weak with amusement.

The only sensible thing Clyde had done on the venture was to hire his girlfriend, Charlie Getz, who operated Charlie's Fix-It, Clean-It. Charlie's business was relatively new. She had only a small crew—just two women—but she did good work. Her cleaning lady was sixty-year-old Mavity Flowers, who was a tiny, skinny creature but a surprisingly hard worker. The other employee, Pearl Ann Jamison, was a real find. Pearl Ann not only cleaned for Charlie, she was handy at light carpentry and could turn out professional Sheetrock work, from installation of the heavy wall-board to mudding and taping. The rest of the work on the building, the wiring and plumbing, Charlie and Clyde were farming out to subcontractors.

Joe finished his breakfast, nosed his plate out of the way, and began to wash, thinking about the burglary. He supposed the antique shop had been the first, as he'd seen nothing in the papers about any other similar thefts. He didn't let himself dwell on the nature of the black tom or where he came from but kept his mind on the immediate problem, wondering what other small village businesses the man and cat planned to hit.

But maybe this had been a one-time deal. Maybe the pair was just passing through, heading up the coast—maybe they'd simply needed some walking-around money. Maybe they were already gone, had hauled out of Molena Point for parts unknown.

Sure. The village should be so lucky.

No, this burglary hadn't been impromptu. The planning was too precise, the team's moves too deliberate and assured, as if they had done their research. As if they knew very well that the quiet village was a sitting duck, and they knew just how to pluck it.

He hated to think that that cat might have been prowling the shops for days—maybe weeks—and he and Dulcie hadn't known about it, hadn't scented the beast or seen him. He imagined the cat and the old man idling in Mrs. Medder's antique shop getting friendly with her, the old man making small talk as he cased the place looking for a safe or a burglar alarm, the black tom wandering innocently rubbing around the old woman's ankles, purring and perhaps accepting little tidbits of her lunch while he, too, checked the layout, leaped up to stare into the drawer of the open cash register, and searched the shadows for an alarm system.

He didn't like that scenario. It was bad enough for a human to steal from the village shops. A cat had no business doing this stuff.

Leaping from the table to the sink, pacing restlessly across the counter and glaring out the window, Joe wished he'd followed those two last night. He wouldn't make that mistake again. Dulcie could find excuses to avoid confronting the black tomcat if she chose, but he was going to nail that little team. Licking egg from his whiskers as he watched the rising sun lift above the Molena Point hills, Joe Grey's lust for justice flamed at least as bright as that solar orb—burned with a commitment as powerful and predatory as any human cop.

4

CHARLIE GETZ had no reason to suspect, when she woke early Saturday morning, that she was about to be evicted from her cozy new apartment, that by the time most of the village sat down to breakfast she'd be shoving cardboard boxes and canvas duffles into her decrepit Chevy van, dumping all her worldly possessions back into her aunt's garage—from which she had so recently removed them. Thrown out, given the boot, on the most special day of her life, on a day that she had wanted to be perfect.

She'd already spent three months sponging off Aunt Wilma, had moved in with Wilma jobless and nearly broke and with no prospects, had lived rent-free in Wilma's guest room after abandoning her failed career.

During that time she'd launched her new venture, put what little cash she had into running ads, buying the old van and used cleaning and carpentry equipment, hiring the best help she could find on short notice. She was twenty-eight years old. Starting Charlie's Fix-It, Clean-It and renting her own apartment, taking responsibility for her own life after wasting six years in San Francisco had been one big strike for independence. A huge step toward joining—belatedly—the adult world.

Now here she was back to square one, homeless again.

She had loved being with Wilma, loved coming home to a cozy house, to a blazing fire and a nice hot meal, loved being pampered, but she valued, more, being her own provider.

Now, waking at dawn before she had any notion that an eviction notice was tucked beside her front door, she snuggled down into the covers, looking around her little studio with deep satisfaction. The one room pleased her immensely, though the furnishings weren't much, just her easel, her single cot, her secondhand breakfast table, and two mismatched wooden chairs. Open cardboard boxes stacked on their sides like shelves held her neatly folded clothes. But through her open windows a cool breeze blew in, smelling pleasantly of the sea, and above the village rooftops the sunrise, this morning, was a wonder of watercolor tints, from pink to pale orange streaked among islands of dark clouds.

The coastal foothills would be brightening now as the sun rose behind them, casting its light down on the small village, onto the narrow, wandering lanes and dark, leathery oak trees and the maze of slanted, angled rooftops, and reflecting from the windows of the little restaurants and shops—the morning sun sending its light into the windows of the Aronson Gallery onto her own drawings, picking out her work with fingers of light.

What a strange sensation, to think that she

belonged to a gallery, that her work was to be part of a real exhibit. She still couldn't believe her luck, not only to be included with six well-known artists but to see her drawings occupying more than half the gallery's front window—a real vote of confidence for a newcomer. The exhibit had been a bonus out of nowhere, unforeseen and amazing.

Four years of art school and two years trying to find her way as a commercial artist, a dozen trial-and-error, entry-level advertising jobs that she knew weren't right for her, nor she for them, had led at last to the realization that she would never make a living in the art world. Her failure had left her feeling totally defeated—a misfit not only in her chosen field but in life. Only now, after she had abandoned all idea of supporting herself in the arts, had anyone been interested in her drawings.

Reaching to her nightstand, she switched on the travel-sized coffeepot that she had prepared the night before, wondering if her flowered India skirt and sandals and the low-necked blue T-shirt *were* the right clothes for the opening or if she'd better try the black dress again, with the silver necklace her aunt had loaned her. She imagined the gallery as it would be tonight, lighted and festive, thinking about the crowd of strangers, hoping she could remember people's names.

As the scent of coffee filled the room she sat up, pushing her pillow behind her, and poured a steaming mug, blowing on the brew to cool it. Coffee in bed was pure luxury, a little moment to spoil herself before she started the day, pulled on her jeans and boots and a work shirt, and hurried out to be on the job by eight, installing Sheetrock and trying to figure out how to do things she'd never done before. She would not, once she got moving, stop again until dark overtook her, except for a hasty sandwich with her girls, maybe with Clyde, and with whatever subcontractor might be working.

Leaning back into the pillows, she planned her day and the week ahead, laying out the work for the plumber, the sprinkler man, and the electrician, and watching, through her open windows, the sky brighten to flame, the sunrise staining the room, and laying a wash of pink over her framed drawings. Her studies of the two cats looked back at her, so alert and expectant that she had to smile. Dulcie had such a wicked little grin, such a slant-eyed, knowing look, as if she kept some wonderful secret.

The portraits of Joe Grey were more reserved. Tomcat dignity, she thought, amused. Drawing Joe was like drawing draped satin or polished pewter—the tomcat was so sleek and beautifully muscled, his charcoal-gray coat gleaming like velvet.

But his gaze was imperious. So deeply appraising that sometimes he made her uncomfortable. Sometimes she could swear that she saw, in Joe Grey's eyes, a judgment far too perceptive, a watchfulness too aware and intense for any cat.

Charlie didn't understand what it was about those two; both cats had a presence that set them apart from other felines.

Maybe she just knew them better. Maybe all cats had that quality of awareness, when you knew them. Her thoughts fled to last night when she had stood alone in the moonlit village looking up at the black rooftops, stood touched by that vast, wheeling space, and had glimpsed two cats leaping between the rooftops across the pale, night sky, and she felt again a wonderful delight in their freedom.

She had gone out to dinner alone, hadn't felt like a can of soup or peanut butter and crackers, which was all her bare cupboard had offered. And she didn't feel like calling Clyde. Their dating was casual; he probably would have been happy to run out for a quick hamburger, but she'd wanted to be by herself. Besides, she'd been with him half the day, working on the house. She'd been tired and irritable from dealing with a hired carpenter, had wanted to walk the village alone, watch the evening draw down, have a quiet dinner and then home to bed. When she had taken on the job of refurbishing Clyde's newly purchased relic of an apartment house, she had bitten off almost more than she could chew. She'd had no intention, when she started Charlie's Fix-It, Clean-It, of becoming a remodeling service. The business was meant to be just what it said: minor household repairs and painting—replacing a few shingles, spiffing up the yard, window washing, gutter cleaning, a good scrub down, total maintenance for the village homes and cottages. Not tearing out and replacing walls, supervising workmen, replacing ancient plumbing. She had no contractor's license, but Clyde was, for all practical purposes, his own contractor. All they had to do was satisfy the various building inspectors.

She'd gotten home from work as the summer twilight faded into a clear, chill night, had peeled off her sweaty jeans and shirt, showered, put on clean denims and a warm sweater. Leaving her apartment, she had walked through the village down to the shore ten blocks south, moving quickly between wandering tourists. This was the beginning of the Fourth of July weekend, and along the narrow streets, NO VACANCY signs glowed discreetly among climbing nasturtiums and bougainvillea.

She had chosen a circuitous route, cutting across Ocean to the south side of the village, slowing to look in the windows of the Latin American Boutique, enjoying the brightly painted carvings and red-toned weavings, admiring and coveting the beautiful crafts and trying not to make nose prints on the glass.

She had met the shop's owner, Sue Marble, a white-haired woman of maybe fifty who, people said, kept the store primarily so she could claim a tax write-off on her frequent Latin American trips. Not a bad deal, more power to her.

But as she had moved along beside the window, a Peruvian death mask gleamed through her own reflection, an ugly face superimposed over her face, framed by her wild red hair. The image had amused her—then frightened her. Swiftly she had turned away, hurried away toward the shore.

She hit the beach at Tenth Avenue, and had walked south a mile on the hard sand, then turned back up Ocean to The Bakery, thinking that a glass of Chablis would be nice, and perhaps crab Newburg. She thought sometimes that she led herself through life only with these little treats, like beguiling a mule with a carrot.

But why not treat herself? Tuck some bits of fun in with the hard work? Hanging Sheetrock all day was no picnic—and the heavy work had left her ravenous.

The Bakery, a rambling structure of weathered shingles, had been a summer-vacation house in the early 1900s. A deep porch ran along the front, facing a little seaside park of sand dunes and low, twisted oak trees spreading like dark, giant hands over the curves of sand and sweeps of dark ice plant. She'd been disappointed that all the terrace tables were taken, but then had spied a small corner table and soon was settled facing the darkening dunes, ordering wine and the Newburg, quietly celebrating the first gallery exhibit of her drawings.

After her father died, it was her mother's subtle control that had eased her in the direction of art school, to develop the talent her mother thought was her strongest. Her mother would not consider that her skills at repair work and at organizing the work of others had any value. Sipping her wine, Charlie thought about her mother with regret and disappointment. Her mother had died a year before she finished art school.

Beyond The Bakery veranda, the breaking waves were tipped with phosphorescence, and above them the night sky flowed like surging water, its light seeming also to ebb and change. She'd been so physically tired from the day's work that the Chablis had given her a nice buzz, and the conversations around her were subdued, a relaxed ambience of soft voices against the hushing surf. When her Newburg arrived she'd made herself eat slowly, not wolf the good dish but savor each bite—had to remind herself this wasn't noon on the job, eating a sandwich with the work crew and with Mavity and Pearl Ann and Clyde, all of them starved. Had to remind herself this was not supper with Clyde. Eating with Clyde was much like eating with the carpenters; she was inclined to follow his lead, devour her meal as if it would remain on the table only briefly and must be consumed before it got away.

But Clyde was good company. And he was honest, quick to see the truth of a situation. If he was lacking in some social graces, who cared? There was nothing put-on or fake about him.

That first morning, when they went up to look at the five-apartment building after he signed the escrow papers, he'd been so excited. Leading her in through the weedy patio and through those moldering rooms, he'd been deep in the grip of euphoria, imagining what the place would look like when they'd refurbished it—imagining he could do most of the work himself, just a little help from her. *Just a little paint, Charlie. A bit of patching.* They'd agreed to exchange labor. She'd help with the house, presenting him with bills that he'd honor by working on her declining Chevy van.

Of course there was more needed than patching, but the five apartments had nice large rooms and high ceilings, and Clyde had envisioned the final result just as clearly as he saw the possibilities in restoring an old, vintage car.

The difference was, he knew what it took to restore a car. Beneath his skilled hands the Mercedeses and BMWs and Bentleys of Molena Point purred and gleamed, as cared for as fine jewelry. But Clyde was no carpenter. To Clyde Damen, carpentry was a foreign language.

In order to pay cash for the building, he had sold his five beautifully restored antique cars, including the classic red Packard touring car that he so loved. The sales nearly broke his heart, he had done every speck of work on those cars himself in his spare time. But he was too tight to pay interest on a mortgage, and she didn't blame him.

As the dining terrace began to empty, she had dawdled over her dinner enjoying her own company, quietly watching the surf's endless rolling, feeling its power—spawned by the interplay of wind, the moon's pull, and the centrifugal whirling of the earth. The sea's unending motion seemed to repeat the eternal power of the universe—its vast and unceasing life.

She relished her idle thoughts, her idle moments, the little pauses in which to let her mind roam.

After the Newburg she had treated herself to a flan and coffee, and it was past midnight when she paid her bill, left the veranda, and headed home through the softly lighted village. The streets were nearly empty. She imagined the tourists all tucked up in their motel rooms, with maybe a fire burning on the hearth, perhaps wrapped in their warm robes nursing a nightcap of brandy.

Walking home, she had paused to look in the window of a sporting goods shop at a beautiful leather coat that she would never buy; she'd rather have a new cement mixer. It was then, turning away, that her glance was drawn to the rooftops by swift movement: Two dark shadows had sailed between the peaks. She had caught only a glimpse. Owls? A pair of large night birds?

But they were gone, the sky was empty.

No, there they were. Two silhouettes, not flying but racing along a peaked ridge, leaping from roof to roof then dropping out of sight.

Cats! They were cats; she had seen a lashing tail against the clouds and sharply peaked ears. Two cats, playing across the rooftops.

And she had to laugh. There was no mistaking Joe Grey's tailless posterior, and his white paws and white nose. She had stood very still, setting carefully into memory the cats' swift flight against the pale clouds. They appeared again, and as they fled up another peak and leaped between dark ridges, scorching in and out among the tilting roofs, she had itched for a piece of charcoal, a bit of paper.

As she stood watching them, she heard a young couple laughing somewhere ahead, the woman's voice soft. Glancing to the street she didn't see the man and woman, but their conversation was playful, challenging and happy; she couldn't make out their words. Then silence, as if they had turned up a side street.

And the cats were gone. She had stood alone on

the sidewalk, her painter's mind teeming with the two racing felines, with the joy of their carefree flight.

But now, lying in bed, seeing the leaping cats among the darkly angled rooftops, she felt a sudden chill.

Puzzled, sliding out of bed, she refilled her coffee cup and stood before the easel looking at the quick sketch she had done, from memory, before she went to sleep, the swift lines of charcoal on newsprint, her hasty strokes blocking in jutting roof lines against the sky, and the lithe, swift cats leaping across—and a sense of threat was there, that she had not meant to lend to the scene. Studying the drawing, she shivered.

Last night she had been so charmed by the cats' grace and freedom, by their wild joy; she had felt only pleasure in the hasty drawing—but she saw now that the drawing did not reflect joy. Its spirit was dark, pensive. Somehow she had infused the composition with foreboding. Its shadowed angles implied a dark threat.

Threat *to* the cats? Or threat *because* of the cats?

Perplexed, she turned away. Carrying her coffee, she headed for the shower.

The bathroom was tiny. Setting her coffee cup on the edge of the sink basin, she slid under the hot, steaming water of the shower, her mind fully on the sketch.

What had guided her hand last night? Those two little cats were dear to her; she had gotten to know Dulcie well while she was staying with Wilma. And if not for her drawings of Joe and Dulcie, sketching them for her own pleasure, her work would not have been seen by Sicily Aronson. She would never have been invited to join Sicily's prestigious group. Without Joe and Dulcie, there would be no exhibit for her tonight at Sicily's fine gallery.

Letting the hot water pound on her back, reaching out for a sip of coffee, she told herself she had better get her mind on the day's work. She had building materials to order and three subcontractors to juggle so they didn't get in each other's way. Coming out of the shower to dress and make a peanut-butter sandwich, checking over her work list, she forgot the dark drawing.

But then as she opened the front door, carrying her denim work jacket and the paper bag with her lunch, a folded sheet of paper fluttered down against her boot, as if it had been stuffed between the door and the molding. Snatching it up before it blew away, unfolding it, she read the neatly typed message.

Charlie:

You'd be a good tenant, if you didn't clutter up the yard. You've had a week, and two previous warnings, to get your stuff out of the backyard. The other tenants are complaining. They want to lie in the sun back there, not fall over wheelbarrows and shovels. I have no choice. You are in violation of your rental contract. This is a formal notice to vacate the apartment and all premises by tonight. Any item you leave behind, inside the apartment or in the yard—cement mixer, buckets, the entire clutter—will be mine to keep and dispose of.

She set her lunch bag on the porch, dropped her jacket on top, and read the note again. Looking down toward her landlord's apartment, just below hers, she wanted to snatch up that neat little man and smear him all over his neat little yard.

Swinging back inside, she grabbed her stacked cardboard boxes and began shoving dishes and pots and pans in on top of her folded clothes. Jerking her few hanging garments from the closet, she rolled them into a bundle, snatched her framed drawings off the wall, and carried the first load down to her van. Halfway through her packing, she grabbed up the phone and called Clyde, told him she'd be a bit late. Didn't tell him why. And within an hour she was out of there, chalking up another defeat.

5

THE BRIGHTLY lighted gallery, from the aspect of the two cats, was an obstacle course of human legs and feet. They had to move lively toward the back to avoid being stepped on by spike heels, wedge sandals, and hard, polished oxfords that looked as lethal as sledgehammers. Slinking between silken ankles and well-creased trouser cuffs, they slipped beneath Sicily Aronson's desk into shadow where they could watch, untrampled, the champagne-fueled festivities.

In Joe's opinion, the way to attend an art exhibit was from, say, a rooftop several blocks removed. But Dulcie had to be in the middle, listening to the tangle of conversations, sniffing expensive French perfumes and admiring dangling jewelry and elegant hair arrangements. "No one will notice us—they're all talking at once, trying to impress each other."

"Right. Of course Sicily won't notice us. So why is she swooping in this direction like a hungry barn owl?" The gallery owner was pushing through the crowd with her usual exuberance. "On stage," Joe muttered.

"Always on stage." She was dressed in silver lamé evening pajamas that flapped around her ankles, a flowing silver scarf that swung around her thin thighs, and an amazing array of clinking jewelry. Kneeling and laughing, she peered under the desk at them, then scooped Dulcie into her arms. Pulling Joe out, too, she cuddled them like two teddy bears; Joe had to grit his teeth to keep from clawing her, and of course Dulcie gave him that *don't-you-dare* scowl.

"You two look beautiful, so sleek and brushed," Sicily cooed, snuggling them against her silver bosom. "This is lovely to have you here—after all, you are the main models, you dear cats. Did Wilma bring you? Where is Wilma?"

Joe wanted to throw up. Dulcie purred extravagantly—she was such a sucker for this stuff. Whenever she visited Sicily, wandering into the gallery, Sicily had a treat for her, a little snack put aside from Molena Point's Pet Gourmet. And Sicily kept a soft sweater for Dulcie to nap on; she had figured out quickly that to Dulcie, pretty garments, silk and velvet and cashmere, were the pièce de résistance. Only once, when Dulcie trotted out of the shop dragging a handwoven vicuña scarf, did Sicily fling a cross word at her and run out to retrieve the treasure. Now, fawning and petting them and effectively blocking their escape, she reached behind the desk to fetch a blue velvet cushion and laid it on the blotter. "You two stay right here—just curl up and look pretty—and I'll fix a plate for you." Leaning down, she stared into Joe's eyes, stroking him and scratching behind his ears. "Caviar, Joe Grey? Smoked turkey?"

Joe felt himself weakening.

But as Sicily left them, a big woman in a plum-colored dress descended, pushing her way out of the crowd. "Oh, the two little models. Oh, look how sweet."

Joe growled and raised his paw. Dulcie nudged him. "Isn't that cute. Look at him put up his paw to shake hands. Just like a little dog."

The lady's male companion had sensibly stepped back from Joe. But the woman reached for him. "Oh, they look *just* like their portraits. Such dear little cats. Come and pet them, Howard. Look how sweet, the way they're posing here on the desk, so obedient." She patted Joe on the head like a dog, a gesture guaranteed, under most circumstances, to elicit a bloody stump. He held his temper with heroic effort, but he calmed as she chose a slice of ham from her plate and gave them each a share.

He was beginning to feel more charitable when a woman in a white dress joined them. "Oh, the darling kitties, the kitties in the drawings." And an elderly couple headed their way, practically cooing. A regular crowd was gathering. Joe eyed them sourly. Even the good party food wasn't enough to put up with this. As other guests circled the desk reaching to pet them, Joe lost it. Lashing out at the nearest hand, he leaped past it, hit the floor running, sped out the door and across the street and up a bougainvillea vine. Didn't stop until he was on the roof of Mara's Leather Shop, pacing among the vents.

Dulcie didn't follow him. Probably she'd stay in there all night, lapping up the attention.

Stretching out beside a warm chimney, he dozed intermittently and irritably. His view from the roof was directly in through the gallery's wide windows and open front door, where the crowd had gathered around a white-clothed table as a tuxedoed waiter served champagne. It was more than an hour before Dulcie came trotting out between a tangle of elegantly clad ankles, scanned the rooftops, and saw him looking over. Lifting her tail like a happy flag, she crossed the street and swarmed up the vine to join him.

"You didn't have to be so surly. You knew we'd be petted. Cats in a public place always get petted."

"*Petted?* Mauled is the word. You said no one would notice us."

She settled down beside him, her belly against the warm shingles. "You missed some good party food."

"I'll have my share in the alley."

"Suit yourself. I had duck liver canapés from the hand of my favorite movie star." She sighed deeply. "He might be sixty-some, but he's some macho hombre."

"Big deal. So some Hollywood biggie feeds you duck liver like a zoo animal."

"Not at all. He was very polite and cordial. And he's not from Hollywood; you know very well that he lives in Molena Point. What a nice man. He treated *me* like a celebrity—he told me I have beautiful eyes." And she gave him a clear green glance, bright and provocative.

Joe turned away crossly. "So where are Charlie and Clyde? Fashionably late is one thing. Charlie's going to miss her own party."

"They'll show. Clyde told Wilma he'd keep Charlie away until there was a real mob, until she could make a big entrance."

"This *is* a mob. And Charlie isn't the kind for a big entrance."

"She will be, tonight."

Joe snorted.

"It's her party. Why not a grand entrance?"

"Females. Everything for show."

"I've seen you make a big entrance—stroll into the living room when Clyde has company. Wait until conversation's in full swing, then swagger in so everyone stops talking. Starts calling to you, *kitty kitty kitty*, and making little lovey noises."

"That is a totally different matter. That is done for a specific purpose."

Dulcie cut her eyes at him, and smiled.

The game was to get the crowd's attention and then, when they were all calling and making a fuss, to pick out the person who remained withdrawn and quiet. Who did *not* want to pet the kitty.

Immediately one made a beeline for the cat hater. A jump into their lap, a persistent rubbing and kneading and waving your tail in their face, and the result was most rewarding. If your victim had a really severe case of ailurophobia, the effect was spectacular.

When the routine worked really well, when you had picked the right mark, your victim would turn as white as skimmed milk. If you could drool and rub your face against theirs, that was even better. There was nothing half as satisfying as a nice evening of ailurophobe harassment. Such little moments were to be treasured—such fleeting pleasures in life made up for all the millions of human rebuffs, for centuries of shabby human slights and maltreatment.

"Here they come," Dulcie said, pressing forward over the roof gutter, her ears pricked, the tip of her tail twitching with excitement.

Clyde pulled up directly in front of the gallery, his yellow '29 Chevy convertible commanding immediate attention. This was the car's maiden appearance. The top was down, and the machine was dazzling. He had completely overhauled the vintage model, had given it mirror-bright metal detailing, pearly, canary-toned paint, pale yellow leather upholstery, and of course the engine purred like a world-champion Siamese. The car's creamy tones set off Charlie's flaming hair to perfection.

Her red, curling mane hung loose across her shoulders over a dark tank top, and as Clyde handed her out, her flowered India skirt swirled around her ankles in shades of red, pink, and orange. The cats had never seen Charlie in high-heeled sandals, had never seen her in a skirt.

"Wow," Joe said, hanging over the roof, ogling.

"Oh, my," Dulcie said. "She's beautiful."

Tonight they saw none of Charlie's usual shyness. She looked totally wired, her cheeks flaming as she took Clyde's hand and stepped to the curb.

Clyde's chivalry prompted them to stare, too, as he gave Charlie his arm and escorted her into the gallery. Clyde himself looked elegant, scrubbed and shaven and sharply turned out in a black sport coat over a white turtleneck and a good-looking pair of jeans. For Clyde, this was formal attire.

"There's the mayor," Dulcie said, "and his wife. And look—the president of the art association."

Joe didn't know the president of the art association from a rat's posterior. Nor did he care. But he cared about Clyde and Charlie. He watched with almost parental pride as they pushed into the gallery and were mobbed with greetings and well-wishers. Crouched on the edge of the roof, the two cats totally enjoyed Charlie's happy moment. They remained watching as the party spilled out onto the sidewalk among a din of conversation and laughter, and the scents of perfumes and champagne and caviar caressed them on the night breeze.

But later when two waiters headed away toward Jolly's Deli carrying a stack of nearly empty trays that they had replaced with fresh servings, the cats left the roof, padding along behind them, their attention on those delectable scraps.

Jolly's Deli catered most of the local affairs, the gallery openings and weddings and the nicest parties. And whatever delicacies were left over, George Jolly set out on paper plates in the alley for the enjoyment of the village cats.

Of course the old man put out deli scraps several times every day, but party fare was the best. An astute cat, if he checked the *Gazette*'s social page or simply used his nose, could dine as elegantly, in Jolly's alley, as Molena Point's rich and famous.

And the alley provided more than a free handout. Through frequent use, it had become the city version of a feline hunting path, a communal by-way shared by all the local cats.

Some people view cats as reclusive loners, but that is not the case. Any cat could tell you that a feline is simply more discerning than a dog, that cats take a subtler view of social interaction.

When several cats happened into the alley at one time, they did not circle each other snarling like ill-mannered hounds—unless, of course, they were toms on the make. But in a simple social situation, each cat sat down to quietly study his or her peers, communicating in a civilized manner by flick of ear, by narrowing of eyes, by twitching tail, following a perceptive protocol as to who should proceed first, who merited the warmest patch of sunshine or the preferred bench on which to nap.

The village cats had established in Jolly's alley, as well, a center for feline messages, a handy post office where, through scents left on flowerpot and doorway, one could learn which cats were with kitten or had had their kittens, which ladies were feeling amorous, or if there was a new cat in the village.

Only in the hierarchy of the supper plate did the

biggest and strongest prevail—but George Jolly did not tolerate fights.

Such social commerce pleased Joe and Dulcie despite the void that separated them from normal cats. After all, every cat was unique. The lack of human language didn't make the other cats imperceptive or unwise; each could enjoy the world in his own way. And, Joe thought, how many cats would *want* to read the newspaper or use the phone?

But tonight they had the alley to themselves, the little brick-paved retreat was their own small corner of civilized ambiance, softly lit by the wrought-iron lamps at either end of the lane, perfumed by the jasmine vine that concealed Jolly's garbage cans.

The two waiters had disappeared inside, but George Jolly must have been watching for visitors, because as the cats flopped down to roll on the warm bricks, the back door opened and the old man was there, his white apron extending wide over his ample stomach as he knelt to place a paper plate before them, a little snack of smoked salmon and chopped egg and Beluga caviar.

They approached the offering purring, Dulcie waving her tail, and George Jolly stood smiling and nodding. Jolly loved providing these little repasts—he took a deep delight in the cats' pleasure.

Kneeling for a moment to stroke them, he soon rose again and turned away to his kitchen like any good chef, allowing his guests privacy in which to enjoy their meal. They were crouched over the plate nibbling at the caviar when, above them, a dark shadow leaped across the sky from roof to roof, and the black tom paced the shingles looking down at them—observing the loaded deli plate.

Dropping to an awning and then to the bricks, he

swaggered toward them snarling a challenge deep in his throat, a growl of greed and dominance.

Dulcie screamed at him and crouched to slash; Joe flew at him, raking. At the same moment, the back door flew open and George Jolly ran out swinging a saucepan.

"No fighting! You cats don't fight here! You cats behave in my alley!"

Joe and Dulcie backed away glancing at each other, but Azrael stood his ground, snarling and spitting at Jolly.

"Stop that, you black beast. Don't you challenge me!" Jolly hefted the pan. "You eat nice or I don't feed you. I take the plate away." He looked hard at the three of them. "I don't put out my best imported for you to act like street rabble—you are Molena Point cats, not alley bums.

"Except you," Jolly said, glaring at Azrael. "I don't know you, you black monster. Well, wherever you come from, you snarl again, you get a smack in the muzzle."

George Jolly could never have guessed the true effect of his words. He had no idea that the three cats understood him, he knew only that his tone would frighten and perhaps shame them. He glared hard at Azrael—Azrael blazed back at him, his amber eyes sparking rage, and he began to stalk the old man, crouching as if he would spring straight into Jolly's face.

"Don't you threaten me," Jolly snapped, swinging the saucepan. "You learn some manners or you'll be snarling at the dogcatcher." He stood glaring until Azrael backed away switching his tail, his head high, and turned and swaggered off up the alley—until the formidable Death Angel vanished into the night.

Joe and Dulcie did not see Azrael again until some hours later as they prowled the rooftops. Pale clouds had gathered across the moon, and there was no sound; the bats had gone to roost or perch or whatever bats did hanging upside down in their pokey little niches beneath the eaves. Who knew why bats would hunt one night and not the next? Presumably, Joe thought, it had to do with how bright the sky was—yet why would bats care, when they hunted by radar? On the roofs around them, the shadows were marbled by moonlight. Above them they heard a barn owl call, sending shivers. Even Joe Grey respected the claws and beak of the barn owl.

When the clouds parted and the full moon brightened the rooftops, across the moon's face the owl came winging. He swooped low and silent. The cats crouched to run. Screaming a booming cry, he dove, heading for the shadows beyond them.

They heard the boom of his wings beating against the roof, and heard screaming—the owl's scream and a cat's scream, then the frantic flurrying of feathers, the thud of bodies . . .

The owl exploded into the sky and was gone.

And in the moon's gleam the black cat sauntered out swaggering and spitting feathers.

Unaware of them, he slipped along seeming none the worse for his encounter. Pausing as before at each window and skylight, looking in, he lingered at a thin dormer window. He reared suddenly, clawing at the frame.

A wrenching creak slashed the night as the casement banged open.

Below on the street the cats heard footsteps, and when they fled over the roofs to look, they saw Azrael's human partner pacing, peering impatiently in through a glass door below a liquor store sign, his gray hair tangled around the collar of his wrinkled leather jacket, his boots, when he fidgeted, chuffing softly on the concrete.

The instant the door opened from inside, the old man slipped in. The cats, dropping down onto the hanging sign then to the sidewalk, crouched beneath a car where they could see through the plate glass.

Within, a faint, swinging light shone as the old man shielded his flashlight behind his hand, directing its beam along rows of bottles where Azrael paced, his tail lashing against the rich labels.

At the cash register, the old man bent over the lock and inserted a metal pick, his thin face lined and intent.

Within minutes he had the drawer open and was snatching out stacks of bills. Cleaning out the shallow tray, he lifted it, spilling loose change onto the floor as he grabbed at the larger bills that lay beneath; the night was so still they heard every coin drop.

"Why do shopkeepers do that?" Dulcie whispered. "Why do they leave money in the register?"

"Because the village has never had that much trouble. Don't you wonder if this old boy knew that—if he knew what an easy mark Molena Point is? Yet he has to be a stranger—I'd remember that old man."

They watched him stuff wads of bills into his pockets while, behind him, Azrael wound back and forth along the liquor shelf smiling and rubbing against the bottles.

"Cut the purring!" the old man snapped. "You sound like a spavined outboard. And don't leave cat hair stuck to everything."

"I never leave cat hair. Have you ever seen me shed?"

"Of course you shed. Everything I own is covered with black fur."

Azrael leaned from the shelf, peering over his partner's shoulder. "Get those tens—they can't trace tens so easy."

"Who's going to trace anything? No one marks their money in this burg. You're talking like some big-assed bank artist."

"How do you know they don't?"

"Don't be so paranoid."

"It's you that's paranoid—getting jumpy because I purr and grousing about cat hair."

The old man smoothed his thin gloves where they had wrinkled over his fingers and closed the register, and the two slipped out the front door.

"Don't forget to lock it," the cat hissed.

"Don't be so damn bossy."

"Don't get smart with me, old man. You'll be running this party alone."

The man and cat stiffened as, half a block away, a prowling police car turned into the street. As it shone its light along the storefronts in routine inspection, the two burglars slid through the shadows into the alley, were gone as completely as if they had never been there.

The patrol car didn't slow. The moment it had passed, the two appeared again, heading up Ocean. As they moved away, Joe and Dulcie followed, slipping along beneath the parked cars. Joe was determined to stay with them tonight, to see where they went to ground. Dulcie didn't like this, but she was unwilling to stay behind.

The two burglars proceeded up Ocean for four blocks, then turned down toward the Fish Shack. The old man paused before entering. "You want the cod or the shrimp?"

"The shrimp—what these stateside yokels pass off

as shrimp. Poor substitute for what we get at home."

"You're not at home, so stop bitching." The little man disappeared inside. The cat turned away to the curb where he sniffed at the messages left by passing four-legged citizens. If he scented Joe and Dulcie over the smell of other cats and dogs and fish and axle grease, he gave no indication. His partner returned dangling a white paper bag liberally splotched with grease.

"No shrimp. You'll have to eat fish and chips."

"Couldn't you have gotten crab?"

"Didn't think to ask. Let's get on, before the law comes back." And off they went, man and cat walking side by side bickering companionably, two swaggering lowlifes with the cocky walk of drunks leaving a cheap bar.

6

BEYOND WILMA'S open shutters, the neighborhood was drowned by fog, the cottages and trees hidden in the thick mist, the gnarled branches of the oak tree that ruled her front garden faded as white as if the tree had vanished and only its ghost remained. Standing at the window sipping her morning coffee, she thought that it was the coastal fog, as much as Molena Point's balmy days, that had drawn her back to her childhood village to spend her retirement years. She had always loved the fog, loved its mystery—had wandered the foggy neighborhoods as a little girl pretending she had slipped into a secret and magical world.

At dawn this morning, she had taken a long walk along the shore listening to the breakers muffled and hidden within the white vail, then home again to a hot cup of coffee and to prepare breakfast for her company.

Behind her, the Sunday paper lay scattered comfortably across her Kirman rug, and beside the fire, Clyde sprawled on the velvet loveseat reading the sports page. On the other side of the hearth, lounging in the flowered chaise, Bernine Sage pored over the financial section. Neither had spoken in some time. Clyde's preoccupation was normal; Bernine's silence came across as self-centered and cold.

She would not ordinarily have invited Bernine to breakfast or for any meal, but this morning she'd had no choice. Bernine had been at her door late last night when she arrived home from the opening. Having fought with her current lover, needing a place to stay, she seemed to think that it was Wilma's responsibility to offer her a bed; she hadn't asked if Wilma *had* company or if her presence would be inconvenient. "Why I ever moved in with that idiot—what a selfish clod. And not a motel room left. I've called and called. Damn the holidays."

After getting Bernine settled, Wilma had left a note on the kitchen table hoping Charlie would see it.

Bernine is in the guest room with you, I'm sorry. She had a fight with her live-in.

Charlie had seen the note, all right. When Wilma came out at five this morning, the scrap of paper was in the trash, wadded into a tight ball.

Bernine had dressed for brunch this morning not in jeans like everyone else, but in a pink velvet leisure suit, gold belt, gold lizard sandals, and gold earrings, and had wound her coppery hair into a flawless French twist decorated with gold chains—just a bit much in this house, in this company, Wilma thought, hiding a smile. Her own concession to company for breakfast had been to put on a fresh white sweatshirt over her jeans. And Clyde, of course, was nattily attired in ancient, frayed cut-offs, a faded purple polo shirt with a large ragged hole in the pocket, and grease-stained sandals.

Bernine had greeted him, when he and Joe arrived,

with a raised eyebrow and a shake of her elegant head. "You brought your *cat*? You brought your cat to breakfast? You actually walked over here, through the village, with a cat tagging along?"

Clyde had stared at her.

"Well," she said, "it's foggy. Maybe no one saw you."

"What difference if someone saw us? We—I do this all the time, take the cat for a walk."

"I'm surprised that a cat would follow you. What do you do, carry little treats to urge it along? Don't people laugh—a grown man walking a cat?"

"Why should anyone laugh? Why should I *care*? Everyone knows Joe. Most people speak to him. And the tourists love it; they all want to pet him." Clyde smiled. "Some rather interesting tourists, as a matter of fact." And he turned away, snatching up the Sunday paper, looking for the sports page.

Now the cat in question lay patiently awaiting the breakfast casserole. Stretched across the couch beside Dulcie, the two of them occupied as much of the blue velvet expanse as they could manage, comfortably watching the fire and dozing. Their occasional glances up at Wilma communicated clearly their pleasure in this lazy Sunday morning before the blazing fire, with their friends around them—and with the front page of the Molena Point *Gazette* lying on the floor where she had casually dropped it so that they could read the lead article. As they read, their little cat faces keen with interest, she had busied herself at the coffee table rearranging the magazines, effectively blocking Bernine's view. But then the cats, finishing the half-page account of the liquor store burglary, had put on dull, sleepy faces again, diligently practicing their best fuzzy-minded expressions.

The two cats looked beautiful this morning,
Wilma thought, sleek and healthy, their coats set off by
the blue velvet cushions, Dulcie's curving, chocolate
stripes as dark as mink, her pale, peach tinted ears and
paws freshly washed. And Joe always looked as if he
had groomed himself for a formal event, his charcoal-
gray coat shining, his white paws, white chest, and
white nose as pristine as new snow.

Wilma didn't speak to them in front of Bernine,
even to prattle baby talk as one would to ordinary pets;
their responsive glances were sometimes more intelligent than they intended, and Bernine was far too
watchful. The history that Bernine had picked up from
a previous boyfriend, the Welsh mythology of unnatural and remarkable cats that had peopled the ancient
world, was better not stirred even in the smallest way.
Better not to set Bernine off with the faintest hint of
immediate feline strangeness.

In fact, having Bernine in the house with Dulcie
was not at all comfortable. She just hoped Bernine
would find a place soon. And certainly Bernine's intru-
sion into the guest room was not a happy situation for
Charlie who, half an hour ago, had disappeared in the
direction of the garage, silent and uncommunicative.
Wilma knew she would be out there sulking as she
unloaded her possessions from the van. Already cross
at the eviction from her apartment—though she hadn't
let her anger spoil last night's gallery opening—her
sullenness was multiplied by Bernine's unexpected
presence. Bernine was not Charlie's favorite person.

Earlier this morning when the two young women
had coffee in the kitchen, Charlie had made no effort
to be civil, had hardly spoken to Bernine. Wilma
hoped that when Mavity arrived, her old friend would
ease the atmosphere, that her earthy temperament

would soften their various moods. Mavity might be ascerbic, without subtlety or guile, but her very honesty made her comfortable to be near.

As she picked up the coffeepot from the desk and moved across the room to fill Clyde's cup, she watched the cats sniffing the good smells from the kitchen and licking their whiskers. She could just imagine Bernine's sarcasm when the cats were fed from the same menu as the guests.

Clyde lowered the sports page and held out his cup. "Charlie going to stay out in the garage all morning? What's she doing?"

"Unloading her tools and equipment—she'll be in shortly. You could go out and help her."

Clyde sipped his coffee, shook his head, and dug out the editorial section, burying himself again. Bernine watched him, amused. Very likely, Wilma thought, Bernine understood Charlie's temper—and the reason for it—far better than did Clyde.

Dulcie watched Clyde, too, and she wanted to whop him, wished she could chase him out to the garage with Charlie. Didn't he know Charlie was jealous? That she was out there sulking not over the eviction, or simply over Bernine's presence, but over Bernine's proximity to Clyde himself? Males could be so dense.

But you didn't need female perception, or feline perception, to see that Bernine's sophistication and elegant clothes and carefully groomed good looks, coupled with her superior and amused attitude, made big-boned Charlie Getz feel totally inadequate. You didn't need female-cat intelligence to see that Charlie didn't want Bernine anywhere near Clyde Damen.

Scowling at Clyde, she realized that Bernine was watching her, and she turned away, closing her eyes and tucking her nose beneath her paw, praying for patience. *Must* the woman stare? It was hard enough to avoid Bernine at the library, without being shut in, at home, with that cat hater.

Why were anti-cat people so one-sided? So rigid? So coldly judgmental?

And how strange that the very things Bernine claimed to value in her own life, her independence and self-sufficiency, she couldn't abide in a sweet little cat.

Beside her on the couch, Joe was avoiding Bernine's gaze by restlessly washing, his yellow eyes angrily slitted, his ears flat to his head. He'd been cross and edgy anyway, since last night when they followed the old man and Azrael and lost them. And then the front page of the *Gazette* this morning hadn't helped, had turned him as bad-tempered as a cornered possum.

The Molena Point *Gazette* didn't concern itself with news beyond the village. Problems in the world at large could be reported by the *San Francisco Chronicle* or the *Examiner*. The *Gazette* was interested only in local matters, and last night's break-in occupied half the front page, above the fold.

SECOND BURGLARY
HITS VILLAGE

A break-in last night at Jewel's Liquors netted the burglars over two thousand dollars from a locked cash register. This is the second such burglary in a week. Police have, at this time, no clue to the identity of the robber.

Police Captain Max Harper told reporters that though the department performed a thorough investigation, they found no mark of forced entry on the doors or on the window casings and no fingerprints. The crime was discovered by the store's owner, Leo Jewel, when he went in early this morning to restock the shelves and prepare a bank deposit. When Jewel opened the register he found only loose change, and loose change had been spilled on the floor.

Captain Harper said the burglar's mode of operation matched that of the Medder's Antiques burglary earlier this week. "It is possible," Harper said, "that the burglar obtained duplicate keys to both stores, and that he picked the cash register's lock."

Leo Jewel told reporters he was certain he had locked both the front and the alley doors. He said that no one else had a key to the store. He had closed up at ten as usual. Captain Harper encourages all store owners to check their door and window locks, to bank their deposits before they close for the night, and to consider installing an alarm system. Harper assured reporters that street patrols had been increased, and that any information supplied by a witness will be held in confidence, that no witness would be identified to the public.

Dulcie wondered if the police had collected any black cat hairs. She wondered what good the stolen money was, to Azrael. *So the old man buys him a few cans of tuna. So big deal.* But she didn't imagine for a minute that any monetary gain drove Azrael. The black tom, in her opinion, was twisted with power-hunger, took a keen and sadistic pleasure in seeing a human's hard-won earnings stolen—was the kind of creature who got his kicks by making others miserable. For surely a chill meanness emanated from the cat who liked to call himself the Death Angel; he reeked of rank cruelty as distinctive as his tomcat smell.

When the doorbell blared, she jumped nearly out of her skin. As Wilma opened the door, Mavity Flowers emerged from the mist, her kinky gray hair covered by a shabby wool scarf beaded with fog. Beneath her old, damp coat, her attire this morning was the same that she wore for work, an ancient rayon pants uniform, which, Dulcie would guess, she had purchased at the Salvage Shop and which had, before Mavity ever saw it, already endured a lifetime of laundering and bleaching. Mavity varied her three pants uniforms with four uniform dresses, all old and tired but serviceable. She hugged Wilma, her voice typically scratchy.

"Smells like heaven in here. Am I late? What are you cooking?" She pulled off the ragged scarf, shook herself as if to shake away remnants of the fog. "Morning, Clyde. Bernine.

"Had to clear the mops and brooms out of my Bug. Dora and Ralph's plane gets in at eleven. My niece," she told Bernine, "from Georgia. They bring everything but the roof of the house. My poor little car will be loaded. I only hope we make it home, all that luggage and those two big people. I should've rented a trailer."

Dulcie imagined Mavity hauling her portly niece and nephew-in-law in a trailer like steers in a cattle truck, rattling down the freeway. Bernine looked at Mavity and didn't answer. Mavity's minimal attention to social skills and her rigid honesty were not high on Bernine's list. Yet it was those very qualities that had deeply endeared her to Wilma. Mavity's raspy voice echoed precisely her strained temper this morning; she had been volatile ever since her brother arrived two weeks ago.

Greeley Urzey visited his sister every few years, and

he liked to have his daughter and her husband fly out from the east to be with him; but it took Mavity only a few days with a houseful of company before she grew short-tempered.

"That house isn't hardly big enough for Greeley and me, and with Dora and Ralph we'll be like sardines. They always have the bedroom, neither one can abide the couch, and they bring enough stuff for a year, suitcases all over. Greeley and me in the sitting room, him on the couch, me on that rickety cot, and Greeley snoring to shake the whole house."

Dulcie and Joe glanced at each other, suppressing a laugh.

"It *is* a small house," Wilma said kindly, sitting down on the couch beside Dulcie and patting a space for Mavity.

Mavity sat stroking Dulcie, then reached to pet Joe. "You're a nice cat, Joe Grey. I wish all tomcats were as clean and polite."

She looked at Wilma, shaking her head. "Can you believe that Greeley brought a *cat* with him! A great big, ugly cat. Carried it right on the plane with him. He found it on the streets of Panama; it probably has every disease. My whole house smells of tomcat. I can't believe Greeley would do such a thing—a cat, all that way from Panama. Took it on board, in a cage. Three thousand miles. I didn't think even Greeley could be so stupid.

"He could have left it home, could have paid some neighbor to feed it. They have maids down there— everyone has a maid, even Greeley, to clean up and take care of things. The maid could have fed an animal. Greeley never did have any sense. Who in their right mind would travel all that way carting a stray cat? It's sure to get lost up here, wander off, and then Greeley will have a fit."

Bernine had put aside the financial page. "Can't you board it somewhere?" she asked coldly. "Surely there are kennels for cats."

"First thing I told Greeley, but he wouldn't hear of it."

Bernine shrugged and returned to the newspaper. Dulcie, fascinated, sniffed at Mavity's uniform searching for the cat's scent.

But she could smell only the nose-itching jolt of Mavity's gardenia-scented bath powder. Leaping to the floor, she sniffed of Mavity's shoes.

No hint of cat there. Mavity's white leather oxfords smelled of shoe polish and of a marigold Mavity must have stepped on coming up the walk; the flower's golden color was streaked up the white leather. Frustrated with her inability to scent the strange tomcat, she curled up again on the couch, quietly regarding Mavity.

"I told Greeley that cat could do its business outdoors. Why ever not, when I live right there on the edge of a whole marsh full of sand? But no, even if the cat goes outside, it still has to have a fresh sandbox, right there in the kitchen. Talk about spoiled—talk about stink.

"I told Greeley it's his job to change the sand, go down to the marsh and get fresh sand, but I have to keep telling and telling him. And to top it off, the cat has sprayed all over my furniture—the whole house reeks of it. Oh, my, what a mess. I'll never get it clean. Why do tomcats do that?"

Dulcie almost choked with suppressed laughter. She daren't look at Joe for fear she'd lose control.

"Well, in spite of that beast, it's good to have Greeley. It's been four years since he was here. After all, Greeley and Dora and Ralph—they're all the family I have."

Mavity grinned. "I guess my little car will hold the two of them and the luggage; it always has before." She glanced at Bernine and reached to stroke Dulcie. "It's not every day your only family comes for a visit."

Swallowing back her amusement, Dulcie rolled over, her paws waving in the air. Mavity was so dear—she could complain one minute, then turn around and do something thoughtful. She had cooked all week, making cakes and casseroles for Greeley and his daughter and son-in-law so they would enjoy their stay.

Dulcie didn't realize she was smiling until Wilma scowled a sharp warning and rose hastily, pulling Mavity up.

"The frittata's done," Wilma said. "It will burn. Let's take up breakfast." She headed for the kitchen, urging Mavity along, shooting Dulcie such a stern look of warning that Dulcie flipped over, flew off the couch, bolted through the house to the bedroom and under Wilma's bed.

Crouched in the dark she swallowed back a mewing laugh—at Mavity, and at Wilma's look of anger because she'd been smiling—trying not to laugh out loud. It was terrible to have to stifle her amusement. Didn't Wilma understand how hard that was? Sometimes, Dulcie thought, she might as well plaster a Band-Aid over her whiskers.

Lying on her back on the thick bedroom rug, staring up at the underside of the box springs, she considered Greeley and his tomcat.

Were these two the burglars?

But that was not possible. It would never happen, the solution to a crime fall into their furry laps as easy as mice dumped from a cage.

Last night she and Joe had followed the old man and Azrael clear across the village before they lost them. Keeping to the darkest shadows, they had tailed them to the busy edge of Highway One, had drawn back warily from the cars whizzing by—had watched the cat leap to the old man's shoulder and the man run across between the fast vehicles where no sensible animal would venture.

Pausing on the curb, their noses practically in the line of fast cars and breathing enough carbon monoxide to put down an ox, they had argued hotly about whether to follow the two across that death trap—argued while Azrael and the old man hurried away down the block.

"You can go out there and get squashed if you want," she'd told him, "but I'm not. It's dark as pitch, those drivers can't see you, and no stupid burglar is worth being squashed into sandwich meat."

And for once she had been able to bully Joe—or for once he had shown some common sense.

But then, watching the pair hurry two blocks south and double back and cross the highway again, toward the village, their tempers blazed.

"They duped us!" Joe hissed. "Led us like two stupid kittens following a string—hoping we'd be smashed on the highway." And he crouched to race after them.

But she wasn't having any more. "We could tail them all night. As long as they know we're following, they're not about to go home."

"They have to go home sometime—have to sleep sometime."

"They'll sleep on a bench. Just see if they don't."

But Joe had shadowed them for over an hour, and she tagged along—until Joe realized that Azrael knew they were still following, knew exactly where they were on the black street, that the cat had senses like a laser.

But now—what if Mavity's brother and his cat were the burglars?

Certainly everything fit. Greeley had been here for two weeks. Both burglaries had occurred within that time. The old man looked the right age to be Mavity's brother, and, more to the point, he was small like Mavity, with the same wiry frame.

There was, Dulcie thought, a family resemblance, the deeply cleft upper lip, the same kind of dry wrinkles, the same coloring. Though Mavity's hair was gray, and the burglar's was ordinary brown, with gray coming in around his ears.

If the burglar *was* Greeley, then, as sure as mice had tails, he had stashed the money somewhere in Mavity's cottage. Where else would he hide it? He didn't live in Molena Point; it wasn't as if he had access to unlimited hiding places. Greeley was practically a stranger in the village.

As she flipped over, clawing with excitement into the carpet, wondering when would be the best time to slip into Mavity's cottage and search for the stolen cash, beside her the bedspread moved and Joe peered under, his yellow eyes dark and his expression smug.

"So," he whispered. "This one dropped right into our paws. Did you smell Azrael on her?"

"No, I didn't. We can't be sure . . ."

"Of course we're sure. There's no such thing as coincidence." He looked at her intently. "New man in town, brings his cat all the way from Panama. Why would he bring a cat all that way, unless he had some use for it? And that old burglar," Joe said, "even looks like Mavity."

Twitching a whisker, he rolled over, grinning, as pleased as any human cop who'd run the prints and come up with a positive ID.

7

CHARLIE HAULED the last duffle from her van and dumped it in Wilma's garage, enjoying the chill fog that pressed around the open garage and lay dense across the garden—but not enjoying, so much, shifting all her gear once again.

As a child she had loved to play "movers," filling cardboard-box "moving vans" with toys and sliding them along a route carefully planned to bring all her family and friends together into a tight little compound. At six years old, moving had satisfied a yearning need in her. At twenty-eight, hauling her worldly goods around in pasteboard boxes was right up there with having a double bypass.

Stacking her cartons of jumbled kitchen utensils and clothes against the wall beside Wilma's car, she sniffed the aroma from the kitchen, the delicious scent of ham and onions and cheese. But, hungry as she was, she didn't relish having to sit at the table with Bernine.

She considered making an excuse and skipping breakfast, but that would hurt Wilma. It wasn't Wilma's fault that Bernine had moved in uninvited; she could hardly have let the woman sleep on the street—though the image *did* appeal. And not only had Bernine taken over the guest room, she was sitting in there with Clyde right now, all cozy beside the fire, and Clyde hadn't made the slightest effort to come out and keep *her* company.

Coming home last night from the opening, she'd been on such a high, had returned Clyde's kisses with more than her usual ardor; they'd had such a good time. And now, this morning, he seemed totally distant.

Slamming the last box into place, she wheeled her cement mixer out of the van and rolled it around behind the garage, parking it next to her two wheelbarrows, throwing a tarp over the equipment to keep out some of the damp. Wilma's backyard was as narrow as an alley, stopping abruptly at the steep, overgrown hillside. The front yard was where Wilma's flowers bloomed in rich tangles of color between the stone walks. Wilma, having no use for a lawn, had built an English garden, had worked the soil beds with peat and manure until they were as rich as potting mixture, creating an environ where, even beneath the oak tree, her blooms thrived.

Closing the van's side door, Charlie stood a moment gearing herself to go back inside. Last night when Clyde gave her a last lingering kiss and drove off in the yellow roadster, waving, she had headed for bed wanting to stretch out and relive every lovely moment of the evening, from the festive arrival Clyde had planned for her, and all the compliments about her work, to Clyde's very welcome warmth. But then, coming into the guest room, there was Bernine in *her* bed, on the side of the room she thought of as absolutely her own, and Bernine's clothes scattered all over as if she'd moved in forever. Bernine had been sound asleep, her creamy complexion glowing, her red hair spread across the pillow as if she were about to have her picture taken for some girlie magazine or maybe welcome a midnight lover.

A silk skirt lay across the chair, a pink cashmere sweater was tossed on the dresser, and Bernine's hand-made Italian boots were thrown on the other bed beside a suede coat that must have cost more than six cement mixers. Surveying the takeover, feeling as if she'd been twice evicted, she'd gone back into the kitchen to cool down, to make herself a cup of cocoa. It was then that she found the note, folded on the table and weighted down with the salt shaker.

She'd read it, said a few rude words, wadded it up, and thrown it in the trash. Had stood at the stove stirring hot milk, thinking she would sleep in the van.

But of course she hadn't. She'd gone to bed at last, dumping Bernine's boots and coat on the floor, creeping into the other bed deeply angry and knowing she was being childish.

This morning, coming down the hall from the shower, she'd avoided looking at Bernine sleeping so prettily—and had avoided looking in the mirror at her own unruly hair and her thousand freckles, had pulled on her jeans and her faded sweatshirt, her scuffed boots, tied back her wild mane with a shoestring, and slipped out of the room only to catch a glimpse of Bernine's slitted eyes, watching her, before she turned over, pulling the covers up.

Then in the kitchen she'd hardly poured her coffee before Bernine came drifting in, yawning, tying a silk wrapper around her slim figure. And now the woman was in there with Clyde, all dressed up and smelling like the perfume counter at Saks. She hoped Bernine's soured love life, or whatever had left her temporarily homeless, had been suitably painful.

An old boyfriend once told her that her temper came from insecurity, that her anger flared when she felt she was not in control of a situation, that if she would just take positive action, put herself in control, she wouldn't get so raging mad.

Maybe he was right. She was considering what positive action she would like to take against Bernine when Mavity's VW Bug pulled to the curb, its rusted body settling with little ticks and grunts like some ancient, tired cart horse.

Watching Mavity slide out, small and quick, and hurry to the front door, Charlie began to feel easier. Mavity always had that effect. And at last she went on in, across the roofed back porch to the kitchen.

Wilma's kitchen was cozy and welcoming with its blue-and-white wallpaper, its patterned blue counter tile and deep blue linoleum. The big round table was set with flowered placemats, Wilma's white ironware, and a bunch of daisies from the garden. Charlie poured herself a cup of coffee as Wilma and Mavity came in, Mavity's short gray hair kinky from the fog, her worn white uniform freshly washed and pressed.

As Wilma took a casserole from the oven and put a loaf of sliced bread in the microwave, Charlie mixed the frozen orange juice, and Mavity got out the butter and jam. Clyde schlepped into the kitchen hitching up his cut-offs, looking endearingly seedy. His disheveled appearance cheered Charlie greatly—why would Bernine be interested in a guy who looked like he'd slept in some alley?

On the table, the frittata casserole glistened with melted cheese; the Sicilian bread came out of the oven steaming hot. The bowl of fresh oranges and kiwi, mango and papaya was aromatic and inviting. As they took their places, the two cats trooped in, licking their whiskers, and sat down intently watching the table. Charlie wished she could read their minds; though at the moment there was no need, their thoughts were obvious—two little freeloaders, waiting for their share.

When they were seated, Wilma bowed her head, preparing to say grace. Charlie liked that in her aunt. Wilma might be modern in most ways, but true to family tradition she liked a little prayer on Sunday morning, and that was, to Charlie, a comfortable way to start the week.

But the prospect of a morning prayer seemed to make Bernine uneasy; she glanced away looking embarrassed. As if the baring of any true reverence or depth of feeling was not, to Bernine, socially acceptable—or, Charlie thought, was beyond what Bernine understood.

"Thank you for this abundance," Wilma said. "Bless the earth we live upon, bless all the animals, and bless us, each one, in our separate and creative endeavors."

"And," Clyde added, "bless the little cats."

Amused, Charlie glanced down at the cats. She could swear that Dulcie was smiling, the corners of the little tabby's mouth turned up, and that Joe Grey had narrowed his yellow eyes with pleasure. Maybe they were reacting to the gentle tone of Clyde's and Wilma's voices, combined with the good smell of breakfast. Now the cats' gazes turned hungrily again to the table as Wilma cut the frittata into pie-shaped wedges and served the plates. Five plates, and a plate for Joe and Dulcie, which she set on the floor beside her chair, evoking an expression of shock and pain from Bernine.

Wilma passed Clyde's plate last. "How's work going on the apartments?"

"A few complications—it'll be a while before we're ready for you to landscape the patio. But between Charlie's expertise and my bumbling we'll get it done."

"Thank goodness for Mavity," Charlie said, patting Mavity's hand. "We couldn't do without you."

"Couldn't do without Pearl Ann," Mavity said.

"I'm the scrub team," she explained to Bernine. "But Pearl Ann does other stuff. I don't know nothing about taping Sheetrock. Pearl Ann's a regular whiz—she can tape Sheetrock, grout tile, she can do anything. She says her daddy was a building contractor and she grew up on the job sites."

Clyde passed Mavity the butter. "Pearl Ann would be just about perfect, if she'd improve her attitude."

"I invited her to breakfast," Wilma said, "but she planned to hike down the coast this morning." Pearl Ann Jamison, tall and plain and quiet, was fond of solitary pursuits, seemed to prefer her own dour company to the presence of others. But, as Mavity said, she was a good worker.

Mavity glanced at her watch. "I don't want to be late, leave Dora and Ralph sitting in the airport."

"They don't get in until eleven," Wilma said, and she dished up another helping of frittata for Mavity. "Maybe they won't stay too long," she added sympathetically.

"One of those night flights," Mavity told Bernine. "Catching the shuttle up from L.A. They bring enough luggage for a year."

"Yes, you said that," Bernine told her dryly.

"And with my brother here, too, my little place is straining at the seams. Maybe one of these days I can afford a bigger house," Mavity rambled amiably. "Two guest rooms would be nice. I plan to start looking when my investments have grown a bit more. That Winthrop Jergen, he's a regular genius, the way he's earned money for me."

Bernine gave Mavity her full attention. "You have someone helping you with your—savings?"

"Winthrop Jergen," Mavity said. "My investment counselor. Doesn't that sound grand? He lives right there in Clyde's upstairs apartment, was living there when Clyde bought the place."

"Oh," Bernine said. "I see." As if Mavity had told her that Jergen meted out his financial advice from the local phone booth.

"He has clients all over the village," Mavity said. "Some of Clyde's wealthiest customers come to Mr. Jergen. They pull up out in front there in their Lincolns and BMWs."

Bernine raised an eyebrow.

"He moved here from Seattle," Mavity continued. "He's partly retired. Said his doctor wanted him to work at a slower pace, that his Seattle job was too frantic, hard on his blood pressure."

She gave an embarrassed laugh. "He talks to me sometimes, when I'm cleaning. He's very young—but so dedicated. That conscientious kind, you know. They're hard on themselves."

"And he does your—investments," Bernine said with a little twisted smile.

"Oh, yes, the bit of savings we had before my husband died, and part of my salary, too." Mavity launched into a lengthy description of the wonders that Winthrop Jergen had accomplished for her, the stocks he had bought and sold. "My account has almost tripled. I never thought I'd be an investor." She described Jergen's financial techniques as if she had memorized, word for word, the information Jergen had given her, passing this on with only partial comprehension.

Bernine had laid down her fork, listening to Mavity. "He must be quite a manager. You say he's young?"

"Oh, yes. Maybe forty. A good-looking man. Prematurely silver hair, all blow-dried like some TV news anchor. Expensive suits. White shirt and tie every day, even if he does work at home. And that office of his, there in the big living room, it's real fancy. Solid cherry desk, fancy computer and all."

Bernine rewarded Mavity with a truly bright smile. "Your Mr. Jergen sounds most impressive."

Dulcie, watching Bernine, envisioned a fox at the hen coop.

"But I do worry about him." Mavity leaned toward Clyde, her elbows comfortably on the table. "You know that man that watches your apartment building? The one who's there sometimes in the evening, standing across the street so quiet?"

"What about him?"

"I think sometimes that Mr. Jergen, with all the money he must have—I wonder if that man . . ."

"Wonder what?" Clyde said impatiently.

Mavity looked uncertain. "Would Mr. Jergen be so rich that man would rob him?"

Clyde, trying to hide a frown of annoyance, patted Mavity's hand. "He's just watching—you know how guys like to stand around watching builders. Have you ever seen a house under construction without a bunch of rubberneckers?"

"I suppose," Mavity said, unconvinced. "But Mr. Jergen is such a nice man, and—I guess sort of innocent."

Bernine's eyes widened subtly. She folded her napkin, smiling at Clyde. "This Mr. Jergen sounds like a very exceptional person. Do you take care of his car?"

Clyde stared at her.

Dulcie and Joe glanced at one another.

"Of course Clyde takes care of his car," Mavity said. "Mr. Jergen has a lovely black Mercedes, a fancy little sports model, brand-new. White leather seats. A CD player and a phone, of course."

The little woman smiled. "He deserves to have

nice things, the way he helps others. I expect Mr. Jergen has changed a lot of lives. Why, he even signed a petition to help Dulcie—the library cat petition, you know. I carry one everywhere."

Wilma rose to fetch the coffeepot, wondering if Mavity had forgotten that Bernine sided totally with Freda Brackett in the matter of Dulcie's fate.

This was the second time in a year that petitions had been circulated to keep Dulcie as official library cat, and the first round had been only a small effort compared to the present campaign. At that time, the one cat-hating librarian had quit her job in a temper saying that cats made her sneeze (no one had ever heard her sneeze). The furor had been short-lived and was all but forgotten. But now, because of the hardhanded ranting of Freda Brackett, all the librarians, except Bernine, and many of the patrons had been walking the village from door to door getting signatures in support of Dulcie. Even Wilma's young friend, twelve-year-old Dillon Thurwell, had collected nearly a hundred signatures.

Mavity busied herself picking up her dishes, and she soon left for the airport, her decrepit VW ratting away through the thinning fog. Strange, Dulcie thought, that at breakfast no one had mentioned the two burglaries. Usually such an incident in the village was a prime topic of conversation.

She guessed Bernine had been too interested in Winthrop Jergen to think about burglaries, and certainly Clyde wouldn't mention them in front of her and Joe; Clyde hated when they got interested in a local crime. He said their meddling complicated his life to distraction, that they were making an old man of him—but Clyde knew he couldn't change them. Anyway, their interests gave him something to grouse about. As she and Joe slipped out into the fog through her cat door and headed up the hills, their thoughts were entirely on the burglaries and on Mavity's brother, Greeley, and his traveling tomcat.

"If Greeley is the burglar," she said, "we need some hard evidence for Captain Harper."

He looked at her quizzically. "Why the change of mind? You were all for keeping this from Harper."

"I've been thinking—if Harper doesn't find the burglar and make an arrest, he'll set up a stakeout. And what if they see Azrael break into a shop? That would really tear it. What if the *Gazette* got hold of that?"

"Harper isn't going to tell the press that kind of thing."

"But one of his men might. Maybe the uniforms on stakeout would tell someone. What if Lieutenant Brennan or Officer Wendell sees Azrael open a skylight and slip in, and then there's a burglary and they start blabbing around the department?"

Joe sighed. "You're not happy if we finger the old man, and you're not happy if we don't. I swear, Dulcie, you can worry a problem right down to a grease spot. What is it with females? Why do you make things so damned complicated?"

"We don't make things complicated. We simply attend to details. Females are thorough—we want to see the whole picture."

Joe said nothing. There were times when it was better to keep his mouth shut. Trotting across the grassy park above the Highway One tunnel, they headed up a winding residential street, toward the wild hills beyond.

"And," she said, "if Brennan and Wendell did see Azrael break in, they'd start putting things together— remembering the times *we've* been under their feet at a crime scene."

"Dulcie, who would believe that stuff? If a cop talked like that, they'd laugh him out of the department. No one would believe . . ."

"People *would* believe it," she said impatiently. "The story's so bizarre, the press would love it. The papers would have a field day. Every tabloid would run it, front page. And every nut in the country would believe it. People would flock to Molena Point wanting to see the trained burglar-cat. Or, heaven forbid, the talking cat. If *that* got in the news . . ."

"Dulcie, you're letting your imagination go crazy."

But he knew she was right. He cut a look at her, kneading his claws in the warm earth. "If we can find the stolen money and get it to Harper, and if the guy's prints are on it, Harper will make the arrest without a stakeout. And the cops will never know about Azrael."

"If there *are* any prints on the money, with those gloves the old man was wearing."

"Likely he'd count the money after he stole it," Joe said. "Why would he wear gloves then? Harper gets the prints, arrests the old man, and you can bet your whiskers that tomcat won't hang around. He'd be long gone. And good riddance."

"Except," she said, "that old man might *tell* the cops about Azrael, just to take the heat off himself. Figure he could make himself famous and create enough interest, enough sympathy for the talking cat, enough public outcry, that he'd be acquitted."

"That's really way out."

"Is it? Look at the court trials just this year, where public opinion has swayed the verdict."

He looked at her intently. She was right. "Talking cat confesses to robberies. Verbose kitty discovered in California village."

She twitched her whiskers with amusement. "Tomcat perjures himself on witness stand."

"Speaking cat insults presiding judge, is cited for contempt."

Dulcie smiled. "County attorney goes for feline conviction. Judge rules that jury must include proper quota of cat lovers."

"Or cats," he said. "Tomcats sit on jury . . ."

"Cat excused because she's nursing kittens . . ." She rolled over, convulsed with feline glee.

"But," she said at last, "what about the murders? We don't . . ."

"What murders?"

"The three deaths. Azrael said he saw death— three murders."

"You don't believe that stuff. Come on, Dulcie, that's tomcat grandstanding. *There will be murder in this village* . . ." Joe mimicked. "*I smell death, death before the moon is full* . . ." He yowled with amusement. "*I see you two little cats standing over the bodies* . . . Oh, boy, talk about chutzpah."

"But . . ."

"So who is going to be murdered over a couple of little, two-bit burglaries? Come on, Dulcie. He was giving you a line. That tomcat's nothing but a con artist, an overblown bag of hot air."

But Dulcie lashed her tail and laid back her ears. "There *could* be truth in what Azrael said." With all his talk of voodoo and dark magic, *was* the foreign tomcat able to see into the future?

Certainly there was a sense of otherness about Azrael—a dark aura seemed to cling around him like a grim shadow. And certainly when she read about cats like themselves, a thread of dark prophetic talents wound through the ancient myths.

Who knew, she thought, shivering, what terrifying skills the black tom might have learned in those far and exotic lands?

8

DORA AND RALPH Sleuder's shuttle from L.A. was due to land at 11:03, and as Mavity headed up the freeway for Peninsula Airport, her VW chugging along with the scattered Sunday traffic, the fog was lifting; the day was going to be pretty, clear and bright.

Wilma's elegant breakfast had been a lovely way to end the week; though the pleasant company made her realize how much time she spent alone. It would be nice to have Dora and Ralph with her, despite her crowded little house. She did miss her family.

She really ought to entertain them better, ought to get Wilma's recipe for that elegant casserole. All she ever made for breakfast was eggs and bacon or cereal. Well, of course she'd be making grits. Dora couldn't face a morning without grits—she always brought instant grits with her from Georgia. The first time Mavity heard of instant grits, which were more common in the south than instant oatmeal, she'd doubled over laughing. But after all, it was a southern staple. And Dora worked hard at home. On the farm, breakfast was a mainstay. Dora grew up in a household where her mother rose every morning at four to fix grits and eggs and salty country ham and homemade biscuits from scratch, a real farm breakfast. Biscuits and redeye gravy became Greeley's favorite after he married a southern girl at eighteen and moved south to her father's farm.

Greeley and his wife had had only the one child, only Dora, and for thirty years he had lived that life, so different from how he grew up here in California. Imagine, getting out to the fields every morning before daylight. You'd think Dora would want to get off the farm, but no, she and Ralph still planted and harvested and hauled produce to market, though they had some help now. And now they had that junk car business, too. Ralph called it a "recycled parts exchange."

For herself, she'd rather clean other people's houses than do that backbreaking field labor. After a day's work, her time was her own. No sick cows to tend, no broken water lines or dried up crops to worry over. She could come home, make a nice cup of tea, put up her feet, and forget the world around her.

And maybe Greeley hadn't liked it all that well, either, because the minute Dora's mother died—Dora was already married—Greeley hit out for Panama, and the next thing she knew, he'd learned to be a deep-sea diver. That had shocked everyone. Who knew that all those years, Greeley Urzey had such a strange, unnatural longing?

Well, he was happy living down there in Central America, doing his underwater repairs for the Panama Canal people, and Dora and Ralph were happy with their farm and their junk business. *And I'm happy*, Mavity thought, *except I wish Lou was still here, that he wasn't taken away from me so soon*. She shoved aside the word *lonely,* pushed it down deep where it wouldn't nudge at her. She knew she'd soon be grousing because of too much family, longing for some loneliness—well, for some privacy.

Never happy. That's the trouble with me. Maybe that's the trouble with everyone, always something that doesn't suit. I wonder what it'll be like in the next world—I wonder if you really are happy forever?

She had given herself plenty of time heading for the airport, and in the brightening morning she took pleasure in the Molena Point hills that flanked the little freeway, the dense pine and cypress woods rising dark against the blue sky, and the small valleys still thick with mist. Ahead, down the hills, the fog was breaking apart over the wide scar of the airport that slashed between the houses and woods. Greeley had wanted to come along, and she could have swung by the house to get him if she'd had room, but he ought to have known the Bug wouldn't handle another passenger plus a mountain of baggage. Even though Dora and Ralph traveled with all those suitcases, she'd never seen either of them wearing anything but jeans and T-shirts or sweatshirts printed in Day-Glo with some crazy message. Besides, they were not small people. Each time she saw her niece and Ralph, their girth had spread a little, expanding like warm bread dough.

But they were a sweet couple, and she'd get them tucked into the car one way or another. Maybe by their next visit she would have a bigger house, three nice bedrooms, one on the main level for herself, two upstairs for company. Not too big, though. Too much to clean. Maybe a place up in the hills. She wondered why Wilma didn't open an account with Mr. Jergen and increase her own pension. Sometimes she didn't understand Wilma; sometimes she thought Wilma's career as a parole officer had left her with no trust at all. Wilma relied on her close friends, but she didn't have much faith in other folks.

Turning off the freeway into the small airport, she drove slowly past the glass doors of the little terminal but didn't park in front. You could never depend on that fifteen-minute parking. They'd give you a ticket one second after your time was up—as if the meter maid was lurking just around the corner, hungry to make her quota. Continuing on down the hill, she pulled into a short-term space, locked the car, and headed double-time back up the steep incline.

Pushing open the glass door, her frizzy gray hair was reflected, and her thin old body, straight as a stick in her white uniform. She might look frowsy, but she was in better shape than most women half her age. She wasn't even breathing hard after the steep climb—and she didn't have to pay some expensive gym to keep fit. She *got* paid for doing her workouts scrubbing and polishing and sweeping, right on the job.

Greeley was the same as her, as lean as a hard-running hound. Dora, being Greeley's daughter, ought to be the same, but she took after her mother. Ample, Greeley said.

Still, Dora didn't have Greeley's quick temper, and that was a blessing.

Peninsula Airport was so small that most of its flights were commuter planes. The runways would take a 737 if some airline ever decided to put on a straight run, but no one had. Crossing the lobby toward the three gates, she saw that all three of the little glassed-in waiting areas were empty. To her left at the Delta desk a lone clerk stood staring into space as if sleeping on his feet.

In the larger general waiting room to her right,

only three travelers occupied the long lines of worn chairs. Two men sat slumped and dozing, as if they might have traveled all night or maybe waited there all night huddled down into the cracked leather. She couldn't see much of the man behind the pillar, just his legs. She had the impression of limpness; maybe he was asleep, too.

She thought she'd like a cup of coffee but, checking her watch by the airport clock, there really wasn't that much time. Anyway the airport coffee was expensive and not worth hiking upstairs, throwing away a buck and a half. Wilma's coffee was better. And where would she put another cup? She was so full of breakfast her ears bulged.

Choosing a seat in the middle of a row of attached chairs, she settled down where she would be able to see the incoming plane but away from the overflowing ashtrays and their stink of stale cigarettes. After one week with Greeley smoking in the house, she longed never to see another cigarette; her little cottage smelled not only of cat, but like a cheap bar as well.

She could have put up one of those THANK YOU FOR NOT SMOKING signs in the living room. Not that Greeley would pay any attention. He'd pitch a fit if she tried to make him go outdoors to smoke. Between the stink of cigarettes and the stink of that cat, she'd have to burn her home to the ground to get the smell out.

Mavity's cottage, anywhere else but Molena Point, would be called a shack. It was a low-roofed, California-style clapboard, one step up from a single-wide trailer. But in the upbeat seaside village, it had value. Well, she thought, the land had value. Located right on the bay, it was real waterfront property, even if the bay, at that point, was muddy and smelly.

One would think, from looking at the Molena

Point map, that her house faced a wide bathing beach. In fact, her little bit of land occupied a strip of marsh between the bay and the river—oh, it had patches of beach sand, but with heavy sea grass growing through. And the marsh was sometimes in flood. All the foundations along the shore were real high, and in bad weather one wanted to have buckets handy. The lower part of her house was stained dark with blackish slime that, as many times as she hosed and scrubbed it, just kept getting darker.

She hadn't thought much about her property value until Winthrop Jergen pointed out just how dear that land might be and had explained to her how much she could borrow on it, if she chose to invest more heavily. But she hesitated at the thought of a mortgage. She would hate to have something happen, though of course nothing would happen.

She did love the view from her porch; she loved the marsh and the sea birds, the gulls and the pelicans and terns. The land just above her place, up the hill where the old Spanish mission rose against the sky, was pricey property. There were fine, expensive homes up there bordering the valley road; and the old mission was there. She loved to hear its bells ringing for mass on Sunday morning.

Dora said the bells brought her right up out of a sound sleep. But what was wrong with that? Being southern, they got up for church, anyway. They always trotted off to mass, even if they weren't Catholic. Ralph said it was good for the soul to worship with a little variety.

The airport loudspeaker crackled, announcing the incoming commuter flight from L.A., and she rose and moved into waiting area number three and stood at the window. The runway was still empty, the sky empty.

It had been a long time since she'd seen Dora and Ralph, though they had talked on the phone quite a lot recently. Now that Greeley was considering moving back to California, she thought the Sleuders might decide to come out to the coast, too, maybe settle down inland where property was cheaper. Since they had that terrible financial loss last year, she supposed they didn't have a lot of money. Well, the only reason *she* could afford to be here was because she and Lou had bought their little place nearly forty years ago when prices along the marsh were nothing. And both of them always worked, too. Their cottage had been only a couple thousand dollars, back then, and was called a fishing shack.

She'd buried Lou in the Molena Point Cemetery thirteen years ago last April, and she had to admit, if only to herself, she *was* lonely—lonely and sometimes afraid.

Well, maybe she wasn't the only one who was lonely. Before Ralph made their plane reservations, Dora had called her four times in one week, long chatty calls, as if she, too, needed family. Then Dora surprised her by deciding to head out her way, when they didn't even know if Greeley was coming. Usually it was Greeley who set the dates, far in advance, when he could get off work.

The small, twin-engine commuter flashed across the sky. Mavity pressed against the glass watching as it came taxiing back, its turbo engines throbbing, and slowed and turned and pulled up before the building. She watched two men push the rolling metal stair up to its door, watched the baggage cart run out to the plane, and stood looking for Dora and Ralph. There was no first class on the commuter, so they might even be first in line.

Waiting for her family, she did not see the thin-faced man behind the pillar shift in his chair for a better view of the plane—a pale, waxen-faced man with light brown hair hanging down his back in a ponytail, pale brown eyes. His brown cords and brown polo shirt were deeply wrinkled, his imitation leather loafers pulled on over bare feet.

Half hidden behind the post, Troy Hoke had observed Mavity since she arrived, and now, watching the disembarking passengers, he smiled as Dora and Ralph Sleuder came ponderously down the metal steps and headed across the tarmac toward the building. Dora's T-shirt said GEORGIA PEACH, stenciled over the picture of a huge pink peach, and Ralph's shirt told the world that he was a GEORGIA BULLDOGS fan. As they came into the glass-walled waiting room, Hoke lifted his newspaper again. The two big people surged inside, laughing and engulfing Mavity in hugs. He kept the newspaper raised as the three stepped to the moving baggage belt and stood talking, waiting for the luggage. He had parked at the far end of the long-term section and, coming up into the terminal forty-five minutes before Mavity arrived, he had loitered in the gift shop reading magazines until he saw Mavity's old VW Bug pull by the glass doors heading for the parking lot. Had watched her come quickly up the hill again, in that familiar, impatient jerking way she had, and swing in through the glass doors to check the flight postings.

The luggage was being unloaded, the two baggage handlers throwing it off the cart onto the belt. It took a while for the Sleuders to retrieve their suitcases, slowly building a tilting mountain of baggage. He watched the two hefty folk and Mavity slide and drag suitcases across the lobby to the main door, where

Dora and Ralph waited beside their belongings while Mavity went to get her car, pulling into the loading zone. He was amused at their efforts to stow all the bags into the interior of the VW and in the hood. They rearranged the load three times before they could close the doors. Dora sat in the front seat balancing a big duffle on her lap. Ralph, in the back, was buried under three suitcases. Not until he saw the VW drive off and turn toward the freeway did the thin-faced man leave the terminal, taking his time as he walked to his car and then headed for Molena Point.

Mavity's little car was so loaded she thought its springs would flatten right down to the ground. Leaving the terminal, she was certain the tailpipe would drag along the concrete. Before she left home she'd removed all her cleaning stuff—brooms, mops, her two vacuum cleaners, the canister model and the old Hoover upright, and her scrub buckets and plastic carrier fitted out with bottles of cleaning solutions and window scrapers and rags—had left it all in the carport hoping Greeley's cat wouldn't pee on everything. Now, beside her, Dora sat pinned down by the big duffle bag and by her bed pillow, which she always carried when she traveled because without it she couldn't sleep. Dora's arm pooched over the gearshift, and her thigh squished against it so hard that they might have to drive the freeway in low gear.

"Where's Greeley?" Ralph asked, looking around the VW as if he expected his father-in-law to materialize from beneath a suitcase.

"He's really anxious to see you," Mavity said. "Too bad there wasn't room in the car."

"How long is it to the house?" Dora said nervously. "I should have stopped in the ladies' room."

"Ten minutes," Mavity lied, cutting the time in half.

"You remember. Only a little while. You can hold it."

"Is there a Burger King near? We could stop there for the restroom. Or a McDonald's?"

Patiently Mavity swung down an off-ramp to McDonald's and watched Dora make a trip inside. When Dora wedged herself back into the car she was toting a white paper bag emblazoned with the golden arches and smelling of hamburger and onions. She handed Ralph a double burger, its wrapping damp with mustard, and shoved a giant paper cup between her knees.

Mavity, pulling onto the freeway again, was glad the Sunday traffic wasn't heavy. Already she was beginning to feel like a sardine packed too tight. She tried to keep her mind on the cool, piney sea wind blowing in through her open window. Ahead, as she turned toward Molena Point, the wide expanse of sea with the sun on it eased the tight feeling across her shoulders. But when they turned off the highway into the village, Dora said, "I'd love to see where you work, where they're doing that remodeling. Could we stop by there?" Dora loved anything to do with houses.

"We can come back," Mavity told her. "After we unload. Or this evening after supper we can take a run up, the four of us." If she didn't get out of the crammed car soon she was going to have one of those shaky attacks that left her feeling weak.

But Dora's face crumpled with disappointment.

"Or what about tomorrow morning?" Mavity said quickly. "You and Ralph and Greeley can drop me off for work, take your time looking at the building—though it's just a mess of lumber and Sheetrock—then you can have the car for the day, go out for a nice lunch, and pick me up at five. How would that suit you?" She seldom offered her car when they were visiting, because she needed it for work, and she knew Dora wouldn't refuse.

Dora nodded, despite the disappointment that pulled down her soft jowls. Mavity only hoped she could show them through the apartments quickly tomorrow, without getting in everyone's way. Dora seemed totally set on seeing the project, and when Dora got her mind on something, it was hard to distract her.

They found Greeley at home in the kitchen frying chicken. He made drinks for Dora and Ralph, and they sat in lawn chairs out on the grass, looking at the bay, talking and catching up, until Dora and Ralph got hungry.

Dora didn't mention the apartment building again during dinner, but Monday morning she and Ralph were up early getting themselves ready, getting in Mavity's way as she tried to wash and dress.

And up at the apartments, they insisted on poking through every room, bothering the two carpenters and chattering to Pearl Ann and Charlie, who were busy hanging Sheetrock, slowing everyone's work until Pearl Ann opened a can of paint thinner and accidentally spilled some on Dora, and that sent Dora off with Ralph in the VW to change her clothes.

She thought it strange that Dora had seemed to avoid the patio, keeping to its roofed walkway or inside the apartments, but glancing out often—almost as if she didn't want to be seen, though there was no one living in the apartments, only Mr. Jergen, and his office lights weren't burning; the upstairs windows were dark as if he had gone out. Maybe Dora, looking out at the flower beds, had developed an interest in landscaping. Heaven knew, the patio could use some nice plants and bushes; it must look to Dora like last year's dried-up farm stubble.

Well, despite Dora's peculiarities, it was good that she had gotten her mind off her troubles; this was not an easy time for the Sleuders. Mavity guessed she ought to be a bit more tolerant of Dora's irritating manner.

9

AT THREE O'CLOCK on Tuesday morning across the moonlit village nothing stirred, no hush of tires on the damp streets, no rumble of car engines beneath the cloud-veiled moon; the tangle of cottages and shops and sheltering trees was so still the village might have been cast beneath some hoary wizard's hundred-year enchantment. The white walls of Clyde Damen's cottage and its ragged lawn were patterned with the ancient scriptures of tree shadow as still as if frozen in time. But suddenly a shadow broke away, racing across the mottled lawn and up the steps and in through the cat door, his white paws flashing.

Tracking mud across the carpet, Joe Grey trotted through the sleeping house accompanied by comforting and familiar sounds; the creak in the floor as he crossed the hall, Clyde's irregular snoring from the bedroom, and beyond the kitchen door, old Rube gently snuffling his own doggy snores. Joe pictured the Labrador sprawled on the bottom bunk in the laundry, among the tangle of cats, all sleeping deeply. The four household animals had slept thus ever since Barney died, dog and cats crowding together to ease their loneliness for the elderly golden retriever.

Joe missed Barney, too. The old golden had been a clown, always into something, dragging Clyde's Levis and gym equipment all over the house, huffing and growling in the kitchen as he goaded the white cat to knock a pack of cookies off the top of the refrigerator.

Moving swiftly down the hall, Joe's nostrils were filled with the stench of human sleep laced with beer and garlic. Loping across the bedroom's antique rug, he sprang onto the blankets inscribing muddy pawprints, avoiding Clyde's stomach by leaping over his housemate. Kneading the empty pillow, he stretched out across it and began to wash.

Around him, the room was a montage of twisted tree shadows, as dense as if he resided in a jungle—though the thought of jungle irritated him, reminded him of the invading tom. As he washed, Clyde stirred and moaned—and woke, leaning up to stare.

"What the hell are you doing? You're shaking the whole damned bed."

"How could I shake the bed? I was simply washing my face. You're so sensitive."

Clyde snatched up the digital clock. "It's three A.M. I was sound asleep."

"You wouldn't want me to go to sleep unbathed."

"I don't care if you never take a bath—if you call that disgusting licking *bathing*." Clyde flipped on the bedside lamp, scowling at him.

"My God. I might as well have a platoon of muddy marines marching across the sheets. Can't you wash outside? When I go to bed, I don't drag half the garden in. And I don't do all that stomping and wiggling."

"*You* have hot and cold running water and a stack of

nice thick bath towels. All I have is my poor little cat tongue."

Clyde sighed. "I presume the hunting was successful, by the amount of blood on your face. And by the fact that you are not out in the kitchen banging around clawing open the kibble box, ripping through the entire supply of cat goodies."

"When have I ever done that after a night's hunt? Of course the hunting was successful. Was, in fact, very fine. The full moon, even with clouds streaked across it, makes the rabbits wild.

"It's the lunar pull," Joe told Clyde, giving him a narrow leer. "Oh, the rabbits danced tonight. Spun and danced across the hills as if there wasn't a cat within miles. Lovely rabbits. Such tender little rabbits."

"Please. Spare me your feline sadism."

"What we do is certainly not sadism. We are part of a complicated and essential balance of nature—a part, if you will, of the God-given food chain. An essential link in the necessary . . ."

Clyde snatched up his pillow and whacked Joe. *"Stop talking. Stop washing. Stop shaking the bed. Shut up and lie still and get the hell to sleep."*

Joe crawled out from under the pillow, his ears back, his head ducked low, and his bared teeth gleaming sharp as knives.

Clyde drew back, staring at him. "What? What's the matter? I hardly tapped you."

"You didn't *tap* me. You *whacked* me. In all our years together, you've never hit me. What's with you? How come you're so irritable?"

"*I'm* irritable? You're the bad-tempered one—I thought you were going to take my arm off." Clyde peered closer, looking him over. "You and Dulcie have a fight?"

"You're so witty. No we didn't have a fight. I simply don't like being hit. Fun is one thing, but that was real anger. And why would Dulcie and I fight? For your information, I left Dulcie on Ocean Avenue staring in the window of that new Latin American shop, drooling over all that handmade stuff they sell. And why are *you* so edgy? You and Charlie have a fight?"

"Of course not. She . . ." Clyde paused, frowning. "Well she was a bit cool."

"And you're taking it out on me. Venting your bad mood on a defenseless little cat. What did you fight about?"

"Nothing. She was just cool. She's been cool ever since Sunday morning. Who knows what's with women?"

"Bernine," Joe said and resumed washing his paws.

"Bernine *what*?"

Joe shrugged.

"You mean she's in a bad temper because Bernine's staying with Wilma? But why get angry at me?"

"You figure it out. I'm not going to draw pictures for you. I don't suppose you would want to get up and pour me a bowl of milk. I'm incredibly thirsty."

"You're not saying—Charlie's not *jealous*. Jealous of Bernine Sage?"

"Milk is good for the stomach after a full meal of raw game. A nice chilled drink of milk would ease my mood, and would wash down that cottontail with just the right dietetic balance."

"Why the hell would she be jealous of Bernine? Bernine Sage is nothing—a bimbo, a gold digger. Doesn't Charlie . . . ? Bernine doesn't care about anything but Bernine. What's to be jealous of?"

"If you would keep a bowl of milk in the refrigerator where I can reach it, I wouldn't have to ask. It's demeaning to have to beg. I have no trouble opening the refrigerator, but without fingers and a thumb I really can't manage the milk bottle."

"Please, spare me the details."

"And have a glass yourself—it will help you sleep."

"I was asleep, until you decided to take a bath. And now you want me to get up out of a nice warm bed and freeze my feet on the linoleum, to . . ."

"Slippers. Put on your slippers. Put on a robe—unless you really enjoy schlepping around the kitchen naked, with the shades up, giving the neighbors a thrill."

"I am not naked. I have on shorts. I am not going to get out of bed. I am not going to go out to the kitchen and wake up the other animals, to pour you a bowl of milk. I can't even describe the rudeness of such a request—all so you can wash down your bloody kill. That is as barbaric as some African headhunter drinking blood and milk. The Watusi or something."

"Masai. They are not headhunters. The Masai are a wise and ancient people. They drink milk mixed with the blood of their cattle to give them strength. It is an important Masai ritual, a meaningful and religious experience. *They* know that milk is nourishing to the soul as well as to the body of a tired hunter. And if you want to talk disgusting, what about those Sugar Puffs or Honey Pops or whatever you eat for breakfast with all that pyridoxine hydrochloride and palmitate, to name just a few foreign substances. You think that's not putting strange things in your stomach?" Joe kneaded the pillow; its springy softness gave him the same sense of security he had known in kittenhood kneading at his mother's warm belly. "There's a fresh half-gallon of milk in the refrigerator, whole milk."

Clyde sighed, rose, and began to search for his slippers. Joe watched him for a moment then galloped along past him to the kitchen.

And as Joe drank milk out of his favorite bowl, which Clyde had placed on the breakfast table, and below him on the floor the other animals slurped up their own hastily supplied treats, Clyde sat at the table drinking cold coffee left over from the morning before.

"I hope you killed that rabbit quickly and didn't tease it. I don't like to think of you and Dulcie torment-ing . . ." Clyde shook his head. "For two intelligent beings, you really ought to show more restraint. What good is it to be sentient, to be master of a culturally advanced language, and, supposedly, of advanced thought patterns, and still act like barbarians?"

"The rabbit died quickly. Dulcie broke its neck. Does that make you happy? It was a big buck—a huge buck, maybe the granddaddy of rabbits. It clawed her in the belly, too. For your information, a rabbit can be as vicious as a Doberman when you . . ."

"Wouldn't you be vicious if someone was trying to flay you for supper?"

"We're cats. We're hunters. God put rabbits on the earth for cats to hunt—it's what we do. You want we should go on food stamps?"

Finished with his milk, he dropped to the cold linoleum, Clyde turned off the light, and they trucked back to bed again. But, getting settled, clawing his side of the blanket into a satisfactory nest, Joe began to worry about Dulcie.

When he had left her in the village, not an hour before, he thought he glimpsed a shadow moving across the rooftops. Probably a raccoon or possum had climbed to the rooftops to scavenge bird's nests. And even if it had been Azrael, Dulcie would be in control;

she was quite capable of bloodying Azrael if he got fresh.

Or, he hoped she was.

The moon's light cast the sidewalk and shops into a labyrinth of confusing shadows, but the street seemed empty, and Dulcie heard no sound, nor had noticed anything moving except, high above her, the little bats darting and squeaking. Her attention was centered on the shop window against which she stood, her paws pressed to the glass, the bright colors of weavings and carvings and clay figures softly illuminated into a rainbow of brilliance. Oh, the bright art drew her. Pushing her nose against the pane, she sniffed the exotic scents that seeped through, aromas no human would detect; the faint drift of sour foreign dyes, of rare woods and leathers, the heavy stink of sheep fat from the handmade wool rugs and blankets. Studying the bold Colombian and Peruvian patterns, she thought that their strange-looking horses and deer and cats were closer akin to mythological animals than to real beasts.

Closer akin to me, she thought.

The notion startled her, shocked her, made her shiver.

The idea must have been playing on her mind without realizing, from the myths she had read—the notion that she was strange and out of sync with the world.

It isn't so. I am real flesh and blood, not some weird mythical beast. I am only different.

Just a little bit different.

And stubbornly she returned her attention to the bright and foreign wares.

She had, coming down the street, paused at each shop to stand on her hind paws and stare in, admiring handprinted silk blouses and cashmere sweaters and handmade silver jewelry, her hunger for those lovely embellishments making her purr and purr with longing.

Now, dropping to all fours, she slipped into the garden that ran beside the shop and trotted along to the back, staring up at the transom above the back door.

She did not intend to steal—as she had, in the past, stolen silky garments from her neighbors. She meant only to get nearer the lovely wares, to sniff and feel and enjoy.

Swarming up a purple-blooming bougainvillea vine that climbed the shop wall, forcing up between its tangle of rough, woody limbs, she clung above the back door, clawing at the narrow transom until the hinged window dropped inward. It stopped halfway, held by a chain.

Crawling through on the slanted glass, she jumped down to a stack of packing crates, then to the floor.

She was in the shop's storeroom. It smelled of packing straw and the sour scent of the raw mahogany crates that had been shipped from South America.

Trotting into the big showroom, she was surrounded by primitive weavings and carvings and paintings, was immersed in a gallery of the exotic, every tabletop and display case filled with unusual treasures. Leaping to a counter, she nosed at straw figures and clay beasts, at painted wooden animals and medieval-looking iron wall hangings and appliqué pictures made from tiny bits of cloth. Lying down on a stack of wool sweaters as soft as the down of a baby bird, she rolled luxuriously, purring and humming a happy, half-cat, half-human song of delight.

It had been a long time since she'd coveted anything so fiercely as these lovely creations.

Choosing the softest sweater, a medley of rust and cream and black that complemented her own tabby coat, she forgot her good intentions. Dragging it between her front paws—like a leopard dragging an antelope—she headed across the floor to the storeroom. There she gazed up toward the high window, her head swimming with the heady pleasure of taking, all for herself, something so beautiful. She was crouched to leap when a sharp thud made her spin around, bristling.

She could smell him before she saw him. In the inky gloom, he was a whisper of black on black, his amber eyes gleaming, watching her. Sauntering out of the darkness, he smiled with smug superiority. "What have you stolen, my dear?"

She crouched, glaring.

"My, my. Would you report me and Greeley to the police, when you're nothing but a thief yourself? Tell me, Dulcie, where are you taking that lovely vicuña sweater?"

"I'm taking it to nap on it," she lied, "in the store-room, away from the display lights. Is there a law against that?"

The tomcat sat down, cutting her a wicked smile. "You don't steal, my dear? You have never stolen from, say, your neighbors? Never slipped into their houses and carried away silk underwear, never stolen a black silk stocking or a lace teddy?"

Her heart pounded; if she had been human, her face would have flamed red.

"My dear Dulcie, I know all about your little escapades. About the box that your Wilma Getz keeps on her back porch so the neighbors can retrieve their stolen clothes, about Mr. Warren's chamois gloves that were a present from his wife, about Wilma's own expensive watch that was 'lost' under the bathtub for nearly a year."

She watched him narrowly. Where had he heard

such things? All her neighbors knew, but . . . *Mavity*. It had to be Mavity—she could have heard it anywhere. She'd probably told that cute little story to Greeley, having no idea she would hurt Dulcie.

"Mavity thinks you're charming," Azrael told her, "dragging home the neighbors' underwear."

The tomcat twitched his whiskers. "And Greeley, of course, was most fascinated by your display of, shall we say, perspicacity and guile."

He looked up to the shelves above them, drawing her gaze to a row of ugly black carvings. "Those figures up there, my dear, those ugly little feathered men—you *do* know that those are voodoo dolls?"

"So?"

"That dark voodoo magic is of great importance." His smile was oily.

"It is that kind of darkness in you, Dulcie, that entices you to steal. Oh, yes, my dear, we are alike in that.

"You know the tales of the black cat," he said softly, "of the witch's familiar. Those are the tales of the dark within us—that is the darkness that invites the joy of thieving, my dear. That is the darkness speaking within your nature."

She had backed away from him, her paw raised to slash him, but his golden eyes held her, his pupils huge and black, his purring voice drawing her, enticing her.

"You and I, Dulcie, we belong to the dark. Such magic and passion are rare, are to be treasured.

"Oh, yes, the dark ways call to you, sweet tabby. The dark, voodoo ways." He narrowed his eyes, his purr rumbling. "Voodoo magic. Black magic. Shall I say the spells for you, the dark spells? The magic so dear to your jungle brothers? Come, my Dulcie . . ." and he slid close against her, making her tremble.

She spun away from him hissing and crouched to

leap to the transom, but he blocked her way. She fled into the showroom. He followed.

"In the jungle, my dear, the voodoo witches make dark enchantments, such exotic and exciting spells—spells to sicken and waste your enemies—and love spells, my dear . . ."

She leaped away but he was there pressing against her. When she lashed out at him, his topaz eyes burned with amusement and his black tail described a measured dance.

"My dark powers fascinate you, sweet Dulcie. My cunning is human cunning, but beneath my black fur, my skin is marked by the spots of the jungle cat.

"I have teased jungle dragons as big as two men and have come away unscathed. I have hunted among constrictors twenty feet long, have dodged snakes so huge they could swallow a dozen cats." And the tomcat's words and his steamy gaze filled her with visions she didn't want.

"I have hunted in the mangrove trees, dodging hairy beasts with the faces of ghosts, creatures that hang upside down among the branches, their curving claws reaching as sharp as butcher knives, their coats swarming with vermin." The black tom purred deep in his throat. "I have witnessed human voodoo rites where an image of Christ is painted with goat's blood and common cats are skinned alive, their innards . . ."

"Stop it!" She twisted away, leaping to the top of a cabinet—but again he was beside her, his eyes wild, her distress exciting him. "Come run with me, Dulcie of the laughing eyes. Come with me down the shore under the full moon. Come where the marsh birds nest, where we can suck bird's eggs and eat the soft, sweet baby birds, where we can haze the bedraggled stray cats that cower beneath the docks, the starving common cats that crouch mute beneath the pier. Come, sweet Dulcie . . ."

His words, frightening and cruel, stirred a wildness in her, and the tom pressed her down, began to lick her ear. "Come with me, sweet Dulcie, before the moon is gone. Come now while the night is on us." His voice was soft, beguiling, dizzying her.

She raked him hard across the nose and leaped away, knocking sweaters to the floor, tipping a tall wooden man that fell with a crash behind her as she fled through the storeroom and up the pile of crates and out the transom.

Dropping down the vine to the mist-damp sidewalk, she fled up the side lane and across Eighth, across Seventh and then Ocean past the darkened, empty shops, never looking back, her heart pounding so hard she couldn't have heard a dozen beasts chasing her, certainly couldn't have heard the soft padding of Azrael's swift pursuit.

But when, stopping in the shadow of a car, she crouched to look behind her, the sidewalk and street were empty. Above her, along the rooftops, nothing moved.

What had happened to her back there? Despite her anger, she had been nearly lost in a cocoon of dark desire.

Pheromones, she told herself. *Nothing but a chemical reaction. His sooty ways have nothing to do with real life.*

Shaken with repugnance at herself, she spun away again racing for home, speeding past the closed shops and at last hitting her own street, storming across Wilma's garden, trampling the flowers, up the back steps and in through her cat door, terrified of the dark stranger and terrified of herself.

Crouching on the linoleum, she watched her door swinging back and forth, unable to shake the notion that he would come charging through.

But after a long time when the plastic door grew still and remained pale, without any looming shadow, she tried to calm herself, washing and smoothing her ruffled fur and licking at her sweating paws.

She felt bruised with shame. She had for one long moment abandoned Joe Grey—for one moment abandoned the bright clarity of life and slipped toward something dark, something rancid with evil.

Azrael's twisted ways were not her ways.

She was not an ignorant, simple beast to whom a dalliance with Azrael would be of no importance. She was sentient; she and Joe Grey bore within themselves a rare and wonderful gift. With human intelligence came judgment. And with judgment came commitment, an eternal and steely obligation and joy from which one did not turn away.

In her gullible and foolish desire, she had nearly breeched that commitment.

There would never be another like Joe Grey, another who touched her with Joe's sweet magic. She and Joe belonged to each other; their souls were forever linked. How could she have warmed, for the merest instant, to Azrael's evil charms?

Pheromones, she told herself, and defiantly she stared at her cat door ready to destroy any intruder.

10

LATER THAT MORNING, in the patio of the Spanish-style structure, where piles of new lumber lay across the dry, neglected flower beds, from within a downstairs apartment came the sudden ragged whine of a skill-saw, jarring the two cats as they padded in through the arch past a stack of two-by-fours. The air was heavy with the scent of raw wood, sweet and sharp.

Joe couldn't count how many mice he and Dulcie had killed in the tall grass that surrounded this building, before Clyde bought the place. Situated high above the village, the two-story derelict stood alone on the crest of the hill facing a dead-end street. The day Clyde decided to buy it was the first time Joe had gained access or wanted to enter the musty rooms. Even the exterior smelled moldy; the place was a dump, the walls stained and badly in need of paint, the roof tiles faded and mossy, the roof gutter hanging loose.

That day, trotting close to Clyde entering the front apartment beneath festoons of cobwebs as thick as theater curtains, he was put in mind of a Charles

Addams creepy cartoon; beneath the cobwebs and peeling wallpaper hung old-fashioned, imitation gas lights; under Joe's paws, the ancient floors were deeply scarred as if generations of gigantic rats had dug and gnawed at the wood.

"You're going to buy this heap?"

"Made an offer today," Clyde had said proudly.

"I hope it was a low offer. What are they asking for this monstrosity?"

"Seven hundred."

"Seven hundred dollars? Well . . ."

"Seven hundred thousand."

"Seven hundred *thousand*?" He had stared at Clyde, unbelieving.

Over the sour smell of accumulated dirt he could smell dead spiders, dead lizards, and generations of decomposing mouse turds. "And who is going to clean and restore this nightmare?"

"I am, of course. Why else would I . . ."

"You? *You* are going to repair this place? Clyde Damen who can't even change a lightbulb without a major theatrical production? *You're* going to do the work here? *This* is your sound financial investment, and you're going to protect that investment by working on it yourself?"

"May I point out that one apartment *has* been refurbished, that it looks great and is rented for a nice fifteen hundred a month? That most of what you're seeing is simply dirt, Joe. The place will be totally different when it's cleaned and painted. You take five apartments at fifteen hundred each . . ."

"Less taxes. Less insurance—fire insurance, liability insurance, earthquake insurance—less yard maintenance, utility bills, general upkeep . . ."

"After expenses," Clyde had said patiently, "I

figure ten, maybe twelve percent profit. Plus a nice
depreciation write-off, to say nothing of eventual
appreciation, a solid capital gain somewhere down the
line."

"Capital gain? Appreciation?" Joe had sneezed with
disgust, imagining within these walls vast colonies of
termites—overlooked by the building inspectors—
chewing away on the studs and beams, weakening the
interior structure until one day, without warning, the
walls would come crashing down. He had envisioned,
as well, flooded bathrooms when the decrepit plumbing gave way and faulty wiring, which at the first
opportunity would short out, emit rivers of sparks, and
ignite the entire building.

Which, he thought, might be the best solution.

"It *is* insured?"

"Of course it's insured."

"I can't believe you made an offer on this. I can't
believe you sold those five antique cars—those cars
that were worth a fortune and that you loved like your
own children, those cars you spent half your life
restoring—sold them to buy *this*. Ten years from now
when you're old and feeble and still working on this
monstrosity and are so in debt you'll never . . ."

"In ten years I will not be old and feeble. I am in
the prime of my life. And what the hell do you know
about houses? What does a cat know about the value
of real estate?" Clyde had turned away really angry,
hadn't spoken to him for the rest of the day—just
because he'd pointed out a few obvious truths.

And, what was worse, Dulcie had sided with
Clyde. One look at the inside of the place and she was
thrilled. "Don't be such a grouch, Joe. It's lovely. It has
loads of charm. Big rooms, nice high ceilings. All it
needs is . . ."

"The wrecking ball," Joe had snapped. "Can you imagine *Clyde* fixing it up? Clyde, who had to beg Charlie to repair our leaky roof?"

"Maybe he'll surprise you. I think the house will be good for him." And she had strolled away waving her tail, padding through the dust and assessing the cavernous and musty spaces like some high-powered interior designer. Staring above her at the tall windows, trotting across the splintery floors through rooms so hollow that her smallest mew echoed, Dulcie could see only fresh paint, clean window glass, deep windowseats with puffy cushions, soft carpets to roll on. "With Charlie's help," she had said, "he'll make it look wonderful."

"They're both crazy, repairing old junkers—Clyde fixing up this place, Charlie trying to save that heap of a VW. So he rebuilds the engine for her, does the body work, takes out the dings and rust holes, gives it new paint . . ."

"And fits out the interior," Dulcie said, "with racks and cupboards for her cleaning and repair equipment—for vacuum cleaners, ladders, paint, mops, cleaning chemicals. It'll be nice, too, Joe. You'll see."

Charlie had made it clear that her work on the apartments would be part-time, that her other customers came first. Her new business was less than a year old; she couldn't afford to treat her customers badly or to turn customers away. She was lucky to have Pearl Ann on the job. Pearl Ann Jamison, besides having useful carpentry skills, was steadier, Charlie said, than most of the men she'd hired. Except for her solitary hikes up and down the coast, Pearl Ann seemed to want no other life but hard work. Pearl Ann's only faults were a sour disposition and a dislike of cleaning any house or apartment while the occupant was at home. She said that the resident, watching over her shoulder, flustered her, made her feel self-conscious.

Now, the cats sat down in a weed-filled flower bed, listening for any mole that might be working beneath the earth. The patio was sunny and warm. The building that surrounded them on three sides contained five apartments, three up and two down, allowing space on the main level for a bank of five garages that were entered from a driveway along the far side of the building. Winthrop Jergen's apartment was directly above the garages. Strange, Joe thought, that well-groomed, obviously well-to-do and discerning Winthrop Jergen, with his elegant suits, nice furniture, and expensive Mercedes would want to live in such a shabby place, to say nothing of putting up with the annoyance of a renovation project, with the grating whine of skill-saws and endless hammering, as he tried to concentrate on financial matters in his home office. But despite the noise, Jergen seemed content. Joe had heard him tell his clients that he liked the privacy and that he was totally enamored of the magnificent view. From Jergen's office window he had a wide vista down the Molena Point hills to the village rooftops and the sea beyond; he said the offbeat location suited him exactly.

And Clyde was happy to have the rent, to help pay for materials while he was restoring the other four units.

Dulcie and Joe watched, through the open door of the back apartment, Charlie set up a stepladder and begin to patch the living-room ceiling; the patching compound smelled like peppermint toothpaste. Above them, through an upstairs window, they could hear the sliding *scuff, scuff* of a trowel and could see Pearl Ann mudding Sheetrock. All the windows stood open except those to Jergen's rooms; Winthrop Jergen kept his office windows tightly closed to prevent damage to his computer.

As the cats sunned in the patio, Mavity Flowers came out of the back apartment and headed upstairs, hauling her mop and bucket, her vacuum cleaner, and cleaning caddy. The cats, hoping she might stir up a last, lingering mouse, followed her as far as the stairwell, where they slipped beneath the steps.

The dusty space under the stairs still smelled of mouse, though they had wiped out most of the colony—mice as easy to catch as snatching goldfish from a glass bowl, the indolent creatures having lived too long in the vacant rooms. Winthrop Jergen's only complaint when Clyde took over as landlord was the persistence of the apartment's small rodents. A week after Joe and Dulcie got to work, Jergen's complaints ceased. He had no idea that the cats hunted in his rooms; the notion would have given him fits. The man was incredibly picky—didn't want ocean air or dust to touch his computer, so probably cat hair would be the kiss of death.

But the mice were gone, and it was while hunting the rodent colony that they had found the hidden entrance into Jergen's rooms.

To the left of the stairs was a two-foot-wide dead space between the walls, running floor to ceiling. It could be entered from a hole beneath the third step, where the cats now crouched. Very likely Clyde would soon discover the space, which ran along beside the garages, and turn it into a storage closet or something equally useful and dull. Meantime, the vertical tunnel led directly up to Winthrop Jergen's kitchen. There, a hinged flap opened beneath the sink, apparently some kind of clean-out access for the plumbing, so a workman could reach through to the pipes—an access plenty large enough to admit a mouse, a rat, or an interested cat into Jergen's rooms.

Now, scrambling up inside the wall from fire block to fire block, they crouched beneath Jergen's kitchen sink listening to Mavity's vacuum cleaner thundering back and forth across the living-room rug; the machine emitted a faint scent of fresh lavender, which Mavity liked to add to the empty bag. They could not, this morning, detect any scent of new mice that might have entered the premises, but all visits to Jergen's rooms were of interest, particularly to Dulcie with her curiosity about computers—she was familiar with the library functions but spreadsheets were a whole new game.

Waiting until Mavity headed for the bedroom, they crossed the kitchen and sat down in the doorway, ready to vanish if the financier turned around. He sat with his back to them, totally occupied with the numbers on the screen.

Jergen's office took up one end of the spacious living room. His handsome cherry-wood desk stood against the front windows, looking down the Molena Point hills—though all the cats could see from floor level was the blue sky and a few clouds, whose dark undersides hinted of rain.

The light of Jergen's computer cast a faint blue gleam across his well-styled silver hair. His busy fingers produced a soft, constant clicking on the keys. His pale gray suit was smoothly tailored. His shoes, in the cats' direct line of sight, were of soft, gleaming black leather. Everything about Winthrop Jergen presented an aura of expensive good taste.

To Jergen's right stood two cherry file cabinets, then a row of tall bookshelves filled with professional-looking volumes. The thick Kirman rug was oversized, fitting nearly to the pale walls, its colors of ivory and salmon forming a soft background to the creamy leather couch and the rose silk easy chairs. The six etchings on the left wall were delicately detailed studies of far and exotic cities, each with unusual rooftops: conical roofs, fluted roofs, straw ones topping stone huts, and a vista with sharply peaked domes. Each city flanked a seaport, as if perhaps the etchings embodied Jergen's dreams of far and extensive travel. The vacuuming ceased, and the cats backed into shadow. As Mavity returned with a lemon-scented cloth and began to dust the end tables, Jergen stopped typing.

"Mavity, would you hand me that file? There on the credenza?"

She picked up a file from the cherry credenza, brought it across to him, her work-worn hands dry and wrinkled compared to Jergen's smooth hands and neatly manicured nails.

"And that book—the black account book."

Obediently she brought the book to him, complying as a kindergartner might obey a revered teacher.

"Thank you, Mavity. Your Coca-Cola stock is doing very well; you should expect a nice dividend soon. And though I can't be certain, it appears the Home Depot stock should split this month, and that will give you a really handsome bonus."

Mavity beamed. "I don't know no way to thank you, Mr. Jergen, for all you're doing for me."

"But, Mavity, your good fortune is in my interest, too. After all, I enjoy a nice percent of your earnings."

"Oh, and you deserve it," she said hastily. "You earn every penny and more."

Jergen smiled. "It's a fair exchange. I expect your niece and her husband have arrived by now, for their visit? Didn't you tell me they were coming this week?"

"Oh, yes, all tucked up in my little place, and enjoying the beach." Mavity began to wind her vacuum cleaner cord, turning away to straighten it.

Jergen smiled briefly and returned to his computer; he began to work again, deep into columns of numbers. Dulcie's eyes widened at the large amounts of money flashing on the screen and at the names of the impressive financial institutions—firms mentioned with serious respect in the library's reference department. But soon both cats grew impatient with a world so far removed, that they could not smell or taste or deal with directly, and they slipped away, leaping down within the dark wall, crouching at the bottom.

In the musty shadows of the narrow, hidden space, Dulcie's eyes were as black as midnight. "Mavity trusts Jergen totally. She thinks he hung the moon. Why does he make me uneasy?"

Joe looked at her and shrugged. "Don't start, Dulcie. There's nothing wrong with Jergen. You're just bored—looking for trouble."

She hissed at him but said nothing as they padded out beneath the stairs into the sunny patio. And they both forgot Winthrop Jergen when a pale blue BMW pulled up in front.

Bernine Sage swung out and came into the patio, her high heels clicking sharply across the worn bricks. Pausing, she glanced through the open doors of the two first-floor apartments.

In the back apartment Charlie had stopped work. She stood quietly on her ladder watching Bernine, but she did not call out to her. Not until Bernine headed purposefully in her direction did Charlie come down the ladder. "Looking for Clyde?" Her tone was not cordial.

"I have an appointment with Winthrop Jergen," Bernine said cooly. "Is it upstairs? How do I . . . ?"

Charlie pointed toward the stairwell. Bernine said nothing more but headed across the patio.

Behind her, relief softened Charlie's face. And from an upper-floor window, Pearl Ann stood at the glass watching the little scene with a dry, amused smile.

The cats listened to the clink of Bernine's heels on the stairs, then her soft knock.

"She doesn't waste any time, does she?" Dulcie said with a cutting little mew.

Joe shrugged. "She'll start off talking investments, then come onto him. The woman's a leech." He curled up in the sunny weeds, yawning.

Dulcie curled up beside him, watching and listening. And it wasn't half an hour later that they heard the upstairs door open and heard Bernine say softly, "Twelve-thirty, then. See you tomorrow." And she clicked down the steps and left the patio with a smug, self-satisfied expression. Her fast work, even for Bernine, piqued Dulcie's interest like the sound of mice scratching at a baseboard.

She watched Bernine drive away, then looked up at Jergen's apartment. "Does he realize she's a little gold digger? He seems smarter than that."

"Maybe *he's* playing at some game—maybe he sees right through her."

Dulcie smiled. "I want to see this. I want to see how he looks when he leaves to pick her up, what he's wearing . . ."

"That's incredibly nosy. What difference . . ."

"What he's wearing," she said with patient female logic, "will indicate what he has in mind—what he thinks of Bernine."

• • •

And Dulcie's curiosity drew them back the next day to the patio, where they lay napping in the sun as Winthrop Jergen left his apartment. The sight of him made Dulcie laugh.

"Just as I thought. Trying to look like a twenty-year-old."

He was dressed in a black turtleneck sweater that set off his sleek silver hair, tight black slacks, a tan suede sport coat, and suede boots. "Right," Dulcie said, smirking. "Bernine made a big impression. Don't be surprised if she takes him for a nice sum—she has a way with her lovers."

But Joe was watching Pearl Ann gathering up her cleaning equipment as Jergen's Mercedes pulled away. Joe rose as she headed for the stairs.

"This isn't Jergen's regular cleaning day," he said, as Pearl Ann slipped quickly inside. "Come on."

In another minute they were crouched beneath Jergen's sink, waiting for the customary cleaning sounds, for Pearl Ann's vacuum to start. They heard only silence, then the jingle of keys and a file drawer sliding open.

Slipping to the kitchen door, they watched Pearl Ann sitting at Winthrop Jergen's desk examining the hanging files in an open drawer. Her keys dangled on their familiar gold chain from the drawer's lock.

Searching through the files, she removed one occasionally and laid it on the desk, paging through. Then she turned on Jergen's computer. She seemed quite at home with the machine, scrolling through vast columns of numbers. But every few minutes she rose to lean over the desk, looking down at the street below, her jumpsuit tight across her slim rear. The scent of her jasmine cologne was so sharp that Dulcie had to press her nose against her paw to keep from sneezing. After a long perusal of both hard copy and computer files, she removed a floppy disk from her pocket and slipped it into the machine.

"Copies," Dulcie breathed against Joe's ear. "She's making copies. She's using a code. How does she know his code?" At night in the library, after some instruction from Wilma, she found the computer a challenge, though she still preferred the feel of book pages beneath her paws. She knew about codes, Wilma had shown her that; Wilma kept a few things on her computer she didn't want the whole library to know.

When Pearl Ann seemed finished with the financial sheets, she pulled up a file of Jergen's business letters, quickly read through them and copied them, then dropped the disk in her pocket and turned off the machine. As she turned to put away the files, a whiff of her perfume engulfed the cats, and without warning, Dulcie sneezed.

Pearl Ann whirled and saw them.

"Cats! My God! Get out of here! What are you doing in here! He'll have a fit. How did you get in here!"

Crouching, they backed away. Neither Joe nor Dulcie cared to run beneath the sink and reveal their secret entrance. And the front door was securely closed.

"Scat! Go on, get out!" She snatched up her mop, shaking it at them.

They didn't move.

"You nervy little beasts! Go *on*, get out of here!" Her voice was hoarse with impatience.

They turned toward the front door, hoping she'd open it, but they weren't fast enough. She shouted again and lunged at them, exhibiting a temper they hadn't guessed at.

They'd never gotten friendly with Pearl Ann, nor

she with them. She did her work, and they went about their business, all perfectly civil. But now that they were in her way, they saw a more violent side to Pearl Ann Jamison. Swinging her mop, she advanced on Dulcie, trapping her against the file cabinet. "You nasty little beast."

Dulcie fought the mop, enraging Pearl Ann, who swooped and grabbed her, snatched her up, avoiding her claws, and shook her hard.

Joe leaped at Pearl Ann, clawing her leg to make her drop Dulcie. Gasping, she hit him and swung Dulcie up. "*Damn* cats! Damn!" she croaked. Jerking the door open, she pitched Dulcie down the stairwell.

Joe barely skinned through as she slammed the door; below him Dulcie fell, unable to find her footing. He flew down the stairs, ramming against her, pushing her into the baseboard to stop her headlong tumble. Pressing against her, he could feel her heart pounding.

"You okay?" he asked, as they crouched shivering on the steps.

"I think so. I couldn't get my paws under me."

"What was she so angry about? What's with her?" He licked her face, trying to calm her. "Do you hurt anywhere?"

"I'm all right. I guess she doesn't like cats. I never saw that side of her before." Her voice was shaky. She licked hard at her left shoulder.

"Whatever she was doing in there, she was nervous as a rat in a cement mixer. Come on, let's get out of here."

They beat it out through the patio, didn't stop until they were across the street on their own turf, hidden in the tall grass.

"So what *was* she doing?" Joe said, nosing at Dulcie's hurt shoulder. "Is she trying to rip him off? First

Bernine came onto him, and now Pearl Ann's nosing around." He looked intently at Dulcie. "What, exactly, was she doing at the computer?"

"I couldn't make much of it, all those numbers make my head reel. You'd have to have an accounting degree."

"Maybe she's running a scam. Hire onto a job, look for something to steal. But what would she . . . ?"

"Could she be the law?" Dulcie wondered. "Or a private detective? Maybe checking on Jergen?"

"Checking on him for what?"

"I don't know. Or maybe investigating one of his clients?"

Joe frowned, the white mark down his nose squeezing into a scowl. "Anything's possible."

"Whatever she was doing, and in spite of getting sworn at and tossed downstairs, I'm as much on her side as Jergen's. Sometimes that man makes me twitch. Always so smooth and restrained—and always *so* well-groomed."

Joe grinned. "Not like Clyde—earthy and honest." But then he sat lost in thought.

"Did Bernine get Jergen away so Pearl Ann could snoop?" Dulcie asked.

Joe looked at her and said nothing. Was there a crime here, or were they painting more into this than was there?

She said, "Pearl Ann was snooping for some reason. And Bernine—even for Bernine—really did come onto him pretty fast."

The cats looked intently at each other, the two incidents, together, as compelling to them as a wounded bird fluttering before their noses.

11

WALKING ALONG Dolores Street carrying a bowl of potato salad and a six-pack of beer, Charlie glanced up as Wilma nudged her, nodding ahead to where a black Mercedes convertible had slowed to turn the corner. From the driver's seat, Winthrop Jergen raised his hand in greeting. Sitting close beside him, Bernine gave them a tight little smile, cold and patronizing. The tall redhead was elegantly dressed in a sleek black, bare-shouldered frock, her russet hair coiled high and caught with a band of black.

"She doesn't waste any time," Charlie said. "Lunch yesterday and now dinner. Wonder where they're going."

"Somewhere expensive, if I know Bernine." Wilma shifted the bag of French bread to her other hand and reached up to steady Dulcie, who was riding on her shoulder. "Mavity's remarks on Sunday, about Jergen's financial acumen, were like gunfire to the troops."

"It's amazing she didn't already know him, considering he's a well-to-do bachelor."

"A rare oversight. I've known Bernine half my life,

and she seldom misses such a plum." Glancing around at
Dulcie, Wilma winked. Dulcie narrowed her eyes in
answer. But as the convertible turned the corner and
disappeared, she turned her attention to the shop windows, dismissing Bernine's little games, enjoying the
elevated view from Wilma's shoulder. Her high perch
was a liberating change from being level with the bot-
toms of doorways—from breathing the smell of hot
rubber tires and dog pee and having to stand on her hind
paws to see a store display. One had, at twelve inches
from the sidewalk, a somewhat limited perspective.

Charlie, pausing at a dress shop, stared covetously
in at a creamy velvet cocktail suit, where the sleek,
dark-haired mannequin posed against a background of
city lights. "Wish I could wear that stuff—and could
look like that."

"Of course you can wear it, and of course you can
look like that, or better. That ivory velvet would be
smashing with your red hair."

"Right. And where would I wear it? For four hundred dollars, I'd rather have a Bosch drill, some new
sawhorses, and a heavier sander." Charlie laughed and
moved on, looking around her with pleasure at the
small village. Over the rooftops, the eastern hills were
burnished by early-evening light, the windows of the
scattered hillside houses reflecting gold and catching
images of the sinking sun. Close around them along the
narrow streets, the sprawling oaks, the tubs of flowers,
the little benches, and the used-brick facades and jutting
bay windows caught the light, so brilliant with color and
yet so cozy that she felt her heart skip.

"This village—how lucky we are. The first time I
ever saw it, I knew that I'd come home."

Wilma nodded. "Some people are born for fast
highways, for tall buildings, but you and I, we're hap-

pier with the small places, the people-friendly places, with the little, interesting details—and with having everything we need right within walking distance.

"I like sensing the land under me, too. The way the old cypress trees cling to the great rims of rock and the rock ridges drop away into the sea like the spine of some ancient, half-emerged animal. In the city," Wilma said, "I can't sense the earth. I couldn't wait, when I retired, to move back home.

"I like knowing that these old trees were here before there was a village, when this coastal land was all wild—range cattle and grizzly bear country." Wilma put her hand on Dulcie as they crossed the southbound lane of Ocean, toward the wide, grassy stretch of the tree-shaded median.

"I bet you had enough of big city crime, too."

Wilma nodded. "In Molena Point, I don't have to watch my backside."

Charlie laughed. "People-friendly," she agreed.

And cat-friendly, Dulcie thought. Compared to San Francisco's mean alleys, which Joe had described in frightening detail—the bad-tempered, roving dogs, the speeding cars, the drunks reaching out from doorways to snatch a little cat and hurt it—compared to these, Molena Point really *was* cat heaven, just as Clyde told Joe.

Clyde said Joe was lucky to have landed here. And despite Joe's smart-mouthed replies, Joe Grey knew he was lucky—he just would never admit it.

Beyond Ocean, as they approached Clyde's white Cape Cod cottage, Dulcie could smell the smokey-meaty scent from Clyde's barbeque and could hear Clyde's CD playing a soft jazz trumpet. Pete Fountain, she thought, purring as she leaped down from Wilma's shoulder and in through Joe's cat door.

• • •

In Clyde's weedy backyard, a thick London broil sizzled on the grill. Clyde and Max Harper sat comfortably in folding chairs sipping beer. Harper, lean and leathery, looked even thinner out of uniform, dressed in soft jeans and Western shirt. Above the two men, in the maple tree, Joe Grey sprawled along a branch, watching sleepy-eyed as Dulcie threaded out the back door between Wilma's and Charlie's ankles. The little tabby headed across the yard, slowed by the inspection of the household cats sniffing and rubbing against her and by Rube's wet licks across her face. The old Labrador loved Dulcie, and she was always patient with him; she never scratched him for his blundering clumsiness and sloppy greetings. Trotting quickly across the grass, escaping the menagerie, she swarmed up the tree to settle on the branch beside Joe, her weight dropping them a bit lower among the leaf cover.

Below them the picnic table was set for four and loaded with jars of condiments, paper napkins, plastic plates, bowls of chips and dip, and now Wilma's covered bowl of potato salad. Wilma laid the foil-wrapped garlic bread at the back of the grill and put her beer in the Styrofoam cooler, tossing one to Charlie and opening one for herself. As she sat down, Clyde handed her a sheaf of papers.

Looking them over, she smiled. "What did you do, Max, threaten your men with desk duty if they didn't sign a petition? Looks like you got signatures from the jail regulars, too."

"Of course," Harper said. "Drug dealers, pimps, they're all there."

She looked up at Clyde. "Two of these petitions are yours. You've been intimidating your automotive customers."

Clyde tossed a roll of paper towels on the table.

"They don't sign the petition, they don't get their car—though most of them were pleased to sign it." He tipped up his beer, took a long swallow. "All this damn fuss. If the village wants a library cat, what's the harm? This Brackett woman is a piece of work."

"Next thing," Harper said, "she'll be complaining because my men circulated petitions on their own time."

"She'll try to get an ordinance against that, too," Charlie said.

"She'd have a hard time," Harper said. "Those petitions aren't for financial or political gain, they're for a cat. A poor, simple cat."

Dulcie cut her eyes at Joe. *A poor, simple cat?* But she had to smile. For someone so wary of certain felines, Max Harper had responded to the library cat battle like a real gentleman—though if he knew the petitions were to help one of his telephone informants, he might go into shock.

Clyde adjusted the height of the grill to keep the meat from burning. The aroma of the London broil made the cats lick their whiskers.

Harper looked at Charlie. "So your landlord tossed you out."

"I'm back freeloading on Wilma."

"And you've joined Sicily Aronson's group," he said. "I stopped in the gallery to have a look." He nodded his approval. "Your animals are very fine." Charlie's cheeks reddened. Harper glanced up at Dulcie and Joe as if inspecting them for a likeness. "You make those cats look . . ."

He paused, frowning, seemed to revise what he'd started to say. "It's fine work, Charlie. And the Aronson is a good gallery—Sicily's people sell very well. I think your work will be very much in demand."

Charlie smiled. "That would be nice—it would be great to fatten up my bank account, stop feeling shaky about money."

"It'll come," Harper said. "And Charlie's Fix-It, Clean-It appears to be doing well—except," he said, glancing at Clyde, "you need to be careful about questionable clients."

"If you hit it big," Clyde said, "if you sell a lot of drawings, you could put some money with Jergen, go for the high earnings. A bank doesn't pay much interest."

"I don't like the uncertainty," Charlie told him. "Call me chicken, but I'd rather depend on a small and steady interest."

Clyde tested the meat, slicing into one end, a tiny cut that ran bloody. In the tree above, the cats watched, mesmerized.

Harper passed Charlie a beer. "Have you found a new apartment?"

"Haven't had time to look. Or maybe I haven't had the incentive," Charlie said. "I get pretty comfortable with Wilma."

"There are a couple of cottages empty down near Mavity's place. We cleared one last week—busted the tenant for grass."

"Just what I want. Handy to my friendly neighborhood drug dealer."

"In fact, it's pretty clean down there. We manage to keep them at bay."

Molena Point depended for much of its income on tourism, and Harper did his best to keep the village straight, to stay on top of any drug activity. But even Molena Point had occasional problems. Several months ago, Joe remembered, there'd been an influx of PCP and crack. Harper had made three cases and got three convictions. In this town, the dealers went to jail.

Harper had said that some of the drugs coming into the village were designer stuff, experimental pills.

Clyde said, "I could turn one of the new apartments into two studios. You could rent one of those."

"Your permit doesn't allow for more than five residences," Charlie said.

"Or you could move in here, with me."

Charlie blushed. "If I move in with you, Clyde Damen, I'll sleep in the laundry with the cats and Rube."

At the sound of his name, Rube lifted his head, staring bleerily at Charlie. The old dog's cataracts made his eyes dull and milky. His black muzzle was salted with white hairs. When Charlie reached to pet him, Rube leaned his head against her leg. The three household cats wound around Clyde's ankles as he removed the steak from the grill. But when the foursome was seated, it was Charlie who took up a knife and cut off bits of her steak for the animals.

The CDs played softly a string of Preservation Hall jazz numbers, the beer was ice cold, the steak pink and tender, the conversation comfortable, and as evening drew down, the fog gathered, fuzzing the outdoor lights and enclosing the backyard until it seemed untouched by the outside world. It was not until the four had finished dinner, the animals had had their fill, and Charlie was pouring coffee, that Harper mentioned the burglaries.

There had been a third break-in, at Waverly's Leather Goods. "They got over four thousand in small bills. Didn't take anything else, just the cash." Waverly's was the most exclusive leather shop in the village. "We have one partial print—we're hoping it's his. The guy's real careful.

"The print doesn't match any of the employees,

but it will take a few days to get a make. He may have taken off his gloves for a minute while he was working on the safe."

"Are you still going on the theory the burglar's getting hold of the store keys?" Wilma asked.

Harper shrugged. "We're checking the locksmiths. Or he could simply be skilled with locks." He started to say something more, then hesitated, seemed to change his mind.

In the tree above him, the cats stared up at the sky, following the antics of the diving bats that wheeled among the treetops, but taking in Harper's every word.

Wilma, glancing up at them, exchanged a look with Clyde and turned away torn between a scowl and a laugh. The cats aggravated them both—but they were so wonderful and amazing that Wilma wished, sometimes, that she could follow them unseen and miss nothing.

It was not until the company had left, around midnight, that Clyde vented his own reaction. As Joe settled down, pawing at the bed covers, Clyde pulled off his shirt and emptied his pockets onto the dresser. "So what gives?"

"What gives about what?"

"You're very closemouthed about these burglaries." He turned to look at Joe. "Why the silence? There is no crime in Molena that you and Dulcie don't get involved with."

Joe looked up at him dully.

"Come on, Joe."

Joe yawned.

"*What?* Suddenly I'm the enemy? You think I can't be trusted?"

"We're not interested in these petty thefts."

· "Of course you're interested. And isn't it nice, once in a while, to share your thoughts, to have some human feedback?"

"We're not investigating anything. Three amateurish little burglaries—Harper can handle that stuff."

"You have, in the past, not only confided in me, but picked up some rather useful information, thanks to yours truly."

Joe only looked at him.

"Clues you would surely have missed if Max and I didn't play poker, if you didn't scrounge around on the poker table, eavesdropping. But now you're too good to talk to me?"

Joe yawned again. "I am eternally grateful for your help on previous occasions. But at the moment I am not in need of information. We're not interested." Turning over on the pillow, with his back to Clyde, he began to work on his claws, pulling off the old sheaths.

He and Dulcie already knew who the perp was. As soon as they checked out Mavity's brother, Greeley, and found where he'd stashed the money, they'd tip Harper. And that would wrap it up. If the prints on the stolen bills matched the print from the leather shop, Harper would have Greeley cold.

Biting at his claws to release the sharp new lances and listening to Clyde noisily brushing his teeth in the bathroom, he quickly laid his plan.

Dulcie wasn't going to like the drill.

But she'd asked for it. If she wanted to play cute with the black tomcat, wanted to cut her eyes at Azrael, then she could make herself useful.

12

MAVITY FLOWERS'S cottage stood on pilings across a narrow road from the bay and marsh, crowded among similar dwellings, their walls cardboard-thin, their roofs flat and low, their stilted supports stained with mud from years of soaking during the highest tides. Mavity's VW Bug was parked on the cracked cement drive that skirted close to the house. Beyond the car, at the back, the open carport was crowded with pasteboard boxes, an old table, a wooden sawhorse, two worn tires, and a broken grocery cart. Joe, approaching the yard from across the road through the tall marsh grass, skirted pools of black mud that smelled fishy and sour; then as he crossed the narrow road, Azrael's scent came strong to him, clinging to the scruffy lawn.

Following the tomcat's aroma up onto Mavity's porch, he sniffed at the house wall, below an open window. Above him, the window screen had been removed and the window propped open, and black cat hairs clung to the sill. Mavity might complain about the tomcat, but she treated him cordially enough. From within the cottage, the smell of fried eggs and coffee wrapped around Joe, and he could hear silverware clatter against a plate.

"Eat up, Greeley, or I'll be late."

"Eating as fast as I can," a man replied. "You hadn't ought to rush a man in the morning."

"If you're coming with me, you'll get a move on."

Below the window, Joe Grey smiled. He'd hit pay dirt. That raspy, hoarse croak was unmistakable; he could hear again the wizened old man arguing with Azrael over their takeout fish and chips. Greeley was their man. No doubt about it. Mavity's own brother was their light-fingered, cat-consorting thief.

Luck, Joe thought. *Or the great cat god's smiling.* And, sitting down beneath the window, he prepared to wait.

Once Mavity left for work, taking Greeley with her, he'd have only Dora and Ralph to worry about—if, indeed, they were out of bed yet. Mavity said the portly couple liked to sleep late, and if the great cat god hung around, he might not even have to dodge the Sleuders; maybe they'd sleep through his search.

As for Azrael, at the moment that tomcat was otherwise occupied.

But to make sure, Joe dropped from the porch to the yard and prowled among the pilings, sniffing for Dulcie's scent.

Yes, he found where she had marked a path, her provocative female aroma leading away toward the village, a trail that no tomcat would ignore. He imagined her, even now, trotting across the rooftops close beside Azrael, her tail waving, her green eyes cutting shyly at the tom, distracting him just as they'd planned.

He sat down beside a blackened piling, trying to calm his frayed nerves, wondering if this idea had been so smart.

But Dulcie wouldn't betray him. And as far as her

safety, his lady could whip a room full of German shep-
herds with one paw tied behind. He imagined her dodging Azrael's unwanted advances, subtly leading him on a
wild chase far from Mavity's cottage, handling the situation with such guile that she would not need to smack
the foreign beast.

"Get your jacket, Greeley, or I'll be late." Inside, a
chair scraped and dishes were being stacked, then water
ran in the sink. He caught the sharp smell of dish soap,
imagined Mavity standing just a few feet from him
washing up the breakfast plates. Then the water was
turned off. Soon the door opened, and from beneath the
deck he watched their hurrying feet descend the steps,
Mavity's white jogging shoes and Greeley's dark loafers.

He got a look at him as they headed for her VW.
This was their man, all right.

Greeley wasn't much taller than Mavity. He wore
the wrinkled leather jacket with the cuffs turned up and
the collar pushing at his shaggy gray hair. Joe could see
him again rifling Mrs. Medder's cash register.

The car doors slammed and Mavity backed out,
turning up Shoreline toward the village. Joe did not
enter the house at once but listened for Dora and Ralph.
When, after some minutes, he had heard nothing but
the sea wind hushing through the marsh grass behind
him, he leaped to the sill and slipped in through the
open window.

Pausing above the sink, his nose was filled with
the smell of greasy eggs and soapsuds. The kitchen
was open to the small living room, with barely space
between for the tiny breakfast table pushed against
the back of the couch. A faded, overstuffed chair faced
the couch, along with a small desk and a narrow cot
covered with a plaid blanket. A TV jammed between
the desk and a bookcase completed the decor. The

ceiling was low, the walls pale tan. To his right, from the darkened bedroom, he heard slow, even breathing.

There was only the one bedroom, and through the open door he studied the piled suitcases, the closed blinds, the two big mounds sprawled beneath the blankets. When neither Dora nor Ralph stirred, he padded along the kitchen counter and across the breakfast table to the back of the couch.

At one end of the couch was a stack of folded sheets and blankets and a bed pillow. Dropping down to the rug, he inspected first beneath the furniture and found, under the cot, a battered leather suitcase.

The clasp was devilishly hard to open. Digging at it with stubborn claws, at last he sprang it.

He found within only socks, underwear, a shaving kit, and a pair of wrinkled pajamas. The shaving kit, which was unzipped, had an inner pocket. Pawing this open, thinking Greeley might have stashed some of the money there, he narrowly missed cutting his pad on Greeley's used razor blades. Why would anyone save old razor blades?

Nosing into the suitcase under the false bottom, which was meant to keep the bag rigid, he found nothing but a small notebook containing some foreign addresses and Greeley's plane ticket. Sliding the ticket from its envelope, he saw that Greeley had not yet made his return reservation. Pushing everything back in order, he turned away. Listening to the lonely wind buffet the cottage, he headed for the bedroom.

Long before Joe entered Mavity's cottage, across the village on the dark rooftops where the sea wind scudded and danced, Dulcie slunk along a roof's edge watching the street below. Around her, the dark trees hushed and rattled, and the moon's fitful light jumped and fled; above her, telephone lines swung in an erratic dance, and in an open dormer window white curtains whipped like frantic ghosts. By the strike of the courthouse clock she had been on the rooftops since three, and it was now nearly six. She had not seen Azrael. She was beginning to worry that he had not left Mavity's cottage or had returned to it, surprising Joe in his search.

Had she not marked her trail clearly enough, on her way from the marsh? Or had she marked it too clearly? Rubbing her whiskers on every surface and leaving little damp messages, had she made Azrael suspicious? She prayed that he hadn't guessed their plan and was lying in wait for Joe. She longed to turn back to Mavity's, but she might only lead him there. She could do nothing but keep on searching, casually marking her trail across the rooftops.

Then suddenly, in the shadows of the alley, was that the tomcat? Quickly she dropped down to an oak branch and crossed the six-foot chasm to the roof of the Swiss Cafe.

Stretching out along the rain gutter, she watched the dark montage of shadows that she thought had moved.

Now all was still. No sign of Azrael.

At last she slipped to the corner where she could see the street. She waited there, watching, until the glow of the street lamps began to fade and the sky grew to the color of pewter beneath dark, scudding clouds. The courthouse clock struck six-thirty. Maybe the tomcat *had* returned to Mavity's and at this moment he and Joe were locked in terrible battle.

A lone car hushed along Ocean as an early riser headed for work. A shopkeeper set a box of trash at the curb then began to water his curbside garden of ferns and geraniums. Dulcie was about to turn away, to seek Azrael along other streets when from beneath a parked truck the black tom swaggered out, nose to the gusting wind. Pausing just below her, he licked his paw and washed his whiskers. He seemed restless, kept glancing away in the direction of the marsh. Was he aware of her? Did some sixth sense nudge him? When he started away, Dulcie followed quickly along the roof's edge.

But then he paused at the Red Skillet Cafe, stood peering into the patio, sniffing deeply the scents from last night's grilled salmon and halibut. As Dulcie hunched on the rooftop, he padded through the wrought-iron gate to wind among the tables. Immediately a mockingbird, snatching up crumbs, attacked him—and exploded in a storm of feathers, with a naked backside. The black tom smiled, licked his whiskers, and prowled among the tables, gulping bits of charred fish like some half-starved stray—but still he seemed edgy and unsettled, glancing away again and again in the direction of Mavity's cottage.

Quickly Dulcie, her heart pounding half with fear, half with excitement, dropped to the pavement and hurried after him.

Beyond the iron gate, Azrael was turned away. But his ears flicked. His tail lashed. His body stiffened as he sensed a presence behind him. As she slipped in through the bars, he whirled to face her.

She paused, her paw softly lifted.

His gaze narrowed to a sly caress.

They stared at each other in silence. Azrael flattened his whiskers, offered subtle body talk meant to set the stage for mating.

Dulcie gave him a slow smile. This wasn't going to be easy, to delay him yet avoid the snuggling games. She felt like a lady cop playing street hustler.

"Where is your friend, my dear? Your little gray friend? Does he know you're out alone?"

She wound among the chair legs, her tail high, her stroll sultry, her heart pounding so hard she could hear it. Azrael trotted close to her, his amber eyes deep and golden; when he bowed his neck, towering over her, she felt small suddenly, and frail.

Dora and Ralph Sleuder slept deeply, their even breathing unchanged as Joe prowled the dim bedroom. Pawing through a suitcase that lay open on the floor, he dug into its pockets and searched under the clothes, taking considerable trouble to push everything back in the same jumble as he'd found it.

He was nosing into a big duffle bag when the bedsprings creaked and Ralph stirred and sneezed. Fleeing to the kitchen, Joe leaped on the table and shot to the top of the refrigerator. Crouching behind a metal canister and a bag of potato chips, he watched Ralph swing to the floor and pad away toward the bathroom, nattily attired in striped green boxer shorts that dropped beneath his bare belly.

Making himself comfortable behind the chips, he was careful not to brush its crinkly cellophane or against the package of cookies. Amazing what a person could cram atop a refrigerator. Clyde favored beer, and an assortment of cat and dog kibble—all the essentials readily at hand.

The bedsprings squeaked again, and Dora rose, her ample curves voluminous in a pink-and-green flowered nightie. Not bothering to wash or comb her hair, she padded into the kitchen, looked out the window, and glanced into the living room.

Returning to the bedroom, she began to open the drawers in the tall dresser, carefully examining the contents of each, her movements quick and watchful.

From the bathroom, the toilet flushed, and Ralph returned to start on the other dresser, pawing through Mavity's personal belongings.

"Nothing," Dora said at last, closing the bottom drawer. "She must have a lot of time on her hands, to keep her drawers so neated up."

Ralph slammed a drawer closed. "Maybe in the living room."

"Start on the desk. I'll look in the bookcase. Daddy'll have dropped her at work by now, so she won't come charging back forgetting her lunch or whatever. That gave me the cold sweats yesterday when she did that."

"What about your daddy? How soon will he be back?"

"Depends. If he decided to drive over to Monterey—haircuts are cheaper over there—he'll be a while."

Watching Dora go through the bookcase, pulling romance novels from the shelves to look behind then shoving them back, watching Ralph finger through the contents of Mavity's desk, Joe grew so interested that he backed into the cookies. The brittle crunch brought both Dora and Ralph swinging around to stare toward the kitchen. He remained frozen behind the canister, as still as one of those plaster amusement park cats—a gray plaster cat with white markings.

"Heat," Ralph said, seeing no one in the kitchen. "Thought it was that stinking Azrael coming through the window, but it was just heat—them chip bags pop in the heat. Makes 'em rancid, too."

Joe watched, puzzled, as the two pudgy people resumed their investigation. If they were looking for Greeley's stolen money, why had they searched Mavity's bedroom? Why not go directly to Greeley's suitcase, as he himself had done?

But maybe they'd already searched there. Or did

they think that Mavity had hidden the money? Did they think she was Greeley's accomplice?

Not Mavity. He couldn't think that.

The smell of chips was so strong he could taste them. What did they put in that stuff? Looking out, he watched Ralph remove papers from the desk drawers and shuffle through them, scanning Mavity's letters and bills, and he grew certain Ralph wasn't looking for the money. But what, then?

The desk had seven drawers. Digging into the bottom drawer, Ralph raised up, fanning a stack of white paper. "*Got it! I got it!*"

Dora hurried in, her short, flowered nightie flapping around her meaty white legs, and snatched the papers from him. Leaning against the desk, she rifled through— then waved the papers and laughed, hugged Ralph and did a little dance around him, wriggling provocatively.

"Take a good look," she said, handing them back, "while I get set up." And she vanished into the bedroom. Joe heard a click, as if a suitcase had opened. She returned carrying a small copier machine. Glancing out the window toward the drive, she set it on the kitchen table and began to search for an outlet.

"Hurry up. Unplug the toaster. A haircut doesn't take forever. Your dad . . ."

"I am hurrying. Give me the statements." Jerking out the toaster cord, she jammed in the plug, flipped the switch, and stood shuffling through the sheaf of papers until a green light came on.

Slipping to the edge of the refrigerator, Joe could just see a letterhead above Mavity's name and address. WINTHROP JERGEN, FINANCIAL ADVISOR.

Dora made two copies of each page and separated them into two piles. When she was halfway through, Ralph stopped her. "You better call him. I'll finish."

"You call him."

"No. You're the one started this. You do it."

Sighing, she fished a slip of paper from her pocket, picked up the phone from the desk and carried it to the coffee table dragging the cord, sat down on the couch where she could be comfortable. "I hope he's there."

"He said he'd wait for the call."

"Why is it so hard to get him on the phone?"

"Just call, Dora. Before your daddy gets back."

While Ralph ran copies, she punched in seven clicks. No area code, so it was a local call. Waiting for her party to pick up, she glanced directly toward the refrigerator. Joe held his breath, didn't twitch a whisker.

Abruptly she returned her attention to the phone. She didn't say hello, she offered no cordial introduction, just started talking.

"We have them."

A pause.

"I can't. Dad has the car. He took Mavity to work. He's getting a haircut—I told you he'd get one today. He'll be back any minute."

Silence.

"All right. But hurry."

She hung up. "He's on his way." She headed for the bedroom and in a few minutes returned dressed in tight jeans and a T-shirt that told the world she liked hot cars and champagne, carrying a large leather briefcase. Ralph finished up the copies, straightened the two stacks, and put the originals back in the bottom desk drawer. Dora carried one stack into the bedroom, then unplugged the copier and slipped it into the briefcase, tucking the other set of pages on top.

When Ralph padded into the kitchen to make coffee, Joe froze again. The couple sat at the table, not five feet from him, sipping coffee and waiting.

"Where can he be?" Dora grumbled. "What's taking so long?"

After twenty minutes by the kitchen clock, she fetched a plate of cake from the cupboard and cut two thick slices.

Ten minutes more, and another ten. They had poured the last of the coffee and Joe felt ready to pitch a fit—it was an interminable wait for both the Sleuders and their silent audience. At last a car came down the street.

"That has to be him. Where has he been?" Dora patted her hair and straightened her shirt. "What in the world took him so long?"

But the car went on by. Joe heard it stop a block away, heard the car door slam. In a minute, footsteps came up the street, turning to the house.

"That's him," Ralph said. A shadow loomed beyond the louvered glass: a thin man. Dora pulled the door open.

"Had car trouble," the man said, stepping inside. "Left it up the block. It's running rough as a paint shaker."

Joe, watching him, was rigid with amazement.

He was of medium height and slight of build, his light brown hair tied in a ponytail that flopped over the hood of his blue windbreaker.

This was the man who lingered around the apartments. The silent watcher. Joe caught a whiff of motor grease as he moved past Dora to the table.

"Let's have a look."

Dora opened the briefcase and handed him the copies.

"Shuffle them out, Dora. My hands are greasy from the car."

She spread the statements across the kitchen table;

he stood scanning them as she sorted through, then looked up at her, smiling.

"This is what we want. Exactly. You've done a good job here." He winked at her. "You two are quite something."

The man watched as Dora put the papers in a neat pile again and slid them back into the briefcase on top the copier, carefully closing the lid.

Removing a white handkerchief from his pocket, he wrapped it around the handle. "No need to get grease on the leather. I'm just filthy." He smiled again, holding the briefcase away from his pantleg, and moved toward the door. "Wish me luck, folks, that I can nurse the old car into the village."

"I could phone for a tow truck," Dora offered.

"I'll take it slow. I think it's the carburetor, but I should be able to make it to the garage all right." He stared down at his dirty hands, let Dora open the door for him.

The man's name was never spoken. When he had gone, Joe endured what seemed eternal confinement between the chips and cookies while Dora fixed breakfast and the two folks ate a never-ending meal of fried sausage, fried eggs, instant grits, toast, and coffee. At first the smells made him hungry, but after prolonged exposure, he wanted to throw up. He woke from a fitful doze as Dora began to do the dishes, running hot water into the sink, plunging her hands into the suds.

When she had put the dishes in the drain, she hurried to the bedroom and returned wearing a yellow-and-purple mumu and flipflops and carrying a blanket and a beach umbrella. Ralph padded out dressed in skintight black exercise shorts and a red tank top straining across his considerable girth. Joe watched them toddle down the steps and plow through the muddy, sandy marsh to a streak of sand at the edge of the water, watched them spread their towels on the fish-scented shore. As Ralph put up the beach umbrella, Joe leaped down from the refrigerator and resumed his own search, swiftly prowling, poking with a nervous paw.

He found no other suitcase smelling of Greeley. He dug into the bags belonging to Dora and Ralph, then looked for the money beneath the beds and up under the bedsprings and under the couch cushions, all the while listening for footsteps on the porch or the sound of a car—or the soft thump of paws hitting the windowsill.

He tossed the bathroom, too, then pawed open the kitchen cabinets. He fought open the refrigerator but found no wrapped package that might contain money. Standing on the kitchen counter, he was just able to open the freezer, a favored place for householders to hide their valuables according to Max Harper. Leaning into the cold, he sniffed several paper-wrapped packages, but the smell of each matched its handwritten label: pork chops, shrimp, green beans. He nearly froze his ears off. Being practically inside the freezer, trying to listen for intruders, feeling as nervous as a mouse in a tin bucket, he backed out gratefully into the warm kitchen.

When he could think of nowhere else to look— couldn't figure a way to take the top off the toilet tank or remove the light fixtures—he gave up, sprang out the open window, and trotted up the hill behind the cottage. Fleeing the scene through the woods, he hit the wide gardens above, galloping between those substantial homes wondering where Greeley had hidden the money and what Dora and Ralph were up to. Telling himself that Dora Sleuder wouldn't rip off her own aunt Mavity.

13

WINTHROP JERGEN liked to tell his
clients that he was a sentimental nonconformist, that he
would endure almost any inconvenience so he could
enjoy the magnificent view from his out-of-the-way
office-apartment.

In fact, the view meant nothing. That wondrous
vista down the Molena Point hills wasn't even visible
when he sat at his desk, only the tops of a few ragged
trees and empty sky. He had to stand up or move to the
couch before the glare of sun-glazed rooftops stabbed at
his vision. And this morning the so-called view was a
mass of wind-churned trees and ugly whitecaps. That
was the trouble with being close to the water, these violent winds whipping inland. Now, standing at his desk
looking down to the dead-end street below, observing
the weeds and the three battered service trucks parked
behind Charlie Getz's rusting van, he wondered why he
tolerated this disreputable display.

According to the provisions of his lease, he could
have refused to let Damen undertake the remodeling,

but he thought it better to endure a few months' annoyance in order to acquire a more respectable environ. And it was always possible that Damen would overextend himself, sink more money into the project than he could manage, and would be in need of cash, perhaps a personal loan.

Glancing at his watch, he left his desk and in the bathroom removed his sport coat, tucked a clean bath towel over his white shirt and tie, ran hot water into a washcloth and steamed his face, bringing up a ruddy color and relaxing the tightness that prevailed after he'd been at work for several hours. He brushed his teeth, used the blow-dryer to touch up his hair, removed the towel, and washed his hands. He was to pick up Bernine at twelve-thirty. He'd had trouble getting a reservation on a Saturday, but Bernine had raved about the Windborne. The restaurant was indeed charming, a rustic, secluded aerie clinging to the seacliffs south of the village. Bernine said she liked the ambiance. The moneyed ambiance, he thought, amused. As long as Bernine wasn't buying. If he kept this up, lunch or dinner every day, she could prove to be expensive.

He wasn't sure whether Bernine Sage would become a client or a lover, or both. It didn't matter. One way or another, she would be useful. She was blatantly obvious in coming onto him, but she was a good-looker, kept herself groomed and dressed in a style that commanded attention. A nice showpiece. And she seemed to know her way around, knew a lot of worthwhile, influential people.

As long as they understood each other, the relationship could be mutually entertaining. With Bernine on his arm he got plenty of appraising looks. She attracted interest, and interest, in a certain strata, meant money.

Straightening his tie and slipping back into his sport coat, he returned to the computer screen to finish up a last group of entries. He checked his figures, then closed and secured the file with a code and punched in the screen saver, a slowly wheeling montage of various foreign currencies. Putting his backup disks safely in the file cabinet, he locked it and locked the desk, left no disk or hard copy accessible. And without the code, no one could access his hard drive.

Surely no one around here had reason to snoop, or very likely had the knowledge to override his code. But he made it a point to follow set routines. He was successful in large part because he did not deviate from carefully chosen and rigorously observed procedures.

Two incidents of the morning did bother him, however. Small mistakes he must have made, though he abhorred carelessness.

He had found a number error in the Benson file. And he had found, in a hard copy file for the Dawson account, two spreadsheets out of order. Such small inefficiencies could lead to far more serious errors. He did not allow such carelessness in others, and he certainly couldn't sanction it in himself.

Locking the apartment, heading down the stairs jingling his keys, he paused at the bottom of the steps glancing to his right into the weedy patio at the stacks of lumber, the sawhorses, and crated plumbing fixtures. He hoped this project wouldn't last forever. Turning left from the stairwell, he stepped out onto the driveway and to the bank of garages. Activating his pocket remote, he opened his single garage door, backed the Mercedes out, and headed down the hills.

Molena Point's shops and cottages were appallingly picturesque. In his opinion, a regular Disney World, though he would not say that to anyone. As for

the crowds of tourists, those people might as well be in
Fantasyland, they were so busy spending money on
foolish whims. No thought to solid investment. No,
the tourists weren't for him. It was Molena Point's
established residents who made up the predictable
cadre of his clients.

Parking in the short-term green zone in front of
the Molena Point Library, he had intended to wait for
Bernine in the car, but on impulse he swung out and
moved through the deep garden, along the stone walk,
and in through the dark, heavily carved doors of the
sprawling Mediterranean building.

The central reading room was brightly lighted, its
white walls and spaciousness offsetting the dark tables
and bookcases. Through an office door he could see
Bernine, dressed in a short pink suit, standing near a
desk beside the head librarian—Freda something—a
frowsy scarecrow of a woman who seemed to be
scolding a third party standing nearly out of sight
beyond the door. Interested, he wandered in that
direction, pausing beside the book stacks.

He could see a bit of the third woman, with her
back to him. Red sweatshirt, long gray hair caught
back with a silver clip, faded jeans. That would be the
Getz woman, the person Bernine was staying with.

Plucking a book from the shelf, something about
Scottish bed-and-breakfasts, he stood slowly turning
the pages, listening for any stray information that
might be useful.

They were arguing about a cat. *A cat*—that cat that
had caused all the fuss in the newspaper, the animal they
called the library cat. Freda was giving the tall, gray-
haired woman a real dressing-down. And she had considerable skill at it, too; she handled her authority with
style, splendidly high-handed and thorough.

And certainly Bernine, standing at full attention, was being very politic; her few comments, when Freda spoke to her, were as smooth as butter. How insane, all this fuss over some cat. You couldn't walk the street without someone wanting you to sign a petition.

He turned away as this Wilma person came out. She was actually carrying the cat, holding the animal across her shoulder like a baby. She crossed the reading room rigid with anger and disappeared through an office door.

From behind the closed door he heard her talking to someone, softly arguing. Curious, he moved closer. The other voice was so soft he could not make out the words, but both women were angry. He had a strong desire to see the other speaker, such a sudden, intense curiosity that he was tempted to push open the door.

Shutting the door behind her, Wilma set Dulcie on the desk. "That woman! How did we ever get saddled with her?"

"I'd like to slash her," Dulcie hissed, her green eyes blazing. "Eviscerate her like a dead toad."

Glancing at the door, Wilma lowered her voice. "She frightens me. We don't know what she might do." She reached to stroke Dulcie. "Won't you agree to leave the library for a while?"

Dulcie's eyes widened.

"She could be capable of anything. I don't want you hurt."

Dulcie glared, her ears flat. "I can take care of myself."

"I know that. I know you can be all teeth and claws. But Freda is bigger, and she has the advantage of any number of large, heavy weapons. She could block your cat door and corner you, trap you in one of the offices.

She might even turn on the gas. This petition movement has her in a rage. She's livid that the town and her own staff are trying to override her."

"You think she'd turn on the gas and risk blowing the place up? Don't be silly. And so she blocks my cat door. You know I can open any door in this library—the back door, the front door, the door to the side street. I can turn the knobs and, with a little time, I can turn every one of these dead bolts."

Wilma stroked her diffidently. "I know how skilled you are. And I know your hearing and eyesight are far superior, that there's no way she could slip up on you. But you refuse to admit that, simply because of size, a human might have some advantage. She's cruel, Dulcie. And she's angry!"

Dulcie turned away and began to wash, every lick across her tabby fur telegraphing her disdain.

Wilma walked around the desk and sat down facing her. "Please, won't you stay in my office during the day? Near your cat door? And stay away at night until the petitions go to the city council?"

Dulcie leaped off the desk, lashing her tail, and without another word pushed out her cat door. She'd had a difficult morning already, before Freda started in, and now Wilma. Tired and cross beyond toleration from leading Azrael around the village while trying to avoid his intimacies, she had come into the library needing a long nap, and there was Freda making another fuss. And now Wilma roiling at her. She felt as irritable as a bee trapped against the window; she wanted only to be left alone.

Azrael had pretended to enjoy her company as she gave him the grand tour, showed him the best places to hunt wharf rats, demurely led him along the shore and into the warehouses; as she showed him the meanest dogs to avoid and where the best restaurant garbage was judiciously hidden out of sight of wandering tourists— not that any village cat frequented such places. Why should they, when they could enjoy George Jolly's offerings? But the entire morning she didn't dare let her guard down. He had only one thing on his mind—he *would* keep nuzzling her. She had swayed on a tightrope between seeking to distract Azrael while Joe searched Mavity's cottage—and fighting her own distressing fascination. She didn't want to find Azrael charming; she didn't want to be drawn to him.

Well he *was* a good storyteller. Lying in the sun on Molena Point's fishy-smelling pier, he had told her wonderful tales of the jungle, had shown her the jungle's mysterious, leafy world awash in emerald light, the rain approaching like a silver curtain to drench the giant leaves and vines then move on again, a silver waterfall receding, glinting with the sun's fire.

He had shown her the steaming city sidewalks crowded with dirty children begging for food and stealing anything their fingers touched, had shown her black buzzards bigger than any street cat hunched above her on the rooftops, diving heavily to snatch garbage from the sidewalks; had shown her tangles of fishing boats tied to the wharves, then buckets of silver cod dumped flopping on the pier. His stories were so vivid that she could smell the stench of the open market where fly-covered sides of beef hung rotting in the tropical sun— and the tomcat's soft-spoken Spanish phrases enticed her, caressed her, though she did not understand their meaning.

She had ignored the darkness surrounding Azrael, the cloying heaviness beneath his sweet Spanish phrases—until he repeated his ugly predictions of murder.

"The people in this village, that woman Bernine Sage, and this investment person, and your Wilma Getz and her niece and that auto mechanic, all of them are drawing close to death. As unable to pull away as leaves blown to the edge of a dark pool." And Azrael had smiled as if greatly enjoying the prospect of human death. Rising, he had peered down into the shadowed world of mud and pilings below them, where Molena Point's small colony of stray cats eked out a meager living.

Suddenly, lashing his tail, he had leaped off the pier and shouldered into the shadows below, snarling and belligerent, routing the cowering strays, tormenting and bullying those thin cats, had sent them slinking away into dark niches to crouch terrified between the damp boulders.

Shocked, she had stormed after him and driven him back with steely claws. To hell with guile and sweet smiles.

But at her attack, his amber eyes had widened with amazement. "What's the matter? They're only common cats. They're not like us. Come on, Dulcie, have a little fun—they're only stupid beasts."

"You think they're stupid because they can't speak? You think they're without feelings? Without their own sensibilities and their own unique ways?"

He had only looked at her.

"Common cats have knowledge," she had said softly. She was hot with anger, but she daren't enrage him—not until Joe had finished with Mavity's cottage. "Can't you see," she had mewed gently, "that they have feelings, too?" All the while, she wanted to tear the stuffings out of him, he was *so* arrogant—this cat couldn't see a whisker-length beyond his ego-driven nose.

Disdainfully he had flicked his tail at her silly notions and stalked away. And she, chagrined, had swallowed her pride and galloped after him, sidling against his shoulder.

He'd glanced down at her, leering smugly again, turning on the charm, rubbing his whiskers against hers. She had held her tongue with great effort and spun away from the wharf, laughing softly and leading him a wild chase through the village. The cat was so incredibly boorish. Who needed a tom that viewed other cats so brutally, who viewed a female not as an interesting companion or hunting partner, but as a faceless object meant only to mount, only for male gratification?

And when at long last she heard the tower clock strike ten, and knew that Joe would have left Mavity's, she gave Azrael the slip. Making a tangled way among and through the shops, through enough varied scents—spices, perfumes, shoe polish—to hide her trail, she had slipped into the library guessing that, even if Azrael tracked her, he wouldn't follow her into that sanctuary of strict rules where he'd likely be thrown out on his lashing black tail.

Alone at last, she'd had a little wash and settled into the shelves of medieval history for a quiet nap. But it wasn't two hours later that she woke to Wilma and Freda arguing.

Alarmed, she had leaped down and trotted into Freda's office to rub against Wilma's ankles—whether out of support for Wilma or out of curiosity, she wasn't sure. And Wilma had picked her up and cuddled her, as together they took the blast of Freda Brackett's temper.

Jergen watched his lunch date emerge from the head librarian's office looking like a million dollars in the pale pink suit, its tight skirt at midthigh, the low-cut jacket setting off a touch of cleavage and Bernine's golden tan. Her red hair, piled high and curly, was woven with a flowered silk scarf in shades of red and pink. The minute she saw him, she turned on the dazzle, gave him a bright and knowing smile.

"Ready for champagne?" he said, offering his arm. "Our reservations are for one." Escorting her out, their passage was followed by the envious stares of several women behind the checkout counter. They made, Jergen was fully aware, an unusually handsome couple, well turned-out and enviable.

Crossing the garden, he stopped to pick a red carnation for Bernine. He was handing her into the car when, glancing across the street, he saw a portly couple entering an antique shop. He forgot Bernine and froze, stood staring—felt as if his blood had drained away.

But, no. Surely he was mistaken. That could not have been the Sleuders. Not Dora and Ralph Sleuder.

How would those two get here to Molena Point, and why would they come here? No, he had only imagined the resemblance. Taking himself in hand, he settled Bernine within the Mercedes, went around and slipped behind the wheel. The Sleuders wouldn't be here, three thousand miles from Georgia. If those two hicks took a vacation anywhere, it would be to Disney World or to Macon, Georgia, to look at the restored southern mansions.

But, pulling out into the slow traffic, he continued to watch the antique shop. Now he could only catch a glimpse of the couple. Behind him, the traffic began to honk. Damn tourists. Moving on to the corner, he made a U-turn and came back on the other side, driving slowly. He was glad he had put the top up, so he was less visible. Passing the shop, he caught a clear look at the woman.

My God. It *was* Dora Sleuder. Or her exact double. And then Ralph moved into view—the heavy chin, the receeding hairline and protruding belly.

This could not be happening.

What earthly event could have brought those people here? Brought those two bucolic hicks across the country? *No one* knew *he* was here. He had taken every precaution to cover his trail. He drove on by, trying to pull himself together, very aware of Bernine watching him, every line of her body rigid with curiosity.

Someone once said that wherever you traveled, even halfway around the world, in any group of a hundred people you had a 50 percent chance of meeting someone you knew, simply by coincidence, by the law of averages.

Surely this was coincidence. What else could it be?

But the worst scenario was that the Sleuders *had* come here to find him.

So? What could they do if they did find him?

Circling the block, he tried to puzzle out who could have sent them to Molena Point. Who, among his acquaintances, might be linked to them?

So far as he knew, only one of his clients had any ties to the east coast, and that was Mavity Flowers, whose niece came from one of the southern states. Mavity hadn't mentioned the niece's name and he hadn't any reason to ask.

What a nasty coincidence if Dora turned out to be Mavity's niece.

But no, that was too far-fetched. That sort of concurrence didn't happen, would be quite impossible.

However, the fact remained that those two dull people were here. He had to wonder if, despite their simple rural set of mind, they had somehow tracked him.

Whatever the scenario—happenstance or deliberate snooping—the reality was that if he remained in this small, close town where everyone knew everyone's business, the Sleuders would find him.

He began to sweat, considering what action to take.

Beside him, Bernine was growing restless. Smiling, he laid his hand over hers. "The couch in that antique shop, that dark wicker couch. It's exactly what I've been looking for. I want to go back after lunch. If it's as nice as it looks, it will fit my apartment perfectly—just the contrast I want to the modern leather."

Bernine looked skeptical.

"Imagine it done up in some kind of silk, perhaps a Chinese print. You know about that kind of thing; you have wonderful taste. Would you have time, after lunch, to take a look?"

He could see she wasn't buying it but that she appreciated the lie.

"I'd love to. Maybe we can find the right fabric in one of the local shops."

He liked the speculative way she watched him, trying to read his real purpose, almost licking her lips over the intrigue. Strangely, her interest calmed him. Perhaps, he thought, Bernine could be useful, if he needed help with the Sleuders.

But as the Mercedes turned off Ocean, picking up speed heading down the coast, neither Jergen or Bernine had seen a woman watching them from an upstairs window as they slowly circled the block.

14

FROM THE FRESHLY washed windows of her new apartment, Charlie, taking a break from cleaning, watched Bernine Sage and Winthrop Jergen leave the library across Ocean looking very handsome, Bernine in a short-skirted pink suit, Jergen wearing a tweed sport coat and pale slacks. The couple, in less than a week, had become an item. And that was all right with her.

She had come to the window for the hundredth time, she thought, amused at herself, to admire her brand-new view of the village rooftops and of Ocean's tree-shaded median and the library's bright gardens. Now, watching Jergen lean to open the passenger door for Bernine, she saw him suddenly go rigid, straightening up and seeming to forget Bernine as he stared across the median at something on the street below her.

Craning to look down, she could see nothing unusual, just window-shoppers, two shopkeepers hurrying by, probably on their way to lunch, and a meter maid marking tires. Directly below her, lying on a bench in the sun, a huge black cat was stretched out, ignoring the people who surged around him, in a most uncatlike manner. Most cats didn't want to sleep anywhere near strangers, but this one seemed to think he owned the sidewalk. Winthrop Jergen was still staring but then he seemed to shake himself. He turned, handing Bernine into the car.

Pulling away from the curb, he crept along slowly, still looking, until irate drivers behind him began to honk. He speeded up only a little, and when he reached the corner where Ocean Avenue stopped at the beach, he made a U-turn and came back up the northbound lane, pausing just below her window and tying up traffic again before the bleating horns drove him on. The cat, on its bench, stared irritably at the noise. Charlie left the window to resume her cleaning, to finish scrubbing the kitchen alcove. A new home was never hers until she had dug out the crevice dirt and scoured and burnished every surface.

She finished cleaning just after one and headed for Wilma's to pick up her clothes and tools and meager furniture, thankful that Bernine wouldn't be there watching her pack, making sarcastic comments. She'd had enough of that this morning. When Clyde picked her up for an early trip to the plumbing supply houses, he had come in for coffee and of course Bernine was up, looking fetching in a tangerine silk dressing gown.

"A breakfast date," Bernine had purred smugly. "Now, isn't that romantic." She had looked them over as if she'd discovered two children playing doctor in the closet. "And where are you two off to, so early?"

"Plumbing supply," Clyde had said gruffly, gulping his coffee. "Come on, Charlie, they open in thirty minutes." Turning his back on Bernine, he had gone on out to the truck. Charlie had followed him, smiling.

They had had a lovely morning prowling through plumbing showrooms looking at showers, basins, at elegant brass faucets and towel racks. Not everyone's idea of fun, but the excursion had suited them both. She had been back in Molena Point in time to pick up the key from her new landlord and get her studio ready to move into.

Now, parking in Wilma's drive, she let herself into the kitchen, went down the hall to the guest room and began to fold her clothes into a duffle bag. As she was hiking her stuff out to the van, Wilma pulled up the drive beside her.

"Short day," Wilma said, at her questioning look. "I took off at noon." She looked angry, as if she'd not had a pleasant morning. Little tabby Dulcie sat hunched on the seat beside her, sulkily washing her paws. Wilma looked at Charlie's tools and bags piled on the drive, looked at Charlie, and her disappointment was clear.

"I found an apartment," Charlie said softly.

"Is it nice?" Wilma smiled, doing her best to be pleased. "Where is it?"

"Just across from the library—I can run in anytime, and you can run over for lunch or for dinner." Charlie reached to touch her aunt's shoulder. "I love being with you. How could I not, the way you spoil me? It's just—I feel a burden, coming back again after being here so long."

Wilma grinned. "It's just that you like your privacy—and detest being stuck with Bernine."

Charlie shrugged. "That, too. But . . ."

"Ever since you were a little girl," Wilma said, "you've valued your own space. I'm going to make a chicken sandwich. You have time for lunch?"

"Sure, I do."

Charlie finished loading up and went into the kitchen where Wilma was slicing white meat off a roast chicken. She sat down, stroking Dulcie who lay curled up on a kitchen chair. Wilma said, "I hadn't much choice, about Bernine."

"I know that. You have enough problem with her at the library. No need to antagonize her any more— until the petitions are in. She's a troublemaker." She got up to pour herself a glass of milk. "But maybe she'll be in a nicer mood for a while, now that she's dating Winthrop Jergen. I saw them coming out of the library at noon, like they were having lunch."

"Who knows how that will turn out?" Wilma said. She set the sandwiches on the table. "Tell me about your apartment."

"It's one big room—fresh white paint, a wonderful view of the village, and there's a garage off the alley, for storage. The stairs go down to a little foyer between the antique shop and the camera store; you can go from there to the street or back to the alley. There's a deli down at the corner, but not as good as Jolly's, and . . . But you know every shop on that street."

Wilma nodded. "You'll enjoy living there."

"You and Dulcie are invited to dinner as soon as I get settled." She finished her sandwich quickly, petted Dulcie again, and headed back to her new apartment to unload her boxes and tools. Seemed like she'd spent half her life lately carting her stuff around. After hiking her duffles and folding bed up the stairs, she put fresh sheets on the bed, slapped new shelf paper in the cupboards, and unpacked her few kitchen supplies. By three o'clock she had stored her tools in the garage and was headed back for the job to check on the plumber, see if he'd finished roughing in the changes to the ground-floor bathrooms.

Parking before the building, coming in through the patio, she glanced up at Winthrop Jergen's windows and was surprised that they were open—this wasn't his regular cleaning day, and he never opened the windows, only the girls did. Then she saw Pearl Ann through the bathroom window, working at something, and remembered that he'd wanted some repairs done. She hoped Pearl Ann would close up when she left or they'd all hear about it. Heading across the patio into the back apartment, she saw that Pearl Ann had finished mudding the Sheetrock in those rooms, and had cleaned her tools and left them dry and shining on the work table, had left the container of mud well sealed. Pearl Ann was always careful with her equipment.

Many women didn't like to mess with Sheetrock, partly because the drywall panels were hellishly heavy for a woman to handle. But Pearl Ann was good at the work, and she used a specially made wedge to lift the panels without straining so she could nail them in place. And her taping and mudding was as good as any full-time professional. She used the big float, giving it long, bold sweeps; she said she had learned from her dad.

Charlie was in the kitchen of the back apartment, which they used as an office and storeroom, when she saw the two cats come trotting into the patio from the hills below. It always amazed her how far and how quickly cats could travel. Less than two hours ago, she'd been feeding Dulcie bits of her chicken sandwich in Wilma's sunny kitchen.

But these two roamed all over the hills; according to Clyde and Wilma, they were excellent hunters. She could imagine Joe Grey killing most anything, but it was hard to think of soft little Dulcie with blood and gore on her claws. Now, watching Dulcie roll on the

sun-warmed bricks, she could almost feel in her own
body the cat's deep relaxion and well-being.

But soon Dulcie rose again, looking around
eagerly—as if all set to rout a colony of mice. She
looked secretive, too. As if, Charlie thought, she was
about to embark on some urgent clandestine mission.

I have too much imagination.

Maybe I never grew up—still carting around my child-
hood fancies.

But the two cats did bother her. So often they
appeared bound somewhere with intense purpose—
bound on a specific errand, not just wandering. Cats
not aware only of the moment but focused on some
future and urgent matter.

These, Charlie Getz, are not sensible thoughts you're
having. You ought to be making a building supply list.

Yet even as she watched, the cats rose and trotted
purposefully away across the patio in a most responsi-
ble and businesslike manner.

Maybe they knew it was nearly quitting time.
Maybe they were waiting for Clyde; he usually showed
up about now. A dog would go to the door at the time
his master was due home, so why not a cat? A dog
would show up at the bus stop to escort his kid home
from school. Certainly cats were at least as smart as
dogs—she'd read some startling things about the abil-
ities of cats. She watched the cats cross the patio, looking up at Winthrop Jergen's windows as if watching
the flashes of Pearl Ann's polishing cloth. Sweeping
across the glass, it must look, to them, like some
trapped and frantic bird.

But suddenly they glanced back and saw her looking
out. They turned away abruptly to sniff at the edge of a
flower bed. Turned away so deliberately that she felt as if
she'd been snubbed. Had been summarily dismissed.

Amused by her own imaginings, she opened the kitchen door and told the cats, "Clyde's not here yet."

They looked around at her, their eyes wide and startled.

"He's bringing some kitchen cabinets. If you're looking for a ride home, just wait around, guys."

The cats gave her a piercing look then closed their eyes, in unison, and turned away—as if the sound of her voice annoyed them. And when, half an hour later, Clyde arrived with the cabinets, Joe and Dulcie had disappeared.

"They'll come home when they're ready," he said.

"Don't you worry about them? Don't you wonder where they go?"

"Sure I worry. They're cats. People worry about their cats. Every time some village cat doesn't show up for supper, you can hear his owner shouting all over Molena Point."

He looked at her helplessly. "So what am I supposed to do? Follow Joe around? I can't lock him in the house, Charlie. Do that, and I might as well put him in a cage."

He seemed very intense about this. Well, she thought, Clyde loved his cat.

They unloaded the kitchen cabinets and set them in the front apartment; this was the only apartment to get new cupboards, thanks to the last tenant who had painted the old ones bright red. The new units were pale oak and prefinished. When Clyde was ready to head home, the cats were nowhere to be found, though he shouted for Joe several times. If the tomcat was around, he would usually come trotting to Clyde's summons, as responsive as any dog. Clyde called him again, waited, then swung into his truck.

She stared at him.

"They'll come home when they feel like it." He searched her face for understanding. "I can't keep him confined, treat him like an overcontrolled lap dog. What good would Joe's life be, if I told him what to do all the time?"

She watched him turn the truck around at the dead end and pull away toward the village, his words resonating strangely. *What good would Joe's life be, if I told him what to do all the time?*

A puzzling turn of phrase. For some reason, the question, thus stated, left her filled with both unease and excitement.

Tossing some tools in through the side door of the van, she went back inside to get a ladder. Slipping it in on top of the tools, she pulled the door closed. She wanted to hang some drawings tonight and put up bookshelves. As she locked up the building, she called the cats, checking each apartment so not to shut them in.

She didn't find them. No sign of the little beasts. She didn't know why she worried about them. As Clyde said, they were off hunting somewhere.

But when she slid into her van, there they were on the front passenger seat, sitting side by side, watching her as expectantly as a taxi fare waiting for the driver, urging him to get a move on.

15

JOLLY'S ALLEY was no longer a pretty retreat for either tourist or village cat. Beneath the darkening sky where the first stars shone, the cozy brick lane with its little shops looked like a garbage dump. The light of its two wrought-iron lamps shone down upon a mess of greasy paper wrappers, broken eggshells, sandwich crusts, and chewed chicken bones. Wadded paper napkins and broken Styrofoam cups spilled from the two overturned refuse cans, and the smears of cold spaghetti and slaw and potato salad were stuck liberally with tufts of torn-out cat fur—a dozen colors of fur, telling the tale of a huge battle.

Joe and Dulcie, pausing at the alley's entrance, surveyed the mess with amazement, then outrage. Dulcie's ears went back and her tail lashed. Joe crouched as if to spring on whatever feline culprit remained.

But no culprit was visible, the battling cats had fled. Only the tufts of fur told the story, and their pawprints deep in the potato salad—and the stink of fear that lingered, as sharp as the smell of gunpowder after a front-line skirmish.

And, stronger even than the fear-stink, was the odor of the perpetrator—the belligerent reek of the black tomcat.

Sniffing Azrael's scent, Joe and Dulcie padded across the greasy bricks, peering into the shadows beneath the jasmine vine, searching for him.

Suddenly above them a shadow exploded between the rooftops and dropped down within the jasmine vine, dark and swift.

The black tom sauntered out of the foliage, his bullish shoulders swaggering, his amber eyes burning. Looking around at the devastation, he smiled and licked his whiskers.

Joe's growl was deep. "I suppose you waited until all the cats congregated for an evening's snack, then attacked them. Did you trap the smallest ones behind the garbage cans, so you could bloody them?"

Azrael widened his amber eyes. "And what business is it of yours, little cat? What are you, keeper of the village kitties?" Crouching, he circled Joe, his teeth bared, his eyes blazing.

Joe leaped, biting into Azrael's shoulder, raking his hind claws hard down Azrael's belly. Azrael clawed him in the neck. They spun, a tangle of slashing and screaming, then Azrael had Joe by the throat, forcing him down. Joe twisted free and bit him in the flank as Dulcie lunged into the fray. Together they pinned the tomcat. Under their violent double assault, he went limp. When they drew back, he fled to a safer position.

Now suddenly he was all smiles, waving his tail, curving and winding around a lamppost, the change swift and decisive. Chirruping and purring, he fixed his gaze on Dulcie.

"If I had guessed, my dear, that you would be here this evening, we could have feasted together—after I routed that rabble, of course. Or perhaps," he said softly, "you would have enjoyed that little skirmish—a little playful challenge to get your blood up. Hold!" he said as Joe moved to attack. "I have news. Information that will interest you."

But Joe leaped tearing at Azrael's ear and shoulder, and again the two were a screaming whirlwind—until the deli door crashed open and George Jolly ran out swinging a bucket. A cascade of dishwater hit them. Azrael bolted under a bench. Joe backed away, shocked, licking greasy dishwater from his whiskers.

"*Look at this mess! At the mess you cats made.*" Jolly fixed his gaze on Joe. "What kind of behavior is this? I go away for half an hour and you trash my alley! And on a Sunday, too—with the village full of visitors. You! I'd thought better of you, gray tomcat. Why would you do this?"

He looked hard at Dulcie. "Tomcats! Stupid fighting tomcats. All this over a lady? *Shame. For shame.*" He shook his head sadly. "I feed you no more, you tomcats. I feed no one. You disappoint me. You're nothing but common street rowdies!"

Turning his back, he went inside. But he was out again at once, carrying a broom and dustpan. Irritably he righted the garbage cans and began to sweep, filling the dustpan over and over, dumping garbage back into the metal barrels. Azrael had disappeared, and as Jolly unwound a hose, Joe and Dulcie fled to the end of the alley.

Bouncing a hard spray across the bricks, Jolly washed up every smear, hosing the last crumbs into the drainage grid. Giving Joe a disgusted look, he disappeared inside. As he shut the door, Azrael dropped down from the roof. Ignoring Joe, he sidled up to Dulcie, looking incredibly smug.

"Such a charming companion you were the other morning, my dear Dulcie—diverting me so cleverly, while your crude friend, here, tossed Mavity's cottage."

He eyed Joe narrowly. "What were you looking for, gray cat, prowling Mavity's home while Dulcie performed her little ruse?"

Joe washed his paws, sleeking the white fur, and spread his claws to lick them dry.

"If you so enjoy snooping," Azrael told him, "if you *like* poking into human business—which I find incredibly boring—you might be interested in last night's telephone conversation. Though I would prefer to share my information privately, with the lady," Azrael said, purring.

Dulcie looked at him coldly. "Share it with both of us. One does not hunt another's turf without shedding blood. What was this conversation? Why would we be interested?"

"An invitation to dinner," Azrael told her. "Someone in the village has invited Dora and Ralph out to dinner—without Mavity or Greeley."

"Humans go out to dinner frequently," Dulcie said, yawning.

"They are keeping this dinner a secret. They've told no one. The reservation is at a very fancy restaurant, much too elegant for those two Georgia hicks."

Dulcie yawned in his face. "Who made such an invitation?"

"They got a phone call, so I only heard one side. Heard Dora say *Winthrop*. Couldn't tell if she was talking *to* Winthrop Jergen or about him. You know Jergen—Mavity's financial guru."

"We know him," Joe said, turning from Azrael to wash his hind paw.

Azrael sat tall, puffing himself up, lashing his thick black tail. "Why would a big-time financial advisor take those two rednecks to dinner? And why wouldn't they tell Mavity and Greeley? Not a word," Azrael said, narrowing his amber eyes.

"Maybe the Sleuders want to invest," Dulcie suggested. "Surely Mavity bragged about Jergen—about how much money he's earned for her."

"Then why not invite her along? But what a laugh—*she* hasn't any business investing, she's nothing but a scrub woman. A bad-tempered, mean-spirited scrub woman, the way she treats visitors."

Dulcie looked hard at him. "The way she treats dirty-mannered tomcats? At least her money is her own. She didn't steal it, like her brother."

"If she'd learned from Greeley she wouldn't be mopping floors—not that I care what happens to that one."

"Where is this dinner?" Dulcie said. "What restaurant?"

"Pander's. Real fancy, people all dressed up, BMWs and stretch limos, street lined with Lincolns and New Yorkers. You should have seen Dora swoon. The minute she hung up the phone she rushed into the bedroom, fussing about dresses, pulling clothes out of her suitcase, holding them up and looking in the mirror."

Azrael smiled. "But when Mavity got home, Dora was suddenly real busy doing up the dishes, cleaning up the kitchen. No hint of the big invitation."

"Why didn't *you* tell Greeley?" Dulcie asked.

"Waiting to see what happens," Azrael said cooly. "To see where this little adventure leads." He licked his paw, smug and self-assured. "Sometimes it pays to hold back a little something from Greeley."

He rose, lashing his tail. "Greeley's blind when it

comes to Dora. He'd never believe that Dora lied to him. When it comes to Dora, he wouldn't believe even me." And for a moment, the black tom looked almost pitiful.

"Greeley didn't believe that Dora nearly killed me with that damned frying pan," he hissed. "The minute he leaves the house she starts throwing stuff—but he says I'm lying."

"When is this fancy dinner?" Joe said. "And why are you telling us?"

Azrael's face became a sleek black mask. "I told you—that night on the rooftops, I told you. I sense death." He looked at Joe almost helplessly. "This dinner . . . Visions of death. I do not want it to touch Greeley."

The black tom shook himself. "If I spy on Dora and Ralph, if they see me prowling the restaurant, Dora'll pitch a fit, have the whole place down on me." He looked at Joe a long time. "She'd pay no attention to you—you'd be just a neighborhood cat lurking. You can slip under the tables. Try the terrace first. She seemed impressed that they might sit on the upstairs terrace, with a view down on the village." Azrael gave a toothy laugh. "What's the big deal about rooftops?" He fixed Joe with another level look. "You can find out what Dora and Ralph are up to—find out if it will harm Greeley."

"Why would his own daughter do something to hurt him?" Dulcie asked.

"Maybe she wouldn't mean to harm him. Maybe she wouldn't understand the implications."

"You're making too much . . ." Joe began.

"I sense death around Greeley," the cat yowled. "I see death."

"Even if you do, why should we get involved?" Joe asked coldly. "What's in it for us?"

The black tom gave Joe a deep and knowing look. "You will do it. You dance to curiosity as some cats dance to catnip. You two are riven with inquisitiveness.

"And with righteousness," Azrael continued smugly. "If you think the law will be broken, that there's a crime, that a human will be harmed, you little cats will do it."

Joe crouched to rake him again, but the tom ignored him, twitching a long black whisker.

"You nosed into every possession Dora and Ralph have. You left your scent on every smallest bit of clothing. If you thirst for knowledge and justice, if you stalk after lawbreakers, how could you *not* run surveillance—as your Captain Harper would say—on this intriguing little meeting?"

They watched him intently, Joe angrily, Dulcie with increasing interest.

"Tonight," Azrael said softly, narrowing his flamegolden eyes. "Seven-thirty. They're to take a cab." And he slipped away, vanishing among the shadows.

Dulcie looked after him with speculation.

Joe said, "What's he trying to pull? There's no crime, nothing has happened. What a lot of . . ."

She kept looking where Azrael had vanished, and an eager, hotly curious expression gleamed like fire in her wide green eyes.

"He's setting us up, Dulcie."

"Why would he set us up? I don't think so. Did you see his eyes when he talked about Greeley? That was—that was a plea for help."

"Come on, Dulcie. A plea for help from the likes of him? That cat cares about no one."

"He cares about Greeley." She gave Joe a deep green look. "He loves Greeley. I'm going over there to Pander's."

"Come on, Dulcie. You let him sucker you right in."

"Into *what*? What could he do? What harm can come of it?"

"Dulcie . . ."

"Do as you please," she hissed. "I want to know what this is about." And she trotted away, switching her tail, heading for Pander's.

Joe galloped after her, leaned down and licked her ear. "Totally stubborn," he said, laughing.

She paused, widened her eyes at him, purring.

"Hardheaded." He licked her whiskers. "And totally fascinating."

She gave him a green-eyed dazzle and a whisker kiss.

"So what the hell?" Joe purred. "So we slip into Pander's, maybe cadge a scrap of fillet. So what could happen?"

16

CROUCHING close together beneath a red convertible, the cats licked their whiskers at the delicious smells from Pander's, the aroma of roast lamb and wine-basted venison and, Dulcie thought, scallops simmered in a light sherry. But the elegant scents were the only hints of Pander's delights, for the building itself was not inviting. From the street it looked as stark as a slum-district police precinct.

The brick face of the plain, two-story structure rose directly from the sidewalk with no architectural grace, not even a window through which to glimpse the restaurant's elegantly clad diners. The closed door was painfully austere, with no potted tree or flower or vine beside it, in the usual Molena Point style, to break the severity. Only the expensive cars parked at the curb and the delicious aromas wafting out hinted at the pleasures of Pander's as the cats waited for Dora and Ralph Sleuder to appear.

Despite the gourmet allure, Joe would just as soon be home catching a nap as spying in that rarified environ, dodging the sharp eyes and hard shoes of unsympathetic waiters.

"What if we can't get in?" Dulcie said softly, studying the blank, closed facade.

"Should have phoned for a reservation. We'd like two cushions laid on a corner table, my good man. We'll have the venison—you can dispense with the silverware."

She just looked at him.

"We'll go over the roof," he said more gently. "Drop down onto the terrace." The second-floor dining terrace, at the back, boasted no outer access, only the stairs from within the main dining room.

"But, Joe, the minute we look over the edge of the roof and the terrace lights hit us, we're like ducks in a shooting gallery."

"Who's going to look up at the roof? They'll all be busy with their menus and drinks and impressing each other." He looked hard at her. "I still say it's a setup. I don't trust anything that lying alley cat tells us."

"He looked really worried. I think he truly wanted our help. Maybe his prediction of murder isn't all imagination, maybe Greeley is in danger, and we can find out why."

Joe shrugged. "Maybe Jergen found out that Greeley's stealing. Maybe he's going to hit Dora for blackmail—she forks over or he turns in her father."

"That sounds flimsy. How would he even know Greeley? For that matter, how does he know Dora and Ralph?" Her green eyes narrowed. "Why this dinner so soon after Dora and Ralph copied Mavity's financial statements?"

"As to that, what about Pearl Ann snooping into Jergen's computer? Is there some connection? And," he said, "need I point out again that there's been no crime committed? That this is all simply conjecture?"

She gave him that don't-be-stupid look, her eyes round and dark. "When people start prying into other people's business, copying their personal papers, accessing their computer files, either a crime's been committed or one's about to be. *Someone's* up to no good. We just don't know who." And she settled closer to Joe beneath the convertible to await Jergen's little dinner party.

The Sleuders had not yet made an appearance when Pander's door opened, a middle-aged couple came out, and the cats glimpsed, within, a tuxedoed maître d' of such rigid stance that one had to assume, should he discover a trespassing cat, he would snatch it up by its tail and call the dog-catcher. They had been waiting for some time when they realized they were not the only observers lingering near Pander's closed door.

Across the street a man stood in the shadowed recess between two buildings, a thin, stooped man, pale and very still, watching Pander's: the Sleuders' mysterious friend and courier. The man who loitered, in the evenings, outside Clyde's apartment building.

"He gives me the shivers," Dulcie whispered. The cats watched him for a moment then slipped away beneath the line of cars and around the corner to the back alley.

They hoped to find the kitchen door propped open, a common practice among Molena Point restaurants during the summer to release the accumulated heat of the day and to let out the warm breath of the cookstove.

But the rear door was securely shut, the entire building sealed tighter than Max Harper's jail.

"Spotlights or not," Joe said, "let's hit the roof." And he took off for the end of the building, swarming up a bougainvillea vine through clusters of brick red flowers. With Dulcie close behind him, they padded across Pander's low, tarred roof toward the blinding light that flowed up from the terrace. Soft voices rose, too, and laughter, accompanied by the tinkling of crystal.

Crouching at the edge, their paws in the roof gutter and their eyes slitted against the glare, they peered down onto two rows of snowy-clothed tables and the heads of sleekly coiffed women in low-cut gowns and neatly tailored gentlemen; the tables were set with fine china and heavy silver, and the enticing aromas engulfed the cats in a cloud of gourmet nirvana. Only with effort did they resist the urge to drop onto the nearest table and grab a few bites, then run like hell.

But they hadn't come here to play, to create chaos in Pander's elegant retreat, as amusing as that might be.

Along the terrace wall, dark-leafed, potted trees stood judiciously placed to offer the diners a hint of privacy between their tables. The cats did not see Dora and Ralph. But a serving cart stood directly below them, and in a flash of tabby and gray they dropped down onto it then onto the terrace, slipping beneath the cart, finding their privacy in the shadows between its wheels.

From this shelter, their view down the veranda was a forest of table and chair legs, slim ankles, pant cuffs, and gleaming oxfords. A waiter passed, inches from their noses, his hard black shoes creaking on the tiles. To their right, a pair of glass doors opened to the interior dining room. They knew from their housemates' descriptions that Pander's had four dining rooms, all richly appointed with fine antique furniture and crystal chandeliers, and the tables set with porcelain and sterling and rock crystal. Both Wilma and Clyde favored Pander's for special occasions, for a birthday or for the anniversary of Wilma's retirement. The staff was quiet and well-trained, none of the *my-name-is-George-and-I'll-be-your-waiter* routine, and none of the overbearing showmanship of some expensive but tasteless restaurants that catered to the nouveau riche, waiters with bold opinions and flashy smiles. Pander's existed for the comfort and pleasure of its guests, not to put on a floor show.

When Wilma did dine at Pander's, she would bring home to Dulcie some small and delectable morsel saved from her plate, wrapped by her waiter in gold foil and tucked into a little gold carton printed with Panders' logo. Once she had brought a small portion of beef Wellington, another time a little serving of pheasant stuffed with quail. She had served these to Dulcie on the good china, too, making of the occasion a delightful party. Pander's was one of the human institutions about which Dulcie liked to weave daydreams, harmless little fantasies in which she was a human person dressed in silk and diamonds and perhaps a faux-leopard scarf, little imaginary dramas that delighted her and hurt no one.

But now she began to worry. "What if they didn't get a terrace table? If they're not here when the courthouse clock chimes eight, we'll have to try the dining rooms, slip along under the dessert cart when they wheel it in that direction."

"I'm not going through that routine again. Creeping around on our bellies between squeaking wheels. I had enough of that in the nursing home."

"At least you didn't have to worry about your tail getting under the wheels." She cut him an amused glance. "A docked tail does have its upside.

"And," she said, "your short tail makes you look incredibly handsome—even more macho. The drunk who stepped on your tail and broke it—he didn't know he was doing you such a big favor."

The terrace was filling up, several parties had entered; only two tables remained empty, and no sign of the Sleuders. The cats were crouched to make a dash for the inner door when they saw Dora and Ralph coming through.

"There they . . ." She stopped, staring.

Joe did a double take.

The Sleuders' host was not Winthrop Jergen.

Dora and Ralph's dinner companion, gently ushering them in behind the maître d', was Bernine Sage, her red hair wound high with bands of gold, her orange-and-pink flowered suit summery and cool—making Dora and Ralph look so shabby that Dulcie felt embarrassed for them.

Dora had chosen a black dress, possibly to make herself appear thinner, but the black was rusty and faded, as if she had owned the dress for a very long time, and her black stockings were of the extra-support, elasticized variety. Ralph was dressed in a gray pinstripe suit with amazingly wide lapels, a shirt that should have been put through a tub of bleach, and a broad necktie with black-and-white dominoes printed across it. His socks were pale blue.

As the three were seated, the cats flashed across open space and beneath the table nearest to their cart. Slipping behind a potted tree to the next table, winding between silk-clad ankles and satin pumps and polished Balley loafers, they were careful to avoid physical contact with the clientele, not to brush against someone's ankle and elicit startled screams and have waiters on them as thick as summer fleas.

Moving warily, their progress alternating between swift blurs and slinky paw-work, they gained the end of the terrace and slipped under the Sleuders' table, crouching beside Bernine's pink high heels and nude stockings, Dulcie tucking her tail under so not to tickle those slim ankles.

Dora's black shoes were a size too small. Her skin pooched over and her thick stockings wrinkled. Ralph was wearing, over his baby blue socks, black penny loafers with dimes in the slots. The threesome was seated so that the Sleuders could enjoy the view out over the village rooftops. Bernine's vantage commanded the terrace tables and their occupants; she could watch the room while seeming to give the preferred seating to her guests. Their conversation was hesitant, almost shy. Above the cats, a menu rattled. Dora shifted in her chair, rearranging her feet so Joe had to back away. She asked Bernine about Molena Point's weather in the winter, and Ralph inquired about the offshore fishing. The cats were starting to doze when a waiter came to take the drink orders. Dora ordered something called a white moose, Ralph liked his Jack Daniel's straight with no chaser, and Bernine favored a Perrier.

When the waiter had gone, Bernine said, "How is Mavity feeling—is she all right? She's working so hard. I worry about her. House cleaning is terribly heavy work for a woman of her years."

Dora's voice bristled. "Mavity has always worked hard."

"I know Charlie is shorthanded," Bernine confided, "but Mavity isn't so young anymore."

"Hard work is the way she and Daddy grew up; they thrive on it. Both of them worked in the family grocery since they were in grammar school. It was right there on Valley Road when this part of Molena Point was mostly little farms," Dora told her. "Mavity and Daddy wouldn't know what to do without hard work. Daddy was the same on the farm, always working."

"Well, I suppose she does want the work just now,

since she's investing every penny. She's so excited about increasing her savings."

There was a pause as their drinks arrived, the waiter's hard black shoes moving around the table, the sound of ice tinkling, the sharp scent of alcohol tickling the cats' noses. "But I do wonder," Bernine said, "about these investments of hers. Mavity is thrilled with the money, but this Winthrop Jergen . . ." Another long pause. Dora began to wiggle her left toe. Ralph's feet became very still. Bernine said tentatively, "I wonder sometimes if Mr. Jergen is—quite to be trusted."

No one responded. Under the table, Ralph tapped his foot softly. Dora shifted position, pressed one foot tightly against the other.

Bernine said, "The kind of money Mavity's making seems—well, nearly too good to be true.

"Though I don't see how Mr. Jergen could cheat her," she hastened. "After all, she must get a regular monthly statement. And she told me herself, she drew two hundred dollars from her profits just last week to do a few things to the house, buy some new dishes."

Dora made a strange little sound. "Oh, the dishes are lovely. Real Franciscan pottery, just like Mama had. Well, she didn't have to do that, just because we were coming. Didn't have to do anything for us."

"She wanted to," Bernine said. "And I guess she can afford it, all right. I'd love to invest with Mr. Jergen, but I—I don't know. Investments make me so nervous."

"Investing with that Je . . ." Ralph began. Under the table, Dora kicked him.

"Still," Bernine went on smoothly, "if Mavity can make that kind of money . . . Well, maybe I *would* like to try."

Ralph cleared his throat. "I—I wouldn't do that." Dora kicked him again, barely missing Joe, and the cats backed away against the terrace wall. There was another pause, as if Bernine might have looked at Ralph with surprise.

"Do—do you have any—special reluctance?" she asked. "I know so very little about investments."

Dulcie cut her eyes at Joe, amused. This was hugely entertaining. Whatever Bernine was playing at, she must seem, to Dora and Ralph, the height of sophistication—it must be a heady experience for Ralph to find Bernine Sage asking his advice.

Ralph leaned closer to Bernine's chair. "I would be careful about investing with Jergen." And Dora's heel pressed hard against his ankle.

"Oh?" Bernine said softly. "You're not telling me there's something wrong?"

The waiter approached and they heard the tinkle of fresh drinks. There was a long interval concerned with ordering, with crab mornay, with a salad of baby lettuces, cuts of rare fillet, and a broiled lobster—a discussion that left the cats sniffing around under the table for any leftovers from previous diners.

"I can't believe . . ." Bernine began when the waiter had gone, "I can't dream that Mavity's Mr. Jergen . . . Are you saying that Mr. Jergen . . . ?" She paused delicately, her hand beneath the table seeming to accidentally brush Ralph's hand. The cats watched, fascinated, as Ralph tentatively stroked Bernine's fingers. Dulcie could picture Bernine giving him a steamy gaze from beneath her mascara-heavy lashes.

Ralph cleared his throat and shifted his hand guiltily as if he thought Dora might have noticed his preoccupation. "I would not invest with Mr. Jergen," he said bluntly.

"Ralph . . ." Dora said.

"We—Dora and I—we are very worried about Mavity."

"But she's made such wonderful money," Bernine said. "She told me her profits have been . . ."

Dora sighed, pressing one toe against the other as if to relieve her tension. "I don't think we should be talking about this, Ralph. After all, we . . ."

"Dora, be reasonable. Do you want this poor girl to . . . Do you want the same thing to happen to Bernine?"

Bernine leaned forward, tucking her sandaled toe behind her ankle in a little spurt of elation. As if she had whispered to herself, *Bingo! Gotcha.*

"All right," Dora said reluctantly. "If you want to do this, Ralph, all right. But we have been far too trusting in the past, and I . . ."

"Dora, this is different. Can't you see this is different?"

Dora sighed.

Ralph leaned close to Bernine, clutching her hand earnestly beneath the table, as if in a spasm of heart-to-heart communication. "Winthrop Jergen—it's hard to tell you this, my dear. But Winthrop Jergen is a—professional confidence artist."

Bernine caught her breath.

"We have the proof," Ralph said. "All the court proceedings are available, back in Georgia."

"You mean he's—been to jail?"

"Jergen wasn't convicted," Ralph told her, "but he's guilty as sin."

"We only hope," Dora said, "that we can convince Mavity of this. That she will accept the truth. We haven't told her yet. We wanted . . ."

This time it was Ralph's turn to kick, his black loafer thumping Dora's ankle.

"We only hope that she can pull out of this in

time," Ralph said. "Before Jergen gets away with her money. She doesn't . . ."

The waiter returned with their salads. In the island of silence as he served, the cats curled down more comfortably against the wall. When he had gone Ralph leaned, again, toward Bernine.

"Winthrop Jergen, my dear, robbed us of nearly all our life savings."

"Oh. Oh, don't tell me that. Oh, how terrible for you. I can't believe this." Bernine's toe wiggled with excitement.

"We've gotten none of our money back," Ralph told her. "All gone. Police couldn't find a trace, not a bank account, nothing."

Dora uncrossed her ankles, setting her feet solidly. "Jergen arranged his little scheme so his partner went to prison. Jergen got off free—went totally free."

"But where did this all happen? And when?" Bernine asked, puzzled.

"In Georgia, and not many months ago," Dora told her. "Not long before Christmas—it was a terrible Christmas for us. Terrible."

"But what brought him here? How did you know he was here? Did Mavity . . . ?"

"Mavity told us about her wonderful investments," Ralph said. "She hoped we might be able to make back some of our losses."

"And," Dora said, "when she described Jergen, we began to suspect that this might be Warren Cumming—that's his real name."

"Seemed impossible it could be the same man," Ralph said. "But when we checked Cumming's phone in Georgia, it had been disconnected. And when we went to his office, it was empty; he'd moved out. Mavity's description of Jergen sounded so much like Cumming that we decided to find out. So when we told . . ."

Dora kicked again. Poor Ralph was going to have a black-and-blue ankle.

"When we told our Georgia friends we were coming out here," Ralph mumbled, "they wished us luck. You have to understand how angry we were, that Jergen got off free."

"Scot-free," Dora said. "Looks like he came right on out here, took a new name, started right up again, cheating people—cheating my own aunt."

"But . . ." Bernine began.

"I suppose he got a new driver's license," Dora said. "Got all those fake cards like you read about, social security, who knows what else?"

Ralph shifted his feet. "All we can do, now, is try to convince poor Mavity of the truth. She thinks that man hung the moon. But with some proof . . ."

"Now," Dora said loudly, pressing her knee against his, "now all we can do is help Mavity cope with this. That's all we can ever do."

As their entrées were served, the conversation deteriorated to a replay of everyone's concerns for Mavity, punctuated by the sounds of cutlery on china and occasional smacking from Ralph. The cats had nearly dozed off again when the main course was concluded and their waiter took the plates and brought coffee and the dessert cart. Bernine declined dessert. Dora chose a pecan and caramel torte with whipped cream. Ralph selected a double cream puff with chocolate sauce. Dulcie was partial to the small custard tart on the bottom shelf. Lifting it gently from its pleated white doily, she and Joe indulged. Above them, the conversation turned to Molena Point's tourist attractions, then back to Mavity, to how shocked Bernine was and how worried they all were for Mavity's well-being. When again the dessert cart passed their table, the cats went away beneath it, licking cream from their whiskers.

As the waiter parked the cart at the end of the terrace and turned away, the cats sprang to its top shelf skillfully missing cakes and pies and tortes. Leaping to the roof, they dislodged one small piece of cherry pie, sent it skidding across the terrace. They heard it hit and didn't look back, sped racing across the roof and didn't stop until they reached the end of the block.

Pausing beside a warm heat vent, they had a leisurely and calming wash to settle their nerves. "What's that hussy up to?" Joe said, licking his paws.

"Don't forget, she worked for years as a secretary for the San Francisco probation office. That's where Wilma first knew her."

"So?"

"She must know a lot of probation officers and law enforcement people. And those guys, when they retire, sometimes start private investigative services. Wilma knows several P.O.s who . . ."

"You think she's *investigating* Dora and Ralph? Or investigating Jergen? Come on, Dulcie. Can you picture Bernine doing anything to help the law?"

"She would for money—she'd do anything for money."

"And what about the watcher?" He peered over the roof to see if the man was still there, but he had gone—or had moved to a new vantage. "He appears to have masterminded the copying of Mavity's financial statements," Joe said. "*He* could be some kind of cop—that's more believable than Bernine helping the law."

He began to pace the roof, across the warm, tarry surface. "And what about Pearl Ann, snooping on Jergen?" He looked at Dulcie intently. "Who's the cop, here? And who's the rip-off artist?"

As they discussed the puzzle, thirty feet below them the sidewalk was busy with tourists, the after-dinner crowd heading home, lingering at the shop windows, and late diners coming from art exhibits or leaving the local theater, heading for various village restaurants. They saw, scattered among the crowd, two women and an elderly man carrying library cat petitions, stopping each tourist to show newspaper clippings with Dulcie's picture.

"Who's checking those signatures," Joe said, amused. "These people aren't village residents."

"They use the library, though," she said defensively. "Lots of visitors do. Wilma makes out temporary cards all the time."

Directly below them a couple in jeans stood arguing about whether to drive on to San Francisco or stay in Molena Point, and up at the corner three college-age girls flirted with their male escort, each angling prettily for his attention. Ordinarily the cats enjoyed watching tourists, they liked hanging over the roof making fun of people, but tonight their attention returned quickly to Bernine and the Sleuders, worrying at the tangle as intently as they would worry at an illusive mouse.

But, as it turned out, they had little time to circle the quarry before Azrael's prediction came true. Before there was, indeed, a murder. An event that sucked in Joe and Dulcie like flies into a spider web.

17

I SEE DEATH around you . . . death before the moon is full, Azrael had told them—almost as if the black tom could himself bring death with his dark magic, as if this beast were indeed the Death Angel. Whatever the truth, two days after Azrael beguiled Joe and Dulcie into spying at Pander's restaurant, death reached out just as he predicted.

It was barely eight A.M., Tuesday morning, as they entered the empty library, slipping in through Dulcie's cat door, their bellies full of fat mice, meaning to curl up on the children's window seat for a little nap before opening time. The cushioned retreat, where the children listened to stories, was at this hour Dulcie's private domain.

According to Freda Brackett, Dulcie had turned the long window seat and the inviting tangle of brightly flowered pillows into a nest of cat hair, fleas, and ringworm, but the children thought differently. They loved finding Dulcie among the cushions to snuggle as they listened to the librarian's stories; they all fought to hold her and sit close to her.

But now this early morning there were as yet no children and the wide bay window was theirs, the only sounds the occasional *whish* of passing cars away across the garden and the distant purling of the sea; crossing the reading room, the cats could feel, through the floor and carpet, the sea's constant muffled heartbeat.

Dulcie thought it so odd that Wilma couldn't feel the surf beating unless she was right there at the shore. How sad, what humans missed. Nor had Wilma, just last week, felt the preearthquake tremors that sent Dulcie under the bed at two in the morning, yowling until Wilma took shelter in the closet, the two of them waiting for the earthquake to hit, for heavy objects to start falling.

The ensuing quake had been nothing, amusingly small, no more damage done than a few drinking glasses broken and a crack in the bathroom wall—by California standards, hardly worth getting out of bed for—though Dulcie had not been able to determine its severity by its preshock tremors.

Now, leaping to the window seat, kneading the pillows, the cats yawned and stretched, ready for a nap—and stopped.

They went rigid, hissing, backing away from the glass.

A smell assailed them, unnatural and alarming.

Not the sweet aroma of little children and candy wrappers and the librarians' subtle perfume.

A stink of death seeped in around the glass—nor was it the scent of a dead animal, not the smell of freshly killed rabbit or squirrel. No. The smell they tasted, flehming and growling, was the stink of human death.

Crouched and tense, they approached the glass, stood pressed against the window looking down into the depths of the tangled garden.

Beyond the window, the building's two wings jutted out to form a partially walled disarray of blooms that reached up thick as a jungle beneath the children's window. Spider lilies, tapping at the glass, were tall and thick, their delicate blossoms curled like reaching hands. Beyond the lilies, flowering bushes glowed, and tangles of blue iris. On the east wall, a mass of climbing yellow nasturtiums shone yellow as sunshine, and above the jungle of blooms the oak trees twisted their sturdy, dark limbs and jade foliage against the morning sky.

Beyond the garden stood Ocean Avenue's double row of eucalyptus trees and then, across the divided street, the crowded, two-story shops. But it was the flower bed beneath the bay window and what lay crushing the blooms, that held the cats' attention, that made every hair rise, that drew Joe's lips back in a keening snarl and made Dulcie catch her breath with a shocked mewl.

Below the jutting window a man knelt. As the cats watched, he reached to touch the two bodies that lay sprawled together unmoving, their fleshy, blue-veined, half-naked limbs shockingly white.

Greeley Urzey knelt stroking Dora's limp hand, reaching to touch her bare, white leg, her naked limbs heavy and comatose. Both Ralph's and Dora's clothes were half-torn off—not as if they had been attacked, rather as if they had flung off their garments in a wild and frenzied dance, an insane gavotte. And across the garden, an erratic path twisted, raw with crushed foliage and flowers, a maddened trail plunging in from Ocean Avenue.

One of Ralph's penny loafers lay yards away from him among a bed of daisies, its dime gleaming in the morning light. The cats could see, across the street, what might be a sweater dropped on the curb.

They drew back as Greeley clasped together his
shaking hands and rose, his whole being seeming to
tremble, the expression on his face frightened and confused.

He stood staring uncertainly around the garden,
then wandered away up the path, his gait slow and hesitant. As he stumbled along Ocean, the black cat
dropped down out of an oak tree and fell into step
beside him.

At the same instant, Joe and Dulcie leaped from
the window seat and scorched across the library and
out Dulcie's cat door. They reached the front garden
just as Greeley and Azrael turned the corner, disap-
pearing into a tunnel of dark, low-growing cypress
trees.

The two cats grimaced at the death smell, softened
by the scent of crushed lilies. Joe placed an exploring
paw on Ralph's arm.

Dulcie nosed at Dora's hand—and drew back from
the icy flesh. She looked at Joe, stricken.

"Greeley didn't do this. Greeley didn't do this terrible thing, not to his own daughter."

"Maybe he just found them. They've been dead
for hours, Dulcie. If he killed them, why would he
come back?"

"But if he just found them, why wouldn't he head
for the police station? He went in the opposite direction."

"Maybe he was too upset. Maybe he'll call the cops
from somewhere. Maybe go home to Mavity, call from
there."

"Oh, Joe, these poor, silly people. What did they
do, that they would die in such—distress?" She pressed
close to him, thinking of the stolen computer print-
outs, then of Ralph and Dora's feet beneath the table at

Pander's, Ralph's penny loafers beside Bernine's silk-clad ankles, thinking of Dora kicking Ralph when his remarks didn't suit her.

"Whatever they did, they were just simple folk. Who would kill them?" She stared at the tangle of pale, twisted limbs, shocked by their raw whiteness. The Sleuders were such very bulgy people, their limbs lumpy and misshapen. It must be terrible not to have a nice coat of sleek, concealing fur to cover your fat places and your rawness. She watched Joe sniff at Ralph's nose and mouth—he made a flehming face, raising his lip and flattening his ears.

He smelled Dora's face, too, scowling. "Drugs? Were they into drugs?"

"Don't be silly. Dora and Ralph Sleuder?"

"What else would smell so foreign?"

She sniffed at the dead couple's faces and backed away sneezing at the strange, pungent odor. "We'd better call the dispatcher."

As they started toward her cat door, he stopped suddenly, pressing her back. "Dulcie, wait."

She paused, one paw lifted. "What? It's nearly opening time; the staff will be coming to work. What's the matter?"

"Isn't children's story hour this morning?"

"Oh! Oh, my! Come on!" She dodged past him. "They'll be crowding in any minute, running to the window." And she took off round the side of the building.

Twice a week story hour began at eight-fifteen. The kids came flocking in, breaking away from their parents, laughing and pummeling each other and heading straight for the window seat, leaping into the cushions in a frenzy of enthusiasm, pressing their noses to the glass to look out. Children were always drawn to windows—as surely as kittens were drawn to dangling string. Entering any room, children flocked to the glass as if, like Alice, they expected to find beyond the pane any number of exotic new worlds.

This morning, beyond this glass, they'd find an exotic world, all right—a scene never meant for a child's viewing. But now, as she leaped for her cat door to call the precinct, Joe barged into her again, blocking her way.

"What?" she hissed, shouldering him aside.

"Listen, Dulcie. What would happen if we don't call the cops?"

She stared at him, shocked. "The children would be . . . We can't let them see those bodies. They'd . . ."

"They'd start screaming," Joe suggested. "Screaming, giggling, making jokes to hide their fear and confusion. Their parents . . ." He licked a whisker and smiled wickedly. "Their parents would see the dead bodies and pitch a fit—that the library would let the children see this."

He began to purr. "Those parents would put Freda right on the hot seat."

She looked at him, her eyes widening. She didn't breathe. What he was suggesting was terrible.

"How embarrassing for Freda," Joe said softly.

"No!" she said, shouldering past him. "I won't do that. It would be dreadful for the children."

"Those kids are tougher than you think. All they'll need is plenty of hugging and a chance to talk it out with their mom or dad—any good parent could put a positive spin on the experience. Turn a shocking situation into something positive—as long as the kids are hugged and loved."

"No!" she said, pressing past him.

But again he blocked her, licking his whiskers. "It

would be the parents who are stressed. And they'd dump it all on Freda—complaints to the mayor, to the city council, letters to the editor, follow-up editorials. Enough fuss," Joe said, his yellow eyes burning, "to get Freda fired."

There was a long silence. Joe's eyes gleamed with the devil's own light.

"No, Joe. We can't! Not frighten the children like that—not to spite Freda, not to spite anyone." Hotly she slashed at him and bolted through her cat door into Wilma's office where she could call the station.

But she was too late.

As she leaped for Wilma's office she heard two librarians talking, heard Freda call out as she came in through the back door, and the next moment she heard children running up the walk past the hidden, flower-shrouded bodies, heard them racing across the reading room straight for their window seat.

18

THE LIBRARY and garden were crawling with cops. From the roof, Joe Grey watched three medics kneel among the lilies beside the bodies of Dora and Ralph Sleuder. Unable to observe all the action from inside, he had streaked up the back of the building to the roof, leaving Dulcie inside on the book stacks doing interior surveillance. The police action upon entering the garden had been swift and precise as each man swung to his appointed job.

But now the medics, unable to help the deceased, rose again and moved away, nodding to the police photographer. He, pushing back his shoulder-length black hair, knelt among the flowers to shoot close-ups first of the victims' faces, then of their raw white limbs, recording from every possible camera position; loading new film, at last he turned from the bodies to photograph the surround, the window above the corpses, the white stucco wall, and the garden itself, calling an assistant to part the lilies so he could shoot the earth beneath. Across the garden, Freda Brackett's angry accusations rose sharply.

She stood before the library's open front door, toe to toe with Max Harper, her words burning like flames. Harper listened to her harangue without speaking, his thin face frozen into complicated lines of distaste that made Joe laugh. Didn't Freda see the deep anger in the police captain's eyes—and the spark of cold amusement?

"What kind of police force *is* this, Captain Harper, to let such a shocking crime occur practically inside the library! This is beyond excuse. You have no idea the damage this will cause the children. What kind of police would subject children to this nightmare? Any well-run police force would have prevented this shocking event. You . . ."

Joe ceased to listen to her—as he suspected Harper had, too. The aftermath of the Sleuders' deaths was turning out pretty much as he'd thought—and as Dulcie had feared. The children, on arriving for story hour and discovering the bodies, had crowded against the window, pushing each other out of the way, shocked at first, then quickly out of control. Staring down through the glass, smearing it with their noses and with sticky fingers, they screamed then laughed, working themselves into a furor of shrill giggles that did not abate until their parents dragged them away. Not even the ululation of sirens careening through the village had quieted them, nor had the arrival of the ambulance and four police cars skidding to the curb; they only shouted louder, fought harder to see every detail.

Out beyond the garden, two officers were clearing the street and putting up cordons at the ends of the block. At both corners, pedestrians had gathered, idle onlookers drawn to tragedy, some out of empathy but most with prurient curiosity. Of all those who crowded to look, Joe was the only observer enjoying a rooftop vantage. Lying with his chin propped on his paws and his paws resting on the roof gutter, his alert gray ears caught every whisper.

He watched the evidence officer lift lint and debris from the bodies and the surround and mark the evidence bags as to content and location. Watched him go over the victims' clothes with the department's tiny vacuum cleaner and wondered if any lint had fallen from Greeley's clothes when he knelt over Dora—or, for that matter, if the lab would find black cat hairs—or traces of their own fur where he and Dulcie had sniffed at the victims' faces.

Well, so Harper found cat hairs. So what was he going to do? There'd been cat hairs at other murder scenes. He watched the fingerprint specialist dust the deceased's clothing and skin and the window and the slick green lily leaves, carefully lifting prints. Watched the forensic pathologist arrive—a white-haired man stepping out of an ancient gray Cadillac—to examine the bodies, place bags over the victim's hands, and wrap Dora and Ralph for transport to the morgue. As the courthouse clock chimed ten-thirty, the forensics team moved inside the library, and so did Joe Grey, heading for the book stack where Dulcie sat twitching her tail, highly amused as she listened to a little group of irate mothers.

Lieutenant Brennan, heavy in his tight uniform, stood talking with the five women and their excited preschoolers, the little ones wiggling and shouting. Three-year-old James Truesdel wanted to know why those people were asleep in the garden, and Nancy Phillips, with five-year-old superiority, told him they were not asleep, they were dead. *She* wanted to know: "How did they get dead, with their clothes off?" And five-year-old

Albert Leddy, trying to drag his mother back toward the window seat from which he had been extricated, pitched such a tantrum, kicking his mother in the shins, that if he'd been a kitten Dulcie would have whacked him hard and nipped his nervy little ears.

But she had to smile, too, because from the temper of the parents, the pro-library cat group had snatched the day just as Joe had predicted, had grabbed opportunity by the tail. As Freda Brackett left Captain Harper and came back inside, nine parents converged on her, and James Truesdel's mother began to question her in a manner that indicated there would soon be a hotly phrased letter in the *Gazette*.

Behind Freda, Bernine Sage manned the three constantly ringing phone lines—word traveled fast in the village—giving dry, uninformative answers. It was hard to tell whether Bernine was an island of efficiency or of total indifference. Dulcie glanced up to the door as a young man bolted in, having talked his way past the police guard.

Danny McCoy was disheveled and breathing hard, his red hair tousled; having obviously rushed over from the *Gazette* offices, he exchanged a look of complicity with Mrs. Leddy.

Danny, too, was a mover and shaker on Dulcie's behalf. He had done several columns supporting the library cat and had made a big deal that library cats were a growing trend across the country. He had done a really nice article on the Library Cat Society, interviewing its president and several of its members and quoting from the society's quarterly newsletters about the popularity of individual library cats in Minden, Nevada, Eastham, Massachusetts, and, closer to home, El Centro. Now, deftly trapping Freda between the checkout desk and a book cart, he began with the standard questions: Who had found the bodies? What time were they discovered? Then he moved on to the question of why the children had been allowed to see the murder victims, why they had not been supervised, to avoid such ugly experience.

"We didn't know the bodies were *there*," Freda snapped. "One does not come to work expecting to find dead bodies outside the children's room. The police are supposed to patrol that street. Why didn't *they* see the bodies? This Captain Harper was extremely lax to allow such an occurrence. This is not New York City. This is a small, quiet town. What else do the police have to do, but keep the streets and public buildings safe?"

"But, Ms. Brackett, why were the children allowed to view the corpses?"

"I told you. We didn't know they were there! Can't you understand me? It was the *children* who discovered the tragedy. *We* don't go into the children's room first thing in the morning. We are far too busy preparing to open the library, preparing the checkout machine, clearing the bookdrop, starting up the computers . . ."

"No one looked out the window before the children arrived?"

"Of course not. Why would we? Don't you listen? We had no reason to look out. The children's librarian was at her desk getting ready for story hour. This work takes a good deal of preliminary attention. My staff does not have time to dawdle, gawking out windows, Mr. McCoy."

"So you let the children run in there, without any supervision, and view a shocking and frightening death scene."

Dulcie smiled with appreciation. Danny was being totally unfair. Taunting Freda and shaping his own biased agenda. The article he was preparing to write would be scathing—he was going to cream Freda.

Purring and rolling over, she watched Joe slip in the front door and across the reading room behind the feet of several officers. He made one leap to a reading table, another to the top of the book stack, landed beside her with a soft thud, purring.

"Where's Mavity?" she whispered. "Did someone go to find her, to tell her about Dora and Ralph? Did they go to look for Greeley?"

"Harper sent an officer to find Mavity. I don't know about Greeley." And he settled down to watch Danny torment Freda, the young reporter playing her as skillfully as any cat baiting an angry rat.

"Exactly what degree of damage, Ms. Brackett, might this event have done to the children? Is it possible, would you say, that some of the children will need psychiatric help? Perhaps trauma counseling? Is the library insured for that kind of . . ."

"The city sees to our insurance, Mr. McCoy. I don't have time for this foolishness. If the children glimpsed a murder scene, that is no different from what they see on television."

Mrs. Truesdel moved closer to join them. "That is not what you told Captain Harper, Ms. Brackett. You said the children would probably need therapy. And as far as television," Mrs. Truesdel said, "I don't let my five-year-old watch violent TV. Nor do my friends. We *try* to protect our small children from undue violence. Certainly we don't expect them to witness two shocking deaths during story hour."

"This experience," Danny said, "will give them far worse nightmares then any TV show." He moved closer to Freda. "Certainly this ugly look at death has been far more harmful to the children than, say, finding a little cat in the library."

"Dead bodies, Mr. McCoy, seen through a window, cannot bite the children or communicate to them some life-threatening disease."

"I don't follow you. The library cat is healthy. What disease do you think she . . ."

"Rabies, Mr. McCoy. Lyme disease. Cat scratch fever—all of which can kill, if not treated. In the past year, in this county alone, there have been fifteen cases of rabies. And the statistics on Lyme disease . . ."

"But Dulcie has had her rabies shots. She has excellent veterinary care—she's not a diseased stray off the streets. And to my knowledge there have been no cases of Lyme disease in this coastal area."

"A cat's bite or scratch," Freda snapped, "is notoriously filthy."

"Has she ever bitten or scratched a child?"

"There is always the chance she will. Cats are half-wild creatures; they are never really domesticated."

Atop the book stack, Dulcie's eyes blazed. If ever she did yearn to bite and scratch, this was the moment. If ever she abandoned her domesticated ways, now was the time.

Beside her, Joe was nearly choking with laughter, his ears and whiskers twitching, his mouth open in a wide grin.

Soon Danny, having taken enough quotes from Freda for a scathing article, smiled sweetly at her, turned away, and approached three other mothers and their children. He was deep into conversation with them, writing down their comments, when another squad car pulled to the curb and an officer hurried up the path looking for Captain Harper, who stood just inside the door talking to the photographer.

"We didn't find Mavity Flowers," he told Harper. "She wasn't at home or at work up at Damen's apartments. And we haven't found Greeley Urzey."

Joe and Dulcie looked at each other. Dulcie whispered, "Has Greeley skipped? *Did* he do it?"

"No way, Dulcie. He . . ." Joe paused, scowling. "Here comes Clyde. He doesn't look too happy."

Hurrying up the walk, stepping over the yellow ribbon barrier and past the police guard, Clyde, like Danny, was disheveled and red-faced. Rushing in, nodding to Harper, he spotted Joe atop the book stack.

Sprinting across the room, he snatched Joe by the scruff of the neck and swung him down onto his shoulder, giving Joe a glare that would turn a Doberman to stone.

"Claws in," he hissed. "Put your claws *in*. And stay right there. Not a move. Not a snarl out of you."

Joe was shocked and hurt. What had he done? And he could say nothing. In public, he had no chance to defend himself.

Clyde looked up at Dulcie more gently. "Would you two like some breakfast?" He reached up for her. She gave him an innocent green gaze and slipped down willingly into his arms, soft and innocent, her claws hidden, her little cat smile so beatific Joe thought he'd throw up; he turned away from her, disgusted.

"It's time you two were out of here," Clyde said softly, meaning: *Stay away from this! Leave it alone! Forget it.* Carrying them out, Joe on his shoulder and Dulcie in his arms, he hurried around the block to his car and plunked them down in the ragged front seat. He was driving his latest acquisition, a battered '32 Ford that sounded like a spavined lawnmower. Starting the engine with a deafening clatter, he headed for Wilma's house.

When Clyde had sold his antique red Packard touring car to help pay for the apartment building, he'd started driving an old Mercedes he'd fixed up.

The car was all right except for its color. Joe had
refused to ride in the baby pink Mercedes. Clyde himself had taken all the ribbing he could stand, then sold
the Mercedes and finished up the last details on the
yellow '29 Chevy convertible in which he had escorted
Charlie to the gallery opening. But then he'd picked
up this Ford; he always had to have some old clunker to
refurbish. Eventually he would turn it into a beauty,
but meantime a ride in the heap was like being trans-
ported in a bucket of rattling tin cans. Driving to
Wilma's, Clyde didn't speak to them. They crouched
together hunched and cross as he parked at Wilma's
curb.

She was on her hands and knees in the garden,
transplanting gazanias, thinning out the low yellow
flowers. As Clyde killed the rattling engine, the cats
leaped out.

Wilma sat back on her heels, looking them over,
her eyes widening with suspicion. "What?" she said.
"What have they done now?"

Dulcie stared at her, hurt.

Joe didn't wait to hear Clyde's biased accusations.
He shot past Wilma through the garden and around
the house and up the hill at the back. To hell with
humans.

Soon Dulcie came trotting along, looking chas-
tened, and they took off up the hills to hunt—to let the
atmosphere cool down.

19

CHARLIE WAS on a ladder painting the downstairs front bedroom when she saw Max Harper's police unit pull up out in front. As he came across the patio, something about his drawn look and the resigned set of his shoulders brought her down the ladder. Wiping her hands, she stepped to the open door.

Lieutenant Brennan had been up earlier looking for Mavity, but he wouldn't tell her why. She'd told him to try Mavity's cottage, that very likely Mavity had slept in, that she did that sometimes, that when she woke up she'd phone the apartments frantic and apologetic. But now, watching Harper, a chill held Charlie. His solemn expression made her stomach lurch.

She hadn't gotten to work herself until ten, had made a run around the coast to Hudson's Building Supply to pick up an order of some special tile and paint, some varnish, five gallons of mud, and some finishing nails. She'd had a cup of coffee with the owner, John Hudson, had helped him load her order then headed back. When she got to work, Mavity's VW wasn't parked in front, nor had Pearl Ann seen her.

Harper stopped in the open doorway.

"Clyde's not here," she said, motioning him on in, searching the captain's solemn brown eyes.

"Clyde's at the library," he said. "Or he was. He left just before I did. I'm looking for Mavity."

"Didn't Brennan find her? He was here."

Harper turned from her, wandered the big room, studying the sanded Sheetrock and the half-painted ceiling. The units were being done so piecemeal that sometimes it even confused her, one room finished and painted while the next room was hardly started; but with their crew, it seemed to be working. Max turned to look at her, his back to the windows.

"What is it?" she said softly.

"Mavity's niece and her husband. They were found dead this morning."

"Dora and Ralph?" She stood a moment trying to take that in. Dora and Ralph Sleuder? "Was—was there an accident? A car accident?"

"We found them in the garden outside the library."

"The library garden? I don't understand. How could . . . Why would . . . ?"

"The call came in around eight forty-five this morning."

She tried to collect herself. "What happened? An accident in the garden? But I didn't see anything—well, but I left around seven." She knew she wasn't making sense.

"You were in the garden?"

"No. Across the street."

"Oh, yes, you moved into that apartment above Joan's Antiques."

She nodded. "I drank my coffee looking out."

"And you saw nothing unusual?"

"The garden was—I saw no one there. I thought I saw something move inside the window, but it was just those pillows against the glass. Dora and Ralph can't be dead."

"You thought you saw something moving?"

"I think it was just the pillows—or it could have been the cat, she sleeps in the window sometimes."

"And you didn't see anyone in the garden? Or on the street?"

"I didn't notice anyone. But I was only at the window long enough to drink my coffee."

"And you saw nothing different about the garden?"

"No." She thought a minute. "Yes. There was some kind of shadow in the lilies. As if something had crushed them. They're so thick and tall, it's hard to be sure. But there seemed to be a dark place, as if maybe a dog had slept there and broken the flowers."

Harper was quiet, watching her. "Did you know the Sleuders well?"

"No. I met them the day after they arrived, they came up to see the apartments—rubbernecking, I guess. Mavity didn't seem too happy about it."

"Have you any idea if they were into drugs—anything Mavity might have said?"

Charlie stared at him. "Drugs? Those two country people? My God, I wouldn't think so. Are you saying—what? They died of an overdose?"

"We don't know yet. Lab's working on it."

"Could they have taken—could it be some medication? I can't imagine drugs. Oh, poor Mavity. Have you told her? No, you came to find her. Have you been to the house?"

"I sent Brennan earlier. No one was home."

She snatched up her purse and keys. "We have to

find her. She could be . . ." She looked at him imploringly. "I want to find Mavity."

In the squad car, as Max spun a U-turn and headed down the hill, he described for her the murder scene outside the children's room. It sickened her to think of Dora and Ralph lying there in the garden dead, half-naked as if they might have been on some wild and terrifying high.

"PCP could do that," Harper said. "Or crack, or one of the designer drugs." His words made her see Mavity lying dead, too; she couldn't shake her concern.

They found Mavity's VW parked in front of her cottage. Mavity was inside, perfectly safe, just finishing breakfast. Charlie grabbed her and hugged her. The little woman stepped back from Charlie, puzzled.

"I just called the apartments," she told Charlie. "I know I'm late. I'm sorry, I meant to call earlier but . . . I went for a walk down the marsh," she said lamely. "The time got away from me." She frowned at Charlie and at Harper. "What? What is it?"

Harper glanced toward the sitting room. Mavity motioned them in, past the kitchen. He sat on the couch taking Mavity's hand and easing her down beside him. Her short white hair was rumpled from the sea wind. Her face had gone deadly solemn.

"Mavity, did Dora and Ralph come home last night?"

"No. That's why I went to the beach. I was looking for them."

She twisted the hem of her white uniform jacket and folded it into a knot. "I thought maybe they got up early, didn't eat breakfast, or went out to eat, and that they were sitting out on the beach. But I . . ." She looked at him intently. "They've never stayed away overnight. And Greeley's gone, too. But Greeley does that. Out at all hours, that's no surprise."

"Were Dora and Ralph home for dinner last night?"

She smoothed her jacket hem and clasped her hands together. "No. Two nights running, they've gone out alone in the evening. Didn't tell me where, didn't tell Greeley."

"Sunday night was the first time?"

"Sunday, yes. They left before I got home from work, and they came home around nine-thirty. They were all dressed up. They went right to bed, wouldn't say where they'd been. What is this about? Where are they?"

Charlie sat down beside her, glancing across her to Max.

"Mavity," Max said gently, "there's been an accident."

She watched him, said nothing.

"Dora and Ralph were found this morning. They were found together. They're dead, Mavity. I'm so sorry."

"They can't be dead. I saw them just last night, all dressed up. They were fine last night." She reached for Charlie's hand. "There must be some mistake. I saw them just last night."

Charlie took both Mavity's hands in hers, held them tightly.

Mavity looked at them nakedly. "A car accident? Was it the taxi? Was there an accident with the taxi?"

"No," Harper said. "Where did they go to dinner? Why didn't you and Greeley go?"

"We weren't asked—neither time. They wouldn't say where they were going." She was squeezing Charlie's hand so hard that Charlie's fingers popped. *"Was there an accident?"*

Charlie glanced helplessly at Harper.

Max said, "No. It was not a car accident. You're sure they didn't come home last night?"

"I don't think so. But Dora always makes the bed, so they might have been here. But Greeley—Greeley wasn't home. He does that. Goes walking at night. Walking all night with that cat. Says it calms his nerves."

"When you got up this morning," Harper said, "no one was here? No beds had been slept in?"

"The beds were made up. No one was here, no dirty dishes in the sink. Neat as a pin." She began to shiver.

Charlie lifted a folded blanket from the end of the couch and wrapped it around the little woman.

"Were they upset about anything?" Harper asked her.

Mavity just looked at him.

Charlie squeezed her shoulder. "Mavity?"

"Nothing really. Just—Greeley and Dora had a fight. Greeley left angry, really mad—but Greeley has a short temper. He doesn't stay mad. He gets right over it."

"What was the fight about?" Harper said patiently.

She shook her head. "No one would say. Wouldn't tell me. That really hurt. All the secrecy. Secrets about where they were going. Secrets about why they fought.

"I can't imagine what they couldn't tell me. I would have driven them if they'd wanted. But no, they didn't want me to bother; they had to have a cab. Was it the cab?" she repeated. "Did it have a wreck?"

"No," Charlie said, "they weren't in a wreck. They may have gotten sick suddenly."

"Sick?" She looked at them, puzzled. "Sick from the food? From their dinner?"

"We're not sure what happened," Harper said. "There will be an autopsy. Were—were they into drugs, do you know?"

"*Drugs?*" Her eyes blazed with shock. "*Dora and Ralph? Of course not.* I can't imagine such a thing." She hugged herself, seemed unable to get warm despite the blanket. "How can I tell this to Greeley? *Drugs?* Oh, you're mistaken."

"The autopsy will tell us," Harper said.

"I don't know how to tell Greeley that Dora . . . She's his only child. She—he didn't see her often, but she's—she was all he had." Mavity shook her head. "Greeley will think it's his fault."

"Why?" Harper said.

"Because they fought, because he left the house angry."

"And you have no idea what they fought about?"

"It was going on when I got home. I guess they didn't hear the car. Greeley was shouting at Dora, that she was making trouble for nothing, that they had no right—then they heard me on the porch and that was the end of it, when I came in. Greeley stomped out with that cat following him, and then Dora and Ralph left all dressed up again, wouldn't say anything more."

Charlie rose, stepped into the kitchen, rinsed out the coffeepot, and refilled it. Mavity said, "It was only a family tiff. Maybe Dora and Ralph, going out alone, made Greeley mad. Who would they go with? They don't know anyone in Molena Point."

"And Greeley was out all night," Harper said.

"I would have heard him come in. He sleeps on the couch right here, and me on the cot. And he always leaves his bed unmade, leaves a mess for me to straighten, sheets half on the floor."

"Are his clothes still here? His luggage?"

"He only has the one bag." She rose and peered in between the recliner chair and the television. "It's here." She picked up the bag, looked in. "Full of clothes." She went to check the bathroom.

"Shaving kit's there on the sink."

Harper said, "Does he always travel so light?"

She nodded. "He never packs much in the way of clothes, says he can buy what he needs. He would have checked the one bag, though, because he carried that cat on board. Right in the cabin, in its cage—one of those carrier things." She opened the washing machine, which stood in a corner of the kitchen, and peered in.

"Left a shirt to be washed, some socks, and a pair of shorts." She looked across at Harper. "Greeley wouldn't go away for good—back to Panama—and not tell me." She pressed her fist to her lips. "Captain Harper, where is Greeley? Greeley has to be all right— Greeley's all I have now."

"We don't know where he is," Harper said. "I'm sure he'll turn up. My officers are looking for him."

They drank their coffee in silence. Max did not light a cigarette but Charlie could tell he wanted one. He asked Mavity if he could search Dora and Ralph's belongings.

"Yes. But what for? Well, it don't matter. They can't complain now," she said, her voice shaking.

"Maybe I'll find something to tell us where they went last night, maybe some scrap of paper with an address, something to help us understand what happened."

"Their bags are in the bedroom—their clothes are in the closet and scattered all over."

Harper rose. "I'd like both of you to come in while I search."

They made a little procession, carrying their coffee cups into the small bedroom. Harper's lean figure moved neatly among the clutter. Charlie stood in the bedroom doorway sipping her coffee, watching Max search for drugs as well as for evidence of the Sleuders' dinner destination. She didn't like having to witness this. The necessity for a search, coupled with Mavity's own distress, made her feel frightened and sick.

She watched him examine each item of clothing, going through pockets, sorting carefully through the contents of each of the Sleuders' five bags and examining the bags themselves, the pockets and the lining. It was in the last bag, a big duffle, that he withdrew a thick packet of legal-size papers divided into two stacks, each held by a metal clip.

"Mavity, I'd like to keep these as evidence. I'll give you a receipt for them."

"Sure you can keep them. What are they?"

Harper looked at her, surprised. "Didn't you know that Dora had your financial statements?" He handed one of the packets to her.

She stared at the papers, at her name and address beneath Winthrop Jergen's letterhead. "These are *my* statements, from Mr. Jergen." She looked at Harper, puzzled. "Dora took my statements? Why would she do that? These are none of her business. Dora wouldn't . . ."

She hurried to the front room. They watched her open the bottom desk drawer, removing a similar stack of legal-size papers.

"But my statements are here."

She looked hard at Harper. Carefully she examined the two stacks.

"She copied them. See where I made some little notes? On the copies, you can barely see the pencil marks."

She sat down on the couch, looking very small. "Why would Dora do that? What could she want with my statements?"

Harper handed her the other set of legal-size papers that he had taken from the Sleuders' duffle bag. These statements had a different letterhead, under the name Cumming, and were dated the previous year, detailing the Sleuders' own stock earnings.

She looked at them, looked up at him. "I don't understand. Dora and Ralph had some investment problems last year, about the time these are dated."

"What kind of problems?"

"They were cheated of a lot of money. The men were caught, and one of them went to prison."

"Is that the name of the firm that cheated them?"

"It could be. Yes, I think it is."

"You said only one of the members was convicted?"

"Yes. Dora was very upset because the other man, Warren Cumming, went free."

"Did Greeley know about the swindle?"

"Oh, yes. He wrote me all about it—he was furious. And of course Dora called me several times. She'd get so angry, with the trial and all." She looked again at the Sleuders' statements.

"Look here, at Dora's little squiggly marks beside some of these stocks. I have some of the same stock. Coca-Cola, Home Depot. Maybe," she said, "maybe Dora was comparing how much she and Ralph made on that stock—before they were swindled—with how much I've made. It doesn't really make sense, but Dora's—was funny that way. And she was so bitter about their loss. Well, anyone would be bitter!"

Harper put his arm around her. "Later today, when you feel up to it, would you come down to the station and give me a formal statement?"

"Yes, if I have to." She was very pale. "I'll look for Greeley first, and then I'll come. I—I'll need to make arrangements—funeral arrangements."

"Not yet," Harper said. "I'll let you know when you can do that. You don't have any idea where Greeley might have gone? Where he might have stayed last night?"

"No. He's a night owl. But he can't go very far without a car—he's too cheap to take a cab."

She moved away from Harper, looking up at him. "Thank you, Captain Harper. Soon as I get myself together I'll drive around the village, see if I can find him. I don't know how I'm going to tell him about Dora."

Charlie stayed with Mavity for a while after Harper left, making her a cup of tea and fetching her an aspirin from the medicine cabinet. When Mavity felt better, she drove Charlie up to work, then went to look for Greeley.

Charlie, getting back to work, kept puzzling over Dora and Ralph. They had seemed such simple folk, plain and uncomplicated, not the kind to deceive Mavity, and surely not the kind to be into drugs. That strange twist, if it was true, put a whole new light on Dora and Ralph Sleuder.

Pulling on her painting shirt and climbing back on the ladder, she was unable to stop worrying over the Sleuders, unable to stop wondering what Harper would uncover when he looked into their background—wondering how much Mavity might not have known about her dead niece.

20

"**Y**OU'D THINK he'd have the courtesy to call me," Mavity complained, "but not Greeley. Always been that way. Walk out, gone a couple of days, and then home again and never a word." She'd pulled herself from the shocked, quiet state she'd been in that morning and was herself again, cross and abrasive, and Charlie was glad to hear the little woman grousing. They were in the back apartment, in the kitchen-office. It was three-thirty in the afternoon and Mavity, after searching futilely for Greeley, had just gotten to work.

"Ever since we were in high school, he's gone off like that. Drove Mama crazy. She called the police once, reported him missing, and when Greeley found out, he pitched a fit. Left home for three weeks, no one knew where." Mavity shook her head. "Mama never did that again—she just let him ramble." The little woman was wound tight, her voice brittle with worry. She had shown up dragging her cleaning things. "I need to do something. I can't bear to stay home by myself. I left him a note, to call me up here."

"If you feel like it, you can go up and help Pearl Ann. Mr. Jergen wanted some extras, and it had to be today. Some repairs—he wants the work done while he's out. Pearl Ann has a dental appointment so she can't stay too long, then she's catching the Greyhound to San Francisco."

"San Francisco? Pearl Ann never goes anywhere. I've never known her to do anything but tramp the cliffs. Hiking, she calls it. Why in the world is she going to San Francisco?"

Charlie laughed. "This will be her first trip to the city, and she seems thrilled. It'll be good for her. She wants to see the Golden Gate, Coit Tower, all the tourist stuff. I've never seen her so talkative. She even showed me the silk pants and blazer she bought for the trip.

"She'll have time to do Jergen's extras, if you help her. He wants the refrigerator cleaned, said the ice tasted bad. Pearl Ann missed it last week. And he wanted some repairs in the bathroom, said a towel rack had pulled out of the wall and the shower is leaking. It needs caulking—these old tile showers. I told him Pearl Ann had to leave early to catch her bus, but what does he care? You sure you feel up to working?"

"I'll feel better keeping busy. There's nothing I can do about Greeley, only wait. The police are looking for him," Mavity said darkly. Finishing her coffee, she headed toward the stairs carrying her cleaning equipment, and Charlie left to take care of the Blackburn house, do the weekly cleaning and half a dozen small repairs. This was her regular work, the kind of miscellaneous little jobs for which she had started Charlie's Fix-It, Clean-It and for which she was building a good reputation in Molena Point. What her customers valued most was being able to make one phone call, have the house cleaned and the yard work and repairs tended to all at once. One call, one stop. Her customers didn't know that every repair was a challenge, that she carried an entire library of helpful volumes in the van, detailed instructions to refer to if she ran into trouble. Only three times, so far, had she been forced to call in a subcontractor.

She was urging the old Chevy up the hill when she saw two cats racing through the tall grass and recognized Joe Grey's tailless gallop and his flashy white markings. Beside him, Dulcie blended into the grassy shadows like a dark little tiger. It still amazed her that they traveled so far. The freedom of their racing flight made her itch for paper and charcoal, and when they vanished into a tangle of Scotch broom, she slowed the van, watching for them to reappear.

They came out of the bushes suddenly and sat down near the street, regarding her van as she moved slowly by. They looked almost as if they *knew* the vehicle, as if they were quite aware that she was at the wheel and wondered what she was gawking at.

She stopped the van and let it idle, to see what they would do.

They glanced at each other, a strange little look between them, then they rose again and trotted away. Turning their backs, they disappeared into the meadow grass as if dismissing her.

Driving on, she couldn't rid herself of the notion that Joe and Dulcie had cut her dead. Had not wanted her snooping, had all but told her to mind her own business. Even after she began the Blackburns' repairs she kept seeing the two cats turning to look at her, seeing their impatient, irritated expressions.

The Blackburn house was a small, handsome Tudor with gray stone walls, brick detailing, and a shake roof. Letting herself in, she did a light weekly cleaning, fixed the sticking latch on the back gate, and put new washers in a dripping faucet. Mrs. Blackburn had left her check on the hall table with a plate of chocolate chip cookies and a note.

Charlie, Becky made a ton of these for school, and I snagged a few. There's milk in the refrigerator.

She sat at the Blackburns' kitchen table enjoying the cookies and milk, then put her plate and glass in the dishwasher and headed back for the apartments.

She arrived just after six. Mavity had left, her VW Bug was gone. She checked the work Pearl Ann had finished, her patches on the back wall of the building so cleverly stippled that, once the wall was painted, no one would ever guess there had been need for repairs. As she headed out again through the patio, she heard a little clicking noise.

Glancing above her, she saw that Winthrop Jergen's windows were open, the louvered metal shade blowing gently against the molding.

She wondered if Pearl Ann had missed her appointment and was still there, because Jergen never opened the windows. Strange that both Pearl Ann and Mavity would forget to shut them, considering the angry exchanges they'd had with Jergen. Though she could hardly blame Mavity for forgetting, with the events of the morning.

Heading up the stairs, she knocked twice and when Jergen didn't answer she let herself in. He didn't much like her having a key, but as long as she contracted to clean for him, both she and Mavity had keys. She thought, when she pushed the door open, that he must be there after all, and she called out to him, because beyond the entry she could see the glow of his computer screen.

He didn't answer. But she could see a spreadsheet on the screen, long columns of numbers. Her attention focused on the room itself, on the overturned lamp hanging off the desk by its cord, on the toppled swivel chair lying amidst scattered in-boxes and file folders. On Winthrop Jergen lying beside the chair, his blood staining the papers and seeping into the Kirman rug.

Charlie remained absolutely still. Looking. Trying to take in what she was seeing.

He lay twisted on his side, his white shirt and pale blue suit blood-soaked. His throat was ripped open in a wide wound like a ragged hank of bleeding meat.

A cleaning cloth lay beside him in a pool of blood, the kind of plaid mesh cloth that she bought in quantity. Though he couldn't possibly be alive, she knelt and touched his wrist. There was, of course, no pulse. No one could live with that terrible wound, with their throat ripped away. She felt nauseated, could feel the cookies and milk want to come up.

Stepping carefully around Jergen's body, trying not to be sick, trying to stay out of the blood, she moved to the desk, fished an identical cleaning cloth from her pocket, and used it to pick up the phone.

But then she quietly laid it down again and grabbed up a heavy postal scale and turned to face the room, appalled at her own stupidity. If the killer was still in the apartment, she had to get out.

What was she was going to do, fend him off with a postal scale?

But she had no other weapon.

Warily she moved into the bedroom, checking the closet, then the bath. Finding those spaces empty, she approached the kitchen, knowing she should run, get out—knowing this was crazy, that this could not be happening. It was bright afternoon in a village as respectable and civilized as a cup of afternoon tea. Through Jergen's front windows, the low sun gleamed gently, sending sparkles across the calm sea and across the village rooftops; this was Molena Point, tame and quiet, not New York or L.A. with their news of bloody daytime murders.

Finding the kitchen empty, she returned to Jergen's desk, and using the cleaning rag to pick up the phone, she called 911.

But even as she dialed, she wondered if she'd locked the front door behind her. And, waiting for the dispatcher, she laid down the receiver and fled to the door and locked it.

She returned to the desk to hear the dispatcher shouting, "Hello? Hello?"

Standing over Jergen's body, holding the phone in the dustrag, she began to shiver. The metallic smell of blood and the smell of other bodily releases sickened her. She gave the address and stood staring down at Jergen's bloody face and bloody, torn throat, unable to hang up or to look away.

The only dead people she had encountered in her twenty-eight years were those from whom all signs of violence or distress had been gently wiped away, bodies thoughtfully groomed and arranged in the clean satin lining of expensive caskets—an elderly neighbor when she was twelve, her mother's cousin Marie two years later. Her father, when she was eighteen, and her mother when she was in art school. All the deceased were dressed in their Sunday best, their hands calmly folded over their demure chests, her mother's gold wedding band gleaming on her pale finger.

In the room's silence, the faint hum of the computer was like a thin voice whispering to her. Moving past the end of the desk and the two low file cabinets, she saw, for the first time, what appeared to be the murder weapon; though for a long moment she looked at it uncomprehending.

On the rug beside the file cabinets lay the metal divider from an ice cube tray. Blood covered its protruding aluminum handle and had run down into the little squares turning them as red as if someone had ejected a double line of red ice cubes—blood ice cubes. There should be a little wooden stick in each like the frozen orange-juice suckers that mothers made to keep their kids from eating junk.

Sirens screamed, coming up the hill. She backed away from the bloody kitchen utensil and moved unsteadily to the wide window beyond the couch. Standing at the glass, she watched the emergency vehicle careen into the lane, followed by two squad cars, watched two medics jump out loaded with an oxygen tank and black bags—as if her report of death had been faulty, as if the caller might have misjudged the condition of the victim. As if Winthrop Jergen still had a chance at life. Behind the medics, Max Harper swung out of his police unit, and two more uniformed officers from the other squad car double-timed through the patio as she hurried to unlock the door.

21

HIGH UP THE HILLS, a narrow hunting trail led beneath a tangle of toyon bushes, a track no wider than a cat's shoulders, and along the path in a spill of sunshine, Joe and Dulcie crouched feasting on a fat mouse, the last of five sweet morsels they had caught within the hour skittering among the roots and leaves. Above the cats, the toyon's hollylike berries were hard and green, having just emerged from their summer blossoms; the afternoon was warm and still, the only sound was the twittering of some sparrows pottering among the upper leaves.

Suddenly sirens screamed, blasting up from the village.

Rearing tall so they could see down the hills, the cats watched an ambulance career up the winding streets followed by two police units, and skid into the dead-end street below Clyde's apartments—and they took off down the hills, Joe with visions of Clyde falling off the roof, Dulcie's sudden fear involving the power saws. Bolting down the slopes, charging through bushes and tall grass and across the last street, they scorched past the hot rubber stink of the ambulance and squad cars and into the patio.

Men's voices from above them, from Winthrop Jergen's open windows. The police radio. Max Harper's quick commands—and the faint but unmistakable smell of human blood. Racing under the stairs and up the inner wall, they slipped beneath Jergen's sink and pushed the cabinet door open.

The smell of blood, of death.

Slinking across the linoleum, they crouched at the edge of the living room. The instant the uniforms' backs were turned, they bolted under the cherry credenza, peering out at Winthrop Jergen's sprawled body. The smell of his shaving lotion mixed strangely with the stench of death.

The lamps were all lit, every light burning except the lamp that hung over the edge of the desk. The toppled swivel chair and scattered papers and files were all soaked with Jergen's blood. As the medics rose and moved away, the cats got a good look at Jergen, his throat ripped as brutally as if a leopard or tiger had been at him—but this was not a hunting kill, this was the result of human malice.

As the photographer got to work, the flashing strobe lights nearly blinded the cats, forcing them to squeeze their eyes shut. The after-flashes, the blazing white reverse-images of Jergen's body, were as eerie as if his light-propelled spirit kept flashing back, trying to rejoin his corpse.

Beyond the windows, clouds had begun to gather, dimming the late afternoon. The tangle of officers' feet moving carefully across the Kirman rug, skirting around the body, Charlie sitting quietly on the couch out of the way, and the familiar forensics routines filled the cats' vision and minds as the photographer shot his last roll and Officer Kathleen Ray began to collect evidence, her dark hair swinging around her shoulders. The first item she bagged, lifting it carefully from the floor beyond the file cabinets, held the cats' complete attention.

A device from the freezer, the thing that held the ice cubes, but covered with blood, dripping blood, its handle sticking up like a bloody knife, making them see too vividly a human hand jabbing and jabbing that blunt instrument into Jergen's soft flesh.

The cats' own bloodthirst was normal; it was the way God had made them. They were hunters, they killed for food and to train their young—well maybe sometimes for sport. But this violent act by some unknown human had nothing to do with hunting—for a human to brutally maim one of their own kind out of rage or sadism or greed was, to Joe and Dulcie, a shocking degradation of the human condition. To imagine that vicious abandon in a human deeply distressed Dulcie; she did not like thinking about humans in that way.

Pushing closer to Joe, she watched Officer Ray's familiar procedures, the tweezers, the tedious routine of picking up each fleck of evidence, the bagging and labeling, and slowly the thoroughness of her actions began to ease Dulcie. She imagined the intricacies of the laboratory studies that would follow, the carefully established methods, and a sense of rightness filled her.

Then the fingerprinting began, the black powder, the lifting tape, the fingerprint cards, all carefully thought out and calming, techniques that were the result of a wonderful human intelligence.

Humans might be sense-challenged, without a cat's balance and keen hearing and superior sense of touch, to say nothing of the cat's night vision, but the human's

inventiveness and mental skills made up for those fail-
ures—people might be capable of brutality, in a shocking short circuit of the human spirit, but the best of
mankind were still wonderful to observe.

And, she thought, *what are we—what are Joe and I,
that we can understand the achievements of humankind?*

By the time the forensics team had finished, night
had closed around the apartment, the black windows
reflecting the blaze of lights within, turning the room
stark and grim. The coroner arrived, completed his
examination and bagged the body, and slid it onto a
stretcher. As the paramedics carried it out, Officer Ray
collected the last bits of evidence from where the
corpse had lain. No one had touched the computer,
except to lift fingerprints from the keyboard and monitor. The screen still glowed pale green, etching into
the delicate glass the image of a financial spreadsheet.

Max Harper had sent Officer Wendell over to
Mavity's cottage to take her down to the station, and
patrol units were looking for Pearl Ann. Harper sat
with Charlie on the couch, questioning her. "Did you
see Mavity and Pearl Ann come up here to clean?"

"Pearl Ann was up here. I could see her through
Jergen's bathroom window, probably repairing the
towel rack. Mavity was headed for the stairs when I
left, carrying her cleaning things. But, no, I didn't see
Mavity enter the apartment."

"What time was that?"

"Around three-fifteen, I think. I got to the Blackburns' about three-thirty. I usually take Mavity with
me; she cleans while I do the repairs. But today—Jergen had asked for some extras, so I sent her up to help
Pearl Ann."

"What sort of extras?"

"Clean the refrigerator, fix the towel rack that had

pulled out of the bathroom wall, and repair a leak in the shower. He said he had a late afternoon appointment up the coast, wanted the work done while he was out. Mavity was going to do the refrigerator while Pearl Ann took care of the repairs."

"And did you see his car, before you left for the Blackburns'?"

"I wouldn't have; he keeps it in the garage. I thought he was gone. I . . ."

"What?"

"I think he must have been gone. Or—or already dead. Pearl Ann had the windows open, and he would never have allowed that."

"You didn't see his car when you came back from the Blackburn place?"

"No. Isn't it in the garage?"

"There's a black Mercedes convertible parked down the street. We passed it, coming up. I've sent Brennan to check the registration and to check the garage."

Officer Ray came out of the master suite to say that the towel rod had been reset and that there was fresh caulking around the bottom of the shower and between some of the tile. Soon Lieutenant Brennan returned. The garage was empty. He had run the plates on the black Mercedes parked down the street. It belonged to Jergen. Harper returned his attention to Charlie.

"What time did you get back from the Blackburns'? Were the two women still here?"

"Around six-thirty. They were both gone. I came up to close the windows, and he—I found him."

"You realize I have to consider you a suspect, Charlie, along with Mavity and Pearl Ann."

"That's your job," she said quietly.

"Was anyone else in the building when you left? Clyde or any other workers?"

"No, just Mavity and Pearl Ann. Clyde hadn't planned to come up. He had a busy schedule at the shop."

"Do you have an address for Pearl Ann?"

"It's that old brick office building down on Valley, across from the mission."

"The Davidson Building?"

"Yes. She rents a room above those pokey little offices. But she'll be on her way to San Francisco by now; she planned to spend the weekend."

"How long have you known about her weekend plans?"

"For weeks. She was really excited—she grew up somewhere on the east coast and she's never seen San Francisco."

"How long has she been in Molena Point? How long has she lived at the Davidson Building?"

"Four months, more or less—to both questions. Said she moved in there the day after she arrived."

"She picked a great place to settle."

"She's very frugal with money. I think she doesn't have much."

"How long has she worked for you?"

"The whole four months."

"Married?"

"No, she's single. And she's a good worker."

"What kind of car?"

"She doesn't have a car—she walks to work."

"What brought her to the west coast? Where does she come from?"

"Arkansas maybe, or Tennessee, I'm not sure. She told me she wanted to get as far away from her overbearing family as she could."

"How old is she?"

"Twenty-seven."

Harper made some notes. "Did you and Mavity talk about the sheaf of statements we found in Dora Sleuder's luggage? Did she give you any idea why Dora might have them?"

"We didn't talk, no." She looked at him questioningly.

"Did Mavity keep a gun?"

"No. She's afraid of guns." She looked at Harper, frowning. "But that—that terrible wound . . . Mavity couldn't . . . A gun couldn't cause that?"

"So far as you know, she did not have a gun?"

"Well, she might. She told me once that her husband kept a gun, that after he died she was afraid to touch it. She asked Greeley to lock it away for her in a strongbox at the back of her closet. She said her husband had always kept a strongbox, a little cash laid by at home in case of some emergency."

Beneath the credenza, the cats tried to follow Harper's line of thought. Was he guessing that Jergen's throat could have been torn *after* a bullet entered and killed him, perhaps to confuse the police?

The cats remained hidden until Harper had sealed Jergen's apartment and Brennan had secured the stairs with crime scene tape. When everyone had gone, Dulcie leaped to the desk.

Though the officers hadn't touched the computer, Captain Harper had called the FBI in San Francisco, arranging for a computer specialist to examine the files. The file on the screen said BARNER TAX-FREE INCOME FUND and was in Winthrop Jergen's name.

"How much will the Bureau agent find," Dulcie said, "if he doesn't have Jergen's code? And, more important, if he doesn't have Pearl Ann's code?" She sat down beside the phone. Lifting a paw, she knocked the receiver off.

"Hold it," Joe said. "Harper's still down there. The police units are still out front—they must be searching the building."

"I'll call him when he gets back to the station." She lifted the receiver by its cord, biting gently, and used her paw to maneuver it back into the cradle. Turning, she sniffed at the computer. "The keyboard smells of Pearl Ann's perfume."

"Could be an old scent—she cleans around the desk."

"Cheap perfume doesn't last very long." She took another sniff and then leaped down, avoiding the bloodstained rug. Leaving the scene, the cats were soon following Max Harper through the lower apartments, padding along in the shadows beyond where lights had been switched on and well behind the photographer as he made bright strobe shots of the various footprints that had been left in the Sheetrock dust.

Too bad the department would have to labor to identify each set of prints, procuring shoes from everyone involved. Enough fuss to make a cat laugh, when Joe or Dulcie could have done the job in a second.

No amount of sweeping could eradicate the fine white Sheetrock dust that impregnated the plywood subfloor, and the cats, living close to the earth, knew intimately each set of prints left there: Charlie's and Clyde's jogging shoes, Pearl Ann's tennis shoes, the boot marks of the two hired carpenters, the prints of various subcontractors. Their quick identification could have been a great help to the police. *How unfair it is,* Dulcie thought, *that canine officers can gather evidence that would stand up in court, but a cat can't.*

A drug dog's sniffing out of evidence was accepted even if he didn't find the drug—he need only indicate to his handler that the drug had been there, and that was legitimate testimony. But similar intelligence, given by a feline volunteer, would be laughed at.

Just one more instance, Dulcie thought, *of prejudice in the workplace.*

Silently they watched the officers bag the workmen's trash, the drink cans and candy wrappers and wadded-up lunch sacks, and scraps of wallboard and lumber. They bagged, as well, Mavity's insulated lunch carrier and thermos, and Pearl Ann's duffle bag containing her dirty work clothes.

Pearl Ann would have changed clothes for her trip, leaving her duffle to take home on Monday. But Mavity's oversight was strange; Mavity never forgot that lunch bag.

Officer Wendell returned to tell Harper that Mavity was not at home, that there was no sign of her car and no answer when he pounded, and that her door was locked.

"I looked through the windows. The house was very neat, the bed made, three cups and saucers in the sink. I took a turn through the village but didn't see her VW."

Watching from behind a stack of crated plumbing fixtures, Dulcie licked her paw nervously. "*Was* Jergen stealing from Mavity? Could she have found out and been so angry that she killed him? Oh, I don't like to think that."

"Whoever thrust that ice tray divider into Jergen's throat, Dulcie, had to be bigger and stronger than Mavity."

"I don't know. She's pretty wiry."

"She might have shot him first."

"*I* don't think she shot him. I don't believe she would hurt anyone. And where was Pearl Ann? Had she already left when his killer entered the apartment?" She dropped her ears, frightened. "Was Mavity there alone? Did she see the killer?"

"Come on, they're leaving. Let's check the bathroom."

But the bathroom where Pearl Ann usually showered and changed was spotless. The shower was completely dry, not a drop of water.

Usually when Pearl Ann cleaned up, she left the shower floor wet, with Sheetrock dust or paint or plaster on the bathroom floor where she'd pulled off her work clothes.

"Maybe," Dulcie said, "she didn't want to pick up any dirt on her clean new clothes. Maybe she mopped up with paper towels, before she got dressed."

"But why would she dry the shower, too? And there are no paper towels in the bathroom trash basket." Nor did they remember the police taking any trash from the bathroom.

"And there's something else," Dulcie said. "Can't you smell it?"

"I do now," Joe said, sniffing at the shower and grimacing. Over the scent of soap and of Pearl Ann's jasmine perfume came a sharp, male odor. A man had used the shower, and recently. Even a careful wiping-up hadn't destroyed that aroma.

"So Pearl Ann had a man in the shower," Joe said. "So maybe she didn't go up to the city alone. Is that a crime?"

"Did you ever see her with a date? You've never seen anyone come by here to pick her up."

"She still could be seeing someone, or maybe living with someone—maybe wants to keep it quiet."

"Could one of the subcontractors have been here and used the shower?"

"There was no sub scheduled for today," Joe said. "Have you ever seen one of the subs use the shower?"

She switched her tail impatiently. "We have to call Harper—tell him there was a man in the shower and give him the codes for the computer. This could be the key to the whole puzzle."

"Before we make any calls and upset Harper, let's have a look at the Davidson Building—check out Pearl Ann's room."

"Don't you think Harper went over there to search? There'll be cops all over the place."

"He won't search without someone at home," Joe said. "You know how he is. Even if he gets a warrant, he won't go in until Pearl Ann gets back. Says it protects the evidence, saves a lot of fuss in court." His yellow eyes burned with challenge, his expression keen and predatory. "Come on, Dulcie, let's go toss Pearl Ann's place—we'll never have a better chance."

22

As A BLUE-CLAD morgue attendant rolled the gurney bearing Winthrop Jergen's corpse into the cooler to await the coroner's knife, as Captain Max Harper sat at his desk in the Molena Point Police Station filling out his report on Jergen's death, and as Joe and Dulcie padded along the top of the fence behind the Davidson Building where Pearl Ann Jamison rented a room, along the lighted village streets Mavity's worried friends searched for her. Charlie, driving slowly past the crowded shops and cottages, stopped frequently to shine her flashlight among bushes and around porches, thinking she might find Mavity wandering confused and frightened. She kept picturing Mavity standing in the shadows of Jergen's hall watching some faceless assailant stab and stab him—then running, terrified.

She was aware of Wilma searching high above her up the dark hills; she caught frequent glimpses of Wilma's car lights winding back and forth along the narrow streets and the beam of her flashlight sweeping the houses and the open meadows.

But next time she glanced up, Wilma's lights had stopped—they were stationary, seemed to be somewhere above the apartment building.

Had she found Mavity?

But then the light swept slowly across the houses and grassy verges as if Wilma was walking the area, searching it again, though they had looked above the apartments earlier, thinking that Mavity might have run up there to escape Jergen's killer.

Wilma, leaving her car, moved among a tangle of gardens and slipped up driveways to shine her beam in through garage windows; she peered into cars parked on drives or in streets to see if they were empty, hoping no one saw her from some darkened house. She didn't need anyone calling the station, reporting a prowler. She couldn't stop thinking that Mavity, having witnessed Jergen's murder and able to identify the killer, had hidden up here.

Yet Mavity could have been struck down by the killer and dragged away, dumped anywhere—the far foothills, the bay . . .

Or had Mavity, driven by hurt and rage because Jergen cheated her, hefted that ridiculous weapon and flung herself at him with enough force to drive the blunt instrument into his soft flesh?

Before she left home, Wilma had examined an ice tray divider from her refrigerator, hefting it, trying to imagine killing with it.

She had put it down again and turned away sickened, appalled at her own lack of faith in her friend.

Earlier this evening as she walked the streets looking for Mavity, she had met Sue Marble closing up her Latin American Boutique, turning out the lights, dimming the window spots that shone across the display of native art. Sue hadn't seen Mavity for over a week. Wilma didn't stress the urgency of her search, didn't mention the murder.

Sue was full of friendly energy, her complexion rosy, her bobbed white hair gleaming. "I have something for you." She had unlocked her shop again and hurried inside, returning with two signed petitions in support of the library cat, her apple face alight with the accomplishment of having gotten fifty more signatures.

"Don't you tell Freda I did this. I'm supposed to be Freda's friend. She'd pitch a fit if she knew I was getting signatures. But I just can't agree with her about your little library cat. The way she's acting almost makes me want to drop her—except she's the only friend I have who likes to play Scrabble. I don't know why she's so down on cats.

"That black cat that visits me, he's such a handsome fellow. Comes right on in the shop, so regal." She laughed. "I'm a sucker for a friendly kitty. I thought at first he was a stray, but he was too sleek and well-fed. And then his master came in, that nice Greeley Urzey, and . . ."

"When was this?" Wilma asked.

"Oh, a couple of weeks ago." Sue colored slightly. "Greeley comes from Panama, so we had a nice visit. Would you believe we know some of the same people?" She pulled the door to, locking it. "I told him I'll be off on another buying trip, as soon as I can find an apartment and get moved."

"I didn't know you . . ."

"I can't stand the noise another minute, Wilma— that trumpet player next door practicing all the time and now a friend has moved in with him, and *he* plays the *drums*. Can you imagine the noise? The police can't be there every minute. And I can't bear the thought of swearing out a warrant—the idea of starting that kind of battle is just too much—I would really rather move. Dear me, is it urgent that you find Mavity? Is anything wrong? I could help you look."

"Nothing at all, of course not. Did you know that Clyde's apartments will be ready soon? He might be willing to hurry one up for you."

"Oh, yes, the girl who draws the wonderful cats— she's doing them up, isn't she? Charlie Getz? Well, of course, she's your niece. I remember seeing her van up there. Are the apartments nice?"

"Lovely big rooms," Wilma said, "and a wonderful view down over the village." She didn't mention that Winthrop Jergen's apartment might be for let soon. Sue would hear that on her own. Tucking the petitions into her pocket, she thanked Sue and went on her way searching for Mavity.

The brick walls of the Davidson Building were black with grime, its closed windows caked with years of accumulated dirt. The plain, two-story building was constructed in the shape of a long U; a garbage-strewn alley separated its two parallel wings, closed at one end by the building itself, and at the other end by a board fence, atop which the cats now crouched looking up at the impenetrable two floors rising above them.

No window was lighted on either floor to indicate human presence save, at the upper level, halfway down, one window reflecting a weak, greasy glow barely visible behind the dirty pane.

Padding along the top of the fence, the cats studied the metal fire escape that hung above them, folded against the bricks. They could see, just above it, a row of narrow, jutting bricks running the length of the building at the base of the upper windows, apparently a half-hearted attempt at architectural detail—otherwise, the structure was as plain as a prison. Nor was the little ledge much of a walkway, maybe wide enough for a broad-shouldered mouse.

They had already circled the building from the sidewalk. The front door was solidly locked, and there was no other way in. They had swung from the door's latch, pressing and pawing, but nothing gave. Now there was nothing left to try but the fire escape.

Crouching, Joe sprang high, grabbing the metal with his claws, fighting to gain purchase on the rusty steel. Dulcie followed him, and together they twisted and raked at the bars until they had pulled themselves up into the center of the folded tangle then onto the brick ledge above.

Precariously balancing, they pawed at the first window, but it was stuck or locked or nailed shut.

Padding around the corner on the thin ledge, they clung close to the long wall, leaning into the bricks, stopping at each dirty pane of glass. All the windows were stuck, and they couldn't see much through the grime. Most of the rooms looked empty. They made out the dim lines of an overstuffed chair, and in another room, when they had pawed dirt from the pane, a lone, unmade bed, its graying sheets wadded in a bundle on a stained mattress. The window halfway down the building where the thin light burned was caked with dirt as thick as garden soil. Dulcie pawed at it irritably.

"Lick the window."

"I'm not licking it. You lick it." She pressed her face against the glass. "And what's to see? A bunch of dusty boxes stacked up." She didn't like schlepping along the precarious ledge past blind windows where, behind the dirty film, anything could be observing them. She didn't like looking down at the dark alley, either, with its jagged cans and broken glass. Contrary to popular human opinion, a cat certainly could fall from high places—or could be pushed. She had the feeling they were being watched, that something was tracking their progress.

Slipping past the light they gained the corner and padded along the short, connecting wall. They had started up the other side when, across the way, the lighted window slid open.

Against the dull glow, a man stood silhouetted. His voice was grainy, thin.

"Come in, you two. Come on in here, if that's what you want." He shoved the window higher, and the light picked out his gnarled hands and wrinkled leather jacket. "Come on in—or go away and quit snooping." Reaching down, he fetched a cardboard box from somewhere beside his feet and fixed it under the raised window.

So this was where the old man was hiding. Had he been here ever since they saw him leaning over Dora's and Ralph's bodies? They remained still, not sure whether to run from him, along the narrow ledge, or to go back and step inside.

"Come on, you cats. Get a move on." He leaned farther, peering across at them. "I know what you are. Do you think I wouldn't know?"

Joe glanced back at Dulcie, where she crouched behind him.

"Who you looking for?" Greeley said. "There ain't nobody here but me—and my friend." Slyly he glanced around to the shadowed crates behind him.

"Who you looking for?" he repeated. "Or are you just out for an evening's stroll, in this delightful portion of the village?"

"We weren't looking for you," Joe said coldly. Dulcie stared at him, shocked, and wanted to slap a paw over his mouth.

But why not speak? Obviously Azrael had told Greeley all about them—thank you very much. And now from the shadows behind Greeley, a voice mumbled, and Greeley laughed harshly.

"Who you looking for, then, if not me?" Greeley said rudely.

There was another comment from behind him, and his eyes widened. "You cats looking for Pearl Ann? Is that it? You come looking for Pearl Ann Jamison?"

They hunched lower, crouching single file on the narrow ledge.

"You two don't want to mess with Pearl Ann. You don't know half about her. What you want with her?"

Joe glanced behind him at Dulcie. She would have to turn around and go first if they were to return the way they had come and approach Greeley.

She flattened her ears, shook her head. She didn't want to do that.

"Go on, Dulcie. Move it. We can't stay here all night."

She crouched, frozen.

He flipped around on the ledge, seeming to hang in midair, then crouched on the ledge facing her, waiting for her to turn back.

She hunched, staring at him, their noses inches apart, her green eyes huge and uncertain. He had seldom seen her afraid—fear was not her nature. Irritated, he tensed to spring over her along the thin protrusion.

She glared at him but at last she switched ends, flipping around precariously on the thin bricks, holding her breath as her three paws struck empty air then hit the bricks again, and she started back reluctantly toward Greeley. At every step she wanted to beat it out of there.

"Go on," Joe growled. "Hurry up."

She padded a trifle faster.

"Move it, Dulcie. What can he do to us?"

She could think of a number of things.

"Go *on*. Show a little spine."

That moved her. She gritted her teeth and headed fast for Greeley, racing along the bricks, her tail low, her ears plastered tight to her head.

As she reached the window the old man stepped aside, and she warily slipped beneath the raised glass, dropping to the floor and backing away from Greeley. Beside her Joe hit the floor with a heavy thud. Immediately Greeley slammed the window. They heard the lock slide home.

23

THE SMALL, crowded room was shut tight, the window bolted, the door securely closed. Around the cats towered cardboard cartons labeled Scotch, rum, bourbon, and vodka, either the supplies for a huge private party or perhaps the extra stock of a nearby liquor store. The room stunk of booze as if Greeley had been happily sampling the various brands. The only light was from a battery-operated lamp of the kind kept for emergency power outages. Anyone who had been through a California earthquake or considered such matters maintained a stock of battery-powered lamps, a radio, bottled water, and emergency food and medical supplies. The cats saw none of these other essentials, only enough booze to weather any quake, and the squat lamp, its light reflecting from the eyes of the black tomcat where he crouched atop the tallest stack of boxes glaring down at them: an ebony statue, the great *el primo gato*.

In the far corner an old, stained mattress lay nested between the cardboard cases, fitted out with a limp pillow ticked in gray stripes, and a wrinkled army blanket laced with moth holes. On a box beside the bed stood four cans of beans, with a can opener, a dirty paper plate, an open bag of chips, and a pair of dirty socks. The opposite corner of the room served as a depository for trash and empty cans.

Greeley's shirt and pants were wrinkled and stained, and he smelled not only of rum but desperately in need of a bath.

"What you want, you cats? You didn't come to this dump sightseeing. Why you looking for Pearl Ann?"

But then the old man's face crumpled. "You didn't come to make condolences, either." He stared hard at them. "You saw her, didn't you. You saw her dead—*I* saw you looking!" He sat down on the mattress, eased a bottle of rum from under the blanket and upended it, taking a long pull. He was so pitiful that Dulcie wanted to pat his face with a soft paw.

"Ought to have swish 'n' swash," he said and took another swig. "But you need a coconut for that." He giggled at a joke the two cats didn't understand; they watched him, unblinking.

"What, for Christ's sake?" he shouted at them. "What you staring at?" He leaped up suddenly, lunging at them. Dulcie flipped away but Joe crouched snarling, ready to strike.

Greeley paused, uncertain.

"Pearl Ann Jamison," Joe hissed. "Where does she live? Which room?"

Greeley's laugh blasted the air, drowning them in the stink of rum. "I knew it. What you looking for *her* for?"

He sat unsteadily on a carton. "She rented the last empty room. All *I* could get was this storeroom."

He smirked at them, pleased. "Rental office let me have it cheap, when I tole 'em I was teetotal." And he belched and scratched his belly.

"So what do you want with her?" he said roughly. "You tell me what's your business with this Pearl Ann, maybe I'll show you which room."

For a moment, no one spoke; the three cats and the old man stared at each other, caught in a vacuum of silence. Then Greeley dug three paper cups from an open carton and set them in a row on the floor.

Pouring several inches of rum into each, he pushed two toward Joe and Dulcie. "Drink up, folks," he said, cheerfully lifting the bottle.

The biting smell of rum burned the cats' noses, made them back away. The old man stood up abruptly, catching himself against the cartons, and on tiptoe he reached to slide the third cup across the cartons to Azrael. Azrael turned his head and slitted his eyes against the fumes.

Greeley drained the bottle. And his face crumpled, tears streaking down.

"They were into something," he said softly. "Dora and Ralph. Playing cop maybe. Or maybe blackmail." He hiccuped and leaned against the cartons, scowling at the floor. He was silent for so long they thought he'd gone to sleep.

But suddenly he snatched up the battery light. "Well, come on!" He glared down at them, his red eyes watery. "I got a key to Pearl Ann's place, if that's what you're after."

His boozy laugh cracked. "*She* don't know I got it. Azrael fetched it. No trick at all for him to slip in through the transom. She thought she lost her key," he said, smirking. "She got another from the rent office. And what do they care?" He unbolted the door and led them down a narrow, dark hall that smelled of mice and human urine.

Padding warily after him along the dirty linoleum, Joe and Dulcie heard a loud thump behind them as

Azrael hit the floor. They turned to see the black tom swagger out, taking up the rear like a guard walking behind two prisoners.

Pearl Ann's room was at the far end of the gloomy hall. Twisting a skeleton key in the lock, Greeley shoved the door open; when the cats hesitated, he laughed.

"Scared, huh? Scared I'll lock you in?" He slapped his knee, giggling, then crossed the room. Pounding on the window frame, he managed to loosen it. Lifting the bottom half, he propped it open with a dented metal wastebasket. "There, that suit you better?"

They padded into the close, sour-smelling room. In one corner stood an iron bed neatly made up with a worn chenille spread faded to the color of a grimy floor mop. The scarred dresser was of the waterfall era that had been popular in the forties, an incredibly ugly piece but one that had enjoyed a recent revival. Joe leaped to its top, onto a film of dust.

It appeared that Pearl Ann had not lived here alone. Before the mirror were two rows of toiletries, one for a man, one for a woman: hair spray and jasmine cologne on one side, can of shaving cream and bottle of shaving lotion on the other.

Two pairs of men's shoes stood in the open closet next to Pearl Ann's jogging shoes, all as neatly aligned as the shoes of soldiers placed for inspection. Above these hung a man's trousers and jeans and polo shirts and, in her half of the closet, four pastel jumpsuits of the kind that Pearl Ann favored for work, a skirt, and two blouses. In the tiny bathroom, which had no counter space but only a basin, the thin scent of shaving cream and aftershave was mixed with Pearl Ann's perfume. The man's odor was strongest around the bed. As the two cats inspected the room, Greeley stood leaning against the door frame with a strange little smile on his face, as if he was secretly amused. Azrael had remained in the hall, separating himself from their investigation with a barrier of disdain.

They had not told the black tom the results of their surveillance at Pander's restaurant, or who Dora and Ralph's host had been; they had not sought him out, to tell him, and Azrael had not come to them. Maybe, Joe thought, Azrael had gone to Pander's after all, had watched *them* watching Dora and Ralph. He didn't like to think that he had been so unaware, so blind to the dark tom's presence.

Now, searching for he knew not what, pawing open the drawers of the waterfall dresser, Joe found only a man's Jockey briefs and socks. No lady's panties or stockings or nighties—as if Pearl Ann didn't have much, as if she'd taken what little she owned with her to San Francisco.

In the doorway, Greeley looked increasingly smug, harboring his amusing little secret. Joe, losing patience, leaped onto the dresser and fixed him with a hard stare.

"You can keep your own council if you choose, Greeley. Or you can trade it."

"What could a cat trade? What would a cat have that would interest old Greeley?"

Joe turned his back and began to wash.

"Well, what?" Greeley shouted.

"This is about your sister," he told Greeley.

"What about my sister?"

Joe looked back at him, remote and ungiving.

"What about her!" Greeley snapped.

"She's gone," Joe said. "She disappeared. You tell me about Pearl Ann—tell me what you're grinning about—and I'll tell you about Mavity."

"Gone where? What do you mean, gone?"

"The cops are looking for her."

"You're lying. Why would the cops ... I don't believe you. Mavity wouldn't be into anything the cops care about. She's as straight as a fencepost. You cats are such liars."

"What do you know about Pearl Ann?"

"You, first. Can't trust a cat to keep a fair trade."

"She might be wanted for murder," Joe said shortly. "Or she might have been murdered. Murdered, while you wallowed here frying your brain in rum."

"You stupid cat—you think I believe what a cat says?"

"She vanished from Winthrop Jergen's apartment this afternoon." Joe looked at Greeley with distaste. "Jergen was found with his throat torn open. And Mavity has disappeared."

Greeley had turned very pale. "She wouldn't kill anyone. No matter what he did, she wouldn't kill him."

Joe stared at him.

Greeley looked back a long time, his glance flicking to Azrael, to Dulcie, to the window.

"Fair trade," Joe said. "Your turn."

Greeley picked up a straight chair from beside the dresser and set it beneath the overhead light.

"Pearl Ann Jamison," he said. "What a sweet little lady." Standing on the chair, he tipped the plastic light cover askew, reached inside, and drew out a thick envelope. Climbing down, he nearly toppled the chair, caught himself against the bed. Glancing out the door at Azrael, almost as if asking permission and receiving only a haughty look from the black cat, he tossed the packet on the chenille spread.

"My partner saw her hide this. He loves looking in windows. He's a regular voyeur." Withdrawing the contents of the envelope, he spread it across the chenille. Joe looked down from the dresser as Dulcie leaped up onto the bed. They studied with interest an airline ticket, a fistful of credit cards, and three driver's licenses.

The airline ticket was partially used, the stub indicating that the holder had traveled from Georgia to L.A., then L.A. to Molena Point. The date of arrival was about the time Pearl Ann had applied for a job with Charlie. The return portion didn't show any reservation. The ticket had been issued in the name of a Troy Hoke.

There was a Georgia driver's license and a Visa and social security cards for Troy Hoke, a second set for a Terrill John, a third set for William Skeel. The pictures were all of the same man: a thin, familiar face, long brown hair tied back in a ponytail. There was no ticket, and no license or charge card or ID for Pearl Ann; presumably she had her cards with her. Greeley leaned against the dresser, giggling.

Dulcie looked the cards over with widening eyes, her ears sharp forward, her tail twitching. Suddenly she leaped for the closet.

But Joe was ahead of her, sniffing at the lineup of shoes.

"All the same size," Joe said.

"And all the same stink," she replied. The cats looked at each other, their eyes dark with excitement.

Greeley began to laugh.

"You got it, you cats. You got it! You been looking for Pearl Ann Jamison." He guffawed, emitting rum-laced fumes, rocking back and forth.

"You got it. This Pearl Ann Jamison," Greeley shouted, spittling rum-laden spray, "this Pearl Ann fits them Jockey shorts just fine."

24

AT THREE A.M., Max Harper pulled into Sam's All Night Burger up on Highway One. He'd been looking for Mavity Flowers but, spotting Clyde's yellow '29 Chevy, he had wheeled in and parked beside it. He sat a moment admiring the car's gleaming finish and boxy, trim lines. Clyde had been working on this one for two years, and she was a beauty. Not many women had this much attention lavished on them—or turned out as elegant, either.

Clipping his phone to his belt beside his radio, he locked the unit and headed into the restaurant. Stopping at the counter to order cherry pie and coffee, he moved on back, where Damen sat hunched over a sandwich and coffee. Sliding into the booth, he picked up the menu out of habit. "Any luck?"

Clyde shook his head. He looked dead for sleep. "Not a sign of Mavity. And I haven't seen Wilma or Charlie for a while. If either one found her, they'd take her back to Wilma's. Her phone doesn't answer."

"I saw Wilma around midnight, up on Ridgeview.

She had hoped Bernine would ride with her, said she guessed Bernine had gone out."

"Only Bernine Sage would party while her latest love interest lies cold in the morgue."

"He isn't her love interest anymore—he's no use to her now." Harper reached for a cigarette, tamped it, stuck it in his mouth unlit. "I wired Atlanta on this Warren Cumming. As Mavity said, charges against Cumming were dropped. His partner, Troy Hoke, was convicted, did a year for theft by fraud against Dora and Ralph Sleuder and five other victims. He's been out just over six months.

"Shortly after Hoke's trial, Cumming left the state. Gave a Florida forwarding address, a private postal box. Forfeited on the lease of his Atlanta apartment, closed his bank account, took the balance in cash."

"Big money?"

"Very small. I'm guessing he had larger accounts in other names and that the Florida move was a red herring."

Billie, the straw-blond night waitress, brought Harper's pie and coffee. She was sixtyish and smelled of stale cigarettes, her thin face dry and deeply lined. Setting the pie down, she spilled cherry juice on the table. Scowling, saying nothing, she wiped it up.

"What's with you?" Harper said.

"Fight with LeRoy," she said shortly. She looked hard at Harper. "What's with these guys? Does he have to mess around with that stupid motorcycle *all* the time?"

"Better than another woman," Harper told her.

"I don't know, Max. Perfume is easier to get out of the laundry than grease."

Harper tried to look sympathetic. When she'd gone, Clyde said, "Why doesn't she leave him?"

"Never will. She just likes bitching about him." But he looked distressed, too. Despite dealing with the dregs of the world, Harper never got used to people staying in a bad marriage. His own happy marriage had ended far too soon, when Millie died of cancer; he didn't have a lot of sympathy for people who put up with anything less than a completely wonderful union. To Max's way of thinking, it was better to be alone. He tasted his pie, ate half of it before he spoke again.

"After Hoke was released, he received several phone calls to his Atlanta apartment." He glanced up at Clyde. "All were placed from the Sleuders' phone. And a few days after the last call, he left the state. That was four months ago."

Clyde had stopped eating, was quiet.

"Shortly before the Sleuders flew out here on vacation, they placed several calls to a Molena Point pay phone a block from the Davidson Building.

"The way I see it, Dora Sleuder stumbled onto Cumming's whereabouts by chance. Try this: Dora makes a casual phone call to her aunt—evidently they talked once or twice a month, family stuff, keeping in touch. During the conversation, Mavity mentions her new investment counselor, brags about how well she's doing.

"She tells Dora how wonderful Jergen is and describes him—you know Mavity, going on about Jergen's youthful looks and silver hair. The description fits Cumming, and Dora starts asking questions."

Clyde nodded. "Like, how old is he? How does he dress and talk? How he furnishes his office, what kind of car he prefers . . ."

"Exactly. Now assume that Mavity's description was so much like Cumming that it got Dora and Ralph wondering, made them decide to check up on this Jergen."

"But . . ."

"They knew that Hoke was just out of prison—they'd kept track of him. And they knew he'd be burning to get at Cumming, for setting him up. Hoke did all the time for that scam. Cumming didn't do a lick.

"Dora and Ralph decide that this Jergen could be Warren Cumming, and they sick Hoke on him, encourage Hoke to come on out here and take a look."

"But how did they find Hoke? Through his parole officer?"

Harper nodded. "We have the parole officer's phone record, and we've talked with him. He remembers a woman calling him, said she was Hoke's niece, that Hoke had some things of her mother's that he'd put away before he went to prison, that she wanted to get them back. Parole officer wouldn't disclose any information, but he took her phone number, passed it on to Hoke—he's obliged to do that. Figures he'll watch developments. This officer keeps good records, the Sleuders' number was there in his logbook.

"So Hoke calls Dora, and she tells him about Winthrop Jergen. According to Hoke's phone bill, they talk for over an hour. The next day Hoke moves out of his apartment, leaves Altanta."

Harper slipped a photograph from his pocket, handed it across.

The man in the picture was thin and pale. Light brown hair, long and tied back. One low shoulder. A bony face, thin eyebrows.

Clyde stared. "The guy who hangs around the apartments. Mavity calls him 'the watcher.' This is Troy Hoke?"

"Yep. And we have Hoke's prints, from the Atlanta file." He mopped up cherry juice with a forkful of crust.

"Did they match the prints from the murder scene?"

"The only prints we got at the scene were for Jergen himself, and for Mavity and Charlie."

"You didn't get Pearl Ann's prints? They should be all over the place. She cleaned for him regularly, and she did the repairs. Except . . ." Clyde thought a minute. "Pearl Ann wears gloves. Has some allergy. Gloves to work on the Sheetrock, to clean, to paint."

"Charlie told me that. Rubber gloves or sometimes a soft leather pair."

Clyde nodded. "She takes them off several times a day, to put on some kind of prescription hand cream."

He looked intently at Harper. "Sounds like this will nail Hoke—but what about Mavity? It won't help us find Mavity." They were speaking softly. At three in the morning, the restaurant was nearly empty. Down at the far end of the counter two men in jeans and plaid shirts sat eating, intent on their fried eggs. In a booth near the door, an elderly couple was drinking coffee, each reading a section of a newspaper. At the counter near them, a striking blond was nibbling at a sandwich and sipping orange juice. As Harper signaled for a refill of coffee, his cellular phone buzzed. Picking it up, he started to speak, then went silent.

Watching him, Clyde thought the call was being transferred. The blond got up from the counter, wrapped her unfinished sandwich in a paper napkin, paid her check and left. Clyde watched through the window as she swung into a Chrysler van with the windows open and a huge white dog hanging his head out, watched her feeding the dog little bites of the sandwich. Across from him, Harper had stiffened.

Harper felt his blood go chill. The voice on the line was female, a smooth voice, a velvety, insinuating voice that made the hackles on his neck rise. He could never get used to hearing this woman. He didn't know her name, had never seen her, didn't know anything about her, but every time she called, the nerves in his stomach began to twitch.

"Captain Harper? Are you still there?"

He said nothing.

"Captain Harper, you have just sealed the scene of a murder up on Venta Street."

"Have I?"

"Your men didn't touch the computer. You left it on, and you have a Bureau man coming down early in the morning to check it out."

Harper remained silent. The pie in his stomach had turned sour. *No one* could know about the Bureau man except his own people and Charlie Getz. He tried to figure who, in his own department, would breach security, would pass along such information. The officers at the scene had been Brennan, Wendell, Ray, and Case. The two medics had left before he called the Bureau.

The caller was waiting for him to respond. He motioned for Clyde to listen. Clyde came around the table and sat down, shoving against Harper, jamming his ear to the phone.

"Captain Harper, there are two code words for the computer that your Bureau man will want. Jergen's code, to open his financial files, is *Cairo.*

"The second code word was used by Pearl Ann Jamison. It should open a set of files that Pearl Ann seems to have hidden from Jergen, on his own computer. That word is *Tiger.* I believe those are both Georgia towns; I looked them up on the map.

"In looking for suspects," the caller said softly, "you need to be looking for a man. Pearl Ann and he are . . ."

She gasped, Max heard a faint yelp of alarm and the line went dead.

Harper sat frozen, staring at the phone. Clyde exploded out of the booth like he was shot, threw a five-dollar bill on the table and fled out the door.

"Hold it," Harper shouted. "What the hell?" He stared after Clyde perplexed, watched the yellow roadster scorch out of the parking lot moving like a racing car and disappear down the hill toward the village.

He wanted to go after Clyde. Instead, he sat thinking about that soft voice.

You need to be looking for a man, Pearl Ann and he are ... And then the gasp or yelp, a strange little sound, and then silence.

The two are *what?*

Working together? Pearl Ann and a man are working together? Involved? Involved in Jergen's death? Pearl Ann and who? Troy Hoke? And then that startled yelp, and Clyde taking off like his boots were on fire.

He motioned for more coffee, and dug in his pocket for some antacid. He didn't want to know where Clyde was headed. He didn't want to follow the yellow car. He didn't want to know who the caller was, with the soft and velvety voice.

25

IN THE DARKEST CORNER beneath
Wilma's bed, Dulcie crouched, listening to the footsteps
coming down the hall, ready to run if Bernine looked
under and found her. At the first sound of someone
approaching she had abandoned the phone and dived for
the shadows, leaving Max Harper shouting through the
receiver. If Bernine heard him and picked up the phone
and started asking questions—and Harper started asking
questions—all hell would break loose. There was no one
else in the house, to have made the call.

But she daren't leap onto the bed again and try to hang
up, there was no time, Bernine was nearly at the door . . .

She'd waited all night to make this call, waited for
Bernine to get off the phone and now here she came
when she should be in bed drifting off to sleep.

It had been nearly one A.M. when Dulcie slipped in
through her cat door exhausted from listening for
hours to drunken Greeley Urzey and breathing his
stink of rum in Pearl Ann's pokey little room. They'd
had to listen to him agonizing over Mavity and to his

wild plans for finding her, which amounted to nothing, because by midnight he had drunk himself into a stupor. Azrael had looked intensely pleased that Mavity might have met with foul play, his amber eyes gleaming with malice. Pure hatred, Dulcie thought. The cat was filled with hate, that was his nature—loathing for anyone who didn't worship him.

Racing home, bolting in through her cat door, she'd realized that Wilma wasn't home; her car wasn't in the drive or in the open garage. She'd pictured Wilma still cruising the dark streets searching for Mavity, looking for Mavity's little VW.

Bernine's car was at the curb, but Bernine had gone out to dinner with a real estate broker. Dulcie hoped she was still out. But then, heading for the phone, she'd heard Bernine's voice.

Slipping through the dark dining room, she'd caught the scent of Bernine's perfume and seen her sitting at Wilma's desk talking on the phone. She'd listened for only a few minutes before she decided Bernine was making up with her estranged live-in. She slipped on into Wilma's bedroom, wishing they had two phone lines.

The curtains had not been drawn, and the faint light from the distant street lamp bathed the room in soft shadows. The bed was smoothly made. Leaping up onto the flowered, quilted spread, she had settled down to wait.

She'd waited for nearly two hours for Bernine to finish, had slipped periodically out into the hall to listen as the conversation swung from mushy love talk to angry argument to sweet words again in a sickening display of human indecision and female guile. Bernine had moved the phone to the couch, lay curled up on *her* patch of velvet, sweet-talking this bozo.

On the bed she'd dozed, waked to listen to Bernine

going on and on, to see the light still burning in the living room and beneath the guest room door and feeling her stomach churn with impatience at the delay.

But then at last she heard Bernine leave the living room, head down the hall, and from the guest room she could hear little rustling sounds. Either Bernine was packing to leave or she was getting ready for bed.

Easing Wilma's bedroom door closed, catching it with her paw just before it latched, she'd leaped to the night table, nosing at the phone.

Her sensible self said, *Wait until Bernine's light goes out—don't do this while she's awake.*

But she'd waited too long. Her impatient self said, *She won't hear you. What are you afraid of? It's practically morning, let's get on with it.*

Lifting the headset by its cord, she had dropped it on the pillow, squinched up her paw and punched in Harper's number, cocking her head to the receiver. Joe was an old hand at this, but she still got nervous. The first time she'd dialed and heard a voice at the other end, she'd felt as weird as if she were communicating with someone on Mars.

When the dispatcher answered, she'd boldly asked for Max Harper.

"Captain Harper is not on duty. Lieutenant Brennan can help you."

"I have information to give to Captain Harper personally. About the Winthrop Jergen murder. Information that Harper must have before the Bureau agent arrives in the morning. I must give it to him now; I cannot call again."

It had taken some time for the dispatcher to switch the call to Harper's cellular phone, a degree of electronic sophistication that further awed Dulcie. The delay made her so edgy that her skin began to twitch, but at last

Harper came on the line. She had tried to speak clearly, but she hadn't dared lift her voice above a whisper.

"Captain Harper, I have some information about Winthrop Jergen."

Harper didn't respond.

"Captain Harper? Are you still there?" He didn't answer, but she could hear him breathing. "Captain Harper, you have just sealed the scene of a murder up on Venta Street. Your men didn't touch the computer. You left it on, and you have a Bureau man coming down early in the morning to check it out."

Only silence and his ragged breathing. Her paws began to sweat. She wondered if Harper was nervous, too. This was so strange, the two of them linked not only by the wonder of electronics but by a far greater phenomenon, by a miracle that she hardly understood herself—and that Max Harper could never bring himself to believe. She imagined herself like those photographs where a cat's face is superimposed over a woman's face, becoming one, and she almost giggled.

"Captain Harper, there are two code words for the computer that your Bureau man will want. Jergen's code, to open his financial files, is *Cairo*.

"The second code word was used by Pearl Ann Jamison. It should open a set of files that Pearl Ann seems to have hidden from Jergen, on his own computer. That word is *Tiger*. I believe those are both Georgia towns . . ."

She was just starting to explain about Pearl Ann and Troy Hoke when she heard the footsteps; gasping a sharp mew, she leaped to the floor and under the bed. Above her Harper's angry voice had shouted, *"Hold it. What the hell?"*

Now as the bedroom door opened and the light flashed on, Dulcie's every muscle was tensed to sprint past Bernine's feet and down the hall to safety. Thank God the phone above her was silent—yet she'd heard no click as if Harper had hung up. She listened for those sharp beeps when the phone was left off the hook. She was so frightened that the sounds in the bedroom hardly registered: the hush of the closet door opening, someone rummaging among Wilma's clothes. All she could think was *If Bernine picks up the phone, what if he's still on the line? No one could have made that call, no one—there's no other human in the house. Only the cat crouched under the bed scared out of her kitty mind.* Shivering, she listened to the *whish* of garments from the closet.

Then she smelled Wilma's scent, Wilma's subtle bath powder.

Peering out from beneath the spread, she saw Wilma's bare feet as Wilma pulled on her slippers. Mewling with relief, she came out, curving around Wilma's ankles, purring so hard she trembled.

Wilma picked her up, stared into her face. "What?" she whispered, glancing toward the closed door. "What's the matter?"

"I thought—I thought you were Bernine," she breathed, snuggling against Wilma.

Only then did Wilma see the phone lying on the bed. She raised a disapproving eyebrow at Dulcie. "You didn't get my note?"

"What note? You left a note? Bernine . . ."

Wilma put her down on the bed, hung up the phone, and went down the hall. Dulcie heard her cross the kitchen and open the back door. She returned with a small, folded paper. "I left it tucked in the frame of your cat door, but only a little bit showing so Bernine wouldn't notice." As she moved to pull the bedroom door closed, Dulcie, peering down the hall, saw that Bernine's light had gone out. Had Bernine gone to sleep? Or was she standing just inside, straining to hear?

Wilma unfolded the paper and laid it on the bed.

Have gone to look for Mavity. Don't stay here alone. Go over to Joe's, now, where you'll be safe.

Dulcie looked at her intently. "Did you really think Bernine would . . ."

"I don't know what Bernine would do. But all night, while we looked for Mavity, I worried about you. Twice I swung by. When Bernine's light wasn't on, I felt easier. She must have gotten home very late."

"She came in about one. But she was on the phone for hours, talking to the guy she was living with. Weeping, shouting. Sweet-talking. What histrionics. Maybe she'll move out. You didn't find Mavity?"

"No." Wilma sat down on the bed, tired and drawn. "And when I think of Jergen's grisly death, I'm afraid for her. If Mavity saw the killer, her life isn't worth much." She looked at Dulcie a long time. "What is his death about? What's happening? Dulcie, what do you know about this?"

Dulcie looked back at her, panicked about what to do.

She had tried to tell Captain Harper, tonight, that Pearl Ann was Troy Hoke. Now, should she tell Wilma?

But what good? Wilma daren't tell Harper. He'd ask how she knew, and why she hadn't told him before. And if she said she'd just found out, he'd want to know *how* she learned Pearl Ann's secret on the same day of the murder. Wilma's sudden knowledge would implicate her in a way difficult to talk herself out of.

Wilma did not lie well to law enforcement, particularly to Max Harper. She was too truthful within her own profession. And if she attempted some hastily contrived excuse, Harper *would* be suspicious. Dulcie looked at her blankly, shrugged, and said nothing.

Wilma was turning down the bed, folding the quilted chintz back while Dulcie prowled across it, when a loud knocking from the back door startled them and they heard Clyde shouting.

Racing for the kitchen, Wilma jerked the door open. Behind her, Dulcie leaped to the breakfast table. Clyde rushed in, his voice loud with alarm. "Where is she? What hap . . . ?"

"Shhh," Wilma whispered, grabbing his arm. "*Don't wake Bernine.* What's wrong?"

Clyde's stubbled cheeks were dark and rough, his dark hair tangled. The underarms of his jogging suit were sweaty. When he saw Dulcie, he stopped shouting. Pulling out a chair, he sat down glaring at her, his face red with frustration. "You just about gave me heart failure. What the hell were you doing? What the hell happened here?"

Dulcie looked at him, puzzled.

"My God, Dulcie. When you called Harper—when you made that awful, frightened cry, I thought someone was killing you." He lowered his voice, glancing in the direction of the guest room. "That was bloodcurdling— that was the next thing to a yowl on the phone!"

"You were listening? Where were you?" Dulcie cocked her head. "And how did you know where I was?"

"Where else would you be? Except maybe my house. I came here first . . ." Clyde sighed. "You *mewed*, Dulcie—you almost *yowled* into the damned phone. Harper looked amazed, looked . . . I thought someone had snatched you up and was wringing your stupid cat neck." He glared hard at her. "These phone calls, Dulcie . . ."

"I didn't yowl. I didn't mew. I simply caught my breath. I thought," she said softly, "I thought I heard Bernine coming."

He simply looked at her.

"I thought she'd catch me with the phone. But then it wasn't Bernine, it was Wilma. What did Harper say?"

"He didn't *say* anything. *I* don't know what he said. I was out of there—came flying down here thinking you were being strangled. We were clear up at Sam's, on the highway. My God . . ."

Dulcie licked his hand. She was really very touched. "How could I know you were listening? I didn't mean to upset you."

"Why the hell wouldn't I be upset? And can you imagine what would happen if Harper heard you really *meow*? With all the questions he already has about you two, don't you think he'd just about go crazy? Questions I can't answer for him, Dulcie. Questions I wouldn't dare answer."

Clyde put his head in his hands. "Sometimes, Dulcie, between you and Joe, I can't handle this stuff."

She patted his hand with a soft paw. He looked so distressed that she didn't know whether to feel sorry for him or roll over laughing.

But still, she thought, Clyde handled most situations very well. From the moment Joe discovered he was endowed with human speech, that he could carry on a conversation in the English language and read the written word, Clyde had weathered Joe's—and her own—unusual lifestyle with a minimum of emotional chaos. He had indulged in very few out-of-control shouting spells. He had exhibited no mind-numbing bouts of terror that she knew of. He had even paid Joe's deli bills without undue grousing.

He had even put up with Joe's reading the front page first in the mornings and demanding anchovies for breakfast. Not until this morning, she thought, had he really lost it.

She patted his hand again and rubbed her whiskers

against his knuckles. "You shouldn't get so worked up—it's bad for human blood pressure. You can see that I'm all right. It was just a simple phone call."

"*A* simple *phone call*? *Simple?* You should have seen Harper's face." Clyde sighed deeply. "You don't seem to realize, Dulcie, how this stuff upsets Harper."

Wilma rose from the table. Turning away, she took the milk from the refrigerator and busied herself making cocoa.

"Every time you and Joe meddle," Clyde said, "every time you phone Harper with some wild tip, he gets suspicious all over again. And he starts making skewered remarks, laying the whole damned thing in my lap."

"What whole damned thing?" Dulcie said softly, trying to keep her temper.

"He starts hinting that he wants answers. But he's too upset to come right out with the real question. And that isn't like Harper. He's the most direct guy I know. But this . . . Dulcie, this stuff is just too much."

She stared sweetly into Clyde's face. "Why is helping him solve a crime a *whole damned thing*, as you put it? Why is catching a murderer, to say nothing of boosting the department's statistics and impressing the mayor and the city council with Harper's absolutely perfect, hundred percent record . . ."

"Can it, Dulcie. I've heard all that. You're beginning to sound just like Joe. Going on and on with this ego-driven . . ."

"Oh, you can be rude!" She was so angry she raised her armored paw, facing him boldly, waiting for an apology.

She would not, several months ago, have dared such behavior with Clyde. When she first discovered her ability to speak, she had felt so shy she'd even been embarrassed to speak to Wilma.

Even when she and Joe began to discover the history and mythology of their lost race, to know that they were not alone, that there were others like them—and even though Clyde and Wilma read the research, too—it had taken all her courage to act natural and carry on a normal conversation. It had been months before she would speak to Clyde.

Wilma poured the cocoa and poured Dulcie a bowl of warm milk. Clyde sat trying to calm his temper. "Dulcie, let me explain. Max Harper lives a life totally oriented to hard facts. His world is made up of cold, factual evidence and logically drawn conclusions based on that evidence."

"I know that." She did not want to hear a lecture.

"How do you think Harper feels when the evidence implies something that he *knows* is totally impossible? What is he supposed to do when no one in the world would believe what the evidence tells him?"

"But . . ."

"Tonight, when Harper's phone rang, the minute he heard your voice, he went white. If you'd seen him . . ."

"But it was only a voice on the phone. He didn't . . ."

"Your voice—the snitch's voice—has him traumatized. This mysterious female voice that he links with all the past incidents . . . Oh, hell," Clyde said. "I don't need to explain this to you. You know what he suspects. You know you make him crazy."

Dulcie felt incredibly hurt. "The tips Joe and I have given him have solved three murders," she said quietly.

Wilma sat down at the table, cradling her cup of cocoa.

Clyde said, "Every crime where you and Joe have meddled, Harper has found cat hairs tainting the evidence—and sometimes pawprints. *Pawprints, Dulcie!* Your marks are all over the damned evidence. Do you think this doesn't upset him? And now, tonight, you yowl into the damned telephone."

"I didn't *yowl.*"

"*You* know the way he looks at you and Joe. *Joe* tells you the kind of stuff Harper says to me. How would you like it if Max Harper ended up in the funny farm—because of you two?"

"There is no way Max Harper is going to end up in a mental hospital. Talk about overdramatizing. Half of Harper's comments are just putting you on. And he only talks that way after a few beers."

Wilma refilled Clyde's cocoa cup and tried to turn the conversation. "You didn't find any trace of Mavity?"

Clyde shook his head.

"We'll start early in the morning," she said. "We can canvas the shops that were closed last night, see if anyone saw her."

"The whole department will be doing that. Mavity is a prime suspect." He reached to stroke Dulcie, wanting to make amends.

Reluctantly Dulcie allowed him to pet her. She couldn't believe that Max Harper would really suspect Mavity of killing Jergen. If he did suspect Mavity, he needed to know about Pearl Ann. She rose and moved away from Clyde, stood looking at him and Wilma until she had their full attention, until Clyde stopped glowering and waited for her to speak.

"Mavity isn't guilty," she told them. "I was trying to tell Harper that, on the phone."

"How do you know that?" Wilma said softly.

"Pearl Ann Jamison is the one Harper wants. I was *trying* to *tell* him that."

They both stared at her.

"Pearl Ann Jamison," Dulcie said, "is a guy in drag. I believe that he's the killer."

Clyde burst out laughing. "Come on, Dulcie. Just because Pearl Ann's strong, and a good carpenter, doesn't mean she's a guy. You . . ."

"Are you saying I don't know what I'm talking about?"

"Of course not. I just think you and Joe . . . Joe's never mentioned this. What would make you think . . ."

"I know the difference between male and female," she said tartly. "Which is more than you and Wilma seem to have figured out. When you get past the Jasmine perfume, Pearl Ann smells like a man. Without the perfume, we'd have known at once."

"She *smells* different? You're basing this wild accusation on a *smell*?"

"Of course he smells different. Testosterone, Clyde. He smells totally male. It's not my fault that humans are so—challenged when it comes to the olfactory skills."

Wilma watched the two of them solemnly.

"Pearl Ann smells like a man," Dulcie repeated. "Half the clothes in her closet belong to a man. The IDs hidden in her room—driver's licenses and credit cards, are for several different men."

Clyde sighed.

"One ID is in the name of Troy Hoke. He was . . ."

That brought Clyde up short. "Where did you hear that name?"

"I just told you. Pearl Ann has an ID for Troy Hoke. If you don't believe me or Joe, then ask Greeley—Greeley knows all about Pearl Ann. *He* let us into her room in the Davidson Building. *He* showed us the driver's licenses and credit cards hidden in the light fixture. He told us where Hoke parks the car he drives, that none of you have seen. An eight-year-old gray Chrysler."

They were both gawking at her, two looks of amazement that quite pleased her.

"That's where Greeley's been all this time," she said patiently. "Camping in a storeroom at the Davidson Building."

"Why didn't you tell us this before?" Wilma said. "It's not like you to keep something . . ."

This was really too much. "I just did tell you," she hissed angrily. Clyde's skeptical questions were one thing, she was used to Clyde's argumentative attitude. But for Wilma to question her—that hurt. "We just found out tonight," she said shortly and turned her back on Wilma, leaped off the table, and trotted away to the living room. If they didn't want to believe her, that was their problem. She'd call Harper back at once and tell him about Troy Hoke.

Leaping to the desk, she had just taken the phone cord in her teeth when the instrument shrilled, sending her careening off again.

The phone rang three times before Wilma ran in and snatched it from the cradle. She listened, didn't speak. She patted the desk for Dulcie to jump up, but Dulcie turned away.

"What hospital?" Wilma said.

On the floor, Dulcie stopped washing.

"How bad is she?" Wilma said softly. "Can we see her?" And in a moment she hung up the phone and hurried away to dress and find her keys.

26

Mavity's hospital room at Salinas Medical was guarded by a thin, young deputy who had been on duty most of the night. His chin was stubbled with pale whiskers, and his uniform was wrinkled. Sitting on a straight-backed chair just outside Mavity's half-open door, he was enjoying an order of waffles and bacon served in a plastic carton. A Styrofoam cup of coffee sat on the floor beside his chair. He was present not only to assure that the suspect did not escape—a most unlikely event, considering Mavity's condition—but to bar intruders and protect the old woman in case she was not Jergen's killer but was a witness to his death.

Mavity's room was not much larger than a closet. The steel furniture was old and scarred, but the white sheets and blanket were snowy fresh. She slept fitfully, her breathing labored, her left hand affixed to an IV tube, her right hand clutching the blanket. A white bandage covered most of her head, as if she were wearing the pristine headgear of some exotic eastern cult. She had been in the hospital since one A.M., when she was transferred there by ambulance from an alley in Salinas where she had been found lying unconscious near her wrecked VW. She had not been able to tell the police or the nurses her name or where she lived. The Salinas police got that information from the registration of her wrecked car. They had notified the Molena Point PD only after an alert was faxed to them that a woman of Mavity's description was missing and was wanted for questioning in last evening's murder.

Salinas Medical was an hour's drive from Molena Point, lying inland where the weather was drier and warmer. The hospital complex consisted of half a dozen Spanish-style buildings surrounded by a circular drive. It was a training facility for medical staff and a bulwark of specialized medical services for the area, including an excellent cardiac unit and a long-term-care wing for patients in need of intensive nursing. Wilma, Clyde, and Charlie arrived at Salinas Medical at five-thirty A.M.

When Wilma had received Max Harper's phone call at four that morning, she and Clyde left her house in her car, making two stops, the first to drop Dulcie off at Clyde's place, an arrangement about which Dulcie was not happy. The last Wilma saw of the little cat, Dulcie was sulking alone on Clyde's steps, her ears down, her head hanging, looking as abandoned as she could possibly manage.

Wilma knew that the instant she drove away Dulcie would bolt inside to Joe, pacing and lashing her tail, complaining about the indignities a cat was subjected to by uncaring humans.

"They won't let you into the hospital," Wilma had told her. "And I don't want you alone here with Bernine."

"I could go in a shopping bag. They'd think I was extra clothes or homemade cookies. Don't you think *I* care about Mavity? Don't you think *I* care that that man might have killed her?"

"Or that *she* might have killed Jergen?"

"Nonsense. *You* know she didn't. I would fit in that canvas book tote. You could just . . ."

"Hospital security checks all parcels. They won't let you in. They'd throw you out in the street."

"But . . ."

"Stay with Joe," Wilma had snapped, and had unceremoniously tossed Dulcie into the car where she hunched miserably on the front seat.

The second stop had been to pick up Charlie, who was waiting in front of her building before the antique shop, sucking on a mug of coffee and snuggled in a fleece-lined denim jacket. She slid into the front seat between Clyde and Wilma, frowning with worry over Mavity.

"Has she remembered her name? Does she know what happened to her?"

"We haven't talked to the hospital," Wilma said. "All I know is what Harper told me when he called, that she was confused and groggy."

"Was she alone in the car?"

Clyde put his arm around her. "As far as we know, she was. They found the VW smashed against a lamp-post, outside a pawnshop in the old part of town. Not a likely place for her to be in the middle of the night."

As they sped east on the nearly empty freeway, the dawn air was damp and cool through the open windows, helping to wake them. On either side of the road, the thickly wooded hills rose dark and solid against the dawn sky. Soon they were inland between flat fields, the crops laid out in long green rows, the dawn air smelling of onions. When they arrived at Salinas Medical, Mavity was asleep, an IV tube snaking up her arm to a slowly seeping bottle. In the corner of the room on a hard wooden chair, Max Harper dozed, his long legs splayed out before him. He came fully awake as they entered.

"I've been here about an hour," he replied to Wilma's questioning look. "Haven't gotten much out of her—she's pretty confused."

Clyde went out to the nursing station to get some chairs, and Charlie went to find the coffee machine, returning with four large cups of steaming brew that tasted like rusted metal.

"She has a cerebral contusion," Harper said. "A lot of swelling. They had a shunt in for a while, to relieve the pressure, to drain off some of the fluid. And she's had trouble breathing. They thought she'd have to have a tracheotomy, but the breathing has eased off. She's irritable and her memory's dicy, but that's to be expected. Not much luck trying to recall yesterday afternoon. And when she can't put it together, she gets angry. They're waking her every two hours." He sipped his coffee. He looked like he could use a smoke.

Wilma smoothed Mavity's blanket. "Were there any witnesses to the wreck?"

Harper shook his head. "None that we've found. We don't know yet whether another car was involved or if she simply ran off the street into the lamppost."

Mavity woke just after six and lay scowling at them, confused and bleary. Her wrinkled little face seemed very small surrounded by the thick white bandage and snowy bedding. When Wilma spoke to her, she did not respond. She frowned at Charlie's wild red hair and glared angrily at Harper. But soon something began to clear. She grew restless, and she reached up her hand to Wilma, trying to change position, kicking out of the blanket with one white, thin leg.

Wilma looked a question at Harper, and he nodded. She sat down on the edge of the bed, helping Mavity to get settled, holding her hand. "You had a little accident. You're in Salinas Medical. We came over to be with you."

Mavity scowled. Wilma smiled back. "Do you remember cleaning for Mr. Jergen yesterday afternoon?"

Mavity looked at her blankly.

"Mavity?"

"If it was his day, I cleaned for him," she snapped. "Why wouldn't I?" She looked around the room, puzzled. "I was fixing supper for Greeley—sauerkraut and hot dogs." She reached to touch her bandage and the IV tube swung, startling her. She tried to snatch it, but Wilma held her hand. "Leave it, Mavity. It will make you feel better."

Mavity sighed. "We had a terrible argument, Dora and Ralph and me. And the hardware store—I was in the hardware store just a minute ago. I don't understand. How did I get in a hospital?"

"You hit your head," Wilma told her.

Mavity went quiet. "Someone said I wrecked my car." She gave Wilma an angry glare. "I've never in my life had a wreck. I would remember if I wrecked my little car."

"When did you make sauerkraut for Greeley?"

"I—I don't know," she said crossly, as if Wilma was being very rude with her questions.

"When did you and Dora and Ralph argue?" Wilma persisted.

But Mavity turned over, jerking the blankets higher and nearly dislodging the IV, and soon she dropped into sleep. They sat in a tight little group waiting for her to wake.

When she did wake, she jerked up suddenly, trying

to sit up. "Caulking," she told Wilma. "Caulking for the shower. Did I buy the caulking? Pearl Ann is waiting for it."

Wilma straightened the bedding and smoothed the sheet. "Pearl Ann sent you to buy caulking? When was this?"

But already she had forgotten. Again she scowled at Wilma, puzzled and disoriented, not remembering anything in its proper order. Perhaps not remembering, at all, Winthrop Jergen's ugly death?

27

IF WILMA GETZ hadn't spent thirty years working with federal criminals, Max Harper would not have placed Mavity Flowers in her custody. Two days after Mavity entered Salinas Medical, she was released to Wilma's care. Wilma drove her home, tucked her up in her own bed and moved a cot into the room for herself. Her official duties, besides helping Mavity, were a perfect excuse to evict Bernine Sage from the guest room, to make room for the twenty-four-hour police guard that Max Harper had assigned. The county attorney agreed that Mavity's care by an old friend might ease her fears and help her remember the circumstances of Winthrop Jergen's death; the case was growing in breadth as law enforcement agencies began to uncover links between Jergen/Cumming, Troy Hoke, and several unsolved crimes in Tennessee and Alabama.

No one knew how much of Mavity's memory loss was due to the cerebral contusion and how much resulted from the shock of what she had witnessed. Under Wilma's gentle questioning, she was beginning to recall more details, to put together the scattered scenes.

But Dulcie's information about Troy Hoke alias Pearl Ann Jamison, which Dulcie passed on to Max Harper during an early-morning phone call, had been—so far as Dulcie and Joe could surmise—totally ignored. Harper felt certain that Troy Hoke had come here to Molena Point to find Warren Cumming; he'd told Clyde that much. So why did he ignore their important and dearly gathered information that Pearl Ann *was* Troy Hoke?

Mavity could remember returning from the hardware store with Pearl Ann's caulking. She could remember crossing the patio and hearing angry shouts from Jergen's apartment. "Two men shouting, and thuds," she had told Wilma. "Then seems like I was at the top of the stairs standing in the open door." But always, at this point, she went silent. "I don't remember any more. I can't remember."

"Did you see the other man?" Wilma would ask. "Did you know him?"

"I can't remember. When I think about it I feel scared and sort of sick."

Now Wilma glanced out toward the living room where the police guard sat reading the paper. "You were standing in the doorway," she said gently, "and the two men were shouting. And then . . . ?"

"A red neon sign, that's what I remember next. Red light shining in my face. It was night. I could hear people talking and cars passing."

"And nothing in between?"

"No. Nothing."

"The red neon—you were walking somewhere?"

"I was in my car. The lights—the lights hurt. I had to close my eyes."

"In your own car?"

"In the back, with the mops and buckets." Mavity looked at her, puzzled, her short gray hair a tangle of kinks, her face drawn into lines of bewilderment. "Why would I be in the back of my own car? I was lying on my extra pair of work shoes. The lights hurt my eyes. Then someone pulling me, dragging me. It was dark. Then a real bright light, and a nurse. I'm in that hospital bed, and my head hurting so bad. I couldn't hear nothing but the pounding in my head."

Wilma was careful not to prompt Mavity. She wanted her to remember the alley where the Salinas Police had found her and to remember wrecking her car, without being led by her suggestions.

"Greeley . . ." Mavity said, "I have to get home— Greeley's waiting. Dora and Ralph . . . They'll be worried. They won't know where I am. I left the meat thawing on the sink, and that cat will . . ."

"The meat's all right—they put the meat away. And they're not worried, they know where you are," Wilma lied. But maybe Dora and Ralph did know, from wherever they were beyond the pale. Who was she to say?

Mavity dozed again, her hand relaxed across Dulcie's shoulder where the cat lay curled on the quilt against her. But then in sleep Mavity's hand went rigid and she woke startled. "I have to get up. They won't know . . ."

"It's all right, Mavity," Wilma reassured her. "Everything's taken care of. Greeley will be along later."

"But Dora and . . ."

Suddenly Mavity stopped speaking.

Her eyes widened. She raised up in bed, staring at Wilma, then her face crumpled. "They're dead," she whispered. She looked terrified. "Dora and Ralph are dead."

Wilma sat down on the bed beside her, put her arm around Mavity. They sat quietly until Mavity said, "Greeley—I need Greeley." She looked nakedly at Wilma. "Is he all right?"

"Greeley's just fine, I promise." *Rolling drunk*, Wilma thought. *But he's all in one piece*.

"I need him." Mavity looked at her helplessly. "How can I ever tell him? Tell him that Dora's gone?"

"He'll be here soon. You won't need to tell him. Greeley knows about Dora. He knows about Dora and Ralph, and he's taking it very well. He'll be along soon, to be with you."

The police had picked Greeley up at the Davidson Building and had held him until he sobered up enough for questioning regarding Dora and Ralph's deaths. When they released him, Max Harper said, he went directly back to the Davidson Building—to the companionship of several more cases of rum. Wilma had no intention of bringing him to see Mavity until he was sober and had cleaned himself up. Dulcie said he smelled like a drunk possum, and Harper said much the same.

The police now knew that Dora and Ralph had died of a drug overdose. The forensics report made it clear that, in Harper's words, Dora and Ralph Sleuder were loaded with enough morphine to put down a pair of cart horses.

"The coroner thinks they ingested the drug during dinner. They'd had a big meal, steak, potatoes, salad with French dressing, chocolate pie and coffee," Max had told them. "We don't know yet who they had dinner with, or where. That was the night after they met for dinner with Bernine."

Harper had learned about the dinner at Pander's from his mysterious informant during the same phone call in which she identified Pearl Ann as Troy Hoke.

Checking with Pander's, Harper had learned that the threesome arrived at seven-thirty and were seated at a table on the terrace. Their waiter remembered what each of the three guests had ordered for dinner, what they had had to drink, what time they departed, and that Bernine paid the bill by credit card.

The doctors had said Mavity might be bad-tempered until her contusion healed, and she was. The four-inch gash in the back of her head was not the result of the car accident; she had been hit on the head from behind several hours before her car was wrecked—very likely she had been knocked out, loaded into the back-seat of the VW, driven to Salinas, and her car deliberately wrecked against the lamppost where it was found. Harper had no intention of allowing Mavity to sustain another attack. Besides the twenty-four-hour guard, patrol units were all over the area.

Now, entering Wilma's pastel bedroom, Max Harper's uniform and solemn, leathery face contrasted in an interesting way with the feminine room, with the flowered chintz and white wicker furniture, putting Wilma in mind of a weathered soldier wandering among the petunias. As she poured coffee for him from the tray on Mavity's bed table, Mavity sat against the pillows, pleased at being fussed over, at being the center of attention. The facts she gave Max, as he questioned her, were the same she had given Wilma. Slowly the jig-saw pieces of her memory were slipping into place.

On the bed beside Mavity, Dulcie lay pretending to sleep as she fitted together Mavity's scenario with what she and Joe already knew.

Winthrop Jergen had left his apartment at about two, telling Mavity and Pearl Ann that he had an appointment up the coast. Charlie arrived at three and left again a few minutes later, headed for the Blackburn house. Pearl Ann was already upstairs in his rooms repairing the towel rack. As Charlie left, Mavity carried her cleaning things up to his apartment.

"When I came in, Pearl Ann said she was nearly out of shower caulking—that good, plastic kind that she likes. She said if I'd go down to the village for some, she'd start on the refrigerator for me, put the ice trays and shelves in a dishpan to soak. She don't mind working up there when Mr. Jergen's not home . . ." Mavity jerked her hand, sloshing coffee on the white sheet.

Grabbing a handful of tissues, she tried to mop up the spill. "I can't get used to it—that he's dead. His throat—the blood . . ."

Wilma took Mavity's cup and wiped the sheets. She handed her more tissues, wiped off the cup, and poured fresh coffee for her. Dulcie rose up from her nest of blankets to rub against Mavity's cheek. Mavity put her arm around the little cat and drew her close.

"Driving back up from the village, I passed Mr. Jergen's car parked three blocks from the apartments, and I thought that was strange. He'd said he was going up the coast. Oh, it was his car, I'd know that Mercedes anywhere, with its two antennas and those fancy hubcaps.

"Well, I thought he must have met his client there and taken their car. Though that did seem odd, that he would park three blocks away. Or maybe he'd had car trouble. I never heard of a Mercedes having car trouble, but I guess they can.

"I parked and hurried in through the patio because Pearl Ann would be waiting for the caulking. Mr. Jergen's windows were open, and I heard him and another man shouting at each other, real angry. It was a strange voice but—something about it seemed familiar.

"And then I heard banging and thuds like furniture being knocked over, and then a gasp. Then silence.

"I ran up the stairs, but I was scared. I was ready to run down again. I listened but I couldn't hear nothing, so I pushed open the door."

She stared into her coffee cup as if seeing a replay of Jergen's murder. When she looked up at Harper, her voice was hardly a whisper.

"He was on the floor. Lying on the floor beside his desk. The blood . . . And Pearl Ann—Pearl Ann kneeling over him stabbing and stabbing . . . Swinging her arm and stabbing into his throat with that terrible ice tray thing."

Mavity sat hugging herself. "I backed away real quiet, out the door. Pulled it closed, praying she didn't hear me, that she hadn't seen me.

"I didn't know where the other man was. I kept looking around for him. I felt weak as jelly. I took off my shoes so she wouldn't hear me going down the steps. I ran down in my socks, to my car. I never stopped for nothing. Kept seeing Pearl Ann kneeling over him stabbing and stabbing . . .

"I dug my keys out of my purse. I was trying to jam the key in the door . . ."

She looked up at Harper. "That's all I remember. Then the red neon sign at night glaring in my eyes, and I was in the backseat lying on my shoes, my face against a dirty shoe. There was a McDonald's wrapper on the floor—it smelled of mustard.

"And then being dragged or something, that's all fuzzy and dark. Then I was in bed in that hospital and you were there, Captain Harper, sitting slumped in the chair." Mavity pulled the quilt up, careful not to disturb Dulcie.

"When you first entered the apartment," Harper said, "before you went out again for the caulking, do you remember anything strange, at that time, anything out of order in the room?"

"No. The room was neat, the way he keeps it. His desk was clean and neat, nothing on it except a few files lying in a neat pile on the blotter. Well, I guess you could say that was unusual. Mr. Jergen always put everything away, always left his desk with nothing but the blotter and the pens, the regular desk things, no papers."

She frowned. "There's one other thing. I'd forgot. I'm sure his computer was off when I first came in. But when I got back with the caulking and saw—saw . . . Pearl Ann . . . I think the computer was on."

Mavity hugged herself. "He shouldn't have been there at all. He had an appointment up the coast. Maybe he forgot to do something at the computer. Maybe he came back to do that."

She looked hard at Harper. "Why did she kill him? Why did this happen?"

"Besides the files and the computer," Harper said, "was there anything else out of order?"

"Not that I noticed. Seemed the same as always, neat, everything in order. Pearl Ann had started working in the bathroom, but she stopped to get the refrigerator started. The kitchen was neat and clean, the way he always left it."

Harper made some notes and rose. There was a tight, hard look about him. Wilma walked him to the door, where he paused, gave her a hug. "You look tired. She'll get through this, Wilma. If we can pick up Hoke, Mavity should be clear, I think we'll have enough to take him to the grand jury."

"And if you don't find Hoke?"

"Let's wait to see what happens."

Wilma leaned against him, very thankful for Max Harper. She would hate to face this, to try to help Mavity, without Max there to go the extra mile.

He stood looking down at her. "I didn't tell you this. Some of the blood on Mavity's white uniform was Jergen's."

She only looked at him, frightened again suddenly.

"The report came in this morning. But from the way the blood was smeared, the lab thinks it was wiped on, possibly by the murder weapon."

"It wasn't spattered or pooled on."

"Exactly. And we're not sure, yet, that the ice tray divider *was* the murder weapon."

He didn't move out the open door, just kept looking at her. "It would strengthen our case considerably, if I knew who our informant was. If I knew who the woman was, who tipped us about Hoke. It might make the case, if she were to testify against Hoke."

"I'm sure it would," Wilma said. "Maybe she'll come forward. Let's hope so." She hated this, hated lying to him.

"She never has. She's helped us on three cases but has never identified herself, never offered to testify." He continued to watch her. "Same voice, same woman."

Wilma widened her eyes. "You think it's me, Max? Are you saying I'm your mysterious informant?"

"No," Harper said. "I don't think that." He looked at Wilma for a long time, then turned away, heading for his car. Wilma moved to the window, watching the patrol unit slide away into the village, thinking what a tangled web had drawn them all in—and, for Harper, what a cat's cradle of leads and unanswerable questions.

28

G REELEY URZEY'S sour, boozy smell
filled Wilma's car thicker than steam in a sauna. Despite
the fact that she drove with all the windows down, the
stink of secondhand rum and stale sweat made her want
to boot the old man out and let him walk to her house—
except, of course, he wouldn't. He'd head back for that
hovel among his cases of 90 proof.

She *could* have stopped by Mavity's cottage and
insisted that he take a bath and change his reeking
clothes, but she hadn't wanted to take the time. Mavity
was so anxious to see him; Wilma hadn't even waited, as
she'd promised herself, for the old man to sober up.

But even as rum-sodden as Greeley was, he seemed
genuinely worried about Mavity. He sat leaning forward, staring hard through the windshield as if to hurry
the car faster—and clutching the black cat in his lap.

She had to smile at the way he'd slipped the cat
in. After the police officer let her into the Davidson
Building and saw her safely downstairs again with
Greeley in tow, she'd waited alone in the dirty hall for

Greeley to go back upstairs and fetch his jacket. She didn't think he'd run out on her—there was no other entry, just the second floor windows. She'd watched, amused, when he returned clutching not only the jacket but the black cat nestled down in the wadded-up leather as if the animal might not be noticed.

Drunk and argumentative, he'd insisted on bringing the beast despite the fact, as she'd pointed out, that Mavity disliked Azrael, and that it was Mavity's comfort they were concerned about here.

Now as she drove across the village, the cat sat possessively on Greeley's lap, a huge black presence which, unlike most cats, made no move to leap out the four open windows. "He'll do as I tell him," Greeley had promised drunkenly, "or he'll know what for."

Well, maybe the cat wasn't as bad as Mavity claimed. Certainly it was a handsome animal; admiring him, Wilma reached gently to stroke his broad black head—and drew her hand back at the blaze of rage that flamed in his slitted orange eyes.

So much for making friends. The animal was as unsocialized as its master.

The cat watched her narrowly as she parked in her drive and killed the engine, its gaze strangely calculating—as eerie as Poe's "The Black Cat" with its chilling stare. *The figure of a gigantic cat . . . I could not rid myself of the phantasm of the cat . . . a large and beautiful animal, entirely black, and sagacious to an astonishing degree . . .*

As she herded Greeley toward her kitchen door, escorting the drunken, smelly old man into her clean house, she felt like she was bringing home a parolee just released from the drunk tank—except that Greeley smelled worse. The instant she opened the door, the cat leaped inside, brushing boldly past their legs with none of the wariness most cats exhibited upon entering unfamiliar rooms. Immediately he scented Dulcie's cat door and flew at it, sniffing and growling, and before she could stop him he turned his backside and drenched the little door with his testosterone-heavy stink, applying liberally the mark of male dominance and possession.

Shouting, she slapped at him with her purse—and jerked her hand away as he sprang at her, his swift claws raking her arm, leaving long red welts oozing drops of blood.

"You make that cat behave, Greeley. Or you'll put it outside."

Greeley shrugged and offered a helpless grin. Wilma found some peroxide in the emergency cupboard, poured some on a paper towel, and scrubbed the wounds, thinking of rare tropical infections and blood parasites. Snatching a spray bottle from the sink, she poured ammonia into it, to mix with the water. "He claws me again or sprays again, Greeley, he gets a shot of this in the face. He won't like it."

The cat glared. Greeley looked back grinning, amused that she would threaten his tomcat. Giggling, he headed for the dining room, stumbling unsteadily past her.

Before the cat could leap after him, Wilma slid through the door and slammed it in the beast's face.

Making sure the latch clicked, that the door was securely shut, she guided Greeley down the hall toward her bedroom. Ushering him in, she wondered if his boozy, sweaty smell would cling in the room forever. Down the hall behind her, she heard the kitchen door click open.

The cat came swaggering out of the kitchen, giving her a stare as sharp as a stabbing knife and pushed past her into the bedroom.

Mavity was asleep. Greeley leaned over his sister and delivered a peckish kiss, surely scratching stubble across her soft skin. Mavity woke, stared up at him vaguely, and drew away, grimacing at his smell.

Unperturbed, Greeley sat down on the bed beside her, taking her hands in his with a gentleness that surprised Wilma.

"Dora's gone," Greeley slurred. "My little girl's gone. And Ralph gone, and that man you set such store by." Glancing to where the cat was sniffing around the dresser, Greeley whispered, "Death sucked them in. Sucked them all in. Death—death before the moon is full." Strange words for the drunken little man. Leaning down, he put his arms around Mavity, holding her close.

The cat watched, seeming almost amused. And as brother and sister comforted each other, the beast began to prowl, nosing into every inch of the bedroom, turning occasionally to observe Wilma, his huge topaz eyes as evil, she thought, as twin glimpses into hell.

Annoyed at her own fear, she went to make some coffee.

But, hurrying down the hall, she could feel the tomcat watching her. And when she glanced back, its eyes on her glowed so intently she turned away, shaken.

What was this beast?

Dulcie hadn't told her the nature of this animal.

Fixing a tray with coffee and sugar and cream and some pound cake, she returned quickly. The cat was not in sight. She set the tray on the night table and checked under the dresser and bed, then went to search the house. She didn't like to think of that creature alone with Dulcie.

She didn't find the animal. When she returned to the bedroom, Greeley was crying drunkenly, the tears rolling down his stubbled cheeks.

". . . feeding those chickens when she was only a little girl, and helping her mama to plant the garden—

my little girl . . . And that old goose used to chase her! Oh, how she would run," Greeley blubbered. "I killed that goose, killed it . . . But now—I couldn't kill whoever hurt her, couldn't save my little girl. So cold—so cold there in all them lilies . . ."

As Greeley doubled over, weeping, the black cat reappeared and leaped onto the bed. Mavity paled and shrank away from it, looked as if she'd like to hit it. Wilma watched, shocked, as it began to stalk Mavity— and thought of the times Mavity had complained about the beast's dirty habits. Surely, there was no love between them. But now the animal looked dangerous. As he crouched to leap, Wilma grabbed him, tossed him to the floor. The black cat landed heavily and jumped at once to the foot of the bed where it began pawing Greeley's jacket that lay crumpled on the blanket.

Clawing at the wrinkled leather, he slid his paw into a pocket, and with a quick twist, dragged out a black-feathered carcass. Taking this in his mouth, his ears back, his head low, he began to stalk Mavity. She jerked away, gasping, as Wilma snatched the blood-streaked bird.

But it wasn't a bird. The thing was hard under her fingers, not soft and limp like a dead bird. She turned it over, looking.

It was a small wooden man, the black feathers wrapped around him like a cloak and tied with red cord. His face was painted with blood red lines like a primitive warrior. His hair felt like real human hair, the side locks stiff with dried red mud, as if he were made up for some primitive ritual.

"Voodoo doll," Mavity whispered, staring at the six-inch man then at Greeley. "You showed me those, in that shop. Where did you get that? Why would you bring that horrible thing here?"

"Only a plaything," Greeley said, patting Mavity's hand. "*I* didn't bring it. The cat—the cat likes a plaything. The cat found it . . ." He reached up to take the carving from Wilma.

She held it away. "Why did you bring this?"

"*I* didn't bring it! The cat brought it. Damn cat—always dragging in something."

"The *cat* put it in your pocket?"

Greeley shrugged. "He digs in my pockets." He grinned sheepishly. "He likes that Latin American shop. I expect it smells like home."

"I'll take it in the kitchen."

The black cat hadn't taken his eyes from the doll. But now he turned from it, fixed his gaze on Mavity, and crept up the bed again, toward her.

"Get him away!"

Grabbing the cat, Wilma drew back a bloodied hand. "Greeley, get the beast out of here."

"Get down!" Greeley scolded. "Get off the bed!" The cat hissed at him but leaped to the floor.

"And stay off," Greeley added ineffectually.

Wilma turned away, carrying the doll, but the tomcat leaped, grabbing for its grisly toy. She swung it at the cat's head until the beast ran. Mavity hadn't exaggerated—the creature gave her more than chills. When she turned to look back, the cat was not behind her and the hall was empty.

She laid the carving on the kitchen table. More than its ugliness bothered her. It seemed to hold around itself a deep oppression. As she stood studying the doll she glimpsed a shadow behind her, slipping along the floor.

She spun as the cat crouched to leap—whether at her or to snatch the doll she'd never know: At the same instant, an explosion of tabby fur hit him, knocking him sideways.

Dulcie was all over him, slashing and clawing. The black cat fought violently in a tangle of raking claws— but he fought only briefly before breaking away, and careened out through Dulcie's cat door, the empty door slapping behind him.

As quick as that, he was gone. Dulcie leaped to the table, looking twice her normal size, and began to lick blood from her claws. Gently Wilma stroked her.

"What a nasty beast. Are you hurt? Where did he hurt you?"

Dulcie spit out a mouthful of fur. "I'm fine. A few scratches. They'll clean right up." Her gaze fixed on the black-feathered doll. "Voodoo," she hissed. "Did Greeley bring this? That old, disgusting drunk . . . Or did Azrael carry it here?" She glared at Wilma, laying back her ears. "Why did you let Greeley bring that cat here—and with *this*?"

"I didn't know. I was trying to keep Greeley happy. I didn't want him making a scene, so I let him bring the cat. I didn't see this thing. And the cat seemed tame enough, seemed just an ordinary cat."

She looked hard at Dulcie. "But he isn't, is he?"

Dulcie studied Wilma a long time. "No," she said softly, "he's no ordinary cat. But he's not like us, either. He's not like Joe Grey—he's horrid." With an angry swipe, she knocked the feathered man to the floor.

"Azrael believes in these voodoo things," she said, hissing. "He believes in dark magic—he said it was a fine way to get back at those who mistreat you.

"I expect he wanted," Dulcie said softly, "to make Mavity sicker—just because Mavity doesn't like him, because she complained about his manners."

She fixed her green gaze on Wilma. "Why else would he bring this terrible idol, if not to torment Mavity and frighten her—or try some wild spell on her? Can that stuff work?" she said, shivering, staring down at the black doll lying like a hunk of tar on the blue linoleum. Wilma snatched up the feathered figure and hurried down the hall. Following, Dulcie watched Wilma shove the ugly little idol in Greeley's face.

"What is this about, Greeley? What did you mean to do?"

"It's only a native doll," Greeley said, laughing. "Indian kid's playtoy. The cat brought it."

"Voodoo doll," Wilma replied.

"*Voodoo?*" He looked at her as if she wasn't bright and choked out a rum-laden laugh. "Child's toy. That Ms. Sue Marble, she's got all kinds of stuff—them Guatamala blankets, all that Panama clutter. Nothing of any use, all that artsy stuff. Even them little gold people aren't worth nothing—not the real thing, not the real gold. Gold birds. Gold lizards. Sue showed me." But suddenly his face colored and he looked embarrassed, his eyes shifting away.

"You must have gotten very friendly," Wilma said, amused, forgetting her anger.

"That nice little woman," Greeley said defensively, "wouldn't have nothing costly." He was blushing; he wouldn't look at her. She had to smile at his discomfiture, at his strange embarrassment.

Was he romancing Sue Marble? But why embarrassment? His distress puzzled her, made her uneasy.

Romancing Sue for her money?

Oh, that would be too bad.

Dropping the doll in the wastebasket, she carried the basket out to the kitchen to empty it with the trash, all the time pondering over Greeley—and keeping her ear cocked for the thump of Dulcie's cat door, for the stealthy return of Greeley's nasty little friend.

29

"WALKING BACK the cat," Max Harper told Charlie as he popped open a can of beer, "means to lay out the evidence and work backward—reconstruct the crime." The five friends sat around a wrought-iron table in the landscaped patio of the freshly painted apartment building. Moonlight brightened the flower beds, which were softly lit by indirect lamps hidden behind the tall banks of Nile lilies that Wilma had planted as background for lower masses of textured ground cover. The brick paving had been pressure-washed, and it gleamed dull and rich, lending to the patio garden a quiet elegance. The new wrought-iron furniture in a heavy ivy pattern—umbrella table, lounge chairs, and chaises—completed the sense of comfort. Harper looked curiously at Charlie. "Where did you hear that phrase, to walk back the cat?"

"I'm not sure. Something I read, I suppose."

Wilma said, "Isn't that a CIA term?"

"I read that in a romance-mystery," Mavity offered. "That's the way it was used, when the CIA was wrapping up a case." The little woman seemed completely recovered. Her memory had returned fully—she had recalled clearly the events surrounding Winthrop Jergen's murder and, once she came to grips with the truth about Jergen, she had been stoic and sensible, her idolization of the financier had turned to anger but then to a quiet resolve. Now she had put all her faith in Max Harper, to recover her savings.

But the fact that Dora and Ralph had come to Molena Point not only to trap Cumming but to keep Mavity from losing her money had hurt Mavity deeply—that Dora had died trying to help her.

Mavity was dressed, tonight, not in her usual worn white uniform but in a new, teal blue pants suit, a bargain that Wilma had found for her. The color became her, and the change of wardrobe, along with her returned health, seemed perhaps the mark of a new beginning.

Of the little group, only Max Harper, stretching out his long, Levi-clad legs and sipping his beer, seemed aware of Charlie's unease. He watched the young woman with interest. She was strung tight, seemed unable to keep her bony hands still, sat smoothing and smoothing her cotton skirt. As he considered the possible cause of her distress, and as he went over in his mind the last details of the Sleuder and Jergen case, while paying attention to the conversation around him, he was aware, as well, of the two cats crouched on the brick paving near the table—uncomfortably aware.

The two animals seemed totally preoccupied with eating fish and chips from a paper plate, yet they were so alert, ears following every voice, the tips of their tails twitching and pausing as if they were attending closely to every word. When he'd mentioned "walk back the cat," both cats' ears had swiveled toward him, and Dulcie's tail had jerked once, violently, before she stilled it.

He knew his preoccupation with the cats was paranoid—it was these crazy ideas about cats that made him question his own mental condition. Of course the two animals had simply responded to the word *cat*, they were familiar with the word from hearing it in relation to their own comfort. *Time to feed the cat. Have to let the cat out.* A simple Pavlovian reaction common to all animals.

Yet he watched them intently.

His gut feeling was that their quick attention was far more than conditioned response.

The cats didn't glance up at him. They seemed totally unaware of his intense scrutiny, as unheeding as any beast.

Except that beasts were not unheeding.

A dog or horse, if you stared at him, would generally look back at you. To stare at an animal was to threaten, and so of course it would look back. One of the rules in dealing with a vicious dog was never to stare at him. And cats hated to be watched. Certainly, with the cats' wide peripheral vision, these two were perfectly aware of his interest—yet they never glanced his way. Seemed deliberately to ignore him.

No one at the table noticed his preoccupation. Charlie and Clyde, Wilma and Mavity were deep into rehashing the reception they had just left.

They had come up directly from the library party, to enjoy a take-out supper in the newly completed patio and to continue the celebration—an affair that had left Harper irritated yet greatly amused. A reception for a cat. A bash in honor of Wilma's library cat. That had to be a first—in Molena Point, and maybe for any public library.

The party, besides honoring Dulcie, had quietly celebrated as well the departure of Freda Brackett. The ex–head librarian had left Molena Point two days earlier, headed for L.A. and a higher paying position in a library which, presumably, would never tolerate a resident cat. A library, Harper thought, that certainly didn't embody the wit or originality—or enthusiasm— to be found in their own village institution.

He didn't much care for cats. But Molena Point's impassioned rally to save Dulcie's position—gaining the wholehearted support of almost the entire village—had been contagious even to a hard-assed old cop.

Dulcie ate her fish and chips slowly, half of her attention uncomfortably aware of Harper's scrutiny, the other half lost in the wonders of her reception. She had held court on a library reading table where she had secretly spent so many happy hours, had sat atop the table like royalty on a peach-toned silk cushion given to her by the Aronson Gallery. And as she was fawned over—as Joe admired her from atop the book stacks—Danny McCoy from the Molena Point *Gazette* had taken dozens of pictures: Dulcie with her guests, Dulcie with members of the city council and with the mayor, with all her good friends.

Danny had brought the local TV camera crew, too, so that highlights of the event would appear on the eleven o'clock news. Young Dillon Thurwell had cut the cake, which George Jolly himself had baked and decorated with a dark tabby cat standing over an open book, a rendering far more meaningful than Mr. Jolly or most of those present would ever imagine. Perhaps best of all, Charlie had donated a portrait of her to hang in the library's main reading room, above a scrapbook that would contain all forty signed petitions and any forth-coming press clippings.

Not even the famous Morris, who must have press people available at the twitch of a whisker, could have been more honored. She felt as pampered as an Egyptian cat-priestess presiding over the temples of Ur—she was filled to her ears with well-being and goodwill, so happy she could not stop purring.

Not only had the party turned her dizzy with pleasure, not only was Freda Brackett forever departed from Molena Point, but Troy Hoke was in jail for Jergen's murder and for the attempted murder of Mavity. And soon, if Max Harper was successful, Mavity would have her stolen money.

Life, Dulcie thought, was good.

Licking her whiskers, she listened with interest as Max Harper walked back the cat, lining up the events that had put Hoke behind bars awaiting trial for the murder of Warren Cumming.

Hoke had not been indicted for the murder of Dora and Ralph Sleuder. That crime, Harper speculated (and the cats agreed), would turn out to have been committed by Cumming himself—but Warren Cumming alias Winthrop Jergen need no longer worry about earthly punishment. If he was to face atonement, it would be meted out by a far more vigorous authority than the local courts.

A plastic bag containing morphine had been found in Jergen's apartment, taped inside the computer monitor, affixed to the plastic case.

"It's possible," Harper said, "that Hoke killed the Sleuders, and taped the drug there after he killed Jergen, to tie the Sleuders' murder to him. But so far we have no evidence of that, no prints, no trace of Hoke on the bag or inside the computer."

"But what about Bernine?" Charlie said. "Bernine had dinner with Dora and Ralph."

"That was the night before," Harper reminded her. "The night Dora and Ralph received the lethal dose, they had dinner at Lupe's Steaks, down on Shoreline—one of the private booths. Not likely they would know about those on their own. And despite Jergen's entry through the back door . . ." Harper laughed. ". . . wearing that pitiful football blazer and cap, one of the waiters knew him."

Harper shook his head. "The man might have been creative with the numbers, but he didn't know much about disguise.

"And Bernine Sage has an excellent alibi for the night of the Sleuders' deaths. She was out with a member of the city council. She was," he said, winking at Wilma, "trying to work a deal to destroy the petitions the committee had collected for Dulcie."

"The library cat petitions?" Wilma laughed. "That was pretty silly. Didn't she know we'd have done them over again?"

In the shadows, the cats smiled, but at once they shuttered their eyes again, as if dozing.

Their private opinion was that though Bernine had an alibi for the night the Sleuders were killed, she had been instrumental in their deaths. If she had not pumped the Sleuders for information, then reported to Jergen that the couple meant to blow the whistle on him, Jergen/Cumming would likely not have bothered to kill them.

"I can't believe," Charlie said, "that I worked with Pearl Ann for three months and didn't guess she was a man. That makes me feel really stupid."

"None of us guessed," Clyde said. "Hoke put together a good act. I swear he walked like a woman—

guys notice that stuff. And that soft voice—really sexy."

They all stared at him. Clyde shrugged. Charlie patted his hand.

"A guy in drag," Harper said, "slight of build, thin arms, slim hands—a skilled forger and a top-flight computer hacker."

Hoke, dressed as Pearl Ann, had been picked up in Seattle carrying eight hundred thousand dollars in cash, sewn into the lining of his powder blue skirt and blazer—money he had transferred from Jergen's accounts to his own accounts in two dozen different names in nine San Francisco banks. It had taken him some time to draw out the money in various forms— cash, bank drafts, cashier's checks, which he laundered as he traveled from San Francisco to Seattle, where he was picked up. The police had found no witness that Pearl Ann had boarded the San Francisco bus in Molena Point. But they located the car Hoke had rented in Salinas, under the name of William Skeel, after deliberately wrecking Mavity's VW and dumping Mavity in the alley beside the pawnshop.

"It looks," Harper said, "as if Jergen had come to suspect Pearl Ann's identity. As if, the day he died, he had set Hoke up.

"He told everyone he was going up the coast, then doubled back hoping to catch Hoke red-handed copying his files. He parked a few blocks away and slipped into the apartment while Hoke/Pearl Ann was working. The hard files he'd left on his desk were bait—three files of accounts newly opened, with large deposits. All with bogus addresses and names that, so far, we've not been able to trace."

Harper sipped his beer. "Hoke comes up to do the repairs, opens those hard copy files with three new accounts, all with large sums deposited, and he can't wait to get into the computer. Sends Mavity on an errand, uses Jergen's code, intending to get the new deposit numbers and transfer the money. We're guessing that he was about ready to skip, perhaps another few days and he meant to pull out for good.

"But then Jergen walks in on him at the computer. They fight, Hoke stabs him with a screwdriver . . ." Harper looked around at his audience. "Yes, we found the real murder weapon," he said gruffly. "Jergen was near death when Hoke stabbed him with the ice tray divider—maybe to lay suspicion on Mavity, to confuse forensics. Or maybe out of rage, simply to tear at Jergen. This is all conjecture, now, but it's how I piece it together.

"He hears a noise, realizes Mavity has returned, maybe hears her running down the stairs. Goes after her, snatches up one of those loose bricks that were lying along the edge of the patio." He glanced at Mavity. "And he bops you, Mavity, as you're trying to get in the car.

"After he loads you in the backseat, he realizes he has the bloody screwdriver. Maybe he'd shoved it in his pocket. He buries it down the hill, with the brick.

"He may have moved the VW then, to get it out of sight. He cleans up and changes clothes, then heads out. Takes his bloody jumpsuit and shoes with him— all we found in the duffle he left was a clean, unused jumpsuit. We may never find the bloody clothes. They're probably in the bottom of some Dumpster or already dozed into a landfill—the Salinas PD checked the Dumpsters in that whole area around where Hoke wrecked Mavity's car.

"It's still dark when he dumps Mavity into the alley by her car and leaves her. He walks to the nearest car rental office, waits until eight when it opens. Gets a car and heads north. He's left his own car in the storage garage a block from the Davidson Building where he kept it—registered in one of his other names.

"We'd like to find the bloody clothes, but even without them we have plenty to take him to court. The money trail alone is a beauty."

The FBI computer expert who had come down from San Francisco to trace Cumming's computer transactions had followed Hoke's transfers from Jergen's accounts, using the code words supplied by Harper's anonymous informer. The Bureau had put out inter-office descriptions of Hoke and of Pearl Ann. Two Bureau agents picked him up at the Seattle airport, in his blue skirt and blazer, when he turned in an Avis rental in the name of Patsy Arlie. He was wearing a curly auburn wig.

"But the strangest part," Harper continued, watching the little group, "is my finding the screwdriver the way I did, the day after Jergen was killed."

He had discovered it the next morning when he came down the stairs from Jergen's apartment after meeting with the Bureau agent. He had been late getting back from Salinas Medical that morning; the agent, using a key supplied by Clyde, was already at work at Jergen's computer. The weapon was not on the steps when he went up to the apartment, nor did Harper see it when he arrived.

But when they came down, it was lying in plain sight on the steps, flecked with dirt and grass seed.

"When we started looking for where it might have been buried—worked down the hill where the grass was bent and broken and found the loose dirt—and dug there, we found the brick, too. The dirt and grass matched the debris on the screwdriver, and of course the traces of blood on it were Jergen's.

"It had been wiped hastily, but there were two partial prints, both Hoke's. Whoever found the weapon," Harper said, "saved the court considerable time and money, and certainly helped to strengthen our case."

He knew he should be fully satisfied with the case against Hoke—they had plenty to hang the man—but this business of the screwdriver, of evidence turning up in that peculiar way, gave him heartburn. This was getting to be a pattern, and one he didn't live with easily.

No cop liked this mysterious stuff, even when the evidence led to a conviction. Unexplainable scenarios were for artists, for fiction writers, for those who dealt in flights of fancy. Not for law enforcement who wanted only hard facts.

The cats, having finished their fish and chips, lay stretched out on the bricks sleepily licking their paws, staring past Harper but watching with their wide vision Harper's frequent glances in their direction. Dulcie, washing diligently, carefully hid her amused smile. Joe, rolling over away from the police captain, twitched his whiskers in a silent cat laugh.

The morning after the murder, just moments after Wilma deposited an angry Dulcie at Clyde's house and Wilma and Clyde and Charlie headed for Salinas Medical, Joe and Dulcie had bolted out his cat door and double-timed up the hills to the apartments, where they settled down to wait for the FBI investigator. How often did one have a chance to observe a Bureau specialist at work?

Crouching in Jergen's kitchen, they had watched the thin Bureau agent deftly scrolling through Jergen's files using the code words *Cairo* and *Tiger* that Dulcie had given to Harper, tracing each money transaction that Hoke/Pearl Ann had hidden. Only when they heard the crackle of a police radio, and a car door slam, did they slip back down between the walls, trotting into the patio in time to see Harper going up the stairs.

Leaving the patio, wandering down the hill to hunt, they had caught Pearl Ann's jasmine scent and followed it with interest through the tall grass. The trail was fresh, maybe a few hours old, the grass still sharp-scented where it had been trampled.

Where they found the earth disturbed, Pearl Ann's scent was strong. Digging into the loose soil, they had pawed out the screwdriver, then the brick. The brick smelled of human blood. They recognized the screwdriver as Pearl Ann's, a long Phillips with a deep nick in the black plastic handle. Gripping the dirt-crusted handle carefully in his teeth, Joe had carried the weapon up the hill and halfway up the stairs, where he laid it on a step in plain sight. They figured, as thorough as Harper was, he'd search for where it had been buried and discover the brick, as well.

But as for the village burglaries committed by Greeley and Azrael, those crimes were another matter. Joe and Dulcie had given Harper no clue.

Maybe Greeley would confess and return the stolen money. If not, the cats still had plenty of time to nail him—Greeley and Mavity would be leaving early in the morning to take the bodies of Dora and Ralph home to Georgia. The funeral had been arranged through the Sleuders' pastor. Dora and Ralph had been active in their church and would be buried in the church plot they had purchased years before.

Mavity and Greeley would remain in Georgia long enough to sell the Sleuders' home and belongings, reserving whatever mementos they cared to keep. Whatever moneys of the Sleuders' might be recovered from Warren Cumming's hidden accounts would be divided between brother and sister. The moneys proven to be Mavity's would of course come to her, once the FBI accountants finished tracing each of Jergen's individual account transactions and Hoke's transfers.

The cats watched Charlie take the lid off a plastic cup of hot tea, handing it to Mavity. "Will Greeley be taking his cat with you on the plane? It seems . . ."

"Oh, no," Mavity said. "He doesn't need to take it. He'll come back with me when we're finished in Georgia—he can get the cat then. He's flying on one of them elderly coupons, so his fare's all the same even if he goes home through Molena Point. And a very nice lady, that Ms. Marble who has the South American shop, she's going to keep the cat. Why, she was thrilled. Seems she's very taken with the beast."

Dulcie and Joe exchanged a look.

"I didn't think," Charlie said, "that your brother knew anyone in the village."

"Greeley went in there because the cat kept going in, made itself right at home. They got to know each other, being as they've both lived in Latin America. It's nice Greeley has found a friend here. Well, she does keep those awful voodoo things . . ."

Mavity stirred sugar into her tea. "I'm sorry Greeley wouldn't come with us tonight. Said he just wanted to walk through the village, enjoy the shops one more time. I've never known Greeley to be so taken with a place."

The cats, imagining Greeley gazing casually into one of the village's exclusive shops while Azrael slipped down through its skylight, rose quickly and, feigning a stretch and a yawn, they beat it out of the patio and across the street, heading fast down the hill.

Watching them, Charlie rose, too, and slipped away.

Standing under the arch, she saw them disappear

down the slope, watched their invisible trail shivering the grass as they hurried unseen toward the village.

They had certainly left suddenly.

But they were cats. Cats were filled with sudden whims.

Except, she didn't think their hasty departure was any whim.

From somewhere below she heard faint voices. The girl's laugh sounded exactly like the female voice she'd heard the night she watched Joe and Dulcie on the rooftops.

She shook her head, annoyed at her wild imaginings. Molena Point was a small village, one was bound to hear familiar voices—probably from one of the houses below her.

But she felt chilled, light-headed.

Hugging herself to steady her shaken nerves, she was gripped by an insight that, until this moment, she would not have let herself consider.

An insane thought.

But she knew it wasn't insane.

A footstep scuffed behind her, and Clyde stepped out from the shadows. He put his arm around her, stood hugging her close, the two of them looking down the hills. After a moment, she turned in the moonlight to look squarely at him.

She wanted to say, *I've suspected for a long time.* She wanted to say, *I know about the cats. I didn't know how to think about such a thing.*

But what if she was wrong?

Leaning her head against his shoulder, she felt giddy, disconnected. She recalled the night she'd walked home from dinner and saw Joe and Dulcie racing across the roofs so beautiful and free—the night she heard those same voices.

And suddenly she began to laugh. She collapsed against Clyde laughing, tears streaming. What if she was right, what if it was true? She couldn't stop laughing, he had to shake her to make her stop. Holding her shoulders, he looked down at her intently. He said nothing.

After a while, as they stood gazing down the empty hill, he said, "Were you really jealous of Bernine?"

"Who told you that?"

"A friend." He took her face in his hands. "So foolish—Bernine Sage is all glitz. There's nothing there, nothing real. She's nothing like you. What's to be jealous of?" He kissed her, standing on the moonlit hill, and whispered against her neck, "My friend tells me I'm not romantic enough—that it takes more than a few car repairs to an old VW van to please a lady."

Charlie smiled and kissed him back. It was a long time later when she said, "Doesn't your friend know how to mind her own business?"

"Oh, meddling is her business. That's how she gets her kicks." He held her tight.

Down the hills, not as far away as Charlie and Clyde imagined, the cats stood rearing among the tall grass, looking up the hill and watching the couple's hugging silhouette, and they smiled. Humans—so simple. So predictable.

Then Joe dropped down to all fours. "So what will it be? We find Greeley and blow the whistle on those two thieves—and maybe open a real can of worms for Harper? Or we find them, try to talk them out of this one last burglary?"

"Or we let it go?" Dulcie offered. "Let this hand play without us?" She went silent, thinking of dark Azrael: Satan metamorphosed. Beast of evil.

Portender of death? Was he really that—really a voodoo cat? A bearer of dark, twisted fate?

"When we charged out of the patio just now," Joe said, "hot to nail Greeley—that was a paw-jerk reaction." He waited to see the effect of his words, his eyes huge and dark in the moonlight.

She said, "I don't think we can stop them. Why would Greeley listen to us? And if we call the station . . ."

If Greeley was arrested and went to jail, and Azrael stayed on with Sue Marble, they might never see the last of his criminal proclivity, of his cruel nature.

She studied the village rooftops, the moonlit mosaic of shops and chimneys and oaks, so rich and peaceful. And she thought of Azrael moving in with Ms. Marble and all her voodoo trappings, and she wondered. *Was* there, unknown to Sue, evil power among those idols? A wickedness that Azrael could manipulate?

Joe said, "Greeley's all that Mavity has. It would break her heart to see him arrested."

"Maybe they'll go back to the jungle," she said, "if we let them go. If we don't interfere. Maybe they'll go where they belong—back to the jungle's dark ways."

Joe considered this. "Maybe," he said, and twitched a whisker. "And good riddance to *el gato diablo*." He looked down at Dulcie, and winked. And where moonlight washed the tall grass, their silhouettes twined together: one silhouette, purring.

FOG LAY SO THICK IN HELLHAG CANYON that Joe Grey couldn't see his paws, could barely see the dead wood rat he carried dangling from his sharp teeth. Moving steeply down the wall of the ravine, the tomcat was aware of a boulder or willow scrub only when his whiskers touched something foreign, sending an electrifying jolt through his sleek gray body. The predawn fog was so dense that a human would have barged straight into those obstacles—one more example, Joe Grey thought smugly, of feline senses far keener than human, of the superiority of cat over man.

The fog-shrouded canyon was silent, too, save for the muted hushing of the sea farther down and the occasional whisper from high above of wet tires along the twisting two-lane, where some early-morning driver crept blindly. Joe had no idea why humans drove in this stuff; swift cars and fog were bad news. As he searched for a soft bit of ground on which to enjoy his breakfast, another car approached, moving way too fast toward the wicked double curve, sending a jolt of alarm stabbing through Joe.

The scream of tires filled the canyon.

The skidding car hit the cliff so hard, Joe felt the earth shake. He dropped the wood rat and leaped clear as the car rolled thundering over the edge, its lights exploding against the fog, its bulk falling straight at him, as big as a hunk of the cliff, a mass of hurtling metal that sent him streaking up the canyon wall. It hurtled past, dropping into the ravine exactly where he'd been crouching.

The car lay upside down beneath a dozen young oak trees broken off and fallen across its spinning wheels. The roof and those tons of metal had likely flattened his wood rat into a bloody pancake—so much for his nice warm breakfast.

Where the careening car had disturbed the fog, and the rising wind swirled the mist, he could make out the gigantic form easing deeper into the detritus of the canyon, the car's metal parts groaning like a dying beast, its death-stink not of escaping body fluids, but the reek of leaking gasoline.

This baby's going to explode, he thought as he prepared to run. *Going to blow sky-high, roast me among these boulders like a rabbit in a stone oven.*

But when, after a long wait, no explosion occurred, when the vehicle continued only to creak and moan, he crept warily down the cliff again to have a look.

Hunched beneath the wreck's vast, dark body— its ticking, grease-stinking, hot-breathed body—he looked up at the huge black wheels spinning above him and listened to the bits of glass raining down from the broken windows that were half hidden among the dry ferns, listened to the big metal carcass settle into its last sleep. He could hear, from within, no human utterance. No groan, no scream of pain or of terror, only the voice of the sea pounding against the cliffs to an accident victim.

Was no one alive in there? He studied the overturned car, listening for a desperate and anguished

```
     #11  09-03-2015 12:34PM
Item(s) checked out to MACLEOD, PATRICIA

TITLE: Cat in the dark
DUE DATE: 09-24-15


Central 979-7151 on the web at jmrl.org
    or call Toll-free 1-866-979-1555
```

cry—and wondering what he was going to do about it. Wondering how a poor simple tomcat was going to render any kind of useful assistance.

He had been hunting Hellhag Canyon since midnight, first at the shore, dodging the rolling breakers, and then, when the fog thickened, moving on up the ravine. He had tracked the wood rat blindly, following only the sound of its scrabbling, had struck and killed it before the creature was ever aware of him. But all night he'd been edgy, too, still nervous from the quakes of the last week; the first instant the skidding car hit the hill and shook the earth he'd shivered as if another jolt were rocking the cliffs, rattling the central California coast.

The original temblor, two days earlier, at 5.2 on the Richter scale, had sent the more timid human residents of Molena Point fleeing from their cottages, to creep back hours later hauling out mattresses and camp stoves and setting up housekeeping in their gardens. All week, as the village of Molena Point experienced aftershocks, people were tense and excited, waiting for the big one, for the earth to crack open, for their homes to topple and giant seas to flood the land.

Well, it was only an earthquake, a natural, God-given part of life—a cat might be wary, but a cat didn't lose perspective. Humans, on the other hand, were hopelessly amusing. Facing a natural phenomenon, the poor, gullible bipeds invariably overreacted.

The earthquake had brought two reporters down from San Francisco, searching for anything sensational, seeking out the displaced and injured, running their cameras in a feeding frenzy, their hunger for alarming news as voracious as the hunger of seagulls attacking a handful of fish innards tossed from the Molena Point pier.

But the quake had disturbed the burrowing wild creatures, the mice and wood rats and voles, driving them from their holes, disorienting the little beasts so they were incredibly easy prey. All week, Joe Grey and Dulcie had gorged themselves.

Though Dulcie refused to hunt down Hellhag Canyon. She had lectured him on the dangers of high, rogue waves after an earthquake, and, when he laughed at her fears, she had turned away disgusted, growling and lashing her tabby-striped tail at what she called tomcat stupidity.

Still listening for a cry for help from within the overturned car, Joe could hear only the drip, drip of gasoline, or maybe radiator water; tensely, he circled the vehicle, ears low, body rigid, ready to spring away if the hulking wreck toppled or exploded.

The broken, fallen saplings that lay tangled across the wreck's greasy, exposed underside half covered the drive shaft and one bent wheel. He found the source of the dripping sound. It came from the left front wheel, where a viscous liquid, a substance as thick as maple syrup, dropped steadily into a pool among the crushed ferns. When he sniffed the little puddle, the stuff *smelled* a bit like syrup: the stink of pancake syrup laced with ether.

Backing away, he approached the upside-down windshield that rose from the bracken, the glass patterned like a spiderweb encased in crystal. And now, over the smell of gas, came the sharp scent of human blood.

Behind the glass he could see the driver, white and still, his contorted body wrapped around the steering wheel and impaled by a twisted strip of metal, his head jammed down into the concavity of the roof. There was no way this guy could be alive, not with his chest pierced through and the amount of blood pooling out. The passenger seat had come loose and lay across him. He hugged it firmly in a rictus of pain and death.

The victim's Levi's-clad backside was jammed against the shattered side window, an edge of broken glass pressed against the billfold that bulged in his hip pocket. The wallet had probably prevented a sharp cut across the buttocks, not that this fellow would have felt it.

There was no passenger. No one else in the car. The young man had died alone. He was maybe thirty, Joe thought. The victim's pale blue eyes stared at some entity that no one among the living would ever see.

His brown hair was neatly trimmed—a better haircut than Joe's housemate, Clyde, would ever spring for. The dead man's bloodstained shirt and torn, camel hair sport coat looked expensive. The scattered items that had fallen onto the inverted headliner included a suede leather cap, a California road map, a Styrofoam coffee cup spilling coffee across the fabric of the headliner, and bits of shattered safety glass decorating the bloody pools and clinging to the dead man's clothes like diamond-bright sparkles for some gory costume party.

The car was a '67 Corvette, a collector's car—you saw many antiques around Molena Point. It was pale blue and, until its mishap that morning, looked to have been in mint condition. The sticker on its license plate indicated that it had been purchased from Landrum Antique Cars in L.A. The wrecked windshield was marked by tape residue where a small piece of paper must have been affixed. He could see no tag ripped away or lying on the floor.

Carefully, Joe reached a paw though a hole in the

crazed glass. Pushing out some of the rounded jewel-like bits, he squeezed his head through, then his muscled gray shoulders, and eased down onto the dead man's bent knee, his weight shifting the body and startling him; but then the victim settled again and was still.

Pressing his nose uneasily to the young man's nose, Joe sought for some hint of breathing. But even as he crouched he could feel, through his paws, a faint drop in temperature as the body began to cool.

Grimacing at the smells that accompanied human death—very different from the smell of a dead rat—he backed away and crept out again, panting for gulps of fresh air. This stranger's death unleashed all manner of past associations for Joe Grey: visions of the police working a murder scene as he crouched watching from the roof above; of a dead man bathed in the green light from a computer terminal; of a man struck suddenly with a bright steel wrench, a memory so vivid that Joe heard again the crack of the victim's skull.

But those deaths had been murders. What he was viewing here was accident, the result of careless driving on a fog-blind mountain road.

Except that something tickled at him, a puzzled unease, some detail of the crash—something he had heard before the car skidded and came thundering down into the ravine.

Frowning, the white strip down his gray face pinched into puzzled worry lines, the big tomcat padded along a fallen sapling between the upturned wheels.

Had this been an accident? Was he sure of that?

Dropping down on the far side of the wrecked car, his mind played back the crash in a quick rerun:

the squeal of brakes, then the skid just about where Deadman's Curve began. Hellhag Hill was famous for that double twist. If a driver lost control on the first bend, he was hard put, when he hit the second one, to regain command. The too-sharp turn was on him, the canyon dropping straight down away from his front wheels. The locals took that road slowly. The warning signs were numerous and insistent—but in the fog a driver wouldn't see them. Even a local might not realize just where he was on the hairpin road.

Had he heard another sound before the squeal of brakes? Had he heard a horn farther away, muffled in the fog? The faint, quick stutter of a warning horn?

He squinched closed his eyes, trying to remember.

Yes. First a faint triple beep, then the skid and the crash and the car careening down at him—but had that earlier honking come from a second car, or had this driver honked at something looming out of the fog? Had there been one car or two, moving blindly along that narrow road?

He thought he remembered the hush of two sets of tires; but had they been coming from opposite directions? Then the faint stutter of the horn, then the scream of brakes and the heart-jolting thunder as the car came careening over.

The other car must have had gone on. Why hadn't it stopped? Hadn't the other driver heard the wreck?

Padding back across a sapling above the car's greasy innards, Joe studied the right front wheel with its thick discharge. The drip was abating now, only an occasional drop still falling, its viscous pool seeping down into the dead leaves. The same syrupy liquid coated the bent wheel. He crouched to look more closely.

The drip came from a short piece of black hose attached to the wheel and to a metal pipe that ran to the engine. The brake line. Padding back and forth along the sapling, studying each wheel with its corresponding hose, he found it interesting that only this one brake line was broken and leaking.

Living with Clyde Damen, his human housemate and a professional auto mechanic, Joe Grey had grown from kittenhood exposed to the insides of every possible motor-driven vehicle, subjected to endless photographs in automotive magazines and to countless boring articles on the intricacies of car engines; as he drowsed in Clyde's lap, he was treated to interminable, mind-numbing hours of Clyde's detailed dissertations on the subtleties of matters mechanical.

He had a clear picture of this car's master cylinder, empty now where the fluid had drained away.

No brakes when the guy hit that curve. Zilch. *Nada*.

He found it most interesting that the broken plastic tube was not ragged as if it had worn through naturally, but was separated by a knife-sharp incision, a cut slicing straight through the hose.

He was debating whether to climb the canyon wall and check the skid marks on the road, to try to get a picture of just what had happened up there, when a noise from above made him crouch.

Someone was descending the cliff, moving downward unseen but noisy, crashing through the fog-blurred tangles in a frenzy, rattling bushes and dislodging stones.

Maybe somebody had heard the crash; maybe the other driver was coming to render assistance after all.

Except, this didn't sound like a man descending. Even a man in a great hurry wouldn't break so many bushes; a man hurrying down that steep bank would be more collected so that he, himself, wouldn't fall. This sounded more like a wild creature running and sliding full out, though the sound was so distorted in the fog that he couldn't really be sure what he was hearing. One minute the approach was loud enough to be a bear, the next instant the noise faded to nothing.

A bear. Right, Joe thought, disgusted. There hadn't been bears on the California coast for a century. A bobcat? No bobcat would follow and approach a wrecked car; no wild beast would do that. Warily, he leaped onto a boulder, ready to fight or run like hell, whichever the situation suggested.

Straining to see above him through the disturbed patches of water-sodden air, he wondered if it could be a horse.

But a horse, escaped from one of the small local stables, wouldn't choose, on its own, to descend the rough and fog-bound canyon. A horse, breaking through his paddock fence, would prefer the slopes of Hellhag Hill above, where the grass was rich and nourishing.

He was considering that perhaps a local horseman had heard the wreck and saddled up to come and render help, when the beast charged out of the mist—not one creature, but two.

Two huge dogs plunged straight at him. Panting and baying, they leaped up the boulder, scrabbling to reach him. Joe, hissing and snarling, prepared to bloody them both. Their eyes were wild, their white teeth flashing.

The boulder wasn't large. It protruded out of the cliff in such a way that if the dogs had thought about it, they'd have gone uphill again and jumped straight down on him. But they didn't think; they were all bark and gnashing teeth, fighting to reach him, their big mouths snapping so close that he could taste their doggy breath. He had raised his steel-tipped paw, ready to rake to ribbons those two invading noses, when he did a double take, studying their thin canine faces.

Joe dropped his armored paw and sat down, watching them, amused.

Puppies.

They were only puppies. Huge puppies, each as big as a full-grown retriever. Big-boned, big-footed pups. And thin. Two bags of canine bones held together by dry, buff-colored pelts, their black-and-white faces so fleshless they appeared skeletal, their whipping tails so skinny they looked like two snakes that had swallowed marbles.

Two oversized puppies, starving and harmless.

They had stopped barking. They grinned up at him, wagging and prancing spraddle-legged around the boulder, their skinny tails whipping enthusiastically.

They had no notion of eating him. Probably they were too young and stupid to imagine that a dog could kill and eat a cat; the idea would not have occurred to them. They simply wanted to be friendly, to be close to another animal. Now that they'd stopped barking, even their doggy smiles were incredibly downtrodden and sad.

They couldn't be more than four or five months old, but were so emaciated that even the weight of their floppy ears and floppy feet seemed to drag them down.

He wondered if they belonged to the dead driver, if somehow they had managed, as the car went over the cliff, to leap free?